NO PLACE LIKE HOME

"Uniquely charming . . . bursting with humor . . . this warmhearted confection is as soothing as a cup of hot cocoa."

—*Publishers Weekly*

THE REAL DEAL

"Exciting contemporary romantic suspense. . . . The exhilarating suspense plot is filled with twists. . . . Will appeal to fans of Nora Roberts and Jayne Ann Krentz."

—Thebestreviews.com

"[A] fast-paced and engaging story from the prolific and entertaining Michaels."

—*Booklist*

"If you are seeking a story of passion, suspense, and intrigue . . . *The Real Deal* is the perfect choice."

—*Romance Reviews Today*

LATE BLOOMER

"Michaels does what she does best [in *Late Bloomer*]. . . . Entertaining, action-packed . . . fun to read . . . engaging romantic suspense."

—*The Midwest Book Review*

"Heartwarming . . . *Late Bloomer* is nothing short of wonderful. You won't want to put it down."

—*Winter Haven News Chief* (FL)

Also by Fern Michaels

FERN MICHAELS

HEY, GOOD LOOKING

POCKET BOOKS
New York London Toronto Sydney

POCKET BOOKS, a division of Simon & Schuster, Inc.
1230 Avenue of the Americas, New York, NY 10020

This book is a work of fiction. Names, characters, places, and incidents are products of the author's imagination or are used ficticiously. Any resemblance to actual events or locales or persons, living or dead, is entirely coincidental.

Copyright © 2006 by MRK Productions, Inc.

Originally published in hardcover in 2006 by Pocket Books

ISBN 978-1-4516-4836-2
ISBN 978-1-4165-2299-7 (ebook)

This Pocket Books paperback edition June 2011

10 9 8 7 6 5 4 3 2 1

POCKET and colophon are registered trademarks of Simon & Schuster, Inc.

Cover design by Lisa Litwack
Front cover photos: woman © Herman Estevez; cat © GK &Vikki Hart/Getty Images

Manufactured in the United States of America

For information regarding special discounts for bulk purchases, please contact Simon & Schuster Special Sales at
1-866-506-1949 or business@simonandschuster.com.

The Simon & Schuster Speakers Bureau can bring authors to your live event. For more information or to book an event contact the Simon & Schuster Speakers Bureau at 1-866-248-3049 or visit our website at www.simonspeakers.com.

I would like to dedicate this book to Claudeen,
my Arizona soul sister,
and to the memory of her beloved Lexi.

Prologue

‿

Ten Years Earlier

The rain that had been holding off for the graduation ceremony finally gave way to a torrential torrent, soaking the graduating class, their scrolls in hand, and their families and guests as they scrambled across the stadium field.

Darby Lane shouted to her friend Russell Gunn. He appeared at her side as if by magic, his handsome face alight with laughter. "Is this great or what?" he shouted to be heard over the melee. They held hands like lovers as they crossed the field, taking their time since they were already soaked to the skin. Though they weren't lovers, they had been inseparable friends since the age of three, and both of them knew the situation would never change. Their laughter rang out as they skipped and stomped in the puddles. Their classmates turned to look at them, shaking their heads in disbelief.

When they finally reached the parking lot, the couple separated. "Meet you back at your place, Darby. An hour at the most."

"Okay," Darby shouted to be heard over the pounding rain. "I'm packed and ready to go."

"We need to make a stop before we head for home. Don't forget anything because we aren't coming back here. Five years is enough! Now we get to do the real thing, mold minds so they can go out and conquer the world. God, Darby, I can't wait to settle into a school and take on a fifth-grade class that's all mine. I hope you get the fourth-grade class you want, too. Look at it this way, you get to prime all those great little kids, then you pass them on to me."

Darby laughed and crossed her fingers that it would happen just the way Russ said. She shrugged off the rain that was soaking into her graduation gown and used the hem of the gown to dry off her dark, curly hair. Russ was right, five years was long enough to spend expanding her brain base. All she wanted now was to go home to the Horseshoe and vegetate for the rest of the summer.

As she fought her way across the parking lot, she craned her neck to wave good-bye to Tulane University. She wondered if she would return for class reunions. Probably not. She knew Russ wouldn't return. Russ's philosophy was do something once, move on, and don't look back. She tended to agree with most of his philosophies.

Darby wondered where Russ wanted to stop. Probably some watering hole to say good-bye to one of his earthy friends. She laughed. Russ was such a good friend. What would she do without him in her life?

She hadn't wanted to come back here for her master's, but Russ insisted. The aunts insisted, too. She'd given in gracefully, and now she had the degree. What she would do with it was anyone's guess. She'd put her foot down, though, when it came to the doctoral program. She'd flapped her arms, screaming, no, no, no! The aunts had looked at her in horror. Russ just stared at her. She'd won that one. The good feeling was still with her.

The driveway leading to the small private house she'd rented for the last five years loomed ahead of her. She pulled in and cut the engine. It didn't seem possible, but it was raining harder. She craned her neck to see if Russ's car was in the driveway four houses down from where she lived, but she couldn't see through the rain. Not that it mattered. If Russ said he would see her in an hour, she would see him in an hour. Punctuality was Russ's middle name.

Darby ran through the onslaught of rain, up a path that bloomed with bright yellow marigolds, on up the four steps to the wide veranda, then indoors, where she dripped gallons of water. She started to shed her clothes, the clinging graduation gown, her sodden tee shirt and shoes as she made her way to the second floor where her bedroom and sitting room were located.

Darby took a minute to notice the small living room, now bare of her treasures, things from home that made the five years bearable. Everything was packed and ready by the front door for Russ to load into her car.

Within minutes, Darby was stripped to the skin, toweling off and pulling clean, dry clothes from one of the packed suitcases. Sandals, wrinkled khaki shorts, bright green tee, and a matching circlet to pull back her long, dark hair. The heck with makeup.

The wet clothes and towel went into one of the lawn bags waiting to be taken to the Dumpster at the end of the street. Like she really wanted that gown or the sodden mortarboard. She was finished with Tulane. She had her diploma, which would go into a drawer someplace when she got home.

Free! No more books! No more papers to write. No more early-morning classes. No more late nights of studying. She felt giddy at the thought.

Darby leaned back on the worn sofa and propped her feet on the coffee table. How many nights had she and Russ sat on the floor eating pizza and studying together? More than she could count. She laced her hands behind her head and waited for her best friend in the whole world to arrive.

A moment later all six-foot-two of him was standing in front of her. He was dressed in baggy shorts and a wrinkled dark blue shirt with an alligator on the pocket.

Worn Birkenstocks covered his size-twelve feet. He was grinning from ear to ear. "Hey, good looking. You ready?" Russ shouted—exuberantly. "We did it, Darby! Now we're outta here. I have to stop at a lawyer's office before we hit the road. It's one of those mandatory things my trust fund calls for. I need to sign my will."

Darby's bright green eyes widened. "You didn't tell me you made a will!"

"It's not something I like to talk about. Usually people don't do that until they're old. What the hell, I figured I'll do it now and forget about it. It's not like I'm thinking about my mortality or anything."

Russ ran both hands through his crop of dark curls. His tone might have been light, but his eyes were dark and angry. He reached down for two of Darby's suitcases. "By the way, you're the executrix."

Darby stopped in her tracks. "No, Russ. What about your brother or your sister? No, I don't want to be your executrix. C'mon, Russ, there must be someone else."

Russ turned around. "Don't go there, Darby. I chose you. You're the only one I trust. Don't even think about arguing with me."

Darby bit down on her lip. She knew Russell, and she knew she could never wear him down or get him to change his mind. "Okay, but I don't like it."

"Don't start fretting now. I plan to live forever, so you'll never have to worry about it. Let's go. You leaving the plants and the small carpets?"

"Yep, the student moving in promised to take care of

the plants. She even has a dog, so the little carpets will come in handy. She's moving in tonight. Does the place look clean?"

"Just the way it was when you moved in. Did you call your aunts?"

Darby took one last look around before she replied. "Yep. And before you can ask, Diddy is cooking. I don't know if Dodo plans on attending or not. I think they were hissing and snarling at each other for a few weeks. They are both so damn temperamental."

They were outside by then, and Russ was jamming the bags and suitcases into the back of Darby's ancient Volvo. "And they live next door to each other! I swear, I don't know which one is nuttier. There's something obscene about a sixty-two-year-old woman who is a black belt." Under his breath, he mumbled, "A sixty-two-year-old woman who only weighs ninety pounds."

"I heard that! I heard that! You're just ticked off that Dodo can wipe up the floor with you and never break a sweat. And Diddy is cooking your favorites, as you requested: jambalaya, shrimp fritters, and pecan pie."

Russ licked his lips as he slammed the trunk shut. "Stay close. The office isn't far from here."

"Okay." Darby slid behind the wheel and turned on the ignition. She eased backward and waited for Russ to get in front of her. He was right, the lawyer's office wasn't far at all.

The waiting room looked like any professional's office. A middle-aged receptionist wearing glasses sat behind a shiny, glass-topped desk. A tired-looking rubber plant with brown edges stood near a table littered with periodicals, outdated business magazines, and a tattered, torn copy of *People* magazine on it. It was easy to see which magazine clients picked up while they waited to get billed, and fleeced. The chairs were burgundy leather and looked uncomfortable.

Darby was about to sit down when the plump receptionist, attired in a tight navy suit, said, "Mr. Lowell will see you now. Go through the door on the left. He's waiting for you."

Russ cupped Darby's elbow in the palm of his hand as he ushered her through the door. "Time is money," he hissed. Darby giggled.

Harrison Lowell rose from behind his desk and extended his hand. He pumped vigorously.

Darby stared at the lawyer. Like his office waiting room, he was classic. Gray hair at the temples, glasses, gray suit, white shirt, conservative tie. Two blank yellow pads waited for him on his desk along with a Mont Blanc pen. The moment the introductions were over, Harrison Lowell sat down and reached for Russell's will. The paper crackled as the lawyer shook it loose. Darby's eyes went to the videocassette that had been attached to the will with a rubber band. It stared up at her like a square black eye. A chill ran up her spine. Why did Russ need a video?

Darby waited while Russ read through the will. He nodded when he was finished.

"Very good," the lawyer said. "Now that everything is in order, my secretary and my associate will be the witnesses to Mr. Gunn's will." Russ signed, the secretary signed, and the associate, a bearded man with a limp who came through the second door to Lowell's office, signed the document just as Russ let loose a huge sigh.

Then he bent toward Darby and whispered in her ear. "You have to watch the video and read the will. That's so the lawyer knows you will carry out my wishes. Five minutes, Darby, then we can head home."

"I don't want to know what's in your will, Russ. It's not my business. I'll do whatever you want where it's concerned should you ... should you die. Why do I have to look at it? I'm not family, I'm just a friend. Please, Russ."

"Five minutes, Darby. Then we can be out of here," Russ persisted.

Resigned, Darby picked up the will and video and walked toward a small room off Harrison Lowell's office, the one through which his associate had entered. The secretary materialized and slid the video into the VCR. She left the room silently as Darby stared at Russ's likeness. Her jaw dropped as she listened to him say that in the event of a terminal illness, no life-support measures were to be used. His voice rose several octaves as he continued. "In the event of my death my organs are *not* to be taken from my body. I do *not* wish to be a donor. Nor do I wish to be cremated. Ashes to ashes, in a traditional burial ceremony, is what I want. I'm trusting you, Darby, to honor my last wishes. Because I trust you, I'm leaving my entire estate to you."

Tears puddled in Darby's eyes when the screen went dark, and Russ's face disappeared. She swiped at her eyes with the sleeve of her shirt. She skimmed the will, and her eyes grew wide: Russ's beneficiary would receive 9 million dollars plus real estate valued at three times that. And Russ's sole beneficiary was one Darby Lane. A lump settled itself in her throat. Oh, my! Okay, she could handle this. Russ wasn't going to die. No one died at the age of twenty-five. Seventy years from now she wouldn't have a problem with it.

Darby's voice was froggy-sounding when she returned to Harrison Lowell's office. "I read the will and watched the video. I'm so grateful, Russ . . . I can't . . . I can't even speak. I don't want to imagine you dying. I do have a question, though. Why don't you want to be an organ donor?"

"I can't believe I've never told you this . . . but I guess dying's not something I like to think about either," Russ said with a crooked grin. "Remember my fraternity brother Adam Messner?"

Darby nodded. She didn't know Adam well, but she remembered when he'd had an accident decorating the frat house for one of their big parties and fallen off the roof. He'd spent some time in a coma, as she recalled, and Russ and his other fraternity brothers had kept a constant vigil by his side.

"Well, what you probably don't know is that after Adam had been in a coma for six months his parents said they were going to disconnect the life-support measures that were in place and donate his organs. I remember how Mrs. Messner cried; Adam was their only son. I begged them not to do it, but they wouldn't listen to me. The doctors were going to disconnect at some point during the next forty-eight hours. During the nineteenth hour, Adam woke up. He's a sportscaster in Philadelphia now."

Darby shook her head in wonder. "That's amazing. His poor family, how awful they must have felt, thinking of what they'd almost done!"

"Exactly," Russ said, "which is why I don't want that even to be an option for me. And now that I know you've seen the video, I know you'll see to it that my wishes are followed," Russ said as he jammed his copy of the will into his back pocket. He carried a copy of the video with him. "Let's go home."

Darby's gaze went to the video on the desk.

"It stays with the lawyer," Russ said. "Where's Darby's copy?"

"Right here," the secretary in the blue suit said. She handed Darby a sealed brown envelope.

Harrison Lowell shook hands with both of them. Then he handed Darby one of his business cards. A crazy thought whipped through Darby's mind. Seventy years from now, Harrison Lowell would probably be dead. What good would the lawyer's business card do her then? She jammed the card into the pocket of her shorts.

Russ tweaked her cheek, then gave her a high five. "Okay, Baton Rouge, here we come. Thanks, Darby. I owe you one for this."

Darby's voice was sober and somber-sounding when she said, "No problem, Russ." Little did she know how she would come to regret those very words.

1

Ten Years Later

The houses on Thornberry Lane near the outskirts of Baton Rouge were always the main draw on the Historical Tour for tourists. No one could explain why or how a cul-de-sac with just five houses could be called a lane or why, since it was outside of the town's historic district, it was on the tour. Some speculated it was because the Lane family owned three of the houses on Thornberry Lane. Others said it was because it was like an oasis, with each house sitting on a full acre of land with an enormous bed of flowers in the middle. Whatever it was, everyone in Baton Rouge agreed Thornberry Lane was the most beautiful sight they'd ever seen.

Gawkers and tourists aside, *Baton Rougies,* as some referred to themselves, were loyal to three of the inhabitants of Thornberry Lane. Not so to the inhabitants of the two houses on the end that belonged to the Gunn family. Outsiders, they said, nouveau riche, others said. The truth was that when Marcus Gunn was finally on the verge of being accepted by the *Rougies*, thanks to the Lane sisters, he up and married his second wife, Bella. The *Rougies* and the Lane sisters closed ranks, and it was a greased downhill slide for Marcus Gunn and his new wife. The Junior Leaguers, along with the members of the Garden Club, Historical Society, and Rotary sniffed that Bella's shady past—which they were convinced included an out-of-wedlock child, something no amount of digging and searching could prove—her bleached hair, her pancake makeup, her faux jewelry, not to mention her *hoity-toity* attitude, would be a disgrace to the *Rougies*. And, the *Rougies* whispered, she was twenty-five years younger than Marcus, which could mean only one thing. Bella was a gold digger and after Marcus's money, of which there was plenty. She was no stepmother to Marcus's three children, they said. *Wicked* stepmother was more like it, they hissed among themselves after they said over and over, "Those poor children; thank God for the Lane sisters and the love they showed the children."

The Lane sisters could attest to that fact, and they did, every chance they got. They fed and took care of the three children as much as was allowed. Bella didn't care as long as they weren't, as she put it, under her feet.

The final consensus on Bella Gunn was that she was

not only white trash, she was tacky as well. That particular statement probably had something to do with the fact that Bella wore a tiara to church services on Sunday morning.

Lydia Lane, oldest of the Lane sisters, and known to friends and family as Dodo, stepped out onto her flower-bedecked veranda and stared across the wide acre of rainbow plantings and cobblestone paths that led out to the street and the main road. She cringed the way she always did when her gaze settled on the two Gunn houses situated at the ends of the horseshoe-shaped lane. They were a blight on the landscape. A deliberate blight, thanks to Bella Gunn. And there was nothing she or her sisters could do about it.

Dodo stared at the rotting wood, the broken windows, sagging verandas, doors hanging on one hinge, and the dilapidated steps that were a danger to any child wishing to explore haunted houses. Every night she prayed that the buildings would collapse or that lightning would strike them. What she was looking at was all the result of Bella Gunn's being denied entrance to the Christmas tour. Bitter and angry over the *Rougies'* refusal to accept her, she'd deliberately allowed the two Gunn houses in the shoe to fall into their present condition. That, and her hatred of the three Lane sisters, who were on the selection committee for the Christmas tour.

Not more than an hour ago, Mary Ellen Prentice had called and said she'd heard from Emma Rangley, who heard from the Baptist minister's own lips that Bella had said in a fit of pique that the reason she was denied entrance to the tour was because of the location of the house she'd designed on the outskirts of town. Now Bella was going to concentrate on the houses in the shoe and reapply. According to Emma, Bella's parting shot had been, "They won't dare turn down a house in the shoe, much less two houses in the shoe."

Just watch me turn you down. There's a young man and his family that belongs here in the shoe, by right of inheritance, not by trickery and chicanery the way Bella was doing. A young man and his family she'd give up all she held dear to know again.

Shielding her eyes from the bright sun, Dodo whistled between her teeth the way a small boy would to attract a friend's attention. Her sister Vivian, better known as Diddy, banged the screen door of her house, which was opposite Dodo's, and waddled over to the veranda railing. "What? Why can't you use the phone like other people do when you want to speak with me? It's not ladylike to whistle between your teeth, Dodo." She was breathless as she, too, leaned on the railing.

The skinny little woman with the spiked hair waved her sister's comment aside. "I swear this is the worst day of my life. I should have killed that woman or, at the very least, pushed her into that grave yesterday. But no, you had to stop me!"

Diddy Lane's plump cheeks flushed crimson. "No Lane has ever been in trouble with the law. I wouldn't do well visiting you in prison, and that's where you would have gone if you had done that. If it's any consolation to you, Dodo, I wanted to do the same thing. We're ladies, and ladies do not go around pushing people into open graves. I just wish . . . Lord, I wish so many things, but mainly I wish Marcus hadn't had that last stroke. He's so out of it he doesn't have a clue as to what is going on. Bella calls the shots these days. Then again, she's been doing that forever, it seems, so I guess it's not new at all. It's just so sad that someone as vital as Marcus could be felled like this."

Dodo looked down from the railing at a border of begonias that were so lush and colorful they looked like they'd been painted on the cobblestones lining the house. "And where is that wayward sister of ours? She loved Russell as much as we did. She said she would be at the funeral. She wasn't there! I'll tell you where she is, she's probably out lollygagging with some young stud forty years her junior," she said vehemently.

Diddy's plump cheeks flushed again. "At least she does her lollygagging off scene in New Orleans. Oh, God! There she is! Would you *look* at her!"

Dodo reared back as her sister Harriet, known to her sisters—and those in town who still remembered her—as Ducky, stepped out of the stretch limousine. She wore a dress that resembled gossamer, or maybe a thousand sheer hankies sewn together, draped on her voluptuous frame. A wide lacy straw hat, with *real* flowers and satin ribbons trailing down the sides and back, adorned her head. Outrageous designer sunglasses finished off her look. Ducky never wore anything that didn't carry a designer's name on it. A purse as big as a suitcase was the only thing she carried. She was boohooing behind the dark glasses as she made her way up one of the cobblestone paths that led to her sisters' houses. The stylish, pointy-toed, backless heels made it a difficult task. Both sisters watched as their sister kicked them off. One landed in the middle of the begonias, and the other settled atop one of the oleander bushes.

Both Dodo and Diddy pursed their mouths at the sight. "Such a lady," Diddy muttered.

The wayward, free-spirit sister removed her sunglasses to see her siblings better. What she saw made her say, "Oh, will you two stuff it already. And before you can ask me where I was, I was attending to business, and as much as I tried, I just couldn't get back in time. I feel awful."

Ducky met Diddy by the steps, and together they walked up them to Dodo's house. "I take it our niece isn't here yet. How are we going to handle all this?" Ducky asked as she quickly bussed each sister on the cheek.

Dodo, a martial arts expert in her prime, pivoted on the balls of her feet before she smacked one hand into the other. "Very carefully," Dodo responded. "I was just telling Diddy I think this is one of the worst days in my life. Darby," she said, "is devastated. She's blaming herself, which is silly, but what can you expect? Russell was her best friend since they were three years old. Why am I telling you something you already know?" she dithered.

The Lane sisters looked at one another. Dodo, age seventy-two, Diddy, age seventy, and Ducky, age sixty-nine, a hair away from seventy, were suddenly squabbling like teenagers as they started to blame one another for their niece's trip to Scotland.

Diddy drew herself up to her full five feet and glared at her sisters. "Tell me, how does one tell one's niece, who, by the way, is thirty-three years old, that she shouldn't travel outside the country. She went on business. Darby does what she wants when she wants. We are not her wardens, Ducky. Is that a nightgown you're wearing?" she sniped.

Ducky hitched up the front of her gossamer dress. "No, it is not a nightgown. It's the latest in fashion. I bought it in Paris two months ago. It certainly beats that . . . that . . . whatever it is you're wearing, Diddy. As for you, Dodo, give up the ninja crap already and dress like a female." Exhausted with her little speech, Ducky sent her straw hat sailing across the veranda. It landed with precision on one of the wicker chairs. She then strode barefoot across the grass-green carpet and sat down on the swing. "Sit! Sit already. We need to make a plan here. Refreshments would be nice."

"Yes, they would," Dodo said as she sat down on the swing next to her sister. It was obvious to both sisters that there would be no refreshments forthcoming.

Ducky reached for one of the fans hanging off the arm of the swing. She started to fan her perspiring face. Fans hanging off chairs and swings on front porches was a Southern thing. "Now, I want you two to tell me what the hell happened to that darling boy Russell."

Diddy glowered at her fashionable-looking baby sister. "He died, is what happened," she snarled. A second later she burst into tears.

"And then they . . . they . . . they donated his organs. Every single one that was . . . *donatable*," Dodo said as she dabbed at her own eyes. "They buried a shell of Russell. Everything was gone, his eyes, his heart, his lungs, his liver . . ."

Ducky stopped fanning herself to stare at her stuttering sister. "I'm getting the picture, Dodo. An organ donor has to be an exceptional kind of person. Russell was young and athletic. I'm sure his organs were in . . . excellent condition. How did the accident happen?"

Dodo jumped up and started wringing her hands. "Do you want the truck driver's version or do you want Bella's version?"

"Both," Ducky snapped. She started fanning herself again.

Diddy whipped a wad of tissues out of her pocket and proceeded to shred them. "The truck driver said Russell veered across the yellow line and hit him head-on. He said he couldn't stop in time. It was one of those eighteen-wheelers, and it happened on a main highway. Bella's version is that Russell committed suicide. I don't believe that for one minute, and neither does anyone else. Something was wrong with the brakes of his car, according to the police. For some reason he was driving his girlfriend Claire's car. Russell was looking forward to Darby's return. As a matter of fact, he was supposed to meet Darby in Atlanta, then they were going to visit friends and drive home together. Does that sound to you like someone who was contemplating suicide?"

A small brown bird flew onto the porch before it settled in one of the luscious green ferns hanging from the ceiling. A second bird flew straight to the fern and settled down between the thick fronds. "They have a nest in there," Dodo said inanely.

The bright, sunny day beyond the front porch suddenly dimmed as gray clouds from the south moved across the summer blue sky. The scent of new-mown grass was like a heady aphrodisiac. Ducky eyed her sisters as they seemed to shrink into themselves.

Dodo started to pace the green carpet. The black-felt slippers she favored, to go with her ninja wear, made scratching sounds that grated on the ears. She bent down to pluck a yellowing leaf from one of the straw baskets full of yellow Gerber daisies that lined the veranda and steps. She tossed it over the railing.

"Marcus should have known his own son's wishes as well as Bella. They didn't bury Russell because there was nothing left to bury but his bones. What I mean is they buried Russell but not all of Russell. God, I don't know what I mean. Now that Darby has inherited all of

Russell's money—which, by the way, is a dizzying amount—do you think she might finally settle down and buy a house of her own? She wouldn't have to travel so much with her little business and could go the catalog route the way a lot of small businesses do. Being a home owner is almost a full-time job, don't you think?" When no one responded to the question, Dodo sat down cross-legged on the porch, dropping her head into her hands.

Just then the rain started to fall, and Ducky said, "Refreshments would be really nice right now."

Dodo turned to look at her sister to see if she was dying of thirst. Satisfied that she wasn't about to expire, she said, "The door's open, fetch it yourself. And, while you're about it, bring something for Diddy and me."

"Feisty, aren't we?" Ducky said, getting up from the swing. "As a hostess you are sorely lacking, Dodo." She swished her way to the front door, her hankie dress clinging to her voluptuous curves.

Diddy walked over to the railing to stare out at the rain, which was coming down like a waterfall. "We need the rain," she said vaguely. "I think you should have thinned out the begonias, Dodo. I love the shell pink color. My lavender ones are just as pretty, don't you think?"

"Shut up, Diddy. I'm not in the mood to discuss rain or begonias. That girl is going to have a nervous breakdown when she gets here. I have a terrible feeling she's at the cemetery. Why would she go there?

Tomorrow would be soon enough. Do you think that's where she is?"

"Yes. I just didn't want to say it out loud. Maybe we should go and get her," Diddy mumbled.

"Maybe we shouldn't. If she wanted us to go with her, she would have come here first. I thought Ben or Mary would have stopped by today." Ben and Mary were Russell's siblings.

The screen door creaked as Ducky elbowed it, a tray in her hands. Three glasses and three bottles of beer, along with a flower in a bud vase and monogrammed linen napkins, graced the tray.

The Lane sisters were beer drinkers in part because of the family-owned business, which was a brewery that distributed beer worldwide.

The sisters clinked their glasses together, their eyes wet and somber.

"Diddy and I think Darby went to the cemetery. She's probably sitting in the rain and the mud crying. We should have gone to get her. Why didn't we do that?"

"Because she wants to be alone with her friend. *If* she even went there," Ducky said as she licked the top of the beer bottle. She seemed surprised that it was empty.

Dodo, who was sitting in a yoga position on the green carpet, unwrapped her skinny legs and entered the house. She returned with three more bottles of beer. She handed one to each of her sisters. All three proceeded to swig directly from the bottles.

The rain continued to cascade from the heavens. The birds in the fern overhead chirped their displeasure as all three sisters' hair started to frizz up from the mist sweeping across the veranda.

"Maybe Darby isn't going to come back here," Diddy said.

Dodo scoffed at the remark. "She has to come back here. This is where her family is."

"Let's face it. Maybe she went to a motel so she wouldn't have to endure all the clucking we'd do over her," Ducky snapped. "She's smart, that niece of ours."

As was their custom when the three of them were together, Diddy lined up the empty beer bottles. She finished her beer with one huge gulp and plopped it down at the end of the line. "I'm going, I'm going. I know it's my turn. Don't talk about anything till I get back. One each or two each?"

"Two," Ducky and Dodo said in unison. Diddy trotted off to complete her mission.

"This is our personal wake for Russell," Ducky said. "I can't believe that snot Bella didn't invite us to the official one. I don't care for myself, but it was so tacky of her. The whole town must be talking this to death." She sniffed to show what she thought about that particular statement.

The rain continued, the birds in the fern kept protesting, the empty beer bottles continued to line up as the sisters sat glumly on the veranda, each worried about what she would do when their niece finally arrived.

It was dusk when the hard, driving rain turned into a steady downpour. The sisters were bleary-eyed but unwilling to enter the house. All three of them refrained from looking at the mountain of empty beer bottles Diddy had tossed into an old bushel basket. "We should eat something. I don't think Darby is coming back tonight."

"What would you suggest?" Dodo asked.

Ducky ran her hands through her frizzy hair, trying to flatten it. A useless struggle. "This is your house, isn't it? You're supposed to play hostess even if you don't feel like it. You must have something in your refrigerator. No bean sprouts or any of those weeds you insist on eating."

"I never did like you, Ducky, so don't go telling me what to do." It wasn't true. All their lives they'd snapped and snarled at one another just to make their lives a little more interesting. It was how they communicated, and none of the three took the comments seriously. The only thing they never argued about or were at odds over was their niece, Darby.

Darby had come to them from the East at the age of three when her parents died prematurely within months of each other, their brother, Germaine, keeling over on the golf course from a heart attack, and dying on the way to the hospital. A month later, his wife, Ann Marie, unable to cope with a child and the loss of her husband, stepped right in front of a car and was killed instantly.

How she wished Gerry were here now. He'd always been their shining light, older by three years and never embarrassed that he had three sisters trailing after him. They'd been such good friends, advisers to each other. Even now, all these years later, the three of them talked of Gerry constantly. What would Gerry think, what would Gerry do? So long ago, Dodo thought sadly. They'd raised Darby as their own, and no child anywhere in the universe could have asked for better stand-in moms, as she referred to them.

"How about peanut butter and jelly? We'll have to use spoons because I don't have any bread."

Diddy pursed her lips. "How will peanut butter and jelly settle in our stomachs with all the beer we drank earlier?"

"That's a very good question, Diddy. My God, it's humid. All right, I'll take the bean sprouts," Ducky said as she again started to fan herself. "The mosquitoes are starting to come out. Should we adjourn indoors?"

Dodo was saved from a reply when she noticed headlights turning into the narrow driveway that was shared by all five houses on Thornberry Lane. "I think she's here, but it doesn't look like her Jeep."

In the blink of an eye, the sisters were at the railing at the top of the steps straining to see into the early twilight.

"It's Ben Gunn!" Diddy said.

"Lord, he's holding up Darby! My God, what's wrong with her?" Ducky squawked. "Did you ever see such a handsome young man?" she added as an afterthought. "She's barefoot."

"So are you, so what's the big deal. My God, she's covered with mud. Look at her hair. That's her favorite yellow linen dress. It's ruined," Dodo said, flapping her arms up and down.

At the foot of the steps, Ben Gunn looked up, and said, "Ladies, I'm bringing your niece home. She could probably use a nice warm shower."

Diddy eyed the handsome young man holding up her niece with suspicion. "She looks like she's drunk!"

"That too. I found her at the cemetery drinking from a whiskey bottle. She bought it for . . . Russ in Scotland. At one of those duty-free shops," he clarified.

Darby was like a rag doll, her legs buckling, as Ben Gunn tried to transfer his hold on her to her aunts. It wasn't working. "Why don't I take her upstairs to the bathroom and just put her in the shower. If you're up to it, you could make some coffee."

"There will be none of *that*, young man!" Diddy said imperiously. "You make the coffee, and we'll see that our niece gets to the shower." Ben shrugged his broad shoulders.

The transfer was made, albeit sloppily, as the three sisters pushed, dragged, and shoved their niece up the long circular staircase. Ben watched until they were out of sight before he made his way to the kitchen. He knew where everything was. As a child, he'd virtually lived in one of the three houses on Thornberry Lane, along with his brother, Russell, and his sister, Mary. The good old days. The happiest days of his life.

While the coffee dripped, Ben sat down, his long legs stretched out in front of him. He looked around. It was the same kitchen he remembered but with updated appliances. He'd done his homework at the round oak table. He'd eaten cookies and had milk at the same table, along with Russ, Mary, and Darby. He'd eaten so many meals in this house and the other two that he lost count. He had his own bed, as did his sister and brother, in all three houses.

It was sixteen long years since he'd been in this house, yet he felt like he'd just returned home even though it was a tragic homecoming. His broad, athletic shoulders slumped, but he straightened back up when Dodo entered the kitchen. She ran to him and hugged him so hard he winced.

"Trust me, Ben, we'll make Bella pay for this."

2

Ben Gunn snapped to attention the minute he heard one of his surrogate mothers speak. He was on his feet a second later. Even though he hadn't heard Dodo's voice in years, he recognized the stern, motherly tone. "Yes, ma'am, we do need to talk. Is Darby okay?"

Dodo shook her head as she stared at the young man she'd always wanted to pair up with her niece. She'd always thought of him as rugged-movie-star material. Tall, muscular, dark hair with a slight wave, matching dark eyes. Thanks to orthodonture, Ben had beautiful, straight teeth that she and her sisters had paid for over Bella's objections. Ben had hugged her the day his braces came off, thanked her profusely, and said he thought girls might look at him from then on. They'd both giggled. He flashed his famous smile now, but it was wary.

Dodo eyed the thick, double lashes covering Ben's dark eyes. Any woman, herself included, would have killed for those eyelashes.

Today Ben was dressed in faded jeans that hugged his legs, and a tee shirt with the words MUSTANG ISLAND sprawled across the front. Both shirt and jeans were damp and sticking to his body.

"What do you want to talk about, Dodo?" His voice sounded vague yet anxious to his own ears.

"For starters, young man, where are you staying, and why aren't you staying here?"

"The Baton Rouge Inn. Mary's staying there, too."

Dodo smacked her hands together. "Nonsense. I want both of you to come here. For heaven's sake, what made you go to the inn?"

Ben raked his fingers through his hair. "It was late when I got in. I waited at the airport for Mary. Her flight got in an hour after mine. It seemed like the thing to do at the time. Neither one of us wanted to wake any of you up in the middle of the night. On top of that, I think we were both in a state of shock. Hell, I'm still in shock. I can't believe Russ is dead." Ben's voice choked up as he swiped at the lashes hooding his eyes.

Dodo opened the refrigerator, twisted off a cap, and handed Ben a beer. "I suppose that makes sense in some cockamamie way. What in the world were you doing at the cemetery today? Never mind, I'm glad you were there to bring Darby home."

"I wanted private time. On the face of it, it sounds

pretty damn stupid. I went there to say good-bye to a shell. My brother isn't in that grave. Jesus, for all I know they donated his brain, too." He choked up again, and Dodo hugged him. "I'd say Russ must be spinning in his grave but there's nothing to spin. Somebody else . . . has . . . has all his parts. He's goddamn well scattered all over the place. Tell me how that could have happened, Dodo. How?" His voice was so tormented, Dodo backed up a step to stare at the bewildered young man.

Dodo started to cry. "I don't know, Ben. You need to speak with your father."

Ben drained his beer and snorted. "Not likely. He leaves everything up to Bella. He's not well, Dodo. He has round-the-clock nurses, so it must be serious. I don't even know what's wrong with him. What little I do know, Russ told me months ago."

"I saw him at the funeral, and he didn't seem to know what was going on or even who I was."

Ben flopped back into his chair. "My father's last stroke has almost incapacitated him. At least that's what Bella told Russ."

Dodo was about to respond when she turned to see her sisters and Darby walking down the hall to the kitchen.

"How's that coffee coming?" Ducky shouted.

Ben jumped up, his eyes going to his old childhood friend. "Is she okay?" He directed his question to the two sisters flanking Darby.

Darby did her best to focus on Ben. "I'm all right. A

steaming-hot shower followed by an ice-cold one tends to bring a person front and center. Thanks for bringing me home, Ben." Her eyes brimmed with tears, but she wiped them away with the sleeve of her robe. "I'm sorry I missed the . . . the funeral."

Ben poured a cup of strong, black coffee and set it in front of Darby. She wrapped both hands around the fragile chinaware, but it still shook in her trembling hands. She looked up at her three aunts, and said, "We should plant some flowers on the . . . grave. Some of your begonias, Dodo. Some of yours, too, Diddy. Different colors. A mix of colors. Russ loved flowers. I'll dig up some of the Gerber daisies that Ducky and I planted in the spring. That way we'll all be represented. Do you think tomorrow will be too soon?" Her words all ran together in one long, jumbled stretch.

The aunts and Ben looked at one another. "Tomorrow will be fine," Diddy said.

"Then in the fall we'll plant some chrysanthemums. Those big pom-poms. Maybe some of those spider mums, too. Bright colors. Then in the winter we'll take evergreens. We should do that, don't you think?" This time the words tumbled over one another only to end on a flat note.

Ben cleared his throat. "Absolutely. I'll help you if you want me to."

Darby again brought the bone china cup to her lips, but her hands trembled so badly that Ben reached out to catch the cup, knowing it was going to fall from her hands. The coffee spilled on the table and ran over its edge. The three aunts rushed for paper towels. Darby started to cry. A wad of paper napkins was shoved into her hands.

Time crawled forward as the aunts seated themselves at the table and waited for Darby to compose herself. Ben walked in circles, his soaking-wet sneakers making squishing sounds on the old pine floor.

Ben couldn't keep his eyes off Darby and hoped the aunts weren't as astute just then as he knew they normally were. He'd loved Darby Lane from the time he was ten years old. Even as a little boy, he'd beamed with pleasure when she smiled at him. When she showed him her two front teeth in a velvet pouch, compliments of the Tooth Fairy, he still thought she looked like an angel. His ears turned pink when he remembered how he'd actually said the words aloud. Both Russell and Darby had giggled. How well he remembered that day.

It was always Russell and Darby. Best friends forever and ever. He wasn't sure if they were lovers or not. Probably. The two of them were stuck together like glue. Over the years that closeness hadn't changed. Because he and Mary were older, they tended to pal around together until Mary made her own friends in high school, leaving him on his own in his search for friends.

People always said Ben Gunn was a loner. He guessed he was, to some extent. The truth was he hated spending time with people who didn't interest him or people he had nothing in common with. He was com-

fortable in his own skin, comfortable with his own company. Seeing Darby now, after all these years, he finally
realized why he hadn't formed any lasting relationships.
He'd given his heart to Darby Lane, and he had never
taken it back.

Ben shook his head to clear away his thoughts.
"Where's Willie?" he asked suddenly, thinking of Russ's
beloved golden retriever.

Darby's head snapped forward. "Willie? Isn't he with
you or Mary? What do you mean, where's Willie?"

The three aunts started to dither.

"Dear God! I think I heard someone say Willie was
in the car with Russell," Diddy said.

"I just assumed Bella took the dog," Ducky said.

"Not in a million years. She wouldn't even allow us
to have goldfish when we were kids," Ben said.

"Maybe the police or the EMS people have him,"
Dodo said. "Dear God, how could we have forgotten
Willie?"

"The pound. Call the pound," Darby said, her voice
quivering in near hysteria.

His angel had spoken. The phone was in Ben's hand
a minute later. They all listened as he dialed the information operator, copied down the number, then called
the Baton Rouge Pound.

Darby reared forward, her hands gripping the sides
of the table when she heard Ben say, "What do you
mean, people are standing in line to adopt Willie? No,
no, that dog belongs to my family. I'll be there in ten

minutes to pick him up. I don't care if your gates are locked. Open them. I want that dog. How did you get him anyway? Mrs. Gunn had her chauffeur bring him in. Well, I'm taking him out in ten minutes."

The four women looked at Ben in awe. "Stay put. I'll go fetch Willie. That damn Bella . . ."

Ben was starting his car in the time it took the sisters to realize that the back door had opened and closed.

"Russ loved Willie. Willie loved Russ," Darby said brokenly. "That woman is so mean. Hateful and . . ."

"We need to discredit that woman for Russ. If we don't discredit her, she's going to turn the shoe into a monstrosity like the one she lives in. The woman has no taste. None at all," Dodo said.

Ducky looked over at Dodo and mumbled. "There's no way on this earth that Bella can get into the good graces of the *Rougies.* She burned her bridges early on when they snubbed her. All those unkind remarks she made, how she refused to donate to anything the town sponsored. The *Rougies* have long memories."

Diddy weighed in. "It's disgusting the way she's been on television. Every time I turn on the news, there she is. She's been saying she just had to be generous even in her time of grief by donating her stepson's organs. I don't trust that woman. She never does anything unless it helps her in some way. It's a sin the way she's playing this up just to ingratiate herself with the *Rougies.*"

"We just need a plan," Dodo said with a glint in her

eye that would have normally sent her sisters running. But this time they knew Dodo was *right*.

"We're all agreed, then," Ducky said. "In the meantime, we really need to eat something." She looked pointedly at the refrigerator. "Ben's probably going to be hungry when he gets here. It's a given that the dog will be starving. Do you have *anything* besides weeds in your vegetable bin, Dodo?"

Dodo huffed and puffed. "I'm a vegetarian, Harriet." The use of Ducky's given name was warning enough that Dodo had had enough of her sister's remarks.

"Come with me, Ducky, to my house. I roasted two chickens early this morning. And, I made a red-velvet cake and two loaves of bread because Darby loves homemade bread. I think I have a potato, onion, and cheese casserole in the freezer. It won first prize last year in the cook-off. With Dodo's vegetables we can certainly put a meal on the table." Diddy loved to cook and could always be counted on to have a full refrigerator and freezer.

Darby gathered the top of Dodo's old robe tightly in her fingers. "Is it always going to hurt this much, Dodo?" she asked when Ducky and Diddy left the kitchen.

Dodo wished her sisters had stayed. This was crucial, important stuff. Darby needed to know Bella went against Russ's wishes. For one brief moment she thought she was having a brain freeze with her niece's question. Sometimes you just had to wing it and hope for the best.

"No, baby, it won't always be like it is today or the day you got the news of Russell's death. It will take time, Darby. This is your grieving time, and that's the way it should be. You take it one day at a time. Willie might be a big help. What did you think of Ben?" she asked, hoping to divert her niece's thoughts.

"Ben?"

"Yes, Ben. He's such a fine young man. Handsome, too. I wonder why he never got married. Most men are married by the age of thirty-five, with a couple of kids. That's another way of saying he's an extremely good catch for some lucky woman."

"That's nice," Darby mumbled.

Desperate to keep the conversation moving, Dodo said, "So, did you get the order for the dollhouse?" The dollhouse she was referring to was a custom-made one created by Darby. Darby Lane Custom Miniatures was the company that Darby started when she graduated from college. With no real home of her own to tie her down, Darby didn't mind all the traveling she had to do with her fledgling business that was more a labor of love than a business and was just now starting to show a small profit. The aunts allowed her to set up shop in the garage, which meant no overhead and allowed her to venture in a very small way into the catalog business at Russ's suggestion.

"Yes, I got the order. The little girl is wheelchair-bound. I showed her father my catalog, and she picked the one I knew she would pick—my favorite house. I'm converting the house to a castle just for her. She was a sweet little girl. Her parents dote on her; they didn't even flinch at the price." She paused then, and looked at Dodo as if her heart were breaking. "What will Willie do, Dodo?"

Dodo had no idea if dogs grieved, or if they just went on with their lives as long as someone fed them. She groped for a response. "I think he'll be fine if you take over his care. I think it's what Russell would want."

"I'll give him one of Russ's shirts to sleep with. He has a teddy bear Russ bought him. Russ always called it Willie's baby. He'd tell him to get it, and he would. I wonder where it is. Willie was really attached to it. We have to find it, Dodo."

A mission. "Maybe it was in the car. They took it to the junkyard. I heard that on the news. Then again, maybe it's in Russell's apartment. Do you think he'd let the dog take it in the car?"

"I don't know. I just don't know, Dodo. My head is buzzing. I feel like I'm caught in the middle of a bad nightmare. What time is it?"

"It's eight o'clock, baby."

Darby nodded as though the time registering on the kitchen clock was paramount. She slid her chair back from the round wooden table that had once belonged to her great-great-grandmother to allow Diddy and Ducky, who had just returned, to place the food in the center.

She watched her three aunts as they busied themselves setting the table and warming the food.

Normally, Darby loved her aunt Diddy's cooking. Now she could only stare at the delectable roast chickens, the casserole, and the red-velvet cake. She'd eaten the same food hundreds of times and loved every mouthful. She knew if she tried to eat it now, she'd get sick. Would she ever be able to enjoy her aunts' food again? Would she ever be able to enjoy *anything* again? Her eyes started to fill again. "I think I should just go on home," she said in a weary voice.

"No, no, no," the aunts chorused. They turned and swooped around her as they crooned words Darby couldn't distinguish. She was saved from being smothered by a wild bark from outside the kitchen door. A second later, the rambunctious golden retriever crashed through the screen in the lower half of the door. He pranced and danced around the kitchen, going from one woman to the other in search of warm pats and scratches to his belly. Darby slid off the chair and tried her best to settle the dog on her lap. He licked her cheeks, snuggling against her. This time she couldn't stop the flow of tears. Sobs shook her slender shoulders.

Willie struggled free of her tight hold and barked as though asking what was wrong. Darby cried harder. The aunts clung to one another, wringing their hands. Ben dropped to his haunches and pulled the dog to him; what he really wanted to do was gather Darby in his arms.

Willie continued to bark, advancing, then backing away, before he tore through the house and up the steps. The little group waited, knowing what was going to happen next.

A subdued Willie returned to the kitchen dragging a well-worn tee shirt that said TEACHER OF THE YEAR on the front. Russell's favorite shirt, presented to him years ago by his fifth-grade class. All eyes were on the beautiful yellow dog as he eyed them all as though trying to decide to whom he should present the shirt. In the end, he carried it over to the door, dropped it, and lay down, his head nuzzling the shirt to savor his master's scent.

Everyone started to jabber at once, uncertain what they should do next.

Ben shifted from one foot to the other. "I think I'll head on out. Mary's waiting for me. I need to spend time with her since she's leaving tomorrow to go back to New York and her travel agency. We'll stop by in the morning before she leaves."

"But . . . don't you want to eat something, Ben?" Diddy asked.

Ben's eyes drifted to Darby. *Ask me to stay.* "I'm not really hungry. I'll come back tomorrow, if that's okay. If you need me, call the inn." He kissed and hugged the three sisters. He dropped down on his haunches again and reached for Darby's hands, forcing her to look up at him.

Darby stared at Ben. He looked so much like Russell

it was unnerving. "Thanks for bringing me home and for getting Willie," she said quietly. "Will you see if you can find Willie's baby. It's a small brown teddy bear with whiskers. One ear is chewed off. I want to keep Willie, if that's all right with you."

Dodo reached out and grabbed her sisters' arms when she heard Ben say, "I think Willie belongs with you. I would never dream of taking him away from you. I'll see you all tomorrow."

Darby turned toward her aunts. "Would you mind terribly if I go to bed? I don't think I could eat even if I tried. I'll take Willie with me."

"No, no, no, you will not take Willie with you. We're going to give him a bath to wash off the smell of the pound. We'll bring him up the minute he's dry. I promise, baby," Dodo said.

At the word *bath*, Willie growled and burrowed into the tee shirt beneath him.

"All right," Darby agreed.

The sisters looked at one another. Ducky looked down at her designer dress and sighed. "Okay, let's get it over with." She advanced one step, then a second. Willie growled and showed his teeth. Ducky backed up. "Okay, Dodo, how do you suggest we get this dog into the laundry tub? He's got to weigh at least eighty pounds, and those teeth of his look pretty sharp. We all take aspirin, so that means our blood doesn't clot normally. I'm waiting, Dodo," Ducky said, tapping her bare foot on the floor.

"I'm thinking, I'm thinking. Would you want a smelly dog sleeping on one of your beds? No, you would not. Let's close all the doors except the door leading into the laundry room. Diddy, fill the tub so when we do get him in there, we can just dump him in the tub."

"Oh, that's a plan all right, you twit! Did you forget about his teeth? What are you going to do, *scare* him into submission?" Ducky exploded.

Dodo's jaw dropped. "Sometimes, Ducky, you absolutely amaze me. That's exactly what I'm going to do. Here's the plan." She whispered so the dog wouldn't hear what she was saying. "Wait right here, I'll be back in a second." Ducky rolled her eyes while Diddy just shook her head, never taking her eyes off the wary retriever.

The dining-room door suddenly blasted open as Dodo burst into the room, a black ninja mask covering her head and face. Only her eyes were visible. Her feet left the floor and came back down in a wide V stance at the same moment she screeched, "Eyowwww!" her arms windmilling all over the place. Willie cowered against the wall, his ears going flat against his head. He whined as Ducky and Diddy scooped him up and carried him to the laundry tub while Dodo brought up the rear.

Within seconds, all three women were soaked to the skin, Ducky's sheer dress hung in shreds from Willie's claws. Diddy's ample bosom heaved as she struggled to soap and rinse the wriggling dog. Dodo stood on the sidelines with an armful of thick towels.

When the spray attachment on the faucet came to life, Willie decided he'd had enough and leaped out of the tub, skidded across the tile floor, righted himself, and beelined for the back staircase, where he disappeared from sight.

All three women started to squawk at one time. Ducky pointed to her designer dress and screeched at her sisters. "It's ruined. Take off that damn mask, Dodo, you look like a . . . like a ninja!"

"Thank you," Dodo said. "Go home. I'll clean this up. The dog was scared. You'd be scared, too, if someone dumped you in a sink of water. Well, maybe you wouldn't, Ducky," she sniped.

"Just a damn minute, Dodo. What the hell does that mean?"

"What I mean was . . . is . . . you were never shy about taking off your clothes in front of people. I remember a time or two when you skinny-dipped in front of men. Don't bother to deny it either."

"What does any of this have to do with giving the dog a bath? Admit it, you're jealous of me. You were always jealous of me."

"True," Dodo admitted. "If I'd been nipped and tucked, sliced and diced as many times as you have, I'd look pretty damn good, too."

Ducky flopped down on one of the kitchen chairs. What was left of her dress dripped water on the floor.

She shrugged. This was all familiar ground that never went anywhere.

"Let's have a beer before we call it a night," said Diddy, ever the peacemaker.

"Okay," Dodo said agreeably.

"I am thirsty," Ducky said.

"We need to make a plan here," Diddy said as she set three bottles of the family beer in the center of the table. "A doable plan. I say we make a plan to run Bella out of town before she gets a firm toehold here in the shoe. Now, let's put our heads together and figure out something before it's too late."

Three beer bottles clinked together before they were upended.

The Lane sisters were on a roll.

3

Bella Gunn was almost out of her mind with happiness as she discarded one outfit after another in her attempt to be the best-dressed woman at the *Rougie* tea. She'd redone her makeup twice, and was now on her seventh outfit. She wished there was someone she could ask for advice. If ever there was a time to be in perfect tune with the women of Baton Rouge, this was it.

She'd been so stunned when Honoria Tribedoux called to invite her to tea, she'd actually been tongue-tied. Somehow or other she'd managed to accept and to scribble down the time and place. An hour from now she would be sitting down to tea at one of the houses in the Garden District that she'd lusted after for years and years. There was a God after all, and he was smiling down on one Bella Gunn.

She should have gone shopping for something new,

but that wasn't the way the *Rougies* did things. They wore clothes that they accessorized and never went out of style. The same little black dress, the same long black skirt, the same shoes with a buckle or a leather flower. They certainly had the means to buy new things but new *things* weren't important to those women.

She'd read up on old money, but she would never understand it. Who wanted to sit on the same smelly old furniture your ancestors sat on a hundred years ago? Still, if she wanted to belong, she was going to have to do the same thing and pretend to like it.

Bella stepped into a sheer flowered dress that looked like it was at least twenty years old and ideal for a lady on a hot summer day. She needed to look *wilted*.

He cologne was summery, too. Light. Lily of the Valley.

As much as she wanted to show up in the Garden District in her chauffeured car, she knew she was going to have to drive herself. The *Rougies* were not ostentatious in any way. She'd actually seen them pedaling bicycles to and fro on their errands. Well, that was never going to happen where she was concerned.

Bella looked in the mirror and wanted to cry. She'd plastered her *poufy* see-through hair close to her head into tight little curls. She thought she looked like a wrinkled Shirley Temple. Oh well, when in Rome . . .

Straw bag in hand, gloves tucked into the handle, Bella started the engine of her car. She'd made three dry runs over the past few days, late at night, to judge the time it would take her to make the short trip to the Garden District. Thirteen minutes if she hit every single green light, seventeen minutes if she hit one red light, and twenty-one minutes if she hit all three red lights.

All the way to the District, Bella did her breathing exercises, hoping to calm her frazzled nerves. This was so important. So long in coming.

And then she was there. There were three other cars parked along the curb. She wasn't the first one to arrive. That was good. Being the last, even though in some circles it was considered fashionable to be late, was not an option.

Bella looked up and down the beautiful street with the angel oaks that dripped Spanish moss, at the colorful flower beds that looked like they'd just been manicured. She'd heard more than once that the garden ladies were out working on their flowers and lawns the minute the sun came up. Like she would ever do something like that. That was why she had gardeners.

The walkway up to Honoria's veranda consisted of hand-painted, colored walking stones with bits of manicured grass growing in between. Each stone had a hand-painted ladybug, dragonfly, or some other winged creature. Bella was careful not to step on the winged creatures.

The veranda was awash in color and smelled heavenly. She looked to her left and saw a trellis with Confederate jasmine that was lush and full. Yellow clay pots full of gardenias sat at each side of the doorway. The scent was almost overpowering. All along the railing were other colored pots with petunias, Gerber daisies, and impatiens. Thick lush ferns hung from the rafters next to paddle fans that circulated the scented air.

The furniture was old wicker, scuffed and scratched. Definitely used. The dark green fiber carpets were also old, almost threadbare.

The last thing she noticed were the windows, nine over nine, as they were called, with the wavy glass that made you sick to your stomach when you looked through it. It was old, original, and valuable.

Bella rang the doorbell as she tried not to look through the screen door into the long hallway with the steep staircase leading to the second floor. She was appalled to see a hole in the screen door big enough to stick her finger through. What *did* these people spend their money on? Maybe they didn't spend it at all, and that's why they said old money was moldy.

"Mrs. Gunn, how nice to see you. Please come in," Honoria Tribedoux said, holding the screen door wide open for Bella to step through.

"It was nice of you to invite me," Bella gushed.

"Come in, come in. We're just waiting for Justine, and she's always late. Usually we're just about wrapping things up when she favors us with her company."

Bella followed her hostess down the long, dark hallway to an equally dark dining room. The house smelled musty and old, the scent fighting with the overpowering smell of fresh flowers that were everywhere.

They were seated around a long, elegant draped table. Sterling silver tea service, exquisite china, priceless silverware that was as old as the house. Heirlooms. Something she did not have. The tablecloth was old, fine linen, and in several places Bella could see that someone had mended it. Obviously another heirloom. Even though she didn't like old things, she suddenly wanted all she was seeing.

"You know everyone, Bethany, Marjorie, Celine, Sarabess, Helene, and Ethel, don't you, Mrs. Gunn? Justine will be along at some point."

Bella's head bobbled around as she acknowledged the women who had refused to admit her into their exclusive circle for so many years. She wondered if they would laugh if she told them how many nights she'd cried herself to sleep over their rejection. "Yes, of course. Please, call me Bella."

"Tea?" Honoria said, assuming her role as hostess. "I made the scones myself this morning. I think, Bethany, they are almost as good as your mama's."

Bella couldn't remember the last time she'd had a cup of tea, and she didn't think she'd ever had a scone either. When in Rome . . .

"I think the decision you made regarding your stepson's organs was magnificent. How hard that must have been for you. I don't know if I could have done that. What was going through your mind when you made that awesome decision?" Celine asked.

Bella lowered her teacup to the saucer, amazed that

her hand wasn't trembling, shocked that she didn't spill her tea. She'd rehearsed this very speech a hundred times over the past few days and had it down pat. She looked around at the women staring at her. She'd hungered for this very meeting, visualizing it over the years. She allowed her eyes to fill with tears. For the first time in her life, she felt important.

"It . . . it was the hardest thing I ever had to do. As you know, my husband is . . . very ill. I tried discussing it with him, but he didn't seem to . . . to understand. His thought processes just aren't the same anymore. Time was of the essence, according to the doctors. When he told me how many lives could be either saved or helped, the decision wasn't that hard. It saddened me, so I couldn't eat or sleep for days. I'm still . . . what I mean is . . . I just have a hard time discussing it. I didn't want to speak on television, but the reporters told me it would help other people make similar decisions."

"Well, I think it was a splendid thing you did. You're a heroine in my eyes," Celine said.

"No, I'm just a mother. Actually, I'm not really a mother, just a stepmother. Not a wicked one, however," she said, with a rueful smile.

"Nonsense," Marjorie said, biting into a scone. "Never hide your light under a bushel, my dear. Now, what is this we hear about your restoring the houses in the shoe that belong to the Gunn family?"

"Oh, my, I didn't think anyone was aware of that. They're an eyesore to the shoe, as you know. Marcus for some reason didn't . . . wasn't . . . I just thought it was a shame for such grand old houses to deteriorate like that. I have my work cut out for me, but I need to channel my . . . thoughts elsewhere. Life was becoming too sad, and I didn't want to wallow." She dabbed at her eyes to make her point.

"Are you going to live there when you finish?" Sarabess asked coolly.

Sarabess would be the holdout. Bella didn't know how she knew that, she just did.

"I certainly hope so. I think Marcus will like going back to the shoe. The Lane sisters are so upset at the way the buildings are rotting away. I'll modernize them and of course we'll move into one of them. I'm hoping Marcus's son Ben will want to move into the other one." *Liar, liar, pants on fire.*

Sarabess's head jerked upright. "What does that mean, modernize the houses?"

"Why . . . I . . . mean . . . an updated kitchen, pretty bathrooms, things like that. Nothing will be changed on the outside. We'll restore the gardens so they flow into the Lane sisters' gardens. The architect I hired has promised to keep everything the way it was for the most part. Do you think that might be a problem, Sarabess?"

"That's for the Preservation Society to decide. Of course, we'll all be watching to see that the contractors stick to the guidelines."

"Of course," Bella said as she folded her hands in her lap. "I wouldn't have it any other way." She knew in her gut that Sarabess was going to be a holdout if a vote of any kind had to be taken.

"Yoo-hoo! I'm here," Justine Bleekman shouted from the foyer. She appeared a moment later in the doorway. "Hello, girls! Ah, you started without me. I forgive you this time, but I do think you could have waited since we have a guest today." She turned and smiled at Bella. "How nice to see you. Wonderful, wonderful thing you did, Bella. The whole town is talking about you. That was so generous, so humane, so wonderful to give other people life. The town should give you a medal. Girls, girls, isn't it time we invited Bella to join our little club and include her in the Christmas tour?"

Bella almost choked as she looked around the dark dining room with all of Bethany's ancestors glaring at her from their gilt frames.

"Good heavens," Bella managed to squeak, "I certainly don't want a medal. I just did what was right." Justine was the ringleader of this little group. And all along she'd thought it was Bethany.

"Bella is going to modernize the Gunn houses in the shoe," Sarabess said. This time her voice was downright cold, so cold, Bella felt goose bumps on her arms.

"About time," Justine said popping a scone into her mouth. "The Lane sisters must be ecstatic. They're such eyesores. The shoe was always so beautiful. Now, what are we discussing today, girls?"

"Nothing," Bethany said. "We just invited Bella to tea to thank her for what she did in regard to the donor program. Things of that magnitude need to be recognized. There is one thing we should make a decision on. The Barkers' veranda is sagging on the left end. It's very jarring to look at it. We need to have a fund-raiser to get some money to have it fixed. A bake sale should do it. Can we count on you, Bella?"

Could they count on her? Did she hear them right? "Of course, I'll be happy to do whatever I can."

"I'm nominating Bella's house for the Christmas tour," Ethel said. "By next year her house in the shoe will be ready so she'll have two different houses in the tour. Now, won't that be something? We've all had the same house year after year. I don't think anyone has ever had two *different* houses. That's probably a good thing."

"Well, I hate to eat and run but I have to stop by Lumosa's to pick up some bulbs and peat moss," Marjorie said. She stood up, walked over to Bella, patted her on the shoulder, and said, "It was nice seeing and talking to you, Bella. I'll take care of getting the forms to you for the tour. I have to warn you, they're extensive and must be filled out in triplicate. We don't let just anybody on the tour. You have to be someone special to get nominated. Bye, everyone."

Bella was so light-headed she didn't know if she would be steady on her feet when she stood up. She was *in*. They were accepting her. She could feel it in her bones.

One by one, the women trickled toward the front door. Sarabess looked Bella in the eye and said, "You know we have to vote on it, so don't get your hopes up, Bella."

"I won't, Sarabess. It was nice seeing you again. Good-bye."

It was Willie who woke her, his nose nudging her to get up. Clearly, he had to go out. Stunned that she'd actually slept, Darby struggled to her feet to lead the way down the steps. She moved quietly so as not to wake Dodo. Willie was just as quiet.

Outside, it was still hot and humid at three-thirty in the morning. Typical Baton Rouge weather that wouldn't change anytime soon.

Darby sat down on the steps to wait for Willie to make his circle of the Horseshoe. He knew every bush, every blade of grass. She allowed her gaze to settle on Ducky's house in the center of the cul-de-sac. Ducky had turned on the porch light. A dim yellow light could be seen on the second floor. The lamp on the little table in the upstairs hallway. In the moonlight, she could see Willie meandering around the yard. She wondered if he'd buried bones on a previous visit and was now looking for them.

The silvery quarter moon rode low in the sky, the perfect complement to the backdrop of twinkling stars. Once, a long time ago, she'd drawn a sky just like the one she was looking at now. She wondered if it was in the little desk upstairs. Her thoughts took her back in time to her childhood when she'd dreamed of one day having a house of her very own in the shoe. Maybe that's why she created dollhouses. Each one was hers for a little while before she had to give it up. When she was little, she'd dreamed of growing up and marrying Ben. They'd live in the shoe and swing on the swing in the evenings when it got dark. They'd hold hands and listen to the tree frogs and watch the fireflies. A little girl's dream. She wondered what Ben dreamed about.

Russell bludgeoned his way back into her thoughts. Now he belonged to her past, the way the drawing of the moon and stars belonged there. She closed her eyes, trying to bring Russell's face into focus. She bolted upright off the steps when it was Ben Gunn's face that formed behind her eyelids.

Darby shook her head to wipe away Ben's face. She needed to do something. She couldn't just continue to sit there watching Willie pee on every blade of grass on the shoe. On wobbly legs, Darby made her way into the kitchen, where she rifled through the cutlery drawer for a large spoon. That would do to dig up the begonias. With the earth soft and moist from all the rain, the flowers and their roots would come up easily. If she dug them up now, they would be ready to take to the cemetery to plant at first light.

The screen door squeaked slightly as Darby let herself back outside into the humid night. Willie heard the sound of the door and bounded over to join her. She reached down to scratch him behind the ears. The retriever followed her around to the front yard, where, with the aid of the moonlight and the bright stars, she dropped to her knees and started to dig through the luscious begonia border. When she'd had enough, she walked across the yard to Diddy's house, where she started to dig again. The flowers came out of the ground with ease. She lined them up, knowing the roots would stay wet until she could plant them on Russ's grave. In her mind, she knew exactly how she would plant them. Two pinks to one lavender. Then the colorful Gerber daisies from Ducky's yard would be planted around the gravestone that would have been set up today except for the rain. The caretaker had told her he planned on setting up the stone early in the morning.

Darby retraced her steps, Willie at her side, to the flower garden in the middle of the Horseshoe. The three aunts had made the garden when she was a little girl. It was beautiful as well as colorful, adding just the right touch to the shoe. It also smelled heavenly, with the Confederate jasmine and honeysuckle that climbed over the huge rocks the boys—Russ and Ben—had rolled to the garden. They'd all been part of the garden, and, as children, it was their job to weed and water the bright blooms, a responsibility all four of them took seriously. Even though there was a full-time gardener for the Horseshoe, he never touched the garden in the center of what the children had nicknamed the shoe.

Willie nudged her leg closer to the little garden. She sat down cross-legged. Willie dropped to the ground to lay his golden head in her lap. She stroked him, trying not to cry. She was so consumed with her own grief she didn't see the lights go on in all three houses on the perimeter of the Horseshoe.

They came from three different directions. Willie growled, remembering it was these three women who had given him that hateful bath. He growled, but it wasn't a serious growl. He knew he was safe with Darby.

No one said anything for a few minutes until Diddy spoke. "We're going to get *piles* if we sit here."

"Hemorrhoids," Ducky said. "*Piles* is an old-fashioned word. It dates you, Diddy."

"Ask me if I care," Diddy said.

"I guess you dug up the flowers, huh?" Dodo said.

"I didn't do the Gerbers yet. For some reason Willie nudged me over here. It's so pretty here, and peaceful, especially at night. Do you remember how we used to run around the shoe catching fireflies?"

"Of course," Ducky said.

"Ben always let them out of the jar when we weren't looking. He could never stand to see anything confined. How long is he staying, do you know?"

"I guess he'll stay as long as he needs to stay. Mary's leaving sometime today. They're supposed to come over in the morning. We need to talk to you about something, Darby," Diddy said.

"Can't it wait till later? I don't much feel like talking right now. I just want to sit here with Willie and my memories."

The three sisters looked at one another. Dodo shook her head.

It was Ducky who took a deep breath, exhaled, then cleared her throat. "No, you need to know this right now. In the morning . . . you might change your mind about going to the cemetery. That's not Russ in the grave. Well, it is, but it isn't. Bella donated all of Russell's organs. It was on the evening news, two hours after the accident. They just buried his bones. For all we know, Bella donated his brain to science." She huffed and puffed to show her total disapproval.

Darby pushed herself erect until she was on her feet. A sound, unlike anything the three sisters had ever heard, escaped from their niece's lips. A second later, Darby was running across the shoe to Ducky's house.

"Maybe we should have waited till morning. Darkness seems to make everything worse," Diddy said sadly.

Minutes later, Darby returned with a powder blue envelope. She waved it threateningly. "I have Russ's will right here. There's a video, too!" Darby screeched. "It's called a living will. You can't ignore a person's last will and testament. Especially a living will."

"Bella did just that," one of the sisters said quietly.

"No, no, you have to be mistaken." Darby waved the blue envelope again. "It's against the law."

"It's done, baby," Dodo said softly. "It can't be undone."

"But . . . do Ben and Mary know? Did they okay it?"

"They know *now*. They arrived after the . . . after the

arrangements were made. The funeral service was almost immediate. At best, there were only a few hours between the time they arrived and the time of the . . . the burial. Neither Ben nor Mary knew about the . . . the donor part. Baby, I don't think Russell ever told anyone. I can't be sure of that. For all we know, Russell may have changed his mind," Dodo said.

"No, no, Russ didn't change his mind. It was the only thing he and I ever argued about, and we really didn't argue as much as disagree. We discussed the donor program at great length. I believe in donating one's organs so that someone else can have a chance at life. Russ didn't want any part of that. His exact words were, 'I don't want someone ripping out my heart and kidneys. I came into this world with all my parts, and I want to leave the same way.' He trusted me to see that his last wishes were carried out, and I failed him. Oh, God, I failed him. How am I supposed to live with that?"

Dodo looked around at the dark night surrounding them and struggled to find the right words. She knew her sisters were struggling, too. Sometimes only the truth worked. She knew what it was like to fail someone you loved so completely. Feeling it and talking about it was not something she was prepared to do. Her heart started to ache at the memory. Yet she had to say something to her niece. Something meaningful. If not meaningful, at least comforting.

"I don't know, baby. What happened was beyond

your control. Do you think for one minute either Bella or Marcus would have listened to you, an outsider? It's too late to do anything. Now we all have to grieve and move on. It's the only thing that's left to us."

Darby waved her arms, stamping her feet at the same time. Russell's will flapped in the humid night breeze. "Like hell!" Darby shouted. "Russell gave the Gunn Foundation a copy of the video and his will. I was with him when he delivered it. The foundation was the reason he made the will in the first place. He made it the day we graduated from college. That means his father and Bella knew about it. Russ said his father was adamant about his making that will. It was tied into some trust and his coming of age, that kind of thing. Someone has to pay for this. Don't think for one minute I'm going to let this matter drop, because I'm not."

The aunts huddled together. Willie whined at Darby's feet.

Darby squared her shoulders. "Good night, every one. I'm going to take Willie in the house, and we're going to bed. I don't intend to sleep. I'm going to think about all of this. We'll talk in the morning. Diddy, I'll be at your house for breakfast at seven o'clock. If it isn't too much trouble, I'd like some banana-macadamia pancakes."

"This is good. I mean, it's really good. This is the Darby we know and love," Ducky said after her niece rounded the corner of the house and was lost to sight.

"I told you we needed to make a plan," Dodo hissed.

"That damn Bella will chew her up and spit her out. The woman's middle name is Vicious. Darby is no match for that witch. We might have to call in our *big gun*." Both Ducky and Dodo fixed their gaze on Diddy, who stepped backward.

"Oh, no. No, no. Don't either one of you two go there. Just forget it. Both of you gave me your solemn word of honor, you promised never to bring that up. No. Do you hear me? No, absolutely not."

"Of course we can hear you. Half of Baton Rouge can hear you," Dodo snapped.

"Sometimes in a crisis, people have to do things they don't want to do. That's another way of saying you'll do it, Diddy, if it comes to that," Ducky said quietly. "And you'll be doing it for all the right reasons. In this particular case, the end will justify the means."

Diddy stared at her sisters in the silvery moonlight. In that one moment she realized the vast difference between herself and her sisters. She considered herself the sane, stable sister, preferring to stay home, making her one-of-a-kind quilts, cooking, canning vegetables and fruits, reading, studying the history of Baton Rouge, knowing that someday she would write her memoirs. A homebody in every sense of the word. Until that one time when she'd stepped off her chosen path.

Ducky was and always had been a wandering gypsy, traveling here and there, soaking up other cultures, meeting new men, never marrying, and living the good life, returning to her roots only when she needed to be rejuvenated by her family. If that didn't work, she treated herself to face-lifts, implants, and anything else she could think of to make herself feel better.

Dodo was a free spirit but in a different way from Ducky. Dodo, perhaps because of her diminutive size, had turned to the martial arts and even studied with some of the great masters in Japan early on in her life. In her own right she was almost as famous as Bruce Lee. Dodo had a fourth-degree black belt. At the age of fifty, she'd hung up her belt and proceeded to teach the art to the people of Baton Rouge. To this day, she still returned to Japan once or twice a year to judge various martial arts exhibitions and trials that garnered worldwide attention and publicity. In doing so, she always made the front page of the *Baton Rouge Advocate*. Dodo knew how to kill with just thumb pressure. She could fell an ox and never break a sweat.

"Be on time for breakfast, and I don't take orders, so you will eat whatever I prepare. I cook, you clean up. Good night."

Without another word, Diddy turned and walked across the lawn, aware that her sisters were watching her. They were probably, right then, that very second, talking about the weight she'd put on, how she hadn't colored her hair, and the frumpy one-size-fits-all dresses she wore. Her plump cheeks burned with embarrassment as she waddled along. She looked this way because she'd been a fool. Not just a plain old fool, a *really big* old fool.

Diddy hated going down memory lane. It was simply too rocky a path to follow. But if she had to get back on that miserable road for Darby, she would. Her plump shoulders slumped but only momentarily. They squared almost immediately as she let herself into her old-fashioned comfortable kitchen. She sighed as she set about making herself a cup of black rum tea. She knew there was no point in going upstairs and back to bed. She might as well sit in the kitchen and plan her breakfast menu.

Across the shoe, in the shell pink room on the second floor, Darby Lane paced, her shoulders rigid, her eyes hot and dry. She looked down at the golden retriever, who was dogging her every step. Dropping to her knees, she started to cry as she told the whimpering animal what she was feeling. "What do I do now, Willie? How am I supposed to go on with my life knowing someone else is viewing life through Russ's eyes? His kind, generous heart is beating in a stranger's chest.

"Will any of those recipients take Russ's fifth-grade class white-water rafting in Colorado next spring the way he planned? Will whoever has his heart know that he planned on giving Claire Bannon an engagement ring this Christmas? Oh, God, Willie, I don't know what to do. I can't think. Why can't I think?"

A second later, Darby was on her feet, running down the hall to Russ's old room. She flung herself into his old, brown, cold chair. With a joyful bark, Willie was next to her, snuggling hard against her side. "It feels right, doesn't it, boy? Maybe I can think in here, come up with some way to make up for not being here to stop Bella from breaking Russ's will." Tucking her legs beneath her, the dog's head in her lap, she sighed.

She was asleep within seconds.

4

While Darby and the aunts were sitting down to a breakfast of banana and macadamia-nut pancakes with banana syrup, a striking blonde carrying a briefcase stared at Ben Gunn in the mirrored walls inside the elevator of the Baton Rouge Inn. Ben was totally oblivious to the woman's admiring looks. Clad in sharply creased khaki slacks and a crisp white shirt whose sleeves were rolled to the middle of his forearms, his dark hair still wet from the shower, he made a striking picture. He respectfully stood aside to hold the door for the young woman to step forward when the doors slid open on the lobby level. The blonde's briefcase banged against Ben's knee—deliberately. She apologized profusely, smiling at the same time. Ben nodded, accepting the apology before he turned left into the lobby, and the blonde turned right to the revolving door.

Ben's eyes raked the crowded lobby for his sister Mary. She was sitting on a dark blue chair, a small suitcase at her feet. From the tip of her head to the case at her feet, her persona shrieked L. L. Bean. Mary spotted him at the same moment he noticed her. His eyes on his sister's face, he bent down to pick up the small suitcase. Mary stopped him.

"You don't have to take me to the airport. I called a car service. Actually, the driver is waiting outside. I wanted to say good-bye."

Ben looked nonplussed, not understanding. "You said you wanted to see the aunts and Darby. Why are you changing your plan? What about Dad?"

Two youngsters raced across the lobby, the smaller one tripping over Mary's suitcase. Ben bent over to pick up the little boy, who started to wail his head off. A stern-looking man delivered a well-placed smack on the boy's backside. The boy wailed louder as his sibling smirked on the sidelines.

Mary shrugged. "That was last night. This is now. I don't belong here anymore. I made a life for myself in New York. Tell the aunts I said good-bye. I'll send them a Christmas card." Her voice was so curt and sounded so flat, Ben winced.

A *Christmas card.* Ben looked at his sister. No one would ever call Mary pretty. Nor would they call her cute. *Plain* was a word attached to Mary by most people. Her thick brown hair was pulled back into a tight ponytail that brushed her shoulders. It was as lusterless as were her light brown eyes. She wore no makeup, and her clothes, while neat and wrinkle-free, were as plain as she was. The suitcase at her feet was bright red, an L. L. Bean special, probably for easy identification like their lemon yellow bags. Mary was such a cold fish that he couldn't help but wonder how she could run a successful travel agency. Maybe she was different with strangers who plunked down money for her services.

"What about Dad?" Ben persisted, unwilling to give up.

"Yeah, Ben, what about him? I don't owe him a thing, and I'm not going to pretend I do. I will not subject myself to a meeting with Bella. Not for you, and not for Russ. And as for our father, where was he when we needed him? I'll send you a Christmas card," she said again.

"You know what, Mary, don't bother." Ben's voice was so bitter it surprised him. "We're all that's left. Me and you. Russ isn't here anymore. Doesn't that mean anything to you?"

"No."

The bluntness of his sister's statement stunned Ben. "Do you want me to deliver any message to Darby?"

"No." The suitcase was suddenly in her hands, the matching backpack on her shoulders forcing Ben to take a step backward. The kid who had tripped was still wailing as his father completed the checking-in process.

"I guess it's good-bye, then."

"Yeah. See you around, Ben. By the way, I left a

standing order with the local florist to deliver flowers every Saturday. That's to show you I'm not heartless."

Ben shrugged as he watched his sister stride through the revolving door. He waited to see if she'd turn and wave. She didn't. Angry at his sister's attitude, Ben made his way to the bank of elevators. The stressed-out father from the registration desk was dragging his squealing kid by his shirt collar, his sibling still smirking. When the elevator door opened, Ben stepped back to wait for the next one. He heard the father say, "You just wait till I get you in the room, Tommy."

Ten minutes later, Ben hung his dark blue suit in a garment bag and zipped it closed. He hadn't really unpacked, so there was nothing left to stow except for his shaving gear. The thick zipper ripped across the oversize suitcase, the sound so loud that it jarred Ben's ears in the quiet room.

Ben slung the garment bag over his shoulder, snapped the handle of his suitcase, and wheeled it out of the room. He was going to the only place he could even remotely call home: the shoe.

Outside, the hot, humid air attacked him like a sodden blanket as he made his way to the inn's parking lot and his rental car.

Twenty minutes later, Ben Gunn whizzed past the road in front of the Horseshoe. He slowed down to take the corner that led to a narrow cobbled lane where two old barns that had been converted to garages stood. As children, they'd played in the barns, swinging from the rafters as they whooped and hollered. In total, the two barns could now house eight vehicles. Four of the parking spaces belonged to the two Gunn houses at the ends of the Horseshoe. With the new white paint, new doors, new windows to match the houses, gingerbread at the peaks, there were no memories here to resurrect. A different place, a different time. Ben felt sad as he parked in front of the closest garage.

He fished out his bags and let himself through an ornate iron gate that led to the back of Ducky's house. He followed a footpath whose cobblestones were worn smooth from many years of traffic back and forth. The path was narrow, bordered by pink, blue, and white hydrangeas. Off to the right, moss dripped, and Confederate jasmine twined around one of the old oak trees. Thick, cushioned grass as green as emeralds stretched across the shoe as far as the eye could see. Mounds of thick, luxurious green moss covered the ground beneath the old trees. He sniffed appreciatively. The lawn must have been mowed recently. The scent of newmown grass mixed with the heady flower scent reminded Ben of his childhood. He remembered giving Darby a daisy once and watching her pluck the tiny petals. He could still hear her childish voice as she said, "He loves me, he loves me not." He couldn't remember what the last petal was on that particular day. What he did remember was Mary standing on the sidelines watching. He'd scurried over to the flower bed to pick a flower for her and had presented it with a flourish. She'd thrown it on the ground and crushed it with the heel of her shoe.

Ben shook his head to clear his thoughts. Some old memories were too ugly to remember.

When Ben reached the end of the footpath he stood still, undecided as to which house he should go to. They were one and the same, and yet they weren't. Ducky's house was out for obvious reasons, leaving either Dodo's or Diddy's as his choices. For some reason he'd always felt closer to Dodo, and her tell-it-like-it-is approach to him, his siblings, and life. On the other hand, Diddy's hugs were so motherly that, as a child, he literally used to swoon with feeling when she gathered him close. Ducky was the one who was a woman of the new century. He liked her free spirit, her roguish wink, her laughter, and her generous spirit.

He turned to walk across the lawn. Dodo's house.

The moment he plopped his garment bag and suitcase on the back porch, Diddy shouted from her own porch. "Ben, come for breakfast!"

Ben didn't need to be asked twice or coaxed. As he leaped over the banister and sprinted across the lawn, he realized he was starved. The last time he'd eaten was the previous morning, and all he'd had then was a bagel and coffee. He blew into Diddy's kitchen like a fresh gust of wind. Willie ran to him and pawed him happily as he barked and pranced around. This was, after all, the guy who'd saved him from the pound. Ben threw back his head and laughed. "Easy, boy, easy!" He spent a few minutes tussling with the dog while Dodo set a place at the table.

Diddy turned the heat on under the griddle. "Wash your hands," she said briskly.

"Yes, ma'am. Cleanliness and godliness." He grinned, showing he remembered the childhood ritual.

"Where's Mary?" Darby queried from her seat at the table.

Ben drew a deep breath and turned to look at Darby.

She was wearing a sleeveless lavender blouse with matching shorts, the same color as the begonias that lined the front of Diddy's house. She had her hair pulled back into a ponytail. She looked sad and woebegone.

What to say? How to say it? *Just say it, Ben,* he told himself. "She's on her way back to New York." Maybe it was the curt words or maybe it was the look on Ben's face that left the four women speechless. Whatever it was, they all busied themselves folding their napkins, slipping Willie tidbits, or, in Ducky's case, putting on her slippers. The awkward moment passed when Diddy slid a half dozen luscious pancakes onto his plate. He wolfed them down within minutes. As soon as he finished the last bite, Diddy slid six more pancakes onto his plate, along with a stack of crisp bacon. Willie was immediately at his side, begging for his share.

Darby tried not to stare at the handsome man sitting across from her. Russ's brother. Almost a stranger but not quite. She thought about her childhood crush so many years ago. How many times she'd dreamed of him in her teenage years. For some reason she felt nervous and jittery being so close to him.

Ben sighed and shoved his plate to the center of the table. He gulped the last of his coffee before slipping the remainder of the bacon to Willie. "That was so good, Diddy. I can't remember the last time I had food this great. It's a super way to start the day. Thank you."

Darby stood up to carry her plate to the dishwasher. "If it's okay, I'm going to go to the cemetery."

"I'll go with you," Ben volunteered.

"Darby, use the new wheelbarrow I bought. It's battery-operated. You can push it with your pinkie," Diddy said. "It's under the back porch steps. Be sure to take some peat moss and manure. It's all in the garage. You better take a few jugs of water as well."

"Okay," Darby said agreeably. Ben held the screen door. Darby rushed through, savoring the scent of his aftershave.

It took Ben only ten minutes to load the flowers, peat moss, and manure into the back of the gardener's pickup truck. He dusted off his hands as he held the passenger-side door for Darby. He hopped into the driver's side, slid the truck into gear, and barreled out of the alley. "Buckle up," he called out.

"Okay, *Dad*." Darby smiled.

If there was one thing he didn't want to be, it was Darby's dad. He struggled for something light to say, something to take away the somber mood of his companion.

"Tell me about your business. Russ just hit the highlights. He did say he designed your Web page. He was always good at stuff like that." *Brilliant conversation, Ben.*

Darby shrugged her lavender shoulders. "I didn't want to teach, so I sort of floundered after college. Unlike Russ, who always knew he wanted to teach kids. It just happened. Ducky lets me stay in her house. I moved my stuff in, and part of that 'stuff' was my collection of dollhouses that had come to me from my grandfather. I have five of them, one for each house on the shoe. Once I tried to give Mary the two that represented the Gunn houses, but she just looked at me and said she didn't want my charity. At the time, I didn't understand what she meant. I don't think she ever liked me. Anyway, one day the housekeeper was cleaning my room and accidentally knocked one of the houses over. It was one of the old ones and it kind of collapsed on itself. I was so heartbroken, I tried to fix it. It ended up looking better than ever. I painted it, and it was as good as new. Voilà! A business was born. Russ helped with the business end of things. He made sure I got off to a good start. The aunts were there every step of the way. Now I have more business than I can handle."

Ben scratched at his head. "And you earn a living doing this?"

A sound Ben assumed was laughter escaped from Darby's lips. "Six figures a year. No overhead, no employees. I charge a lot. I was in Scotland to sell one of the houses when . . . when Russ died. I had a call from this viscount who said his daughter was a semi-invalid, and he wanted to order a custom dollhouse. It was a fifty-thousand-dollar order, that's why I went. He paid for my travel and accommodations."

Ben scratched his head again. "Fifty thousand dollars for a toy! I'm in the wrong business. Do you need a partner?" he joked.

Darby turned to stare at Ben. "No, not really. I don't want to flood the market. That's why I never hired anyone. Thanks for the offer, though. Hey, slow down, there's the entrance to the cemetery. I don't like this place."

"Guess what. I don't like it either. Mary told me she left a standing order with a florist to deliver flowers every week."

Darby hopped out of the truck. "It was a good idea to bring that wheelbarrow. It's a long walk to . . . to where . . . Russ is buried."

Ben dropped the tailgate. The sound was so loud in the quiet cemetery, Darby jumped. She took a deep breath and helped load the begonias into the wheelbarrow. The gardening tools followed the flowers; the bale of peat moss and the bag of manure stayed in the truck. "I'll come back for the rest. You can get started while I do that."

Darby started off, following the brick path. "I like it that the grave is under one of those big trees. The sun here is so brutal." She turned to look up at him. "Do you think there are special things you're supposed to say in a place like this? Or are you just supposed to *think*?"

"I think it's one of those whatever-feels-right things," Ben said, and Darby nodded.

"Oh, look, the caretaker or someone put up the stone. It's so . . . so plain." Darby dropped to her knees. "It just has his name and birthday on it and that one little angel." Darby looked around, pointing to other gravestones. "Look at those. They have big angels and cherubs. Russ deserves better than this."

Ben stepped closer to take her shoulders in his hands. A jolt of electricity rushed through him. "We can always get a bigger stone. Somehow I think Russ would have liked this simple one."

Darby nodded, her shoulders shaking. Ben was right.

Ben whirled around, the wheelbarrow moving on its own. *Brilliant move, Ben, real brilliant.*

Ben was back within minutes. He opened the bag of peat moss with a small knife on his key chain. They worked in sync and were done in thirty minutes. No one was more relieved than he was. He watched as Darby tidied the gravesite, picking up broken leaves and a few stray petals from the blooms. Suddenly, he wanted to bawl his eyes out. Whatever expression was on his face, Darby reacted.

"I want to say something comforting to you, but I don't know the words. I suppose I should say it will be all right, but it won't be all right. I failed him. How do you think I'm going to live with that for the rest of my life. He trusted me. He made me the executrix of his will, and I wasn't even here to see that his last wishes were honored. I have to do something. This"—Darby pointed to the flowers—"was a start. Maybe someone else could leave it at that, but not me."

"You must have loved him very much?"

Darby's head jerked upright. "I did ... do ... love Russ but not the way your tone is implying. No one, even the aunts, ever understood Russ's and my relationship. He was my best friend, the brother I never had. There was nothing romantic between us. He trusted me. I trusted him. It was a special, extraordinary relationship that goes back to childhood. He had this wonderful girlfriend named Claire. He showed me the engagement ring he bought her. He was going to give it to her at Christmas.

"We should go to Russ's apartment and get that ring. I think we should give it to Claire. What do you think, Ben?"

She wasn't in love with Russ. There was no ring on her finger. "Yeah, yeah, let's do that." Suddenly he felt better than he'd felt since learning of Russ's accident. "And after we get the ring, I think we should go see Mr. Bodene."

"You didn't say how long you're staying."

"As long as it takes. I took a leave of absence. Okay, let's go see attorney Bodene."

"Okay."

Darby turned to look at Russ's grave. "I know what you said. I . . . it's a place to come to. Everyone needs a place to go to unburden. His name is on this little space. That makes it his. Maybe . . . maybe I'll bring something from his apartment and . . . and bury it here to make it . . . you know, even more *official*. What do you think, Ben?"

What do I think? Darby was asking his advice. Ben's chest puffed out. "I think it's doable." He held the door for her, aware of her long, tanned legs. He noted the bright red polish on her toenails. He thought that made her adventuresome.

"If Russ was about to get engaged, what would that have done to your relationship?" Ben asked curiously.

"Claire's one of my best friends. In fact, I introduced her to Russ. It was love at first sight for both of them. Claire understood my and Russ's relationship. You look like you find that hard to understand, Ben. Don't you have any close female friends?" She smiled, and his heart melted.

Ben's thoughts raced back to Mustang Island and Mandy Prentice, the young woman he'd dated off and on for the past two years. If he never saw Mandy again, it wouldn't break his heart. He would, however, miss her friendship. "I suppose so," he answered vaguely.

"How did Russ feel when you dated other guys?" He wondered if Darby would see through his transparent question.

"He was forever trying to fix me up with some of his teacher friends. We double-dated a lot. If that's your way of asking me if I'm engaged or seeing anyone on a steady basis, the answer is no."

Yesssss.

They were almost to the shoe when Darby turned in her seat and asked the question that had been on the tip of her tongue all morning. "Ben, I'd like to go see your father after we go to see the attorney. Do you think he'll see me?"

"Probably not. We can try. Bella . . ."

"What about his doctor? Can't we get him to intercede? Or someone from the Gunn Foundation."

"Again, Bella . . ."

Darby's shoulders stiffened. "You have a right to see your father, Ben. I'll go with you; there's strength in numbers."

Yesterday he had been willing to wash his father and Bella out of his life the way Mary had. Today, it was a different story. All because the woman who had plagued his dreams for years and years had asked. "Okay, but be prepared to be disappointed."

Darby merely nodded. The rest of the drive back to the shoe was made in comfortable silence. Ben unloaded the wheelbarrow for Darby to return to its resting place and parked the truck inside the garage.

"I just want to wash up a little and change my clothes. Ten minutes tops, okay?"

If she'd asked him to wait for ten hours, his reply would have been the same. "Sure."

Ben settled himself on a decorative iron bench inside the gazebo. He wasn't at all surprised to see a crystal pitcher full of sweet tea and two glasses full of ice cubes on a silver tray. Linen napkins and colorful coasters sat on the glass-topped table. The aunts must have heard the old clunker coming down the alley. He poured a full glass and downed it in two long gulps. He filled it a second time.

When they were children there was always either juice or tea along with cookies in the gazebo. One minute they would be shinnying up trees, running around like wild Indians, then magically, one or the other would spot the treats. Play would always cease until they finished every drop and crumb. Fortified, they would go back to whatever they had been doing.

Ben closed his eyes, his shoulders slumping. It wasn't his grown brother's face that surfaced behind his closed lids but rather the face of a crying four-year-old Russell who was running toward him, tears streaming down his cheeks as he pointed to his knee and the blood running down his leg. "Can you fix it, Ben? Huh, please. Don't tell Aunt Diddy. She might make me go home. Can you fix it, Ben? I won't cry," the pudgy little boy had said, wiping his eyes on his shirtsleeve.

He remembered exactly what he'd done. He'd

picked up Russ and run across the yard to Diddy's house, where Diddy clucked her tongue and did what mothers have done since the beginning of time — administered tender, loving care.

Sporting a neat white bandage, Russ had allowed himself to be hugged and kissed by Diddy. Then she'd handed out strawberry Popsicles, and said, "Scoot!" And off they went, Ben with Russ on his shoulders.

It was one of his fondest memories of his brother. He brushed at his wet eyes in time to see Darby staring at him. She was dressed in a simple yellow dress with thin straps and matching sandals. A straw bag of some sort hung over her shoulder. She had on lipstick. "Want some tea?" Darby nodded.

"I was sitting here thinking about when we were kids. Do you remember that time Russ fell and cut his knee? Diddy doctored him up, then gave us all strawberry Popsicles."

"I remember. I remember everything, Ben. I'm trying really hard not to think about all that right now. It's simply too painful."

"Where's Willie?"

Darby laughed. "He's exercising with Dodo. She's teaching him to walk on the treadmill. He used to run with Russ in the morning. He had his own water bottle, too. I'll take him for a long walk when we get back. Don't let me forget to look for his baby."

Ben bounded to his feet. "I can do that. I have a phenomenal memory."

"Are you going to pack up Russ's things?" Darby asked, with a catch in her voice. Ben stared off in the distance. He wished he could stay there in the gazebo forever. Barring that, he wished he could turn back the clock to his childhood years. But he knew that wasn't going to happen either.

"Later this week. I'm going to have to work up to that. Would you help me?"

Darby considered the question. No, she did not want to pack up Russ's things. She didn't even want to go to his town house at all. But, this wasn't about her and what she wanted. "Yes, I'll help you."

The minute the young couple left the backyard, Diddy was in the gazebo. She waved to Dodo and Willie, who were standing on the back porch. Dodo's thumb shot into the air. Diddy smiled as she followed the path to her back steps.

5

Ben led Darby back to the car, parked in what used to be Russ's spot at the condo. Retrieving Claire's ring and Willie's baby, and seeing the home Russ would never return to, had been harder than Ben had imagined possible. Ben asked, "Where do you want to go first? Bodene's office or visit my father?"

Darby buckled her seat belt. "It's not a question of wanting, Ben. I need to talk to your father and Bella. I want answers. Maybe instead of going to your father's house, we should go to the foundation offices to see Mr. Bodene first. Russ's will is there, on file with the attorneys. As the executrix of Russ's will I have a legal right to ask questions. They are bound by law to answer my questions. I can always go back to the attorney who drew up Russ's will. What do you think, Ben?"

She wanted his advice. Her eyes were so imploring.

"I think we should go to the foundation first. If we don't like what they tell us, then we'll take it from there."

Darby fiddled with the strap of her seat belt. "It's a given that we're not going to like what they say, but if you're game, so am I. Are you sure you don't mind doing all this, Ben?"

"Russ was my brother. I want answers myself, so he can rest in peace."

Darby reared back, her face draining of all color. Her voice was hard and cold when she snapped, "That's just the point! He's not resting in peace. It could be fifty years, maybe more, before Russ can rest in peace. He's *scattered* all over the damn place. There's no closure there. God, this is so morbid." She knew she was going to cry again out of pure frustration. She knuckled her eyes. Ben pretended not to notice.

"Point taken," Ben said quietly.

"I'm sorry, Ben. I didn't mean to snap at you like that. Are we going to need an appointment?"

"We better not," Ben said grimly as he steered the rental car out of the complex and onto the highway. Fifteen minutes later, he parked the car at the far end of the parking lot of the Gunn Foundation.

The Gunn Building, which housed all their shipping offices as well as the foundation, stood near the river. An old brick structure, it towered over the lower, flat-roofed buildings that surrounded it. Over the years it had received several face-lifts, the brick newer-looking, the windows replaced, the inside gutted, floor by floor.

Confederate jasmine climbed the walls and twined around the pillars and windows. The scent was so heady, Darby felt light-headed as she and Ben moved toward the front door. The lobby, while huge, held only a circular desk, where a lone man sat with an open book, a phone console, and a computer. Ben walked toward the desk, his stride swift and sure, his shoulders stiff with resolve. He reached for the open registry, scrawled his name, then waited while Darby wrote her name. Somehow or other, Darby found her hand in Ben's. It felt right. Later she would think about that moment.

The receptionist looked at the signatures and nodded. "Take the elevator to the eighth floor. I'll call to tell them you're on your way up, Mr. Gunn."

A young man, probably a summer intern, judging from his eagerness, greeted Ben and Darby the moment they stepped from the elevator.

"We want to see Mr. Bodene. Russ called him Bo," Darby whispered.

The intern stopped at a door whose nameplate said it was the office of Eric Lampton.

"No, not this office," Ben said. "We want to see Mr. Bodene." Authority rang in Ben's voice. The intern stepped back, flustered.

"I don't think that's possible. Mr. Bodene never sees anyone without an appointment. I'm sorry."

"Even if that 'anyone' is someone named Gunn? I don't think so. Where is Mr. Bodene's office?"

The intern's eyes flicked toward the end of the hall as he said, "I'm sorry, I can't tell you that." The grim look on Ben's face told the younger man that all hope of employment after his internship was up had just become out of the question.

"Don't worry. I can find Mr. Bodene's office on my own. I'll be sure to tell Mr. Bodene you tried to stop us." Still holding Darby's hand, they walked briskly down the hall. Out of the corner of her eye Darby saw the young man snap his cell phone open.

Eric Bodene opened the door just as Ben put his hand on the knob. His expression said he didn't like the intrusion, even though his voice was welcoming.

"Ben Gunn," Ben said, holding out his hand. "This is Darby Lane, a personal friend as well as executrix of my brother Russell's will."

"It's nice to see you again, Benjamin. And it's a pleasure to meet you, too, Miss Lane. Let's see, the last time I saw you, Benjamin, you were about eleven years old."

"That sounds about right, Mr. Bodene. We need to talk with you. We have questions, and we need answers."

Eric Bodene adjusted his wire-rimmed glasses. Beads of perspiration dotted his forehead and receding hairline even though it was ice-cold in the elegant-looking office. He was a rotund little man who huffed and puffed as he waddled across the carpet to take up his position behind his shiny-topped desk.

Behind Bodene's desk was a solid row of plate glass with a magnificent view of the Mississippi. Pictures of the same river dotted the mahogany-paneled walls. Luscious green plants thrived in the light. His was a high-profile office even though the man behind the desk looked like the Pillsbury Doughboy.

"Please, sit down. Can I offer you some coffee, perhaps some sweet tea?"

Both Darby and Ben shook their heads.

Bodene took the initiative. "I've been expecting you, Miss Lane. I tried calling you several times but only got your answering machine. I since learned that you were out of town. I'm sorry we're meeting under these sad circumstances. However, it's nice to see you again, Benjamin. Now, what can I do for you?"

Darby moved forward on the seat of her chair. Her voice was ice-cold when she said, "You can tell me, Mr. Bodene, how you allowed Russell's organs to be donated when it was his express wish in his living will that nothing like that was to happen. I have a copy of his will, and I also have the video, as does the foundation. I am his executrix. I was with Russ the day he signed his will. I know for a fact he dropped it off here at your offices when he returned home the day we both finished up our master's programs. He said his father insisted on his making the will. Now, how did this happen?"

Eric Bodene leaned back in his chair, his fingers

steepled in front of his face. "Tragic, simply tragic. I was in New Orleans on a probate matter that day. Actually, I was on my way home. Russell died at around four o'clock. The police notified Mr. and Mrs. Gunn immediately. The reports say Russell died on his way to the hospital. Mrs. Gunn was at the hospital when the ambulance arrived. She's the one who made the decision to donate Russell's organs. She has Marcus's power of attorney, so she was able to do what she did, and she did it quickly. I heard about it on the six o'clock news. I rushed to the house immediately, but it was already too late." The lawyer's eyes behind the wire-rimmed glasses implored them both to understand his position. Darby and Ben just glared at him.

"You have to understand, there was a very small window of time."

In shock, Ben sputtered, "My father knew my brother's wishes?"

"Ah, yes, your father knew. The question I suppose you are posing is, did Bella know your brother's wishes? She said she didn't even know Russell had made a will. I tried talking with Marcus, but he's . . . in another world."

"Bella oversees this foundation the way she oversees everything associated with the Gunn name. How could she not know?" Ben snapped.

The attorney mopped at his perspiring forehead. "I don't know, Benjamin. Perhaps you should talk to your father. I cannot tell you how sorry I am about this tragic turn of events. If you can find it in your heart to think kindly about any of this, think that your brother saved many lives by Bella's donating his organs. People who otherwise would have died."

Ben was on his feet, his hands slapping down on the glass-topped desk. "It's not what my brother wanted. He was so adamant about it, he made a video stating his wishes. The way I see it, it was your duty to see that my father and my stepmother knew about my brother's wishes. You failed in your duty to my brother."

Eric Bodene glared at both Ben and Darby. "I don't like what I'm seeing on your face, Benjamin. What are you going to do?"

"Do? I'm going to take matters into my own hands, that's what I'm going to do. Make no mistake, I will *try* to talk to my father. If that fails, then I'm going to go to the newspapers and tell them what Bella did. And how ineffectual you were. Thank you for seeing us, Mr. Bodene."

"Benjamin, wait! What good will that do? You could set the transplant program back years and years. It's a wonderful thing, please don't ruin it. Start thinking with your mind, not your heart, and forget the bad blood between you and Bella. For your own sake, think before you act."

Ben again reached for Darby's hand. Together, they left the office, neither saying a word. Outside in the hot, humid air, they looked at each other. Ben spoke first. "At least we now know *how* it happened. I don't think

Bodene was lying. Everything he said can be checked. It brings it all right back to my father and Bella's doorstep. Where do you keep the will and the video, Darby?"

"At home in the safe. Why?"

Ben's eyes narrowed. "I think you should make another copy and put it in a safe-deposit box. You know, just to be on the cautious side. I bet you five bucks Bodene was on the phone to Bella the minute we left his office. Knowing that, do you still want to go to my father's house?"

"Damn right I do."

Ben smiled. He squeezed her hand. She squeezed back. She looked at Ben out of the corner of her eye. She could see a smile tug at his lips. In spite of her mood, she found herself smiling.

Something was happening here. To cover the confusion and what she was feeling, Darby climbed into the car, buckled up, and squirmed until she was comfortable. "I feel like all I've been doing is getting in and out of cars today," she mumbled.

Ben, his eyes on the road in front of him, maneuvered the car up and down side streets until he was on the main road again before he spoke. "Do you know what I miss about this place?" Not waiting for a response from his companion, he continued. "I miss the river smell and the aunts. That's it. Sad, isn't it?"

"No, not really. You left a long time ago and made a new life for yourself outside of Baton Rouge. That's not a bad thing, Ben. It would have been nice, though, if you had come back once in a while. The aunts missed you. A phone call isn't the same as a visit in person. Birthday and Christmas cards don't quite cut it. I missed you, too. Russ talked about you a lot. Just about a month ago, he told me you were involved with someone, and he said he thought it was serious." Darby was stunned at how flat-sounding her voice was. She looked out the window wondering how the good-looking man sitting next to her was going to respond.

Ben's knuckles gripped the wheel tighter. *Oh, shit.* "I was seeing someone. It wasn't serious. That was brother talk. The *zing* wasn't there, if you know what I mean. Listen, would you like to go to lunch? It's after twelve. Is Soupy still in business?"

Darby laughed. "Soupy is an institution. Of course he's still here. In the same spot, too. His grandchildren help out now. Claire and I manage to go there for lunch at least once a week. Sure, I'd like to have lunch at Soupy's." Was that a lilt she heard in her voice? Obviously it was, since Ben was grinning from ear to ear.

"Good. We can catch up on old times. I'd like to hear about Russ, if it isn't too painful for you to talk about him. Oh, and you, too. I want to know all about the dollhouse business, and I want you to catch me up on the aunts."

"I can do that. It's always going to be painful to talk about Russ, but avoiding discussing him will be worse. I have to put it all in perspective."

"Okay. I think we both could use some cheering up, and reminiscing about good times with Russ should do just the trick."

Fifteen minutes later, Darby cried out in dismay. "Oh, no! Soupy is closed today. Wait, wait, I forgot, today is Bayou Day. Soupy will have a booth there. Let's go, Ben. It's only another fifteen minutes from here. The aunts were talking about it yesterday and trying to decide if they were going to go. You remember Bayou Day, don't you? You did say you missed the river smell."

"Of course I remember Bayou Day. I fell in twice when I was a kid. One time Dodo fished me out. The other time I had to do it on my own. This is so great. A *twofer*. Does Bella go?"

"I don't know, Ben. I haven't gone in years. Diddy said it isn't the draw it used to be. The folks are getting older and the younger ones don't want to be bothered. The Garden Club sets up a booth and so does the Preservation Society. Some of the stores have dropped out over the years, but it's still considered an event. There's not as much entertainment for children like there was when we were kids. They still do the boat ride, though, according to Diddy. I'd like to do the boat ride, but only after we sample some of Soupy's cuisine."

"I'm your man. Makes me feel like a kid again. Did Russ attend?"

"No, he always thought the bayou was depressing. You know, the snakes and gators. Look, there's a parking space. Quick, before someone else snatches it," Darby cried. Ben swerved into the spot, straightened the wheel, and climbed out.

Hand in hand, the two of them walked along the grassy roadway to where the different booths were set up. "I can't smell Soupy's kitchen, can you?"

"No, but I can see it," Darby said, dragging Ben along to Soupy's makeshift kitchen as she dodged a thick strand of Spanish moss swinging from one of the oak trees.

"Snag a table for us and I'll get the food," Ben said. Darby looked around and finally saw a small picnic table that afforded a full view of all the booths as well as the bayou, where the boat sat ready for customers. She laughed when Ben set down two styrofoam bowls of gumbo and two po' boy sandwiches. "You aren't going to believe this, but they have orange dreamsicles. Remember those?"

"I sure do. I also remember the time you snitched six of them from Diddy's freezer and got sick. You didn't share," Darby said accusingly.

They talked of everything and nothing as they munched and crunched their way through Soupy's fare. When they finished, Ben carried off the trash and returned with four dreamsicles. "Eat them quick or they'll melt. It's got to be in the high nineties today."

In the end there was no help for it, the delectable treat dribbled down their chins and onto their clothes. No amount of dabbing and mopping could help. They laughed in delight as they started off. Again, they were hand in hand.

"Let's check out everything and do the boat ride last. Is that okay with you?" Darby nodded happily. When she awoke this morning, she had no idea today was going to be such a wonderful day.

"Uh-oh, look who's at the Preservation Booth."

"It's Bella!" Darby hissed. "What's she doing here?" She yanked at Ben's arm to pull him to the side of a monstrous cypress tree. "This isn't good. The Society has never accepted Bella and that horrible house she built. They look pretty friendly to me. This can't be good, Ben," she repeated. "Russ was on the Preservation board and every year he blocked her plans. That means there is a seat open on the board. Quick, come with me. I have an idea," she said as she approached the Preservation Society's booth, heading straight toward an older gentleman who was arranging pamphlets in the booth's display.

"Mr. Bourdroux, Darby Lane. It's so nice to see you here. The aunts send their regards. You remember Ben Gunn, don't you?"

The old man tugged at his snow-white goatee as he looked from one to the other, trying to place them. A lifelong resident of Baton Rouge and the owner of the only antebellum mansion on the river near LSU, Simon dedicated his life and his money to the Preservation Society. No one, not even his wife, ever went up against Simon once he got an idea into his head about what was good or bad for the society.

"Ah, yes, Mr. Gunn. My condolences on the loss of your brother. He was a wonderful addition to the Society's board. Welcome to Bayou Day."

Darby nudged Ben to keep his eye on Bella while she tackled Simon Bourdroux. "I was wondering, Mr. Bourdroux, if it would be possible to take Russell's seat on the board." Darby lowered her voice and said, "I don't know if you know this or not, but Russell left his estate to me. His *entire* estate. I think I would be a definite asset to the board and would certainly be willing to help with some of the renovations to the older homes. I'm not sure how it all works. Do I have to be voted in or can I just assume Russ's seat?"

The old man fingered his goatee. "I have the power, young lady. I've been in charge of the Preservation Society for the last fifty years. I think you might be an asset as you say. Would you be willing to do some work to the library?"

"Absolutely. Just tell me what you want me to do. When is the next meeting? Do you know what's on the agenda?"

The old man looked miffed at the question. "Of course. Our next meeting is next week. There is one application pending, by Mr. Gunn's stepmother, as a matter of fact," he said, pointing to Bella. "She wants to do some renovations to the two houses in the shoe. I understand she wants to *modernize* them. I can't be having something like that going on."

Darby thought she was going to faint. "How do you think the vote will go?"

"I can't speak for the others. There will be some squabbling. The vote, as you know, is secret."

"What do I have to do to vote this down? Are there forms to fill out? Do I just show up at the meeting?"

"You can fill out the form when you attend the meeting. The committee will welcome you with open arms. We were just discussing who we could get to fill Mr. Gunn's seat. That woman," he said, pointing to Bella again, "has been asking what she had to do to take on her stepson's seat. I squelched that right at the start. There are others who seem to think the woman would be a welcome addition."

"So what you're saying is, nothing has been decided, is that right?"

"That's what I'm saying right now." The old man motioned for Darby to come closer. "You might want to get your aunts to do a little . . . ah . . . *politicking*, if you know what I mean." Darby knew exactly what he meant.

Ben sauntered back to where Darby was waiting for him. "She's gone. Now she's over at the Garden Club booth. Aren't they the ladies who do the Christmas tour?"

"They're the ones," Darby said grimly. "She's buttering them up. They're falling for it, too. Diddy called me last night to tell me she heard at the market that Bella was invited to a tea at Honoria's house yesterday. You know how gossip is in this town. Now here she is. I guess it's all true. We have to find a way to stop her from coming into the shoe and ruining it. Ben, can't you talk to your father? Surely, he won't allow this to happen."

"I don't know if my father is in any condition to make decisions. I can try, but don't get your hopes up. Let's do that boat ride now. I've seen enough. Bella looks like she's going to stay in the booth for a while. She's spreading stuff out. When ladies do that, according to the aunts, that means they're going to stick around."

Darby laughed all the way to the paddle boat. They were the only two passengers. Jethro Beecher, a thick cigar clamped between his teeth, turned on the engine and they were under way.

The bayou was beautiful and yet scary and thrilling with the huge cypress trees, the balls of their roots standing out of the water like giant tentacles of octopuses. Slices of sunlight filtered through the trees cloaking the thick clusters of moss dangling from the lower branches in a sickly yellow light.

Jethro removed his cigar long enough to say, "Don't be dangling your arms in the water. The gators rise up and snap. Sit in the middle of the seat close together." Darby was only too glad to obey the suggestion.

"Do you remember when we were kids and thought pirates hung out here with their treasure? We used to pester the aunts to bring us here to see for sure. I love this river smell. I didn't realize just how much until right now. I've just about made up my mind that I'm not going to go back to Mustang Island."

Darby sucked in her breath and squirmed in her seat. "Really, Ben?"

Ben grinned. "Yeah, really."

"The aunts will be so happy."

"What about you, Darby? Will you be happy if I stay?"

He sounded like he cared about her opinion, and she knew this was no time to be coy. "Yes, Ben, I'd be happy if you stay on. We all need you."

Ben squeezed her shoulder. It felt so right. Or was it just wishful thinking on her part?

The slices of sun disappeared leaving them in eerie semidarkness as the paddle boat churned forward. "There's old Sebastian. They say that old gator is over fifty years old," Jethro said, pointing to a monster alligator that slid into the water.

Ben started to laugh. "Ducky used to threaten us when we were bad. She'd say she was going to bring us down here so Sebastian could get a look at us. Just a look. It scared the hell out of me and Russ. I can't believe that old gator is still in these waters."

The boat suddenly swung around and headed back to the shoreline. Ten minutes later they stood watching Jethro tether his paddle boat. Ben paid for the ride and off they went.

"Now what?" Darby asked.

Ben craned his neck to see if Bella was still sitting

with the garden ladies. She was nowhere to be seen. "We can go see my father now if you like. Just don't get your hopes up that he can help us."

"We won't know if we don't try, but since Bella seems to have left, maybe we should wait until tomorrow morning. We certainly don't want to run into her. Dodo said she goes to the Foundation offices every morning around eleven or so and doesn't go back to the house till around two-thirty. We could show up right after she leaves. Morning might be better for your father, too. Sick people always seem more alert in the early-morning hours. What do you think, Ben?"

"I think you're right. Let's go back to the shoe and talk. We have a lot of catching up to do. You want to tell the aunts about the Preservation seat, don't you?"

"I sure do. I don't know, though, Ben. I think Bella might have beat us to the punch. She was at both booths. That has to mean something. An inside track, so to speak. Right now that awful woman is a celebrity. All because of Russ. Somehow or other, she's managed to bamboozle all those ladies and Simon. Well, not Simon but the rest of them."

"Think positive. The aunts might have some ideas."

"Let's hope so. I don't feel good about this, Ben."

"Only positive thoughts, Darby."

6

A mile away from the shoe, as the crow flies, a building sat among a stand of scraggly trees. It was a house more than just a building, really, a house that defied architectural description. Most inhabitants of Baton Rouge simply called it "the monstrosity." To tourists who asked about what sites they should visit, they were always told, "the Horseshoe and the monstrosity." When the tourists arrived at the house on Gunn Court, they stood back, craning their necks, as they tried to figure out if the house was a Tudor, a Georgian, antebellum, or modern McMansion. They usually walked away shaking their heads in disbelief, asking one another if the house *really* was crooked. Most took pictures knowing they could never describe the house with any accuracy to their friends back home. Nor could they believe the marble plaque stuck in the ground by the ornate iron gates that opened to a code and password. The plaque was simple really, with just a few words: DESIGNED BY BELLA GUNN. The tourists always took a picture of the plaque, too, wondering who in the name of God Bella Gunn was.

The Gunn house, as it was known, was all peaks, sharp angles, sprawling add-ons, gingerbread and curlicues for trim. The windows were tall and angled, coming to a sharp point at their tops like those in a Colorado ski chalet. Skylights could be seen on every section of the roofline. A bright yellow double door completed the Gunn house. It was ugliness personified. And it really was crooked.

The ugliness didn't stop with the exterior but carried inside with a checkerboard floor in the foyer that was bigger than most people's living rooms. Dark burgundy settees, artificial trees, and bamboo tables greeted any guests who cared enough to visit. The rest of the house was a mishmash of odd pieces of furniture, from Western to Chippendale. All reproductions, of course. As were the pictures in ornate gold frames, most gotten from discount stores.

The Gunn house was *not* on the Christmas Candlelight Tour, nor was it on the Spring Tour, an acknowledgment Bella Gunn hungered and coveted. It was said that Bella would gladly give up her oversize porcelain veneers for just one shot at either tour.

"Not in this lifetime," Diddy Lane said.

"Over my dead body," Ducky Lane said.

"I'll kill her first," Dodo Lane said.

Sentiments echoed by most *Rougies*. Most, because there were some who simply didn't care and couldn't be bothered even to discuss such silly things.

Bella Gunn checked her appearance in the long pier glass standing in the corner of her bedroom suite. A suite she shared with no one. She considered it lavish as well as elegant, certainly worthy of a spread in *Southern Living*.

Satisfied with her appearance, Bella minced her way across the thick carpeting to the dresser, where she picked up the jewelry she was going to wear. Two diamond rings, three carats each. Earrings, three carats each; diamond bracelet, twenty-seven carats; Rolex watch studded with diamonds on the bezel. Diamond choker whose carat weight was thirty. A woman could never have enough diamonds. Never, ever.

She was dressed today in a yellow Chanel suit. Yellow was her favorite color because it made her think of warm, golden sunshine. Yellow linen shoes graced her big feet, size twelve. She hated her feet, but it was the only thing she hated about herself.

In the beginning, right after she'd married Marcus Gunn, and the town chose up sides, she'd read an article in the *Baton Rouge Advocate* about herself. The article said she had *dyed*, *big* hair, the kind you could see through. They'd described her smile as tight, then went on to explain it was probably because she was self-conscious about her oversize teeth. It said other things, cruel things she didn't want to remember. She'd canceled her subscription to the paper and forbade her husband ever to advertise in it again.

Bella surveyed her suite the way she did every morning as she prepared to start her day. She'd decorated the rooms herself and was proud of the job she'd done. In the whole of her life she'd never expected to sleep on silk sheets with cashmere blankets. Everything was a light shade of yellow, even the carpet. Life was good. If there were moments late at night when memories of her past rose to the surface and prevented sleep, no one knew about them but she.

Now it was time to visit her husband's suite of rooms like the dutiful wife she pretended to be and silently thank him for giving her the life she was now used to. She usually stayed ten minutes, cooing and gurgling, kissing his cheek and patting his hand for the nurse's benefit.

She walked downstairs to the formal dining room, where she breakfasted on a muffin, half a grapefruit with a ton of sugar on top, and three cups of black coffee. Everything served on Crate and Barrel linen and crockery. Everything was yellow.

She rang the little silver bell next to her plate. One of the three kitchen maids scurried through the door. "Yes, ma'am?"

"I think I'd like a rack of lamb for dinner." A long, lacquered nail tapped at her chin. "No, on second thought, let's have sloppy joes. Marcus loves sloppy joes. A peach cobbler will do nicely. Make sure the vanilla ice cream is fresh. I don't like those little crystals that form on the top. Be sure the Jamaican coffee is freshly ground. I *can* tell the difference. I saw dust on the stairway. I certainly hope it isn't there when I get home. That will be all for now." The little maid scurried back through the open door, trembling.

On her way to the front door, Bella stopped at the downstairs lavatory to check her teeth. The one thing she hated about the porcelain caps was that food stuck in the cracks. She grimaced in the mirror. Sure enough, part of a raisin was stuck between her upper-front teeth. She picked at it with one of her long nails. *The price of beauty*, she thought.

Now she had to go to the Gunn Building to see what it was that had Eric Bodene in such a snit. Like she had nothing else to do but stroke his ruffled feathers.

Outside, under the portico that resembled the portico at the White House, a chauffeur held open the door of Marcus Gunn's Bentley. She climbed inside and settled herself before she fired up a cigarette, her first of the day. "Take me to the offices, Arnold," she said imperiously.

"Yes, ma'am. Be sure to buckle up, ma'am."

"Shut up, Arnold. Don't tell me what to do."

The chauffeur tipped his cap before he slid behind the wheel. Every morning it was the same unpleasantness. He thought of it as a ritual.

As she puffed on her cigarette, Bella thought about the perfect day she'd had yesterday down at the bayou.

She was almost certain she was finally going to be accepted by the *Rougies*. Almost. That old twit Simon wasn't going to win this round of votes. As far as she could tell, and she'd always prided herself on reading people, she had the other members in the palm of her hand.

How they'd gushed over her yesterday, saying how wonderful she was, how compassionate, how caring to think of others even while she was grieving over the loss of her stepson.

Acceptance was in the palm of her hand. She had felt it, sensed it in every pore of her body, then that snip of a girl and Ben Gunn showed up. In a matter of minutes that acceptance had dwindled to doubt when she was told that the seat vacated by Russell's death was going to be filled by Darby Lane.

She'd been shocked to her very being to know her stepson had left his entire estate to that little snip. Marcus had assured her years ago that his son had changed his will and left everything to his brother Ben. A bold-faced lie. But then, Marcus had never told her the truth about anything, and that's why he was in the condition he was in these days. Suddenly there was a new player in the game. A game the Lane sisters had organized years ago to keep her out of everything she coveted. Obviously she was going to have to resort to other measures. The two ramshackle Gunn houses in the shoe would do the trick. They were her ace in the hole. All she had to do was stop by the Preservation offices, pick up her provisional license, and take it over to the contractor she'd hired to dismantle the houses. At the moment the provisional license only allowed her to move equipment to the site. The bulldozers, the wrecking ball, the bush hog, and the huge dump trucks. The minute she had the conditional license in her hands those two buildings were going to come down at the speed of light. Before the hateful Lane sisters could blink.

Ben Gunn leaned back in the booth, looking at the empty breakfast plates in front of him. He told Darby he couldn't remember when he'd eaten so much food at one sitting.

"I don't know, Ben. You did okay with Diddy's pancakes yesterday morning," Darby replied, laughing as she pushed her own plates away. "Well, I'm ready if you are. Are you sure you want to do this, Ben?"

Ben threw his hands into the air. "Today might be one of Dad's good days. If not, oh, well. It's Bella I don't want to see. Every time I see her, I want to strangle her. I will never understand why Dad married her. Someday I want someone to explain it all to me."

Darby reached across the table and held Ben's hand. "Look at it this way, Ben. You might not be the person you are today if things hadn't happened the way they did. I, for one, think you turned into a pretty nice person."

A *pretty nice person.* Ben's chest puffed out.

"Thanks." He rummaged in his pocket for some bills. "Okay. I'm ready as I'll ever be," he said, and Darby's heart broke a little at the sadness she heard in Ben's voice.

Twenty minutes later, Ben parked his car behind "the monstrosity." He grimaced as he always did at the sight of the house. He could see Darby struggling not to laugh.

"I think I'd go out of my mind if I had to live here," Darby said.

"See! You get it! That woman is out of her mind. But that doesn't explain my father living here."

Darby poked Ben on the arm. "Sure it does. He married her. Married couples live together in the same house. Dodo always says, you make your bed, you lie in it. End of story."

Ben rang the doorbell. When strains of "Dixie" resonated throughout the house, Darby started to giggle and couldn't stop. She pretended to cough just as the door opened.

"I'm Ben Gunn. I'm here to see my father," Ben said to the maid who opened the door.

"I'm sorry, sir, but Mr. Gunn is not receiving visitors. Mrs. Gunn handles all the appointments, and you're not in the book for today. Perhaps you can call back or call the offices to make an appointment."

Ben's cheeks reddened, but whether it was from anger or embarassment, Darby couldn't tell. She guessed a little bit of both. "But . . . he's my father. I shouldn't need an appointment to see my father. Please, step aside. You can tell Mrs. Gunn I forced my way in here. Or, you can call the police. Take your pick, but I'm going to see my father." Not bothering to wait for the maid's reaction, Ben took hold of the door with one hand to prevent it from being closed in his face while his other hand reached for Darby. "Come on, Darby."

Together, the duo raced through the tacky foyer, through a room that had a jungle motif and was probably supposed to be a solarium, and up the wide circular staircase and down the hall, past the startled maids who were vacuuming and dusting.

A formidable-looking nurse in starched white spread her arms across the open doorway. Darby ducked underneath while Ben tried to cajole the nurse into allowing him to pass.

Marcus Gunn looked up from his chair, clearly startled by the commotion. He'd been staring out one of the ugly windows at the tree line. On the table next to his chair was a prepared hypodermic needle. He looked down at it, then at Darby. He tilted his head to the side. Darby immediately understood his meaning. She deftly snatched it up, removed the tip. She walked back to the doorway where Ben was still cajoling the nurse. She took careful aim and jabbed the woman in the buttocks. The nurse whirled around, then she swayed from side to side, her arms flapping as Ben caught her.

"Damn. That took guts, Darby," Ben marveled, a

look of admiration on his face. "Help me get her over to the bed."

Funny sounds were coming from the man in the chair. It took only a few seconds for Darby to realize Ben's father was laughing.

"Hi, Dad!" Ben said.

Darby took several steps backward to give Ben personal time with his father. She eyed the drugged nurse on the bed, who appeared to be sleeping peacefully. She wondered what kind of drug she'd jabbed her with. Always a creature of impulse, she was suddenly concerned at what she had done. She moved closer to the bed to check the woman's pulse. Steady and slow. That had to be good.

Darby looked around, stunned at the array of pill bottles sitting on the dresser. Syringes, already prepared, were on a tray along with alcohol and cotton balls. A chart hung off one of the dresser-drawer pulls. She was tempted to read it but wasn't sure if she should or not. But she'd just pumped the nurse full of *something*, and the chart was her best bet at figuring out just what was in that syringe.

Darby risked a glance at Ben and his father. They appeared to be in earnest conversation, at least Ben was. The elder Gunn seemed to be listening. Her gaze swept the room, bathroom on the left, study or another room of some kind on the right. Maybe a dressing room. She inched forward. A small office with desk, chair, computer, telephone, fax machine, and a photocopier. In the blink of an eye she had the chart in her hands. She removed the thick wad of daily reports, put them into the automatic feed of the copier. The pages spit out quickly. In seconds she had the chart back where it belonged and the copies folded and in her purse.

This was a man's room, Darby decided, decorated tastefully in rich colors of brown and harvest gold. Obviously Bella's hand had not stretched this far. What were father and son talking about?

Suddenly Ben stood up, his expression furious. He was almost shouting when he said, "You let it happen, that's how you're to blame. You married her, that was your first mistake. You just threw us away, is what you damn well did. If it wasn't for the Lanes, God only knows what would have happened to us. Yeah, you are to blame. Mary won't forgive you, Russell's dead, and I'm standing here reaming you out. What's wrong with this picture? Where are those Gunn guts you always used to tell us about? Where?"

Ben was about to continue his tirade when Darby, who was standing by the window, hissed, "I just heard a car, Ben. I think Bella's home."

"That's nice. Did you hear that, *Dad?* Your loving wife is home. I think I'll just wait till she gets here so I can say hello and good-bye all at the same time. By the way, excuse my terrible manners. This lovely woman is little Darby Lane, all grown-up. She was Russell's best friend. Bet you didn't even know that. She's also the beneficiary of Russell's estate."

Darby thought she saw a tear in the old man's eyes. How strange. She did her best to smile, and said, "It's nice to see you again, Mr. Gunn." She wasn't sure, but she thought his eyes were pleading with her. Out of her depth, she moved away just as Bella Gunn walked into the room.

"If I had known you were coming by, Benjamin, I would have stayed home. Unfortunately, I had a meeting with the Preservation Society. They granted me a provisional license to bring in the equipment to the shoe. Of course, there has to be a formal vote at the meeting next week to grant me a conditional license, but in the meantime, the equipment will be delivered and be ready to go when the conditional license is issued. The next time you want to see your father, call first. Today isn't one of his better days. Where's the nurse?" she asked coldly.

Ben pointed to the bed. "I'd fire her if I were you. Sleeping on the job. Tsk, tsk," he said, clucking his tongue. "It was a spur-of-the-moment visit. So, we'll just say hello and good-bye." He placed his hand on Darby's elbow to usher her from the room. The funny sound she'd attributed to laughter from the old man followed them from the room.

"She looks like a walking cadaver," Ben said, as they literally ran down the steps.

"I was going to say anorexic," Darby said.

They were outside, both of them aware that Bella was watching them from the upstairs window.

"Ben, what's wrong with your father?" Darby asked, as she buckled her seat belt.

"I don't have a clue," Ben said grimly. "I'm going to find out, though. Off the top of my head, I'd say his last stroke left him in this condition."

Darby dug into her purse. "Maybe this will help. I copied his medical chart. There was a little office off the bedroom. I guess your father or someone uses it for business because it had a computer, a phone, and a fax machine as well as a copier. Maybe the nurse uses it to stay in touch with your father's doctor."

Ben grinned. Darby's heart picked up a beat. "Damn, you did that right under my nose, and I didn't even see you do it. We should go into the sleuthing business."

"I don't think I'd go that far. Did you find out anything from your father?"

"He has difficulty talking, but he was able to blink or nod in answer to my questions. I think he might have had a series of strokes, but he seemed to understand everything I was saying. When I asked him if Bella knew about Russ's will, he shook his head no, then yes, so I don't know. I think we need to talk to the aunts now, Darby. Five heads are better than two."

"I agree, but we have one more stop. We have to open Russ's safe and get the ring for Claire. I don't know why, but I just have a feeling we should give it to Claire as soon as we can. I know she's sitting at home crying her eyes out."

"Okay. Give me directions."

Twenty minutes later a tearful Claire opened the door and literally swooped Darby into her arms. She sobbed, Darby cried, and Ben shuffled his feet. Crying women was something he didn't know how to deal with. Mandy was tough. He seriously doubted she knew the meaning of tears. There was nothing soft or cuddly about Mandy. Now that he could openly compare her to Darby and this strange grieving person, he realized that Mandy was not only tough but hardedged. He knew in his gut she would just move on if he didn't go back to Mustang Island. She'd chalk it up to an interlude in her life that didn't work out. She wasn't the type to send Christmas cards, so he'd probably never hear from her again. A feeling of relief settled over him.

Their tears dried, Claire invited Ben and Darby into her apartment, motioned for them to sit, and asked if they'd like coffee or tea. They declined.

Claire was plain, like Ben's sister Mary, but she wasn't flat or unemotional like Mary. Freckles crunched against a nose that had a slight bump in it near the bridge. Her dark brown eyes were sad and redrimmed. Her lips trembled as did her hands. She kept brushing at her short dark hair.

Probably a nervous habit, Ben decided.

The little apartment was just one big room with a roll-down bamboo blind that covered the kitchen area. He surmised the couch they were sitting on was a pull-out bed. His hands in his pockets, he fingered the key to Russell's town house.

Ben tuned in to the conversation between Claire and Darby. He listened, but his thoughts were on his father and his stepmother.

"It was supposed to be a secret, Claire. Russ was going to give you the ring on Christmas. He had it all planned. He was going to get down on his knees and propose. He practiced on me, but I kept giggling, and finally he got mad and locked up the ring. Listen to me, I don't want us to avoid each other because it's too painful to talk about. We have to get through this together. School will be starting soon, and you'll be able to fill up your days. It's the nights when we'll need each other."

Ben stood up when the two women rose. He fingered the keys in his hand. He spoke for the first time. "Darby and I decided we'd like it if you'd move into my brother's town house, Claire. We know it's what he would want. We can see about signing over a quitclaim deed to you as soon as we get everything straightened out. Russ told me he paid for the town house outright, so you don't have to worry about mortgage payments. Do you have a lease here?"

"No, it's month to month. Can I go there today?" Claire asked tearfully.

"Of course you can. Do you need any help moving anything?"

Claire shook her head. "This is all rental furniture.

I'll just take my clothes, my bike, and my plants. I can fit everything in my car. You're sure it's okay?"

"I'm sure it's what Russ would want," Darby said. "Did you forget? I'm in charge."

Claire smiled tremulously.

Ben watched as the two women cried some more, hugged some more, then patted each other on the back for comfort. They were at the door when Claire said, "Darby, how does it all work? Whoever got Russ's heart . . . does . . . is . . . will the person who has his eyes see things the way Russ saw them? I need to know that."

Darby turned to Ben. "I want to know, too. How can we find out? I'm sorry to say, I am totally in the dark in regard to the donor program. I think we'll all feel better if we know the people who were helped by Russ's death."

"I'll call the hospital and look into it, but I doubt they'll tell me anything. I read somewhere that donor and recipient are never revealed. I don't know why that is but I'll try to find out," Ben said.

He would try to find out. That meant he *really* was staying. Back in the bayou she hadn't been totally sure. Suddenly, her heart felt lighter.

A second later, Ben was heading down the wooden steps on the second floor to the alley where he'd parked the car. "Where to?" Ben asked.

"I want to go home, Ben. I need to think about all this. I need to see Willie." Darby leaned against the door, her gaze and her thoughts far away.

The ride home to the shoe passed in silence.

The minute Ben turned off the ignition, Willie flew through the yard, his bark shrill but welcoming. Darby held out her arms to the dog, while Ben removed the safe he'd taken earlier from his brother's house. Willie whined but wouldn't go near either one of them. Darby watched in dismay as the retriever tucked his tail between his legs and moved off.

"He's picking up Russell's scent, Darby. He knows where we were." With the small metal safe balanced on one knee, Ben slammed the trunk lid.

"Wait, wait. Don't lock the car. I have to get Willie's basket of toys. He'll be okay when he gets his baby. Dogs are so smart, aren't they?"

Darby reached into the backseat for the wicker basket of dog toys and the thick fleecy dog bed they'd picked up before going to breakfast. Willie's well-worn teddy bear was on top. "Come here, boy, look what I have."

Curious, the golden dog advanced, sniffed, and threw his head back and howled. A chill ran up Darby's spine. Ben stopped in his tracks. A second later, the teddy bear in his mouth, Willie ripped across the yard and up the steps to the porch. Ducky opened the door, and Willie rushed through.

"He's okay, Darby. He's got his comfort toy. Russ's scent is on it like it was on his shirt," Ben said, and gave her a wobbly smile. It warmed her heart to know that

Ben was putting on a brave face for her. "Guess I'll see you later."

"Yeah, later," Darby said as she walked toward the house, where Ducky was standing in the doorway.

Darby's shoulders drooped as she trudged past her aunt and into the kitchen. She opened the refrigerator and poured herself a glass of sweet tea. Then she sat down at the table across from her aunt and started to cry. Ducky handed her a wad of tissues. "We really didn't accomplish much, Ducky. The best thing was getting Willie's bed and his baby. We went over to Claire's and told her about the engagement ring Russ meant to give to her on Christmas. We'll give it to her when we get the safe opened. Since I'm the executrix, that shouldn't be a problem. Ben and I agreed she could move into Russ's town house. That was a good thing. I think we're probably going to give her the town house. We both agreed it's what Russ would have wanted."

"That sounds just perfect, Darby," Ducky said.

"We had lunch. That was nice. Ben . . . Ben's really nice. Then we went to his father's house. There's something going on there, Ducky. We only got in because Bella wasn't there. Lord, you should have seen her when she came home to find us there. I . . . you aren't going to believe this, Ducky, but I jabbed the hateful nurse with a hypodermic and knocked her out cold. Mr. Gunn was . . . pathetic. He has difficulty speaking, but Ben was able to communicate with him. We aren't sure if Bella knew about the will or not. Mr. Gunn intimated she did, but then seemed confused, so we aren't sure. He seems to be on a lot of medication."

"Well, that certainly sounds like a jam-filled day," Ducky said.

"You haven't heard the best part. I told you last night what transpired at the bayou yesterday. Well, Bella said the Preservation Society gave her a provisional license to move the heavy equipment into the shoe. She plans to start demolition the minute she receives her conditional license. The society has to take a formal vote next week. She was gloating like it's a shoo-in for her. I don't know, Ducky, I suppose it could happen. I'll vote no. Simon will vote no. I don't know the other members. You, Diddy, and Dodo will have to do some campaigning. Otherwise, she wins."

"Over my dead body," Ducky huffed.

Darby drained her glass and set it in the sink. "Do you want to hear something strange, Ducky? I didn't really think about Russ that much until we got to his town house. When I was at the cemetery planting the flowers I was there but I wasn't there. Does that make sense? When I was with Ben having breakfast or in the car, it was different. It was all so surreal. Now I feel guilty. You don't think I'm having a nervous breakdown, do you?"

Ducky wrapped her arms around her niece. "No, sweetie, you are not having a nervous breakdown. What you're feeling and thinking is normal. Run along and do what you have to do. I'll be here thinking about dinner this evening."

Darby turned around. "But you can't cook, Ducky."

"I know. That's why I said I would be *thinking* about it."

In spite of herself Darby laughed. Now, *that* was normal.

Thirty minutes later Darby was in the workroom that ran the entire length of the garage. Triple French doors in the back provided all the light she needed as she sawed, nailed, and painted her Darby Lane Creations.

Wide, sturdy shelves at eye level held what Russ had always called the prototype for her little business. To her the dollhouse, fashioned by her great-grandfather for the aunts, was a treasure. It was an exact replica of *Dodo's house*. She'd wondered thousands of times how many man-hours went into the creation that was now hers. The house, almost as big as a washing machine, had everything, even running water if she hooked up a tiny hose to a water bottle. When she was ten years old, and the house came to her one Christmas morning, courtesy of the aunts, she thought she was the luckiest little girl in all of Baton Rouge.

Even then, at such a young age, she knew Mary Gunn and the boys weren't interested in playing with dollhouses, so she played alone in the evenings, all by herself, arranging tea parties for all the little dolls she'd collected. From her bed, with the night-light shining directly on the house, she'd always felt extra secure, extra safe, extra loved.

Until one day when it rained. Actually it had rained for days and days, and the aunts were at their wits' end as to how to entertain four rambunctious children. They'd exhausted the attics' treasures, the front-porch games, the snacks, the books, until there was nothing left to do. Cranky and out of sorts, Darby had left the boys on the front porch reading comic books they'd read fifty times already and went upstairs, Mary in her wake. Mary wanted to play checkers, and Darby wanted to play with the dollhouse. An hour into the playtime, the boys appeared, wanting to play Monopoly. She could see in her mind how the next few minutes played out. Ben reached for the game on the shelf at the foot of the bed as Russ cleared the table to set up the game. Mary was next to the huge white pedestal holding the dollhouse. Ben turned and handed the game to Russ just as Mary turned and with one slick, quick elbow move, toppled the dollhouse to the floor, where the third floor shattered into hundreds of small pieces. Darby remembered falling to her knees crying as she tried to gather up the pieces. Mary cried over and over that it was an accident. Darby looked up at her and saw the hatred in her playmate's eyes. Russ saw it, too. She wasn't sure about Ben, though. When the aunts came running and saw what had happened, it was Mary they consoled, not Darby, who was heartbroken. Diddy picked up the pieces, saying the dollhouse could be fixed, while

Ducky gathered up the Gunn children and took them downstairs. Darby sat on the edge of her bed, using the hem of the pink seersucker bedspread to wipe at her tears.

"Shhh, don't cry, honey. We'll get it fixed, and it will be good as new. It was an accident. Sometimes accidents happen for no reason. It's all this rain, it's making us all cranky and irritable," Dodo said.

"No, no, Dodo, it wasn't an accident. Mary did it on purpose. I saw her knock it over. She spoils everything. Why are you taking her side?"

"Shhh, don't say such things. Now, come on, wash your face, and let's go downstairs and make some fudge."

At that precise moment, Darby pitched what she called her first fit. She stomped her way to the bathroom, shouting over and over that she hated Mary Gunn, and the aunts liked Mary better than they liked her. On and on she went until she was exhausted. "I don't want to make fudge," she'd yelled as she flounced back to her room and lay down on the bed, where she curled into a tight ball and tried not to cry.

The incident, that's how the aunts referred to the dollhouse breaking, was never mentioned again. It had been repaired almost as good as new. From that day on, the Gunn children never again entered Darby's room.

Years later, she'd asked Russ if he remembered the incident. She'd been stunned at his blasé response, which was, "Oh, you mean that day Mary deliberately knocked over your dollhouse?" When she'd asked him why he didn't tell the aunts that Mary had crashed the house deliberately, he'd just looked at her like she'd sprouted a second head. "Because she's my sister, and you're just my friend." And that had been the end of *that*.

Darby hitched up the straps of her coverall, her work attire, before she moved over to her worktable. She was going to have to work around the clock if she wanted to fill all the orders that were hanging on her bulletin board. How she was going to do that with all that was going on in her life was a mystery.

Ironically, it was thanks to Russ that her little business had taken off. He told her to think *BIG* and go on from there. He said if she was going to go into business, she had to go into it knowing she wanted to be successful. Well, she was certainly that these days. People from all over the world, rich people who could afford her five- and six-figure prices for their children, clamored for her dollhouses. Just two months ago a rich industrialist from Madrid had arrived in Baton Rouge aboard his own Gulfstream to take back a dollhouse that had taken her four months to build. The man and his wife had been delighted over the dollhouse, a gift for their only child, an eight-year-old daughter. The check had made Darby giddy.

She really had to get to work, sketch out the house she was going to build for the little girl in the wheelchair, the child she'd gone all the way to Scotland to meet. The viscount wanted the dollhouse for Christmas. That meant she had four months to build it. Not quite four months, since the viscount wasn't exactly sure when he would arrive to pick it up from her. Houses were much too expensive, and fragile, to trust to just any shipping company.

Darby looked at the photographs she'd taken of the castle, shots from all angles before she set to work. From time to time she jotted notes to herself about what she had to order. This particular dollhouse—castle, actually—would be built of stone, and it was going to be a definite challenge since the count wanted it authentic, which meant she had to find just the right stones and polish them. Hours and *hours* of work. Darby sighed. Ordinarily, she loved a challenge, and this was going to be quite a challenge, but her mind wasn't on building dollhouses or castles. Her mind was on other things. Things like how many more children she could make happy with all the money Russ had left her. She could expand her business now, hire more help. More manpower meant she would be able to cut her prices to make the dollhouses more affordable and available to more children. By taking Russ's seat with the Preservation Society, she could tell the members she would pattern some of her dollhouses after houses the society had restored over the years. In addition, she could donate monies to help restore other houses when funds got scarce. It was a wonderful idea and one she thought the members would endorse. In her heart she knew Russ would approve. Hadn't he been the one to tell her to think *big*.

While it was small in the scheme of things, it was another example of how Russ's death would help others.

Darby picked up a small piece of molding she was going to sand, then tossed it back onto the worktable. She moved back to the chair in which she liked to take her breaks. She reached over to the small refrigerator to grab a Coke. She uncapped it and drank thirstily. She leaned back, her eyes closed. Who was seeing the world today with Russ's eyes? Who was the person who'd been fortunate enough to receive the gift of sight from Russ Gunn. Whose chest was his heart beating in? She should know that. Didn't she have a right to know? Probably not, since she wasn't a family member. *Does Ben have a right to know? Maybe we can find out.*

Darby's thoughts moved to Ben and the day they'd spent together. What was he doing over at Dodo's house right then, that very minute? Would he walk over later to see her? What was tomorrow going to bring? So many thoughts. She curled into the chair, closed her eyes, and was sound asleep within seconds.

7

$\mathcal{C}$

The heavy equipment arrived at the top of the shoe just as dawn was breaking. It was all parked strategically, then the workers who delivered the equipment climbed into the back of a pickup truck and sped off. At the last second, one of them hopped out of the truck to plaster a yellow sheet of paper onto the side of a bush hog. He leaped back into the truck.

Diddy, who always woke early, walked out to her porch and almost fainted when she saw all the heavy machinery. The urge to scream at the top of her lungs was so great she had to pinch herself to hold back the scream. Instead, she tromped across the lawn and up to the top of the shoe, where she snatched the yellow sheet of paper and read it. This time she did scream. Within seconds Dodo and Ducky were running toward her.

"Look! Look! This is a provisional license for Bella

to have all this equipment set up here. How did this happen?" Diddy screeched so loud her sisters covered their ears.

"I'll tell you how it happened. That . . . that . . . twit used Russell's death to aid her in this crazy scheme. She was on television nonstop for days saying how many lives she was saving or making better. She even likened herself to Mother Teresa, saying she only thinks of others, never herself," Dodo said angrily.

"Darby warned me this was coming. We have to do something. Something drastic. We can't let this happen. We do carry some weight in this town. It's time to act like the eight-hundred-pound gorilla we are. We still have a small window of time to come up with a plan," Ducky said.

Arm in arm, the three sisters walked back to Diddy's house, where she popped sweet rolls into the oven and made coffee.

"We've never been able to discredit that woman before because we can't get anything on her. It's like she was born the day she arrived here. We should hire a private detective to get the goods on her. I bet she has some dark, secret past she doesn't want anyone to know about. She's going to ruin those houses. They're going to look just like that monstrosity she lives in, mark my words. How in the damn hell did she convince the committee to give her a provisional license?" Dodo fumed.

"I told you how. She's using Russell's death to get what she wants. We can't let her get away with this,"

Ducky said. "Not only is it disgraceful, it's sinful for her to use Russell like this. The more I think about it the better I like the idea of hiring a private detective. Maybe one in New Orleans, so no one knows what we're up to."

"That works for me," Dodo said. "Diddy?"

"Whatever it takes. I don't want to see Bella Gunn living in one of those houses. They belong to Ben. Marcus told me once he was leaving one to Ben and one to Russ. I don't know if he made a will to that effect or not. Maybe we should go to the courthouse and see what's on file. I have a dental appointment this morning. I can go to the courthouse when I'm finished."

Dodo felt her eyes grow misty. There were two houses. One for Ben and one for . . . She squeezed her eyes shut so she wouldn't have to give up her dream of another family living in the second Gunn house. She bit down on her lower lip. Sometimes no matter how hard you wished for things, they simply didn't happen. Another dream shot to hell, she thought bitterly.

Ducky nudged her sister, and both busied themselves clearing the table. There were some things that were so private, so personal, one simply didn't acknowledge them.

When Dodo finally had her emotions under control, she said, "Okay, this is what we do. We get dressed up and go visiting. We make our feelings known where Bella is concerned. Ducky, you take on the Garden Club. Invite them all to lunch if you have to. I'm going to see Simon and the members of the Preservation Society. We need to agree that if we have to get down and dirty, we do it. Meaning, of course, that we will shut down the brewery. That will put the fear of God into all of them. Bella or the brewery. A definite no-brainer. Bella is forcing us to resort to her tactics, so she deserves whatever happens."

Hours later, Dodo silently crept out of her room and tiptoed down the steps, grateful that they didn't creak. She quickly called both of her sisters, and within minutes she was carrying a tubful of the family beer to the gazebo in the backyard. Diddy was to bring the ice. Ducky, as usual, brought herself and nothing else.

Meeting in the gazebo late at night was nothing new for the three sisters. They did it on a regular basis in times of crisis, and if there wasn't a crisis, they conjured one up. Now, they huddled around the wooden table, each with a bottle of the family beer in her hands. Dodo took the initiative. "We need a plan, something foolproof. Something that will make this all easier for us to bear. What that boils down to is we have to chop Bella Gunn off at her bony knees," Dodo said, her voice ringing with vengeance. "We have to figure out a way to discredit her."

Diddy squirmed on the bench she was sitting on, knowing what was about to come next. She beat her sisters to the proverbial punch by saying, "No! Don't go there, either one of you. I'll help, but I'm not going to do what you want. I mean it!"

Dodo struggled for a normal tone of voice. "Of course you'll do it. If you don't, I'll have to kill you."

"All you want to do is kill people. Kill me dead, see if I care! Then where will you be? Nowhere, that's where!" Diddy's voice was so belligerent, both sisters patted her arms to show they understood her inner turmoil, knowing that, in the end, Diddy would do what was required of her. This was all about family, and when it came to family, the Lane sisters united.

Dodo tried another tack. "Diddy, don't you think if there was anyone else or another way, we'd try it? You're it! Drink your beer, and let's make a plan." Both sisters waited a minute or two to see what Diddy's response would be. When none was forthcoming, they got down to business.

"I think we're right back where we were earlier this afternoon," Diddy said. "I didn't find out anything at the courthouse we didn't already know. The two Gunn houses are in Marcus's name. There was no way to find out about his will, so I don't know if he kept his promise to leave them to Russell and Ben. It was a total waste of time even though I tried to gossip with some of the older clerks to see if they might have picked up something here or there. No one knew a thing."

"I didn't fare any better with the members of the Garden Club. With the exception of Sarabess and maybe Honoria, they're going to vote to include Bella in the tour. They bought into her good Samaritan crap. Bethany had the gall to tell me I was jealous of Bella.

When I threatened to close the brewery, they just looked at me and dared me to do it. If we three vote no and Sarabess and Honoria vote no, it will be a tie. It's a crapshoot," Ducky said sourly.

The three women sat in silence, each busy with her own thoughts.

A long time later, Dodo squared her skinny shoulders. "It's raining!" she said. "I get brilliant ideas when it rains, for some reason."

"So what?" Ducky snarled. "The worst thing that will happen is our hair will frizz into giant bushes, we'll get wet, and we'll keep drinking Granddad's beer. What kind of ideas?"

Dodo drained her bottle of beer. It never paid for them to allow Dodo to get ahead of them when they were in their serious planning stages. She leaned forward and spoke in a hushed whisper. "Now hear me out and for God's sake let me finish before either of you goes off the deep end. The Garden Club is getting ready to send out the invitations for the Christmas Candlelight Tour. Now, we all know that Bella Gunn would sell her soul to have her house included. It might look like the club is going to approve Bella, but it isn't going to happen, because we are going to stop the process. Right now, Bella thinks she has an inside track, so we'll trade on that. Ducky will invite her to lunch to congratulate her while . . . while . . . Diddy and I go to the house and . . . and snatch Marcus. This is crunch time and we need to pull out all the stops," Dodo said, barely stopping to take a breath. "All in the interests of preserving the shoe and getting Ben to stay in town. Marcus can talk and has alert moments, according to Ben. Marcus must have some kind of dirt on Bella. We need to find out exactly what that dirt is. We don't have a whole lot of time here, girls. The clock is ticking, and that provisional license could turn into a conditional one if Bella puts pressure on the committee. While Ducky is entertaining Bella, Diddy and I go to the house and snatch Marcus. Diddy's the bait. I'm the muscle." Ducky choked on her beer.

Diddy's eyes glazed over. "No," she mumbled.

"Yes. Then we take him to Rayne, to Trixie's house. Trixie and Fred can keep Marcus for a while till we see just what the hell is wrong with him. That way no one can pin anything on any of us. Ducky will be with Bella, and we'll just spirit him away. We have to stop Bella before she ruins the two houses in the shoe. I hate to keep saying this, but the clock *is* ticking. Even if we snatch Marcus, there is no guarantee he will help us. If that happens, we're back to square one, and the clock is ticking faster. I suppose we should give some thought to Plan B if Marcus can't or won't help us. For all we know that witch could have some kind of evil hold on him. Having said that, let's give some thought to hypnotizing Marcus, if all else fails.

"One last thing." Dodo's voice turned fierce when she said, "Family should stick together, be together. That's what life is all about. Family. That's why we're

doing this, and don't forget it. It's all about . . . family."
Her voice cracked and broke as her sisters rushed to her,
their eyes meeting across Dodo's bowed head.

"Aren't you forgetting the nurse and all the household help?" Ducky queried, trying to change the subject.

"I have to work on that a little. What do you think of
the plan so far?" Dodo asked, clearly grateful to put her
mind to the task at hand.

"It stinks," Diddy said. "What makes you think Trixie
and Fred, our oldest and dearest friends in the whole
world, will do this? It's *kidnapping!*"

Dodo sighed. Trixie and Fred McGuire, aka, T. F.
Dingle, writer of blood-and-guts mystery stories, now retired, and training K-9 dogs for police departments all
over the country, were the perfect couple to hide Marcus Gunn. And Rayne was just under two hours away, so
they could easily keep tabs on Marcus and his condition.

"It's not really kidnapping if we can get him out
under his own power. They'll think he just wandered
off. You know how us old people do that from time to
time," Dodo said airily.

"Shut up, Dodo. This is illegal. We could go to jail.
Fred and Trixie could go to jail. Think about *that!*"
Ducky hissed as she uncapped her third bottle of beer.
"I know, I know, you'll just kill anyone who gets in the
way. We need to get real here. Why are we even plan-
ning this anyway?"

"Because Bella did the unforgivable. She ignored Russell's last wishes. She gave away his body parts when he expressly said he didn't want that to happen," Dodo said.

"That's illegal, too," Diddy sniffed. "You can't hypnotize someone against their will. Even I know that!"

Dodo slid off the bench and proceeded to do some limbering-up exercises. "He'll never know he's being hypnotized. That's the beauty of it. Stop worrying. We can do this if we each do what we're supposed to do. Ducky, Bella will be drooling over your invitation. You'll have so much to talk about, your nips and tucks, your designer wear, all those boy toys you play around with, your world travels, et cetera. Your reputation for being as loose as a goose will sit well with Bella."

"Oh, God!" was all Ducky could say.

"I saw Marcus's chart. Darby copied it yesterday. It said the nurse takes Marcus out to the garden every afternoon for lunch, weather permitting. That's when we snatch him. We'll use the pickup truck and take the battery-operated wheelbarrow. We just dump him in it, hoist him into the back, and off we go. All the way to Rayne. You just wait and see, Marcus will thank us when this is all over," Dodo said cheerfully. "See, I'm planning as we talk. That's how a plan comes together. Find one thing wrong with anything I've just said."

"I hate you, Dodo. I can't believe you're my sister," Diddy said sourly. "Your mind is warped."

"Yes, it is. I'm taking that as a compliment. Well, are you in or are you out? I guess your silence means you're in. I'm proud of you."

"What if Trixie and Fred say no?" Ducky asked.

"Think of the excitement, the challenge. Us against that damn Bella. From here on out, I want you both to think positive. Would you look at that rain! I think Ben is smitten with our Darby. She's smitten with him, too, she just doesn't know it yet." She continued. "We're going to need a private dick, too. We're going to get the skinny on that woman once and for all. I'm telling you, Marcus is going to thank us when this is all over. There's no doubt in my mind that we can pull off this caper. I like that word *caper* almost as much as I like the word *specificity*," she jabbered.

Diddy shook the beer bottle in her hand till it was almost all foam and squirted it at her sister. "I'm going to pray tonight that you get lockjaw, Dodo," Diddy said, reaching down to the tub for a fresh beer.

"I second that," Ducky said. "When was the last time we took our clothes off and ran through the rain?"

"A hundred years ago," Dodo said. "Now I'm going to smell like a distillery. Why did you do that, Diddy?"

"Because I hate you. I've always hated you. I will continue to hate you forever." She didn't mean a word of it, and Dodo knew it.

A ripe discussion on each other's naked attributes followed. No one took offense.

"We're old now," Dodo said sadly. "Does either of you ever think about what kind of legacy we're going to leave behind when we . . . you know, *go*?"

Neither sister answered her. Dodo shrugged. The heavy rain continued to beat on the roof of the gazebo. Off in the distance, the tree frogs talked to one another. She loved the sound. She didn't even mind when one or two of them got into the house. She viewed them as company.

Dodo looked toward her house. She could barely see the dim yellow light on the second-floor hallway. A dog barked. She wondered if it was Willie or a dog beyond the shoe. In the scheme of things she realized it didn't matter one way or the other. She looked toward the shoe the way she always did late at night or early in the morning. Then she would daydream about a family living there, a special family. A family with children running and laughing, playing. Dogs, cats, friends. Bicycles, red wagons, roller skates, all the things children needed to be children. If she had a say in the matter, it would happen. It had to happen. Maybe it was time to go in and go to bed. Walking across the yard in the rain would wash away most of the beer smell on her clothes. "What time is it?"

"Almost midnight. The witching hour," Ducky said. "Why do you want to know, and what difference does it make? By the way, in case either of you are interested, I canceled my plans and am staying here. I'm going to let my hair go gray, I'm going to eat like a truck driver, and

I'm going to wear bib overalls so I look like the two of you. I'm just going to get old."

"Really. That's interesting."

Ducky ignored her sisters, her thoughts far away as she wondered if she could adjust to life in Baton Rouge again. With a flip of her frizzy hair, she decided she could. Life here in Baton Rouge would be whatever she made it.

"It's a good thing we decided not to get *nekkid* and romp through the yard. You want to talk about a caper, that would be the ultimate," Ducky gurgled. In the blink of an eye, her nightgown sailed over the railing of the gazebo, and she was running through the rain.

"When in Rome . . ." Dodo said.

"Fools!" Diddy said, as her nightgown landed on top of Ducky's.

On the second-floor balcony, Ben's jaw dropped as he squeezed his eyes shut and ran into the house and into his bed. He pulled the covers over his head to stifle his laughter. He was still smothering his chuckles when he heard Dodo marching down the hall to her room.

Damn, it's good to be home.

The noise was harsh and loud, unlike any noise the Lanes had ever heard in the shoe. The Lane sisters, Ben, and Darby all bolted out of bed and raced to their respective front verandas. The sight that greeted them rendered the sisters speechless. Not caring that they were in their nightclothes, they raced down the steps, across the lawn, and up to the two Gunn houses. Darby was tying the belt to her robe as she joined them. Ben, dressed only in a pair of khaki shorts, brought up the rear.

"What the hell's going on?" he bellowed.

Still speechless, Ducky pointed to the road, where bulldozers, a wrecking ball, assorted trucks, and men were standing. A radio blasted from one of the many pickup trucks; heavy metal sounds that grated on the ears. Two huge dump trucks pulled up, adding to the confusion.

"Who's in charge here?" Ben shouted to be heard over the cacophony of sound.

A big, burly man wearing a hard hat stepped forward, his hand outstretched. "Jay Tigger. Tigger Construction. We're here to demolish these two houses," he said, pointing to Ben's father's houses, which sat opposite each other on the Horseshoe. "I have all the paperwork. Mrs. Gunn signed off on it. She hired us to build two new houses, replicas of her own house."

Ben snatched the sheaf of papers out of Tigger's hands.

"She can't do this. These are historical houses. They can't be torn down. Marcus knows that!" Diddy screeched. "Dodo, go in the house and call the Historical Society and while you're at it, call the police and Simon from the Preservation Club. She can't do this with a provisional license."

"The ladies are right, Mr. Tigger. Historical houses

can rot to the ground, be repaired, but they cannot be torn down." Ben turned to Dodo and said, "Call the mayor and the newspaper." He turned back to Jay Tigger. "I'm Ben Gunn. These two houses belong in my family. You're going to have to wait until someone in authority gets here. My father would never agree to this. Never!" Yet even as he said the words, Ben wondered if what he was saying was true.

Tigger held up both hands, palms out as though to say he did not want any trouble. "My paperwork is in order. Mrs. Bella Gunn has her husband's power of attorney. I checked with the law firm. We were paid to demolish these two houses. I have a signed contract. We'll wait, but you should know time is money in the construction business. I'm not about to break any laws." He turned to his foreman and said, "Go fetch us some coffee and donuts, and turn down that damn radio."

"You better not be doing any littering," Diddy said menacingly.

"She can't do this, can she?" Darby whispered to Ben.

"She's going to try," Ben whispered in return. "I think you should get your aunts to go in the house to get dressed. I'll stay here and keep my eyes on these guys. By the way"—he leaned closer so his voice wouldn't carry—"do you know your aunts romp around naked in the rain at midnight?"

"They do that all the time. You didn't *watch*, did you?"

Ben pretended horror. "What kind of person do you think I am? Of course not!"

"I think I'll get dressed, too. Come along, ladies," she said to her aunts. "We need to get dressed. The whole damn town will be here before you know it."

"Oh, my God!" Suddenly aware of her appearance, Diddy grabbed Ducky's arm and dragged her backward, their nightgowns billowing out behind them.

Dodo met them halfway across the yard. "I called everyone. Now, don't you wish you had let me kill that witch? Where are you all going?"

"To get dressed," Darby said. "Ben is staying to make sure they don't do anything they shouldn't do. Hurry, ladies. I expect Bella herself will be here soon."

The women separated, muttering to themselves as they went along. In mere minutes, they were back at the front of the Horseshoe just as an elegant, austere man, dressed in a full three-piece summer suit complete with straw hat, climbed out of his car with a yellow folder in his hands. He introduced himself as Hudson Duquesne, president of the Historical Society. "The society's attorneys are filing an injunction with the court as we speak. Where is Mrs. Gunn?" His voice rang with authority in the heavy-laden air. Tigger shrugged as he shoved his contract under Duquesne's nose. "This isn't worth the paper it's written on," Duquesne said as he shoved the papers back into Tigger's hand. "It's a provisional license."

Five minutes later it was a circus, with the mayor

looking for his five minutes of fame as the local television personality shoved a microphone under his nose. The chief of police, who was extremely photogenic, inched his way closer to the mayor. He gave a short speech about residents who tried to break the law, and he was the man who would prevent such a thing from happening. He also made sure he put his hand on the gun at his hip. He looked macho, which was his intention.

The reporter backed away to take possession of the microphone, and said, "I think we're in good hands here, folks. Oh, here comes Mrs. Gunn. Maybe she'll say a few words and explain how this all came about. This is Axel Matthews talking to you from the famous Horseshoe in Baton Rouge."

Bella Gunn stepped from the Bentley, her gaze on her stepson. She squared her bony shoulders as she pasted a smile on her face. She looked around at the mayor, the police, the police cars, the hoity-toity man from the Historical Society. She waited for the reporter to approach her. She nodded slightly to Tigger, meaning, just hold on until I take care of this.

"Mrs. Gunn, can you tell us what's going on here?"

Bella flashed her porcelain caps. "I'd love to tell you what's going on. My husband wants these houses demolished. Look at them! They're a hazard and on the verge of collapse. Someone could get hurt. The liability insurance is atrocious. We want to rebuild them so that the Horseshoe can be a thing of beauty again. Our lawyers assure us this is all legal. I do have a provisional license pending the conditional event. Now, if you'll excuse me, I need to speak with our contractor."

The little group standing in the middle of the Horseshoe watched as Bella, dressed in a yellow polka-dot dress with a wide woven-straw belt minced her way not toward the contractor but to the mayor, where she hissed in his ear, the porcelain caps glistening in the bright sunlight. Her hair was even bigger and higher than usual. A bird could have flown into it, nested, and no one would have noticed.

"*Mistah* Mayor, you assured me this wasn't going to happen. It looks to me like it's happening. Take care of it, *Mistah* Mayor, or all those little pet projects my husband and I have been funding are going to come to an immediate halt. I will not tolerate these people making a fool of me. I do have a provisional license, as you know. Do we understand each other, *Mistah* Mayor?"

The mayor nodded, knowing he had a tiger by the tail. What did they expect from him? The Preservation Society had granted a provisional license pending the conditional license. Why they would do such a thing was beyond him. Now the Historical Society was weighing in. There wasn't a darn thing he could do, thanks to the premature granting of the provisional license. Let the Preservation Society and the Historical Society duke it out.

He groaned, knowing the Lane sisters were going to make his life miserable if he didn't at least try to do something. But his hands were tied, thanks to that damn provisional license. He groaned again when he thought about the field day the press was going to have with this mess.

All eyes were on Bella as she sashayed over to the contractor. "I think, Mr. Tigger, that we should let these kind people settle things. I want you to sit here with all your equipment until I tell you otherwise. Is that clear?"

"Yes, ma'am."

Bella turned and waved to Ben. "It was nice to see you again, Benjamin." A moment later she was in the Bentley.

The police started to disperse the small crowd. The mayor and the local newspeople made up their own parade as they, too, packed up to leave.

"I don't know what's worse, looking at those ramshackle houses or having to look at Jay Tigger and all his equipment," Dodo said as she trudged back toward her house. "Meet me in the gazebo. We'll pretend we're going to clean up the mess we left last night," she whispered to Ducky, who in turn whispered the plan to Diddy.

"Would anyone like some breakfast?" Darby chirped. "Ben and I will make it."

The threesome mumbled something that sounded like "bring it to the gazebo." Darby and Ben exchanged glances as they walked up the wide steps of the veranda. "How does scrambled eggs and bacon sound?" she asked.

"You look nice even when you get up in the morning," Ben said.

"So do you," Darby said, her eyes twinkling as she eyed his bare torso. She laughed outright when his ears turned pink.

"I think I'll . . . what I'll do is"—he motioned behind him—"you know, get cleaned up. This is just a guess on my part, but I think your aunts are hatching something, so they're going to be at it for a while."

"I think you're right. Take your time." Darby grinned. She turned away. She was flirting, and she liked the feeling. It was way too long since a man had been in her life. Not that Ben was in her life. But he could be. He definitely could be. She hummed under her breath as she opened the screen door. Willie jumped up and tried to lick her face. "C'mon, big guy, I'm going to take a shower. You can stand guard."

The retriever barked happily as he bounded ahead of her.

Life was suddenly looking just a little sunnier. Now, if she could just figure out what the aunts were up to, life might get even sunnier.

8

Darby smiled as she took in Willie sprawled across her bed, his head on her pillow. She knew he was daring her to make him get off, but she didn't have the heart. "You're going to have to move, Willie, I want to make the bed." Willie stretched, barked his displeasure when Darby shook out the spread, and grudgingly hopped off the bed. She fluffed the pillows, then straightened the colorful spread. She looked at Willie, who was now curled up in his own bed, his silky head on his baby.

Darby dressed quickly in a mint green sleeveless sundress with spaghetti straps. She slipped into leather sandals. She felt ready for whatever the day would bring. But was she? As she made her way out to the hall and the stairs, she thought about the dream she'd had. Later, when the dream wasn't so raw, maybe she would talk to Ben about it.

In the kitchen, she set about preparing breakfast. A quick look out the kitchen window showed her the aunts huddled close together in the gazebo. She wondered what they were up to. Whatever it was, she realized they were a law unto themselves, and nothing she could say or do would alter things. She shrugged. She had more important things on her mind just then than worrying about her aunts' hijinks.

Darby was whipping eggs into a rich, yellow froth when Ben entered the kitchen. Willie jumped up and tried to paw the man who looked so much like his old master. Ben tussled with him for a while before he washed his hands and set the table. Darby smiled at his exuberant greeting as she watched him out of the corner of her eye. Russ had been the same way, exuberant in the morning. They were so much alike and yet unalike. Her heart skipped a beat at how good Ben looked. *Handsome* hardly covered the way he looked in khaki slacks and sky-blue pullover shirt. She found herself smiling again at his resemblance to Russ. The only difference was that Russ had never made her heart skip a beat the way Ben did.

Darby watched as Ben placed strips of bacon on a bacon rack for the microwave oven. Toast was his next project, as Darby set the table for two. "The aunts want breakfast delivered." She grinned. "If you're lucky, you might overhear what they're cooking up." Her voice was breathless when she said, "Do you think Bella will win with the houses?"

"I sure as hell hope not. She only has a provisional license, which means absolutely nothing. All it does is allow her to park that equipment up at the top of the shoe. I'm thinking they issued it to shut her up until they can make up their minds definitively. Let's not panic now. You took Russell's seat on the board, so you have a vote. I think between you, Simon, and Sarabess you have a good chance of turning some of the others who are leaning toward granting the conditional license."

"One swing of that wrecking ball, and it's all over, Ben. If she says her contractor ignored her orders and did it anyway, then it's too late. I heard her say she was going to demolish the houses. She has to *fix* them, not tear them down. She knows it, too. She's planning something devious. I feel it in my bones."

"Darby, that guy Tigger isn't going to put his butt on the line. He knows the law, he could lose his contractor's license if he pulled something like that. Bella's running scared now that she knows you have Russ's vote. The town won't let her demolish those houses. Trust me on that."

"It certainly did upset the aunts. Me, too, for that matter. Can you imagine two houses on the Horseshoe that look like the one she lives in. It would be a nightmare. The aunts offered to buy those houses hundreds of times. The Historical Society intervened on their behalf and even offered to buy them. Bella said no. There was a running commentary for weeks in the paper, then it more or less died off. I think our visit yesterday stirred Bella up again."

Ben removed the bacon from the microwave and placed it on a platter. "You know, Darby, I think you may be right. What are we going to do today?"

We. It sounded so . . . so intimate. "I'm going to see Eric McAllister. He's an old friend of Russ's. He's a lawyer in town. He's a nice guy; you should come along—I'm sure you'd like him. I want a legal opinion on Russ's will. There was something about property he would inherit in the future that I didn't understand."

"Sure, I'd like to go along for whatever good I'll do. How about dropping me off at Russ's place so I can pick up his car. The rental agency is going to pick up my rental this morning, so I'll be without wheels."

Darby removed the scrambled eggs from the frying pan. "I had this . . . this awful dream last night. I think it was right before I woke with all that racket outside. The workers started up all those machines and rap music was playing. In my dream I was at this parade in town and there was a long line of people and they all said their name was Russ. Each one wore a badge saying which body part they inherited. None of them knew me. I was screaming at the man who had Russ's eyes. I kept saying, 'Look at me. You must know me!' He told me to get away from him. It was awful. I've always heard that you can interpret your dreams just by thinking about what's going on in your life. Do you believe that?" she asked fretfully.

Ben nodded, and would have taken Darby in his arms, but he was holding the platter of bacon, and Darby was holding the platter of scrambled eggs. "I had a similar dream two nights ago. It's the not knowing."

"Well, I want to know," Darby said with a sigh.

"Probably. I can research dream interpretation if you like. You do have a computer, don't you?"

"Sure. Let's get this all down to the aunts before it gets cold."

They were back within minutes. Ben buttered the toast, and Darby poured coffee.

Ben stared at her with an intensity that unnerved Darby. "This is nice. I enjoy having breakfast with someone I like. It's a good way to start off the day, wouldn't you agree?"

Darby flushed. "Absolutely." Russ had always told her to be patient where her love life was concerned. He said it would happen when she least expected. Was it happening now? Russ always knew what to say and managed to say it at exactly the right time. A wave of sadness overwhelmed her. She struggled to overcome the feeling. "Do you like being a park ranger, Ben?" she asked, changing the subject.

"Very much. I think I'm in a rut, though. I've been thinking about moving on this past year. I truly do miss home. I didn't realize how much until I got back here. I really missed the shoe when I went off to college. This is home. That other place . . . that place Bella built was never home. You and Russ were the lucky ones, you came back."

"Yes, we were the lucky ones," Darby said sadly. "Russ loved it here. He found his niche and had a wonderful life. He loved his job, the kids, the school. He had great friends, and he had Claire. Next year he and Claire were going to go to Africa on a safari. Their honeymoon. I can't tell you how he was looking forward to it." A sob caught in her throat.

Ben was at a loss as to what to say. He was learning things about his brother he'd never known. Guilt washed over him. He should have called more often, sent more e-mails, come home more often. He said so.

Darby shook her head. "Don't feel guilty. I have enough of that for both of us. Russ talked about you all the time. He used to get such a kick out of your stories about patrolling on horseback. We need to get this all settled in our minds, or it's going to ruin our lives. That's why I'm going to see Eric at his law office. I don't have an appointment, but I'm sure he'll see me. Eric and Russ belonged to the Big Brother organization. They were so good with the kids."

Ben pushed his plate away as did Darby. Willie waited patiently, knowing he was going to get the leftovers. When no one moved to transfer the food to his bowl, he trotted over to his dish, carried it back to the table, and dropped it with a hard thump. He sat back on his haunches to wait. He let out a loud bark, startling both Darby and Ben. Together they stooped and started to scrape their plates into Willie's food bowl. They were so close, their noses touched. Their eyes locked, and then, slowly, Ben leaned forward and kissed her. Darby thought it was the sweetest, gentlest kiss she'd ever gotten. Her breakfast plate dropped from her hands. Ben dropped his as his arms went around her. Willie barked. And barked. Then he barked some more. They separated, their eyes wide with astonishment.

Never bashful, Darby said, "Wow!"

Ben grinned from ear to ear. "Yeah, 'wow' about covers it."

Willie wolfed down his food and ran to the door. "The aunts are coming," Darby said. "Let's not give them something else to stew about, okay?"

"The three of them have been plotting to get us together for years. Didn't you know that?"

Darby flushed as she bent down to pick up the plates. "Yes, and no," she muttered.

Willie danced around, enjoying all the attention the aunts showered on him.

Always astute, they looked smug at the obvious discomfort on the young couple's faces. "Since you cooked, we'll clean up. Why don't you two go about whatever it is you planned for the day. We, ah, might not be here later when you get back, so don't worry about us. Lunch and dinner will be whatever you prepare. Go, go, scoot," Ducky said, making shooing motions with her hands. "Leave Willie with us. We might need

. . . what I mean is we'll feel better with Willie here. You know, all those people out there on the shoe."

"Well, sure," Darby said, certain now that the aunts were up to no good. "I'm going to drop Ben off at Russ's town house so he can pick up the Range Rover. Then we're going to see Eric McAllister to talk about Russ's will and his inherited property. What are you three going to do?" she asked, suspicion ringing in her voice.

"Not much," Ducky said vaguely.

"I was thinking about finishing a quilt I've been working on," Diddy said just as vaguely.

"Why do you want to know what we're doing?" Dodo demanded.

Darby's feet literally left the floor as Ben pulled her forward. "I was just making conversation. Do you need anything from town?"

"No," the aunts said in unison. It was clear they wanted them to leave.

Outside, Darby said, "Don't tell me they aren't up to something. They looked guilty as hell. What do you suppose they're planning?"

"I don't have a clue, but I bet it's something that will make us nuts. Want me to drive?"

"Sure," Darby said, climbing into the Volvo.

"Listen, Darby, what happened back there in the kitchen . . ."

"Are you sorry you kissed me?" Darby asked boldly. "You can't take it back, you know. It happened, and I liked it."

"Hell no. I just don't want you getting the wrong idea, you know, that I go around kissing women just for . . . oh, hell, you know what I'm trying to say."

Darby grinned. "Now why would I get the wrong idea. I said I liked it. Do you have anything else on your agenda?"

"Do I ever." They both laughed self-consciously.

"I just wish I knew what the aunts were up to."

"The only way we'll ever find out is if they tell us," Ben said.

Little did they both know how wrong they were.

Diddy moved away from the kitchen doorway the moment she heard the engine of Darby's Volvo turn over. "Okay, they're gone. Ducky, it would please me greatly if you would make some fresh coffee. We need to fall back and regroup. That damn Bella is one step ahead of us. The woman is a conniver and a manipulator."

Ducky nodded in agreement. "We have to stop her. If we can break Marcus out, our best hope is he'll turn on her. We have to believe that blood is thicker than water, and family is family. I don't see him ignoring family. I refuse to believe he will side with that witch over us when he understands what's been going on. Diddy, you might have to . . . well, you might have to . . . be really nice to Marcus. He'll listen to you before he listens to anyone else." She moved away so she wouldn't have to look at her sister. To her surprise, Diddy didn't argue.

Dodo stood at the kitchen counter, her cup in hand, waiting for the coffee to finish dripping into the pot. "The first thing we should do is call around, maybe New Orleans, for a private detective. It's a given that we can't use anyone here in town. We need to find out all we can about Bella, get to the bottom of her shenanigans." She set her cup down and picked up a blue-and-white-checked dish towel that she proceeded to wring, then tie in knots. She held it up for inspection. "This is what I'd like to do to that woman's scrawny neck."

"You're so vicious, Dodo," Ducky said as she poured coffee into three cups. "Somehow, some way, she hoodwinked Marcus. Which doesn't say much for Marcus." She eyed Diddy, whose face was flushed a rosy pink. She looked away, unwilling to acknowledge her sister's words.

Dodo took a gulp of the steaming coffee. "We can't snatch Marcus today, that's for sure. But that doesn't mean we can't do a little spying, get the lay of the land, so to speak. We can hide in the bushes and see what time the nurse takes Marcus outside. Check the terrain, position the truck for the getaway, that kind of thing. We need to *plan*. I don't think we have to worry about the two houses out front. The town will have to hold meetings, the Historical Society will have to call a special meeting, and the newspapers will have their run with it as well as the local news. It will be at least a few weeks before anything is settled. We'll just have to put up with the circus unless Bella has a change of heart and calls it all off. I don't see her doing that, though."

Ducky sat down with a thump on one of the kitchen chairs. "This has to be kept entirely separate from what Darby and Ben are doing. Simon Bourdroux has the authority to cancel next week's meeting with the Preservation Society if he feels time is getting away from him, and he needs to stall the vote. Bella will gnash her teeth in frustration, but it will work to our advantage. The clock is ticking way too fast, to my liking. With Darby taking Russ's seat on the board, I'm even more hopeful. That young woman can be very convincing when she puts her mind to it. I'm pinning my hopes on her and Simon helping us."

The sisters smiled. "Marcus holds the answer to everything; that's why we have to snatch him."

"This is so crazy," Diddy said. "Bella is going to know it's us."

Dodo snorted as she finished the last of her coffee. "Knowing and proving it are two different things. Alibis are wonderful things. Need I remind you that . . ."

"For God's sake, Dodo, no, you do not need to remind us that you should have killed her. Get the phone book and see if you can find a private detective. When are we going out to Bella's house? Another thing I think we need to think about is Marcus's medicine. What if there's something he absolutely needs, and we don't have it. Then what?" Diddy asked.

Dodo crunched her tiny face into a grimace. "Ben

has his chart. I looked at the meds on it. I faxed the list to Trixie, and she said she knows how to get *everything* on it. Over the years they've made some rather strange friends in all the research they've done for those mystery books they write. She's fixed up a room for him and is going to pick up a wheelchair today. She came up with a better plan than the three of us did. She's driving up here with Flash, that K-9 dog she bought a few years ago before she went into the business of training police dogs," Dodo said. Her excitement was infectious, and her sisters leaned forward to listen more closely. "Listen up, here's the plan. We, as in Diddy and I, are going to snatch Marcus, then turn it all over to Trixie and Flash, who will transport him back to her farm in Rayne. We come home and sit on the front porch. We'll be each other's alibi—we'll tell everyone we both spent the day sitting and talking. Ducky will keep Bella busy at lunch for at least two hours, then join us on the porch. Ducky now has an alibi just as we do. Tell me it isn't foolproof."

"What if Ducky's lunch with Bella doesn't coincide with the time Marcus is taken outside?" Diddy asked fearfully.

"Then we're screwed and will have to go to Plan B as soon as I can figure out what Plan B is," Dodo snarled. "Are you ready, Diddy?"

"No, I'm not ready. Why isn't Ducky coming? What if we have to run or something?"

Dodo tapped her foot impatiently. "In that case, you're on your own. I've been telling you for years to stop eating that damn red-velvet cake and take off those fifty pounds you put on. Did you listen? No, you did not." Diddy started to cry. "Look, I'm sorry, Diddy, I didn't mean that. I know your world ended when Marcus ditched you for Bella. I know all your dreams were shattered. Maybe we can make it right for you. We should have done all this years ago, but you wouldn't let us get to the bottom of it. Therefore, you have to take some responsibility." She handed over the dish towel for Diddy to wipe her eyes. Then she patted Diddy's plump arm in a sisterly fashion. "Let's go. Ooops, wait, let me get my digital camera. We might need it. We can blow the pictures up on the computer. So we can get a close look at the terrain. I'll meet you at the car."

Ducky turned to her sister. Her face was full of awe. "Oh, Diddy, I didn't know you still had feelings for Marcus. After he made such a fool of you for the whole town to see, how can that be?" she asked, not unkindly.

"Marcus was the only man I ever loved. The feeling never went away. It's the only answer I can give you. I really don't want to talk about this, Ducky. I have to go now. Good luck finding a private detective. Make sure he signs a confidentiality agreement."

Dodo settled herself in her small black car, a 1985 Mercedes convertible. She had to sit on two cushions and had wooden blocks on the gas and the brake pedals, much like parents put on children's tricycles, because her legs were too short to reach. She roared out of the alley, jolting Diddy forward. "Buckle up, Diddy."

They tooled along, enjoying the sunny day and the slight breeze in the air. "I never asked you about Marcus, Diddy, not because I didn't want to," Dodo said finally, her voice soft and kind. "I don't want you to think I was uncaring or selfish, but I took my cue from you. Ducky did, too. If it's any consolation to you, I know how you must have felt. I guess the Lane women aren't very good about picking out their partners."

Diddy's head snapped sideways. "Are you saying . . . ?"

"Yes. I met this man, oh, it was about thirty years ago, in Japan. I loved him with every breath in my body. That's why I didn't come home too often during those years. We lived together. He had his own *Dojo*, which I financed, and I helped with the training classes. It was so wonderful, it was downright scary. Our lives were blissful, or so I thought."

Diddy stared at her sister in awe. This was the first time in her whole life that Dodo ever opened up about her life in Japan. She and Ducky had suspected, though. "What happened?"

Dodo turned on her signal light, made a right-hand turn, and started down the paved road that led to Bella and Marcus Gunn's house before she replied. "One night he didn't come home. When he didn't come home the second and third night I knew something was wrong. When I went to the *Dojo* on the fourth morning it was empty. He'd cleaned everything out. I went back to my house and hunkered in for months. I heard through some very good friends that Sobu went to Taiwan with a beautiful, tall blond woman. He sold the *Dojo* right from under me and cleaned out my bank account. That's the end of my story. And before you can ask, no, I never got over it. Maybe it was the rejection, maybe it was love, I just don't know."

"And you never saw him again?"

"Oh, I saw him over the years. The blonde left him. He came back every year or so for the trials. He'd bring one of his students, but they were never as good as the students we trained together. He tried to talk to me once, but I walked away. Like you, Diddy, I don't want to talk about this anymore. I'm apologizing to you, and I hope you accept the apology. Oh, one last thing. Don't think for one minute Ducky hasn't had her share of failed love affairs. Why else is she out there trying to recapture something she thinks she lost and can never have again?"

"I do. Accept your apology, I mean. Thanks for telling me about . . . your life in Japan."

Dodo nodded. "From here on in, we have to be careful. I'll park in that brush over there. It has some excellent overhead cover. There has to be a footpath somewhere other than this driveway. I don't want to go too close to the house. You can wait in the car, Diddy. It's kind of hilly."

"Don't worry about me, I can do it. Besides, I've never been here before. I'd like to see what all the fuss has been about," she said, then she gasped in surprise as she looked up the hill toward Bella and Marcus Gunn's "monstrosity." "That's probably the ugliest house I've ever seen. It suits Bella."

"You're right about that. Okay, let's go. Don't talk, voices carry. I want to find a good vantage point so we can see the backyard. I saw a pictorial spread in the *Advocate* once, and it showed the yard and the big trees. I'm thinking the nurse would park Marcus under a tree in the shade. I'm sure there's a breeze this far up the hill. Careful, Diddy," Dodo warned as she herself slipped on a rock.

Ten minutes later, Dodo stopped in her tracks. Diddy reached out to grasp a sapling to hold on to as Dodo rummaged in her fanny pack for a pair of binoculars. "I can see the yard," she hissed. "I can't see anyone, but I can see the whole yard. It's rather pretty." She looked down at the oversize watch with the glow-in-the-dark numerals on her skinny wrist. She pointed to it for Diddy's benefit. Diddy nodded. Ten minutes past noon. "Hand me the camera, Diddy."

Dodo snapped and snapped, turning this way and that to make sure she got the flower garden from every angle. Satisfied, she handed the camera back to Diddy, who hung it around her neck.

"How are we going to get Marcus down this incline?" Diddy whispered.

Dodo shrugged. "What we need to know is does the nurse stay out here with Marcus or does she go back indoors. There are windows that face the yard. It's a possibility that someone in the house could see us. Uh-oh, someone's coming. Don't make a sound." Diddy obediently clamped her lips shut.

Overhead a pack of squirrels raced down the tree in front of them. Somewhere to the left they could hear a woodpecker having his lunch.

Dodo watched as two maids dressed in gray uniforms with pristine white aprons set up a small wooden table under one of the oak trees. She could hear the clatter of crystal, china, and silver as the table was set for two. Within seconds a nurse appeared at the doorway, pushing a wheelchair. Dodo winced at her sister's indrawn breath. She continued to watch as another maid appeared with a huge silver tray covered with a white cloth. The sisters watched as the maid served lunch. The nurse ate heartily while Marcus stared at his food. After a few minutes, he pushed the plate away. Either he didn't like the food or he wasn't hungry. A snarl escaped Diddy's lips when they heard the nurse say, "If you don't eat this food, I'll have to feed you. You know how you choke and sputter when I do that. I don't want to have to give Mrs. Gunn a bad report this evening when she gets home." The threat worked. Marcus speared something off his plate with his fork and put it into his mouth. He chewed slowly and methodically until his plate was empty.

"At least he understands and can hear. He's able to eat. I don't think there's anything seriously wrong with him, Diddy. I think Ben and Darby might be right—

Bella might be doping him up to keep him quiet," Dodo whispered.

The two maids with the white aprons appeared to carry away the table and the dishes. The nurse moved to a bench under the tree. She removed a copy of the *National Enquirer* and the *Star* and started to read. Marcus leaned back in the wheelchair and closed his eyes.

The sisters waited patiently, sweat pouring down their bodies. Exactly one hour later, the nurse finished reading both tabloids and got up and shook Marcus's shoulder. "Time to go in, Mr. Gunn. Your wife brought home some new videos last night you might like to watch this afternoon."

Dodo and Diddy remained quiet as the nurse struggled to push the wheelchair across the thick carpet of grass. They were at the edge of the lawn when the sprinkler system came to life, water shooting upward and sideways. The sisters waited a good ten minutes before they backed down the incline, Dodo going first.

Back in the car, Diddy started to shake. Dodo placed a comforting hand on her arm. "I really think we can pull this off. I'm going to call Trixie and tell her to leave now. We'll do it tomorrow. Since we don't want to set off any alarms, I'll tell her to get a room at the Baton Rouge Inn. The kids will suspect something if she stays at the house."

"What about Flash?" Diddy asked uneasily.

"She'll say he's a Seeing Eye dog. Stop worrying."

"I was born to worry. What about the nurse?"

Dodo turned in the seat, phone in hand, to look at her sister. She placed the phone on the console and said, "Diddy, I know all the pressure points on a person's body. I know just how much pressure to exert. I can render that nurse unconscious for as long as I want. When she wakes up, she'll think she just dozed off. Now, stop worrying. We can do this. We'll be back home arguing with those people in front of the Horseshoe by the time they discover Marcus is missing."

Diddy leaned back and closed her eyes, as Dodo dialed Trixie McGuire's number in Rayne. Her heart skipped a beat when she heard Dodo say, "The gig's on. Leave now. Make sure you tell the registration clerk that Flash is a Seeing Eye dog. We'll join you for dinner. Think about room service. Call me with your room number so we can go straight to your room without having the desk call you. Okay, bye, Trixie."

"It's all set, Diddy. Relax."

Diddy groaned as she envisioned herself being carted off to jail and her picture gracing the front page of the local newspaper. She voiced the thoughts aloud. "Dodo, it was so . . . strange to see Marcus again in the flesh. I didn't expect my heart to flutter like it did. I thought all those old feelings were dead. They aren't. Oh, Lord, Dodo, what kind of old fool does that make me?"

"A kind, caring old fool. That's the best kind. I'm just glad you aren't bitter and hateful. I was for a while, but you have to move on and hope things will get better. In your case, I think they will. For me, it's too late."

"Oh, no, Dodo, it's never too late. When we're dead, then it's too late. This might not be the time to say this but I, too, would like to see a family in the shoe. Your family, Dodo. We won't talk about this again unless you want to."

Her eyes welling with tears, Dodo simply nodded.

9

Darby could hardly believe her good fortune when Simon Bourdroux called at seven just as she was heading for the shower. In a sly, all-knowing voice, he'd asked if she would like to accompany him and the committee to LSU to look at some properties the committee was considering refurbishing. "It will give us both an opportunity to do a little campaigning," he'd whispered into the phone.

Wily old fox, Darby thought as she hung up the phone and rushed to get showered and dressed. Her offer to pick up Simon had been accepted. He promised to have cinnamon rolls and coffee in hand when she arrived.

Sipping and munching, Darby's eyes on the road, their conversation was limited as they sailed down the road to the LSU campus, where they were to meet up with the others on the quad. As she drove around look-ing for a suitable parking space, Darby let her anxiety show. "Are we going to have any luck, Simon? How do you think the vote will go?"

"Not good," the old man said. "I think our best bet is for me to cancel next week's meeting. I have gout, so it won't come as a surprise to any of the members. I've done it be-fore. We're going to need more time to persuade our members to get them to come around to our way of think-ing. I have to tell you, aside from Sarabess, the others are all on that woman's side. Eleanore Doucette has a nephew that got a donor kidney some time ago, so she's pretty much on Mrs. Gunn's side."

"Simon, Bella Gunn wants to level both houses and rebuild new structures. She will single-handedly ruin the Horseshoe with the kind of buildings she wants to erect. Didn't you see the wrecking ball at the top of the shoe? You've been with the Society forever. Can't you think of something we can do if the vote goes against us?"

The old man looked like he was going to cry. "No, young lady, I can't. The truth is, they want me to resign, to retire so they can bring in new blood. Russell was my protégé, and he felt the same way I did. He didn't want to see the old houses go to wrack and ruin."

"Russ was always so excited about the Society's plans. I only hope I can help carry out his ideas. What else should I know about the area?" Darby asked.

"First off, this used to be a transit town, with people

getting their start in the oil refineries, then moving on. I personally know of a dozen families Russell talked into putting down roots here. He convinced them to buy up some of the old houses around the LSU campus and refurbish them."

"That's right," Darby said. "I remember him talking about how much restoration was being done around campus."

"It was my idea to come here today to throw a guilt trip on the members. They all thought what Russell did back then was so wonderful. Let's see if they still think it was wonderful. There is one house in particular that's owned by one of the oil workers who has fallen on hard times. His house needs a lot of work. I'd personally like to see the committee take it on as our new project."

"That's very clever, Simon," Darby said, getting out of the car. "It's just a short walk to the quad. Can you make it?"

"Of course I can make it. I'd like you to concentrate your efforts today on Clarice Lafaiete. She might be swayed. There's our little group," Simon said, pointing to a small group of women all wearing straw hats with brightly colored ribbons.

Introductions were made as they walked along to Franklin and Anna Baptiste's sprawling white house with the sagging front porch. The grounds were overgrown, the walkway cracked and broken, large chunks of mortar tossed onto the side. The flower beds were choked with weeds and crabgrass.

"Russell loved this old house. Baptiste got it for a song because it was in such bad condition. Most of what was done was done by him. He's a proud man, so we're going to have to be careful how we approach him. He won't take kindly to charity. The others know the man's history. I wanted to bring you up to date. See if you can get close to Eleanore."

The women were chatting among themselves as they made their way up the steps to what should have been a beautiful veranda but was now in need of repair. The beautiful nine-over-nine windows were clean and sparkled as though they'd just been washed. The arched doorway was just as beautiful, but it needed to be sanded and painted. The heavy door reminded Darby of something she'd seen in a monastery.

Simon turned to Darby. "Russell found this door in Charleston, South Carolina. He borrowed a pickup truck from one of his students' parents and drove there one weekend to fetch it back here. He said he got it for a pittance. It's beyond gorgeous."

Darby watched as the women touched the door, whispered among themselves. Twice she heard Russ's name mentioned. She moved closer to Eleanore and tried to strike up a conversation. "I'm going to do my best to follow in Russell's footsteps. To do what he wanted. In fact, I'm going to pattern my next doll-house after some of the old houses the committee has refurbished. I would be remiss if I didn't mention that Russell would be very upset if the committee approves

Mrs. Gunn's application to level the houses on the shoe."

Eleanore Doucette sniffed and took a step away from Darby. "Young lady, are you trying to get me to change my vote?"

Startled, Darby closed the gap between the two of them. "Yes and no would be my answer, Mrs. Doucette. Russell wouldn't want the houses torn down. If I'm not mistaken, one of the houses on the shoe was supposed to go to him on his father's death. The other one was supposed to go to his brother, Ben."

Eleanore Doucette sniffed again. "Russell is no longer with us, but he lives on in others, thanks to Bella Gunn. For her unselfishness in her hour of grief, the very least we can do for her is to allow her to refurbish the houses. I know a thing or two about the donor program since a family member has been a donor recipient. So, if you're fishing to find out if I'll change my mind, the answer is no."

Darby could feel her shoulders start to droop. She forced herself to listen to Simon going on about the magnificent pine flooring and the fabulous crown molding in the foyer. It was beautiful, but the floors needed some work and the crown molding needed to be stripped down and repainted.

How beautiful the staircase was with the carved posts and spindles that looked like they were hand-carved. She made a mental note to try to duplicate the spindles in her next dollhouse.

As she trudged along behind Simon and the little group she could see Eleanore Doucette whispering to some of the other members. That couldn't be a good thing. She moved off toward Sarabess and commented on the old fireplace. Sensing an ally, the woman offered her condolences on Russell's death. Darby was so grateful for her kindness, her eyes filled with tears. "It's so sad, Russ wouldn't want . . ."

"I know, dear." She winked at Darby and raised her voice slightly. "Tell me, my dear, is it true that your aunts are not going to donate any more money to the Preservation Society. I heard that the other night when I ran into Ethan Fox at the library."

Darby raised her voice to match Sarabess's. "That's what they said. They don't want the shoe to become an eyesore. They'd rather live with it the way it is."

Eleanore Doucette whirled around. "I wasn't eavesdropping, Sarabess, but I couldn't help but overhear what you said. That's blackmail, pure and simple."

"Well, it is their money, now isn't it, dear? I think you might have forgotten how powerful the Lane sisters are in this town. I think you just might end up eating that provisional license you were so quick to hand out. And while I'm at it, Eleanore, I'm withdrawing my house from the Christmas Candlelight Tour just the way the Lane sisters are." Sarabess looked to Darby for confirmation, and Darby nodded. "Now, if you ladies will excuse me, I have to be going. Simon, I think this is a worthy project. You have my vote."

"Mine, too," Darby chirped as she trailed behind the group, before deciding to go off on her own to look over the house. So much could be done here. All it would take was a bucketful of money.

When the tour ended, Darby drew Simon aside out of earshot of the others and told him of her two conversations. The old man winked and grinned. "I definitely feel an attack of gout coming on. We can leave now, young lady."

"Where are the owners, Simon?"

"In the garden. Both of them are in wheelchairs and pretty much live on the ground floor. I'd like to install a more efficient and better-looking ramp for them. What do you think?"

"Whatever it takes. The committee isn't going to budge—you know that, right? They're determined to let Bella proceed with ruining the shoe."

"Sadly, my dear, I agree. That's why I'm going to have an attack of gout. A delay is all we can do for the time being."

Her heart heavy, Darby dreaded telling the aunts that she'd failed.

No one waved good-bye as Darby led the old man to her car. "This is beyond sad," she muttered. "Bella has brainwashed the committee. They keep using the word *refurbish*, but Bella Gunn wants to level the two houses. She's not interested in refurbishing them. Don't they understand the difference? Why else would she have a wrecking ball right there at the top of the shoe? Two

wild swings of that ball and the houses are splinters. If
that happens, it's too late, those lovely old homes will be
gone."

"I tried to tell the others the same thing. They said
that would never happen."

"It will happen, Simon."

"I know, my dear. We need to put on our thinking
caps."

If Darby wasn't feeling so angry and frustrated, she
would have laughed at Simon's old-world attitude.

She was beaten, and she knew it.

Ducky Lane checked her makeup and hair before she
got out of the car. At the last minute, she decided to
drive to New Orleans instead of calling around for a private detective. She knew both her sisters were going to
pitch a fit, but she felt strongly that the fewer people
who knew about their business, the better off they were.
And, this way, she could actually interview the detective. If she didn't like what she saw, she'd move on to another agency. Spilling her family secrets wasn't exactly
something she looked forward to. Plus, everyone knew
private detectives were generally a sleazy lot.

Ducky took time to wonder what this man would
think when she came right out and said she wanted him
to find information on Bella Gunn that she could use to
discredit the woman before she ruined the houses on
the shoe. Ducky looked up at what looked like a private
home in the French Quarter, to the second-floor bal-

cony, which was overflowing with flowering plants. Such an odd place for a detective agency. The building appeared to have been restored, unlike its neighbors on both sides. The brick steps looked like they were scrubbed on a daily basis. The intricate wrought iron looked freshly painted, as did the pristine white door. The brass plate was almost hidden behind a luscious oleander. It was a thick plaque, with black lettering that said BRANDON LAUTRIL, and underneath in smaller letters, the word INVESTIGATIONS. This was no fly-by-night agency, Ducky decided as she rang the bell. She was glad now that she had dressed for a day in the Big Easy.

A tall man dressed in a three-piece, lightweight, summer suit, with pale blue shirt and striped tie, opened the door. Ducky sucked in her breath. She couldn't remember when she'd last seen such a handsome man his age, which she quickly estimated to be close to her own. A crop of pure white hair adorned his head. He smiled. "You must be Miss Lane. Please come in. I'm Brandon Lautril. Can I offer you some refreshments? I stock your family's beer, if that will help you make a decision."

Ducky smiled, her dimples showing. "In that case, by all means." So, he'd checked her out after her phone call. She wasn't sure if she was happy about that or not.

"I'll be right back. I'm afraid today, actually all week, I'm on my own here. My secretary is on vacation until the middle of next week and my assistant is up north on a case. Please forgive me if I muddle through this." To prove that he was muddling, he managed to find the beer but couldn't locate the glasses. He looked at Ducky, a helpless expression on his face.

Ducky smiled. "I'm used to drinking out of the bottle. Not very ladylike, I grant you, but sometimes it's necessary." She accepted the bottle and took a healthy swig, as did Lautril. The detective motioned to one of two deep, comfortable easy chairs. When Ducky was seated, he settled himself across from her.

"This is very nice," Ducky said, looking around. "It isn't what I expected."

Lautril smiled. "Were you expecting a grizzled, cigar-chomping, gun-toting detective in a sleazy dark room with a whirring fan overhead?"

Ducky laughed. "I think that's exactly what I was expecting. Do you live here?" she asked, waving her arm about.

"I use the two front rooms for the business. The back end of the house and, of course, the second floor are my personal quarters. Later, if you like, I can show you my courtyard garden. It's quite remarkable. Now, Miss Lane, tell me how I can help you."

Ducky drew a deep breath, her chest expanding, her cleavage obvious. For once in her life, she wasn't thinking about her person but about the matter at hand.

Lautril listened attentively, neither taking notes nor asking questions. The minute Ducky finished her account, she took a deep swallow of beer. "I know it's been twenty-five years, but do you think you can find out anything on Bella Gunn?"

"I can certainly try. That poor young man. I understand your family's anguish. In today's high-tech world, I have more tools at my disposal than my family did when they were in business. How soon would you like me to complete the investigation?"

"I think I speak for my sisters when I say we'd rather you be thorough than rush through things, but time is of the essence. Now, how much is your retainer?"

To Ducky's credit, she didn't blink an eye at the astronomical number Lautril mentioned. All she could hope for was that she would get her money's worth. She stood up and thanked the detective for the beer. They shook hands. Was it her imagination or did he hold her hand a bit longer than necessary? She suddenly felt flustered and wasn't sure why. Sixty-nine years old, and she was flustered!

"I'll be in touch sometime late tomorrow. I expect I'll be driving up to Baton Rouge. I think I want to see this lady with my own eyes." A smart-ass retort in regard to Bella Gunn was on Ducky's lips, but she decided not to utter it. She looked into the rich brown eyes that were staring down at her.

"Thank you for seeing me on such short notice."

"Not a problem, dear lady, nothing much goes on during the dog days of August. Two weeks from now, that's something different. I'll be in touch."

Three hours later, Ducky drove into the alley behind the houses on the shoe. Darby was back, and so were her sisters. That had to mean Ben was at Dodo's. She walked up the path to Diddy's house. She tossed her straw hat onto the table and asked for a very cold beer. "I've been to N'awlins, ladies, and I hired us a dee-tective who almost blew my socks off. Wait till I tell you . . ."

It was six o'clock when Ben turned off the computer in Dodo's home office. He leaned back in the swivel chair to stare at the framed photos on the wall. They were all of Dodo at various martial arts events. As his gaze raked over the photos, he found himself in awe of the little woman. That she had the nerve back in her youth to go into martial arts must have taken not only sheer guts but courage as well. For some reason, his gaze kept going back to one particular photo, actually a series of photos that hung on the wall over the computer. He decided they must be special in some way. A student dressed in white with different-colored belts. From the age of four till the student was in his early twenties, he assumed. Maybe it was the child/young man who was special. He made a mental note to ask Dodo who it was.

Ben reached for the sheaf of papers he'd printed out for Darby. He scanned them, his heart heavy.

"Ben." Dodo's voice startled him from his musings.

Ben whirled around. "I hope you don't mind that I used your computer, Dodo. I told Darby I would see what I could find out about organ transplants." He held out the stack of papers. "Are you going somewhere?" He eyed the black bag at her feet.

"As a matter of fact, I am," Dodo said vaguely. "Ducky and Diddy want to go to Rayne to see Trixie and Fred. Just for a day or so. You don't mind, do you, Ben?"

"No, of course not. Trixie and Fred are your mystery-writer friends, right?"

"Right. Trixie and Fred are retired now. No more blood and guts or chain-saw murders. They train K-9 police dogs now."

"That's interesting."

"Yes, it is interesting," Dodo said vaguely. "I'll call."

"Okay. Is there anything you want me to do while you're gone?"

"No, I don't think so. Keep your eye on that work crew out front and don't let them touch those houses."

"Okay, I can handle that. Is something bothering you, Dodo?"

"Well, hell yes, Ben, there are a lot of things bothering me. That mess out front, your brother's death, that wicked stepmother of yours, and canceling my trip to Japan. But I'll survive. Family comes first, no matter what. Maybe you should take Darby out to a nice dinner. She likes Armand's. You know, a dress-up dinner. A date, Ben," Dodo said sharply.

"Oh. All right, I'll ask her. Have a nice trip. Tell Trixie I've read all her books."

"I'll do that. I'll try. With my sisters, you never know!" Dodo said with a laugh. "Like I said, I'll call."

Ben walked Dodo to the kitchen, where he watched her cross the yard to where her two sisters were waiting. Darby was right, the three of them were up to something, and he didn't have a clue as to what it was. With Dodo's suggestion ringing in his ears, he himself walked across the yard and around back, to where Darby had her little studio. He didn't have to shout or knock. Willie's bark was announcement enough. Darby looked up from what she was doing and smiled as she beckoned him to come indoors.

"I came to invite you to dinner."

Darby wiped her hands on a wet cloth. "The idea of food sounds wonderful. But how would you feel about a loaded pizza and some ice-cold beer as opposed to going out? They can deliver, and we can sit on the front porch. Kind of like a picnic."

"It sounds like a plan. I can do pizza. Are you sure you'd rather not go out to eat?"

Darby smiled as she bent down to tickle Willie behind his ears. "I'm sure. I have the pizza parlor on my speed dial. When I'm here working by myself, I order on a regular basis. They deliver in those hot bags. It's your four food groups," she said airily.

"This new commission looks like it's going to be complicated," Ben said as he walked around Darby's worktable. He looked up at the dollhouse on the pedestal.

"Do you remember the Christmas the aunts said we had to make gifts for each other with our own hands, and it had to be from our hearts, Darby?"

"Sure," she answered with a smile. "We weren't allowed to buy anything. We even had to use our imaginations for the wrapping paper. That had to have been the ultimate challenge for a kid. I couldn't sleep for thinking about it."

"Even Russ was beside himself. We would talk under the covers at night. I can't tell you how frazzled we both were," Ben said, and a faint blush came to his cheeks. "Anyway, I carved you a bench for the dollhouse. As I recall, it was pretty ugly. The paint job wasn't much better. I wrapped it in the comic pages, and when you opened it, you said you loved it. You ran right up to the dollhouse and squeezed it through the opening, which wasn't easy since I made it a little too big. You gave me such a beautiful smile. I think that was the moment I fell in love with you. I was snooping around your dollhouses the other day and imagine my surprise when I saw that you still have that bench in the dollhouse. I guess you couldn't get it out, huh?"

Darby's jaw dropped, her eyes popped wide. She struggled to say something light and teasing, but her tongue felt so thick she could barely speak. "You fell in love with me! I wish you had told me. I had such a crush on you. You know, boy next door, older boy, that kind of thing. I used to dream about you. You're right about the bench, I've never been able to get it out."

It was Ben's turn to have his jaw drop. "You did?"

"Oh, yes. Almost every night. Until Mary told me about the ugly things you used to say about me. I was too skinny, too many freckles, and my braces made me look like a snapping turtle."

Ben stared at her in shock. "I never said any such thing. Not ever. Mary used to tell me you said I was a buffoon. Hell, I didn't even know what a buffoon was until Dodo told me. She said you were going to marry Russell when you grew up. She clinched it when she said Russell made you a daisy chain. Let me tell you, that statement sent me skulking away. As I recall, when a guy made a girl a daisy chain it was serious stuff."

Darby burst out laughing. "We aren't kids anymore, Ben. You can make me a daisy chain anytime you want." Darby smiled and Ben thought he'd never seen a more beautiful sight. Willie barked and danced around Ben's feet, not understanding what was going on.

Anytime you want. Damn, he was going to have to ask Dodo how to make a daisy chain. "Well, sure. Do you have daisies in the garden?"

Darby laughed again as she teased him. "I have tons of Gerber daisies all around the house. All colors. Why do you think I planted them? Because," she said, a wicked gleam in her eye, "I knew you'd come back someday."

I'll be damned. She's flirting with me! Ben suddenly felt like he was sixteen years old again. He shoved the papers he'd printed out for her into her hands. It was something to do to break the moment. Was it his imagination, or did Darby look disappointed.

Darby looked down at the thick wad of papers in her hand. She laid them on the worktable. "This looks like serious stuff. Let's go into the kitchen. I'll look at them later. No sense spoiling our picnic. And anyway, it's Willie's dinnertime." At the mention of his name, the retriever headed for the door leading to the kitchen, where his food bowl waited.

"Do you think he misses Russell?" Ben asked as he followed Darby into the kitchen.

"Yes, he does. Especially at night. He starts out sleeping in his bed with Russ's tee shirt and at some point in the night, he climbs up on the bed with me. He doesn't bring the shirt, though. Sometimes he covers his baby, you know, his teddy bear, with the shirt. He knew we were at Russ's town house the other day because he kept sniffing me when we got home. I guess we brought Russ's scent home with us. He's going to be fine. The aunts love him. I do, too. I worry though that he may still be lonely. I've actually been thinking about getting him a companion. Someone to romp around the yard with."

"That sounds like a good idea. If you don't mind, I think I'll run over to Dodo's and grab a quick shower."

"Sure. I think I'll do the same thing. It will take at least thirty minutes for them to deliver the pizza. What do you like on yours?"

"Everything but anchovies," Ben called over his

shoulder. "I'm partial to pepperoni and green peppers. Garlic, too. Maybe some onions."

Darby laughed. "That's the works minus the anchovies." She was still laughing when she picked up the phone.

A picnic on the front porch with Ben Gunn. *My childhood dream coming true. Oh, Lordy.*

10

It was seven-fifteen when Darby, in her bare feet, trotted across the lawn to the back alley to pick up the pizza from the delivery man. She paid the driver, accepted the pie, turned around, and bumped into Ben, who had a wad of money in his hand. "You can buy it the next time," she said. "Just so you know, Willie gets the crust. Don't you, boy? Dogs can't eat anything that has tomatoes in it. At least that's what Russ said. He was really up on dog stuff." The retriever sniffed and barked.

The next time. It sounded good to his ears. Ben shoved the bills back into his pocket. "I think it's going to rain again," he said, just to have something to say.

"This is Baton Rouge. It rains almost every day when it's this hot. Did you forget?" Darby chided with a smile.

"Sometimes I do forget, and other times I remember everything. Every little thing. I guess I block stuff out I don't like remembering. Let's eat. I'm starved."

They were on the front porch, where Darby had set up a little folding table with paper plates, napkins, and a jar of hot peppers. A small bucket held ice and bottles of the family beer. She opened the box, and said, "Dig in."

Darby eyed Ben over her slice of pizza. He looked handsome, and he smelled wonderful.

They ate in comfortable silence until the entire pie was gone. Willie had a pile of crusts on his plate.

Darby uncapped a bottle of beer. "The aunts should be in Rayne by now. I wish I knew what the three of them are up to."

Ben didn't want to talk about the aunts or Eric McAllister. He wanted to talk about *them*. "Would you like to have dinner with me on Friday night? A date," he mumbled.

Darby felt herself blushing and wondered if her girlhood crush could possibly still be this strong. "You mean like I get gussied up, you ring my doorbell, and off we go?"

"Yeah. Yeah, I can ring your doorbell. I guess you have to get dressed up to go to Armand's."

"Armand's! I hate Armand's. How about Chinese? I love good Chinese. That way we can wear shorts, I don't have to wear makeup. Makeup runs in this humidity."

"Oh. That's certainly reason enough to do Chinese. Dodo said you loved Armand's."

"Dodo loves Armand's. It's a date then. What time?"

"Seven."

"Oh, look, it's starting to rain. I love sitting out here

on the porch. What I really love is watching a good storm. How about you?"

"I might like it if you were with me. I don't think I ever sat around and watched a storm."

Darby tilted her head for a better look at the man sitting next to her on the swing. "You're an odd duck, Ben Gunn. I suspect you were so busy running from your memories you just haven't taken the time to enjoy the little things in life. Am I wrong?"

"I have a lot of regrets, if that's what you mean. But I'm not sure I'd do anything different if I had to do it over again." He stared upward at the lazy circles the paddle fans on the porch ceiling made as they tried to battle the heat.

Darby reached for Ben's hand. "You have to deal with the memories and the regrets, Ben. Otherwise, you can't move forward. Dealing with life isn't for sissies."

Ben laughed ruefully. "How'd you get so smart?"

"Russ. We used to talk it out. During the last few years he was able to leave the baggage behind. He found his niche, his peace. The longer you keep things locked in, the harder it is to let it go. Anytime you want to talk about it, I'm a good listener."

Ben smiled. Darby's heart kicked up a beat. "Do you really think I'm an odd duck?"

"Only in a nice way. Want to take a walk in the rain? I'm already in my bare feet. Remember how we used to pray for rain so we could make mud pies? Then we'd throw them at each other, and the aunts would hose us off. Followed by cherry Popsicles and those fat lemon cookies."

Ben kicked off his Docksiders and reached for her hand. "Let's do it."

They started off by walking across the lawn toward the gazebo. At the halfway point, Darby dropped Ben's hand and raced ahead. She ran, zigzagging this way and that way, daring Ben to catch her. She was soaked to the skin, her clothes cleaving to her slim body. Willie ran interference as she slipped, fell to her knees, righted herself, and ran around the gazebo. They laughed the way they had when they were children, surrendering to the moment. When Ben slipped and went down, Willie raced to Darby, inching her forward. Laughing, gasping for breath, her hands on her knees, she stared at the handsome man she'd lusted after as a young girl. In the blink of an eye, Ben's hand reached up, pulling her down on top of him. He kissed her long and hard, the rain pounding their bodies with relentless force. Willie ran to the gazebo, shook the rain off his silky coat, and settled down to wait for his new mistress.

Ben's voice came from his toes—maybe his gut— when he struggled to say, "Are you sure?"

"Yes. Oh, yes."

The dining room hummed with the bustle of the waiters and the clink of china and silver. It wasn't as crowded as it usually was on a weekday night, allowing the four women to pick the table they wanted in the farthest corner of the room, where they ordered white-wine spritzers they only pretended to drink.

Ducky took a moment to wonder what it would be like to eat a romantic dinner here with the private detective she'd just hired. She shook her head to clear it of such thoughts as she concentrated on her three dinner companions.

"I do like a table set with real table linens," Dodo said. "I particularly like the Inn's wineglasses. Don't you, Trixie?"

"I suppose. I never really gave it much thought. Fred and I pretty much eat on the fly. That means whatever we can pop into the microwave. The dogs take up all our time."

"Okay, ladies, this is the plan we hatched," Ducky began. "I'm going to call Bella and invite her to lunch. To congratulate her. I think she'll fall for it. She's so hungry to be on the tour, I don't think she will question the call at all.

"I will allude to the fact that the Garden Club is getting ready to make plans for the Christmas Candlelight Tour of homes here in Baton Rouge. I'm sure Bella knows she has to have three sponsors just to be *nominated*. We number three. God, I hope I don't choke when I have to say that. That's my contribution, and I want to go on record as saying it's the worst part of this caper."

"*Caper*. I so love that word," Trixie gurgled. "Fred and I wrote sixteen books with the word *caper* in the title. Each one was an instant best seller." The skinny, stringy little woman beamed at them over her wire-rimmed glasses. She was smaller than Dodo, weighed a colossal eighty-seven pounds, and had the tensile strength of steel.

"I wonder how much you're going to like this little *caper* when we get hauled off to the slammer," Diddy groaned. "If that happens, what will become of poor Marcus?"

Trixie shrugged her skinny shoulders. "The object is not to get caught. I've plotted enough books to know the devil is in the details. Now, what you have going for you is that battery-operated wheelbarrow. I didn't know there was such a thing. I sure hope no one steals it. Did anyone see you park the truck in the lot?"

"No. We parked by the Dumpster. That pickup truck is so old, we'd have to pay someone to steal it," Dodo said. "It's nothing fancy like that Lincoln Navigator you showed up in, Trixie."

"Flash requires a lot of room. The Navigator has lots of room. But"—Trixie held up her hand—"that fancy-dancy wheelbarrow will not fit into the cargo hold. That means I'm going to have to drive the pickup with Marcus in the wheelbarrow all the way to Rayne. Flash will guard him."

"And you don't think people will notice?" Diddy squealed in outrage.

Trixie clicked her dentures. "Not with a tarp over him. I'm not stupid, Diddy. Then tomorrow evening,

I'll send Fred back with the truck, and he will exchange it for the Navigator. It's the details," she said smugly. "This is an exceptionally good plot line. I just might come out of retirement to write the story. Fred will love it. But there's still one thing missing. How can we kill off that bitch?"

Three sets of eyes zeroed in on Dodo, who held up her hands and said, "*Yeow!* I can push her nose right up into her brain. Is that gory enough for one of your books?"

"It's perfect. Fred is gonna love this. Okay, back to business. I meet you with the Navigator at the path you two made earlier. Dodo drives the pickup truck. Dodo and I go up the incline. Diddy stands watch with Flash until we load Marcus in the back of the pickup. We wheel Marcus down, dump him in the back, cover him, and off I drive to Rayne. Dodo and Diddy take my Navigator back to the inn to wait for Fred to show up. How'm I doing, ladies?"

"You forgot the part about getting the wheelbarrow up the incline and Dodo knocking out the nurse. Not to mention Marcus. He might get a little *pissy* when he sees he's being kidnapped," Diddy said through clenched teeth.

"That wheelbarrow is better than a billy goat. It can take the incline. Trixie and I can handle it. I'm not going to kill the nurse, I'm just going to put her to sleep. Now let's adjourn to Trixie's room, where we can discuss this further without people watching us.

We can use room service for additional refreshments."

Trixie was off her chair in a nanosecond, ready to go, the leftovers in a doggie bag for Flash.

The worrier of the foursome, Diddy voiced her other fear in the elevator. "In case none of you noticed, it's raining outside. What are we going to do if it's raining tomorrow and the nurse doesn't take Marcus out for lunch?"

Trixie eyed her old friend. "Then we go to Plan B. Or, we create a diversion. We have a killer in our midst," Trixie said, pointing to Dodo, who winced.

"That means shut up, Diddy, and stop worrying," Ducky snapped.

Diddy clamped her lips shut but not before she said. "It's almost two hours to Rayne from here."

"And your point is . . ." Dodo said.

"That's a long time to spend in a wheelbarrow."

"Give it up already, Diddy. The end will justify the means."

"God help us all," Diddy mumbled as she trundled down the hall to Trixie's room.

Bella welcomed the new day. How wonderful it was when things worked out according to a plan. Today she felt like she had a golden aura because everything was finally, finally, going her way. The best thing she'd ever done in her whole life, aside from marrying Marcus for his money, was donating her stepson's organs to the donor program. Who knew such a decision could give her what she'd lusted after for over twenty years?

Right now, right this very minute, she felt like she had the Preservation Society and the Garden Club in the palm of her hand, and the members of the Garden Club had hinted that she would be nominated for the Christmas tour. Then, just last night, one of the members had called to give her a heads-up that they were starting to process the nominations and to watch her mail. She'd been so giddy she hadn't been able to sleep all night long.

Bella looked down at the pile of papers on her dressing table. Phony building orders. For the benefit of all those highfalutin society ladies—especially Sarabess, who had demanded to see the work orders. So, she'd spent a whole day writing out plans that would please the committee, plans that she had no intention of carrying out. The only work order that counted was the one where she *verbally* instructed Tigger to take a wrecking ball to both buildings. For the princely sum of twenty-five thousand dollars in cold hard cash, Tigger agreed to say he misunderstood his client's instructions in regard to the wrecking ball. She knew how to pretend outrage. She practiced daily in front of the mirror.

As Bella preened and primped in front of the mirror she wondered if the Garden Club would give her a "Generous Citizen" award. If they did, she had just the right place to hang it. Right in the foyer where anyone who entered the house could see it. Maybe she would attach a little light over it like they did for priceless paintings.

Now, it was time to visit her husband before she left the house. She could hardly wait to see his reaction.

Bella tripped down the hall to her husband's room. She didn't bother to knock. She smiled as she always did when she cooed to her husband for the nurse's benefit. "Mrs. Engles, Cook just baked some wonderful breakfast pastries and the coffee is freshly ground. I'll stay with my husband while you have some breakfast. Take your time as I'm in no hurry. I just adore spending this time of day with my husband."

When the door closed behind the nurse, Bella started to pace the confines of her husband's sickroom.

Marcus Gunn watched his wife, his brow furrowed. He was startled when he heard her talking to herself. "What?" he mumbled, his speech slurred.

"What? I'll tell you what. It finally happened, my dear. I have to admit, it took a good many years, but this town has finally come to its senses. Our house is finally going to be on the Christmas tour this year. The paperwork is on the way. They told me to watch the mail. How much more definite can that be? In addition to that good news, the Preservation Society has issued me a provisional license to work on the two houses in the shoe. In the shoe, Marcus! Did you hear what I just said? I'm going to build such grand houses. Those Lane women will have to remodel those derelicts they live in to keep up with what I'm going to build."

Marcus started to jabber, spittle dribbling down his chin. In frustration, he wiped at it with the sleeve of his shirt.

"Oh for heaven's sake, stop that jabbering. You can speak properly if you do it slowly. Yes, yes, you've told me a hundred times that those two houses were to go to Ben and Russell. Well, Russell is dead, and Ben doesn't need a house. I want those houses. If you give me one ounce of trouble over this, Marcus, you will force me to tell this town a few things you would rather not have them know. Especially those twisted Lane sisters and your son, Ben. I hope you're listening to me, darling. I've waited too long for this, and I won't have you screwing things up."

"Russell . . . you had no right . . ."

"Stop right there, Marcus. It's over, it's done with, and I don't wish to discuss it. People are now living who might have died; others are living a better life because of what I did. Now, I have to go out to the shoe and talk to my contractor. By the way, I stopped by the library yesterday and got some new books for you. I left them on the hall table. I'll have the nurse fetch them for you. Tell me, darling Marcus, that you understand everything I've said. Just nod. I can't stand that jabbering you do. I think you do it just to get on my nerves. Nod, Marcus." Marcus dutifully nodded.

"What a good boy you are, Marcus," she cooed. And then she smiled, a smile that sent a shiver down Marcus's spine.

11

Darby stirred and stretched out her legs. When her foot touched something other than Willie's soft fur, she froze, realizing she was naked beneath the covers. She cracked one eye to see Ben sleeping peacefully, little tufts of hair poking up around his tousled head. Total recall bombarded her, forcing her to close her eyes. They snapped open a moment later. She fought the urge to reach out and touch the man she'd loved from the time she was five years old, even though she'd valiantly tried to get over him throughout the years. Suddenly, she felt like singing.

Willie took that moment to hop onto the bed, and he tried to figure out who he should jump on. He'd been patient for some time, and it was time to go out. Because Russell had taught him manners, he woofed softly. Darby looked longingly at her sleeping partner as she swung her legs over the side of the bed. She pulled on her robe and proceeded down the steps.

While Willie romped in the early-morning sunshine, Darby made coffee, then went into the downstairs bathroom to brush her teeth and shower. When she was finished, she went into the laundry room to fish clothes out of the dryer. Everything was old and wrinkled. A fashion plate she wasn't, nor would she ever be. Maybe she needed to think about hiring a housekeeper. Someone to cook for her, to fold the clothes in the dryer and maybe iron. Now that Ducky was back, she would insist on getting some household help. Darby shrugged and added hiring a housekeeper to her mental To Do List. She bent down to dry up the puddle of water on the floor from their wet clothes the night before. She picked up the clothes, tossed them into the dryer.

Willie barked at the kitchen screen door. She let him in, turned around to see Ben standing in the kitchen with a towel wrapped around his middle. She suddenly felt hot all over and knew she was blushing. He grinned. "Morning," he said cheerfully. "Is this going to be one of those moments where we stutter and stammer and try to ignore what happened last night, or are you going to come over here and kiss me good morning?"

The blush disappeared, the heat engulfing her body turned up at least ten degrees as she moved with the speed of light. The kiss was something she'd remember all her life. "Howzat?"

"More, more!"

Willie wiggled between the two of them. Didn't they know it was almost eight-thirty, an hour past breakfast. When the retriever saw he wasn't getting anywhere, he picked up his bowl and dropped it on Ben's bare foot.

Darby laughed. "Time to feed Willie. Your clothes are in the dryer, but they won't be dry for a while."

"That's okay, I'll walk over to Dodo's and dress. Walk me to the porch," he said, putting his arm around Darby's shoulder. He didn't ever want to put distance between them again. She leaned into him as they made their way to the back porch, Willie growling his displeasure.

A devil perched itself on Darby's shoulders as Ben started down the steps. She reached out, whipped off the towel, and ran into the house. She locked the screen door, doubling over with laughter. Willie barked ferociously before he sent his food bowl skidding across the tiled floor. Darby continued to laugh as Ben sprinted across the yard as the construction men at the top of the shoe let loose with catcalls and whistles.

"Okay, okay, I'm making it. Bacon and eggs, okay? I had to do it, Willie. I really did." Willie sat on his haunches as his new mistress talked to him. "I didn't think I'd ever laugh again, but look what I just did. Then there was last night. It makes me wonder what kind of person I am. I should be in mourning. I am in mourning, but I know that Russ would say something profound like 'Life is for the living' or 'Just remember me but don't grieve for me.' I know he'd say that, Willie, I really do. I just want you to know something, Willie, Ben is a great guy, and boy can he kiss!"

Willie nosed his food bowl closer to the stove. "Woof."

Darby used the tongs to take the bacon out of the frying pan to finish microwaving it.

The scrambled eggs slid into his bowl. "You know the drill, boy, you have to wait till it cools. I don't know why Russ didn't feed you dog food. I know, I know, he'd say, Willie eats what I eat. No one, not even a dog, should have to eat the same thing day after day."

The microwave buzzed. Darby removed the bacon and crumbled it on top of the scrambled eggs. She gave the mess a good stir before she tested it with her finger. She thought she heard Willie sigh with relief.

Darby poured herself a cup of coffee. She sipped at it as she beat more eggs in a bright red bowl. This time she microwaved the bacon she was making for Ben and herself. Russ, a health nut, said if you microwaved bacon, it took all the bad stuff out of it. She wondered if it was true. She thought it tasted different. Russ said it was her imagination.

The screen door creaked. Darby turned and almost swooned at the sight of Ben in his khaki shorts and bright yellow Polo collared shirt. Instead of his Docksiders, which were now drying in the sun, he wore sneakers. He looked almost as delicious as the breakfast she was preparing.

Ben poured himself a cup of coffee. "Just so you know, Miss Smart-Ass, there were *women* out there. Two in hard hats and some tourists. *They wanted my body!*"

Darby tried not to laugh. "No kidding! Your rear end jiggles when you run. Did you know that?"

"No, I didn't know that. Thank you for telling me. I'll get you for that."

Darby laughed again as she scooped the eggs out of the frying pan. "I'll look forward to it. Look at the time. I cooked, so you have to clean up. What are you going to do today, Ben? I have to work, at least for a while."

"I'm going to drive to Metairie to see if I can get any firsthand information from the Louisiana Organ Procurement Agency. I'm not hopeful, but still, it's worth a try."

"I agree. I know it's like locking the barn after the horse is stolen. I am not forgetting for one minute that people are alive thanks to Russ. Some of whom would have died otherwise. I have to get past the . . . past the part where I think of Russ as *scattered* all over the place. I need to see, to get in touch with the recipients of Russ's organs. I can't go forward until I do that." She changed the subject and said, "I thought the aunts would have called by now. I find this whole visit of theirs really strange."

"They don't need keepers, Darby. Go ahead to your workroom. I'll clean up and leave for Metairie. If I find out anything, I'll call you. Otherwise, I'll see you later this afternoon. I'll leave my cell phone number here on the counter in case you want to call me."

They looked at each other, both their eyes full of awe at what was happening to them. "I'm not going to kiss you, Darby. If I do, I'll never leave, and we both know it."

Darby's head bobbed up and down. "Call me." She touched her fingers to her lips and blew the kiss toward Ben. He smiled, and her world turned upside down, or maybe it finally turned right side up.

"Well, what are you waiting for?" Dodo Lane snapped. "Get on with it, Ducky. It's eight-thirty."

Ducky stared at the cell phone in her hand. "All right, I'm doing it," Ducky said as she flipped on the phone. She waited for the dial tone. As she punched in the numbers she'd memorized, she looked at the three women sitting on the bed. She offered up a sickly smile.

"Gunn residence," a prim voice sounded on the other end of the phone.

"This is Harriet Lane. I'd like to speak to Mrs. Gunn, please. Tell her I'm calling in regard to the Garden Club's Christmas Candlelight Tour."

Ducky drew a deep breath into her lungs as she mumbled under her breath. She had her little speech down pat, but she wanted to be sure it all came out just right. She jerked backward when she heard Bella Gunn identify herself.

"What can I do for you this morning, Harriet?" Bella asked sweetly.

"Actually, Bella, I'm calling to invite you to lunch today. Of course, I understand if you can't make it since it's such short notice. Honoria called me late last night to say the board is considering nominating your house for the Christmas tour. I would have called last night, but it was after eleven, and I thought you might be sleeping. As you know, each nominee needs three sponsors and I've been chosen to conduct the interview with you. This year we're only picking two houses to add to the tour. I thought we could meet at the Baton Rouge Inn at noon if you can make it. If not, we'll have to postpone the interview." Not waiting for a response, Ducky rushed onward. "You and Marcus must be thrilled and delighted that *Architectural Digest* is interested in featuring your house in their magazine. I think that's what prompted the board to add a second name to the nomination process this year." When there was still no response, Ducky plowed forward, rolling her eyes for the benefit of her listeners.

"If this isn't a convenient time to be calling, you can call me back. Just leave a message if I'm not here." This time Ducky waited, the silence on the other end of the phone unnerving her.

Bella's voice was smooth as silk when she replied. "This is short notice, Harriet. I'm looking at my day planner. I think I can cancel a meeting I have at the Gunn Foundation scheduled for eleven-thirty. I have to be honest with you. I thought you would be upset with my plans for the houses in the shoe."

"Personally, Bella, I consider those two houses eyesores," Ducky said through gritted teeth. "I'll see you at noon then. Say hello to Marcus for me."

"I'll be sure to do that, Harriet."

Ducky clicked off the phone and threw it across the room. Sweat dripped down her cheeks. "The lady is one cool customer under fire. She didn't by so much as a word indicate she's been lusting after this nomination for almost thirty years."

"She's probably in a state of shock right this minute. Five bucks says she's rushing around changing her outfit. What are you wearing, Ducky?" Dodo asked.

"My Donna Karan original, what else? Diddy, did you remember to bring the different forms from the committee you ran off from the Society's Web page?"

"Yes, and I can't wait to see how she fills out the personal information. If we can get even a smidgen of background information on her that to date has been the world's best-kept secret, the private detective will have something concrete to go on. We all keep saying it was like Bella was born the day she arrived here. Everyone has a background, we just haven't found hers yet. Bear in mind that people who hide their background have a past they don't want anyone to know about. That's when you ask yourself, why?"

The women exchanged knowing looks. "All right, ladies, in case you didn't notice, it's a bright sunny day,"

Trixie announced, "which means Marcus will be dining outdoors."

The countdown was on for what Trixie McGuire called the Hatch and Snatch Caper.

Ducky closed the door behind Trixie and her sisters at eleven forty-five. Childishly, she crossed her fingers that nothing would go wrong with the *caper* they were about to attempt. She looked down at her watch. She had a good ten minutes until it was time to go downstairs. She spent the time adjusting her hairdo, which was pulled back into a fashionable French twist. Her Donna Karan dress was special. She'd been saving it for just the right occasion. She did so love the color lavender, and the dress fit like it was made for her. She wasn't overdone; nor was she underdone, she decided. Small pearl earrings, definitely understated, graced her ears. She also wore a magnificent canary yellow diamond ring and, of course, her diamond-studded Rolex watch. She stared at the watch and decided she didn't need it to complement her outfit. She removed it from her wrist and dropped it into her purse.

Ducky checked her purse one last time to make sure she had all the forms Diddy said were needed by the Garden Club. She reached for a pen from the hotel desk.

She was ready with five minutes to spare.

Ducky exited the elevator a scant two minutes before Bella Gunn walked haughtily through the plate-glass doors. Ducky watched as Bella nodded curtly to the doorman, sashaying into the lobby, her eyes searching out Ducky.

Bella looked around, trying to gauge the attire of the female guests, wondering if she measured up. She'd taken great pains with her outfit this morning, settling for a beige suit with matching shoes and bag. She wore a single strand of pearls with matching earrings. She wore no rings or even a watch. Her see-through hair twinkled in the overhead lights, thanks to a spray that promised highlights.

She spotted Ducky and waved languidly.

Ducky managed to paste a smile on her face as she walked across the lobby. "It's been a long time, Bella."

"Yes. *Years*," Bella responded.

"Shall we," Ducky said, taking the lead to head for the dining room. Her stomach churned, knowing Bella's eyes were boring into her back. All she wanted to do was to get this over with so she could return to the shoe to wait for Diddy and Dodo. A lump settled itself in her throat when she envisioned herself bailing them out of jail.

A sweet young hostess in a short tight skirt and spike-heeled shoes greeted Ducky with a smile. "It's nice to see you again, Miss Lane. I told Mama you were coming in to lunch, and she sends her regards."

Ducky offered up a sickly smile. "How is Lalie?"

"Just fine. Her arthritis isn't so good in this humidity, but she manages," the hostess said, leading the way to a secluded table. She pointedly ignored Bella Gunn.

The lump in Ducky's throat grew as she looked around the crowded dining room at all the *Rougie* ladies having lunch. She wished they would close their mouths and not stare at her the way they were doing. She did her best to ignore them by whipping open the oversize menu. She was almost afraid to look across the table at Bella Gunn. For a moment, she almost felt sorry for the woman. *Almost*.

A waiter appeared with water and addressed her by name. Ducky smiled. "How are you, Peter?"

"I'm well, Miss Lane, and you?"

"Just wonderful. I'll have a glass of the house red wine. Bella, how about you?"

"I'll have the same." The waiter discreetly withdrew to fill their drink order.

"I can personally vouch for the pecan-crusted salmon. The sweet-potato soufflé is just as good. That's what I'm going to order. Does it appeal to you, Bella?"

"Yes, that sounds fine," Bella answered.

Ducky reached into her handbag and withdrew the forms her sister had given her earlier. "The president of the Garden Club said to give these to you. If you and Marcus wish to be nominated, you need to fill them out, and don't omit anything." She slid them across the table just as their wine arrived. They gave their order to the waiter and looked at each other, Ducky's eyes guileless, Bella's filled with suspicion.

"*Now* they want to nominate me. Now—after *thirty*

years! I'm sure you understand my . . . reluctance as well as my suspicions. Of course I'm flattered," she added as an afterthought.

"I'm sorry about that, Bella. As you must know, I haven't spent all that much time in Baton Rouge in the last thirty years. Personally speaking, I'm not into all that historical . . . *crap.*" Oh, God, did she just say that out loud. Diddy would kill her if she heard such blasphemy. "I can't imagine why anyone would want hundreds of people tromping through their house at Christmastime."

Bella looked uncomfortable as she sipped at her wine.

"How is Marcus?"

"As well as can be expected. He has good days and bad days."

"What exactly does Marcus suffer from, Bella?"

Bella sighed. "Years ago he had a stroke that left him mildly handicapped. Then he had a small heart attack, and after that diabetes settled in. It was time for him to retire, and he knew it. He's doing nicely with his round-the-clock nurses. As I said to you on the phone, we were going to take a cruise in December. I'll have to discuss this with Marcus," she said, pointing to the stack of forms at her elbow.

"Lord, I must be getting senile. Bella, please accept my condolences and please, pass them on to Marcus. Losing Russell must have been devastating for you both."

"Yes, it was awful. I'm afraid it's caused Marcus a terrible setback."

Ducky grappled for something to say. She wished she could look at her watch. "Marcus certainly has had his share of tragedies in his lifetime."

"Yes, he certainly has, but Marcus has a strong spirit. Benjamin and your niece came to see him. They didn't stay long. I don't think Benjamin could bear to see his father in a wheelchair drooling."

Ducky's head jerked upward. "Can't Marcus walk?"

"Oh, yes, but mostly indoors. We have to goad him at times because he gets lazy. The wheelchair is more a precaution than anything else. I certainly don't want him to fall and break a hip. That's something I don't think he could handle. Mobility is terribly hard to give up, especially for someone like Marcus."

Ducky was saved from a reply when their food arrived. The last thing she wanted was food, but she knew she was going to have to choke down the entire meal along with the salad that materialized after the luncheon plates were placed in front of them. Maybe she could forget about the weeds and eat just the salmon and the soufflé. *What time is it? How is the Hatch and Snatch Caper going? The snatch part must already be under way.*

"This is very good, Harriet. I must tell my cook to prepare it at home. I think Marcus might like it."

"I've tried to make it myself, but for some reason it never tastes like this. I'm sure they have a *secret* ingredient they refuse to divulge. They publish the recipe from time to time in the Sunday paper. Everyone says the same thing." Damn. She was babbling. Ducky forced herself to relax. "By the way, Honoria wants me to pick up the forms tomorrow if you decide to have your name go to the nomination committee."

Bella stopped chewing long enough to say, "I'll call you later this evening after I talk to Marcus. Will that be all right?" she asked coolly.

"Absolutely. I'll be home all evening. I promised my sisters I'd help them finish the quilt they're working on." Ducky looked down at her long nails ruefully. "I haven't quilted in years."

"Are you finished traveling, Harriet?" Bella asked in a bored voice.

"I'm enjoying my stay, if that's what you're asking. I came home for Russell's funeral. My sisters tell me it's time to stop, as they put it, gallivanting around the world. I think I was born with wanderlust. Do you and Marcus travel much?" Half the salmon on her plate was gone, and she had to concentrate on the soufflé. Bella was making excellent progress with her meal, to Ducky's dismay. She'd have to make sure they lingered over coffee and dessert. There was no way she could let Bella leave if there was a chance the caper was still under way. *What time is it?*

"Last year Marcus and I took a cruise to Alaska. He hated it, but he was the one who insisted on Alaska. It was just too cold. Our plans and vacations depend on

Marcus's health. We pretty much do things on the spur of the moment these days."

Ducky couldn't eat another bite. She slid her plate to the side and signaled the waiter for coffee. "I think my eyes were bigger than my stomach," she said ruefully.

Bella stopped eating the minute Ducky moved her plate. "I think I agree with you. It was very good, but I rarely eat such a big lunch."

"Dessert, ladies?" the waiter asked, setting their coffee in front of them. Ducky looked at Bella, who seemed to be waiting for Ducky to make the decision. "As much as I love and crave sweets, I think I'm going to order the pecan tulle." Bella seconded Ducky's decision.

"Will you excuse me, Harriet? I want to call home to see how Marcus is doing."

Ducky panicked. "My goodness, Bella, stop fretting. You did say Marcus had round-the-clock nurses, didn't you? Let those nurses earn their money. Luncheon at the inn is special, enjoy it."

"You're right. I do worry too much. It's a habit."

My ass, Ducky thought. She almost exploded with relief. Now it was time to lay on the flattery. "I've been admiring your suit. I can tell it's not off the rack."

"No, it isn't. I bought it in New York when I was there last year. I love the color beige. Your own dress is quite lovely."

Ducky shrugged. "It's off the rack," she lied. "You

know, a knockoff. It just goes against my grain to pay those astronomical prices to wear someone's label." *Liar, liar, pants on fire. What time is it?*

The busboy worked his way to their table. Ducky almost fell off her chair when Bella asked if he had the correct time. The boy looked down at his oversize watch, and said, "It's one-fifteen, ma'am."

"Are you in a hurry, Bella? I hope not. We should finish this coffee, it's flown in from Hawaii." Before Bella could answer, Ducky ordered refills for both of them.

Ducky was so giddy with relief she made a mental note to add a twenty-five-dollar tip to the bill.

"Isn't this coffee delicious. It's Kona. I never knew that. Did you know that, Bella?"

Bella sipped at the coffee in her cup. "I can't say that I did know that, Harriet. I guess that's why the inn is so expensive."

"I think you have to be a coffee connoisseur, which I'm not, to appreciate it. I always use too much sugar and cream. They say you should drink it black. I can't abide black coffee. It makes my nerves twang. Does it affect you like that, Bella?" Ducky babbled. *What time is it?*

"No. Marcus used to drink coffee by the gallon all day long. Now, alas, he drinks herbal tea."

Ducky tried to relax. To her eye, Bella was getting jittery, her gaze flitting around the room. *I'm boring her,* she thought. "I have an idea, Bella. Why don't we ask for a pecan tulle for Marcus. And a small cup of this special coffee. One little treat like that can't hurt him, can it? Oh, dear, you did say Marcus had diabetes, didn't you. That means no sugar. Well, they make the tulle with artificial sweetener. I saw that in one of their ads on television."

Bella looked flustered. "I don't think . . ."

Ducky wagged her finger at her luncheon companion. "We just had this scrumptious lunch. How can you not want to share it with Marcus? Please, let me order it for your husband. It will be such a treat. And it will still be warm when you get home."

I can't stand this. What time is it? Ducky flagged down the waiter and ordered the tulle and coffee to go. "The diet tulle, Peter. It's for Mr. Gunn. Make sure the coffee is black."

Ducky almost jumped out of her skin when Bella asked for the time again. Peter looked again at his oversize watch. "It's one-forty, ma'am."

"You seem concerned with the time, Bella. Do you have to be somewhere soon? I can ask for the check as soon as Peter gets back."

"No need. I'm just not used to eating such a big lunch. It was very kind of you to invite me today, Harriet. If I haven't been as gracious as I should be, it's because I'm worried about Marcus. He had a bad night. Bad nights lead to bad days and doctor's visits."

They talked about Marcus and how depressed he got when it rained for the next ten minutes. Ducky whipped out her credit card, added the generous tip, and waited for the waiter to return with the slip for her to sign.

Bella picked up the to-go bag as she waited for Ducky to gather her purse and keys. She was fully aware that the other customers were watching her. It wasn't a bad thing to be seen dining with Harriet Lane. Not a bad thing at all.

12

⌒

"We're running late," Dodo said as she stomped down on the gas pedal with a vengeance. The clunker of a truck shot forward. Flash, the K-9 who was sitting between her and Trixie, barked his displeasure. "This dog scares me, Trixie. One chomp from those teeth, and I'm toast. He looks like a killer."

"Flash! A killer! This sweet baby is a pussycat. He's been taught to capture and hold. Forever if necessary. You know the story about Flash. His original handler moved on to the FBI, and Flash was retired because he was seven years old. He had severe separation anxiety when that happened. I adopted him. He almost died on me, but I finally figured out what was *really* wrong." She turned to ruffle the hair behind Flash's ears. "He missed going to work. So, I bought an old police cruiser, complete with siren and flashing lights, bought myself a cop uniform and a gun that shoots blanks. Then Fred planted marijuana on the farm. I don't mean he planted plants. You know, a stash. Then I'd take Flash to work, driving the cruiser all over the fields, siren blasting, lights flashing, and him decked out in his bulletproof vest. We've been hiding the same bag of pot for three years now. He finds it every time. He's my best friend now. Don't worry, he knows exactly what to do. This dog is smarter than any human I know.

"You look nervous, Dodo. Relax. This is just like plotting a book. Fred and I got right on it the minute you called. We anticipated every possible contingency. If you're worried about Marcus's meds, let me assure you we can get him everything he needs. He gets the same insulin that Fred gets. He's on a low-dosage high-blood-pressure pill, a low-dosage aspirin, and a cholesterol pill. None of the above is for anything life-threatening. However, they've been giving him some pretty potent sedatives. We can have our family doctor check him over when we get back to Rayne. Now stop worrying, you're in good hands. We'll treat Marcus like a king." Trixie looked over her shoulder to be sure Diddy was following in the Navigator. She was.

Her eyes on the narrow road, Dodo said, "I wonder how Ducky is doing with Bella. That woman's no fool. Even after all these years, I still can't believe Marcus actually married her. He was supposed to marry Diddy. They were inseparable after his wife Myrna died. Then, just like that"—Dodo snapped her fingers—"Diddy was history, and we read about his marriage to Bella. Mind you, that's how we found out, an announcement in the newspaper!"

Trixie clicked her dentures to settle them in place. "How many times do I have to tell you, that woman had some kind of hold on Marcus. Fred and I would have figured it out, but you told us not to stick our nose in Diddy and Marcus's business. Maybe Fred can get it out of Marcus once we settle him in. How much farther is it, Dodo?"

"Not far. A quarter of a mile or so. We need deep brush to hide our vehicles, and this is the best way. One good thing is there's little to no traffic this far out, and we're going in by the back end. No one has ever developed the land out here. Except for Bella. No one has been able to figure that one out either. Then again, it might have something to do with the fact that Gunn Enterprises owns just about all the acreage as far as the eye can see. Marcus talked once about selling some of it off, but nothing ever came of it. Here we go, hold on, it's kind of rocky," Dodo said as she turned the wheel sharply to make a right-hand turn. She steered the pickup to the right so Diddy could pull ahead in the Navigator, enabling the pickup to make a hasty getaway.

The women exited their vehicles in unison. Flash stood still while Trixie strapped on his bulletproof vest. "The vest makes it official," Trixie said. "*Sitz*," she whispered, giving the dog the German command he was used to. The dog obediently sat. While she talked to the dog, Diddy and Dodo removed the wrinkled blue tarp from the battery-operated wheelbarrow.

"Okay, let's go. Not a sound now. This baby," Dodo said, tapping the wheelbarrow, "is like a billy goat. She'll take the incline with no problem. It makes barely any noise, so that's a plus. Supposedly it can carry three hundred pounds and hold its charge for three hours. Do you believe that?" Dodo sounded like she couldn't believe her own words. "It's the super-duper top-of-the-line wheelbarrow."

"I'm impressed," Trixie muttered. She snapped her fingers and pointed to the wheelbarrow. Flash hopped inside and sat on his haunches. He shook with anticipation. Dodo turned on the switch, and the wheelbarrow moved forward, with Dodo guiding it. She could hear Diddy sucking in her breath. She gave her a thumbs-up. Diddy offered up her *middle* finger. In spite of herself, Dodo laughed. She hoped she would be laughing thirty minutes from then.

Overhead, the sun shone brightly, confirming that, aside from the humidity, it was a perfect day for lunch outdoors. Birds chittered as squirrels raced from branch to branch. The same woodpecker was having his lunch in the same old oak tree to the left. The women settled themselves on the ground to wait. Flash remained in the wheelbarrow. Trixie made lowering motions with her hand. Flash dropped on all fours, his eyes alert.

Dodo rubbed her hands together in anticipation.

"Okay, Let's go over the plan. I go first, creeping up behind the nurse. I render her unconscious. I figure she'll be out for at least two hours. She'll look like she's sound asleep. It will take me no more than ten seconds, if that long. Trixie and Flash head right for Marcus. I'll be there to help load him in the wheelbarrow. That might take a minute or two unless he's able to help us. If he fights us, it could take longer. He could also be a deadweight. If he is, you take his arms, and I'll take his legs. Flash will patrol and follow us as we go down the incline to the truck. Shhh, here come the maids."

The women waited as the table was set with the same fine-looking crystal, china, and silver. Today there was a single yellow rose in a bud vase. "It's just like yesterday," Dodo whispered. "Here comes the nurse with Marcus. Shhh." Five minutes later, she said, "It looks like they're having meat loaf and mashed potatoes. Lima beans. Yuck."

Flash sniffed the air but remained quiet. The minute the maid finished serving the couple, Dodo crept from the brush. Trixie in her cop uniform, the fierce-looking dog at her side, followed. The only sound to be heard was the woodpecker, who was still dining on the oak tree. Trixie drew in her breath when Dodo crept up to within an inch of the nurse. She watched in amazement when the woman wilted like a flower left in the sun too long when Dodo pressed down on the pressure points in her neck. Dodo positioned her with her hands folded in her lap.

"How's it going, Marcus?" Dodo whispered. "We're here to spring you. I hope you're ready. Sorry about the vehicle," she said, motioning to the battery-operated wheelbarrow, "but it's all we could manage. It is top-of-the-line, though. Don't make a sound."

Flash circled the wheelchair, his eyes boring into the man, who was stunned speechless. Two minutes later Marcus was in the wheelbarrow, his long legs hanging over the side. Trixie took one handle, Dodo the other. She turned on the switch, and the wheelbarrow streaked off, the women running to keep up with it and the dog, who was running directly ahead.

"Bella . . ." Marcus stuttered.

Dodo yanked at the wheelbarrow to slow it down. "What about her? Do you want to stay here?"

Marcus shook his head emphatically. "Hell no."

"Then shut the hell up, Marcus, and let us get you out of here. Ducky is entertaining your wife. This ain't no Mickey Mouse operation, Marcus." Dodo thought she heard laughter coming from the old man's lips.

At the bottom of the incline, Diddy stood waiting. She was wringing her hands in agitation. Trixie and Dodo both looked away when she dropped to her knees. "Oh, God, Marcus, what happened to you?" Tears streamed down her cheeks.

Marcus reached out a trembling hand. Diddy grasped it.

"You can do all that lovey-dovey stuff later. We have to get out of here," Trixie said. "Help Marcus to stand up so we can get this wheelbarrow into the truck." Marcus stood. He was wobbly, but with Diddy's help he remained upright.

"Make sure the switch is off. In you go, Marcus. Don't worry about anything. Trixie is driving you to Rayne. Flash is going to watch you. There you go." It was a struggle, but the three women managed to get Marcus back into the wheelbarrow. Flash hopped in, nosing the man farther back into the wheelbarrow. He growled menacingly when Marcus refused to slide backward. Another growl, and Marcus did as he was told. The strange sounds escaped his lips again. He *was* laughing. He managed a thumbs-up before the tailgate was locked into place and the blue tarp knotted at the two corners of the tailgate.

"Burn rubber, Trixie," Dodo growled.

The pickup backed up, then shot forward, dirt and rocks flying everywhere in her wake.

Diddy and Dodo spent another ten minutes obliterating the tire tracks by gouging the marks with sticks and scattering the rocks. Diddy moved the Navigator to the shoulder of the road that was full of shale. She got out to peruse the ground. Satisfied, Diddy climbed behind the wheel of the Navigator. Dodo had to run to hop in the passenger side. "Are you nuts? Slow down. We did it. We pulled it off. He's going to be just fine, Diddy. Trixie and Fred will take good care of him. They'll do their best to get information out of Marcus. If anyone can do it, it's Trixie and Fred. Our best hope is that they can convince him to turn on Bella and reunite with Ben. We need this information to discredit her. I'm hoping he's able to help us. It's the best answer I can come up with right now, Diddy."

Diddy sniffled into a Kleenex she had balled in her hand.

"We go back to the inn, pick up my car, and go back to the shoe. I'm just sorry it took Russell's death to motivate us. It doesn't say much for any of us, Diddy."

Diddy blew her nose. She sniffled again. "We're criminals. We'll have a rap sheet. We kidnapped Marcus. He looked awful. Is he going to die? Tell me the truth."

Dodo digested her sister's words. "We are not criminals. Not *real* criminals. They can only charge us with kidnapping if Bella or Marcus press charges against us. And, no, he is not going to die. Well, someday he's going to die, but not now. I'm telling you, Diddy, once all that dope gets out of his system, he's going to be fine. You just wait and see." She crossed her fingers, hoping she was telling Diddy the truth.

"What time is it?" Dodo asked as they pulled into the inn.

"It's one-thirty."

"Damn, we're good. Hustle, Diddy, we have to get to the shoe."

Exactly eighteen minutes later, Dodo parked her car in the alley. The sisters walked back through the alley and around to the front, where Ducky was haranguing the work crew, who were eating a Taco Bell lunch. She was shrilling about the litter they'd left scattered around. She almost fainted when she noticed her sisters. "I think you should call the Board of Health, Diddy. These people are littering. It's not healthful. I'd like to know where they go to the bathroom."

Diddy and Dodo stepped front and center. Diddy looked at her watch. "Isn't it a little late for lunch? It's after two. I'm sick of listening to that awful rap music, too. You've been playing it for the past two hours, and you're giving me a headache. We were watching you from the front porch."

"No law against it, lady," one of the men said.

Damn, we are so good, Dodo thought. *Diddy just established our alibi.* She turned to walk away, her sisters following her. Inside Dodo's kitchen with the door closed and locked, the three sisters fell against one another. They were all trembling, giddy with what they'd done.

Ducky broke away first. "We need to act normal. Normal means we take out our tub of beer and retire to the front porch. One of us should probably let Darby know we're home. Then again, maybe we should let well enough alone. We'll just say we got back around eleven. Conceivably we could have left Rayne early this morning. If the cops come snooping around, Darby won't give up anything. I'll bring the beer. Diddy, bring some munchies. Dodo, bring your cell phone in case Trixie tries to call."

The front porch looked the same. Nothing had changed in the past few hours. The paddle fans whirred overhead. Diddy moved the table closer to the three chairs so she could center her tray of munchies. At the top of the shoe the rap music was still blaring. The three women did their best to ignore the music as they huddled close, whispering among themselves.

Ducky held her beer bottle aloft. "I think we should make a toast to the successful Hatch and Snatch Caper." Three beer bottles clinked together.

"Someone has to know already that Marcus is gone. The nurse should be waking up about now, shouldn't she, Dodo?" Ducky asked. Dodo shrugged. "The first thing they'll think is that Marcus wandered off. Maybe they're still searching the grounds. I say they don't call the police until at least two-thirty." Ducky took a huge gulp of beer.

"That sounds about right," Diddy said, her eyes glazed.

"Trixie should be home by three-fifteen at the latest. I hope she gets in touch with us before the police come to call," Dodo said ominously. "If Fred starts out as soon as Trixie gets home, he should be at the inn by five-thirty. You should see that dog! He is ferocious, and he's so big he's scary. His teeth look like shark's teeth." Dodo leaned back, exhausted from her monologue.

"Shut up, Dodo," Ducky snarled. "Let's just sit here and wait for the police. We need to practice looking stunned when they tell us Marcus disappeared. They'll have to tell us Marcus is gone, so we want to look shocked. Then we have to look angry and puzzled as to why they're questioning us. Diddy—are you even listening to me?" Ducky asked.

"Yes. I thought you wanted us to shut up." Diddy clamped her lips tight, her thoughts on the cargo in the rusty old truck heading toward Rayne.

Trixie heaved a mighty sigh of relief when she turned off the highway and onto the deeply rutted road that led to her sixty-five-acre farm. She really had to get after Fred to get the mile-and-a-half-long driveway paved. She knew she wouldn't do any such thing because Fred wouldn't do it, saying that he was leaving the road as is to discourage unwanted visitors. She swerved to avoid a particularly deep rut and tried to slow the truck at the same time. She heard the tailgate go down, heard Flash's shrill bark as he suddenly streaked alongside of her. Where the hell was Marcus and the wheelbarrow. She saw him a moment later whizzing past the pickup that was now stalled in one of the ruts. She could see Flash was having a hard time keeping up with the battery-operated vehicle. Damn, the start button on the wheelbarrow must have jarred loose when it sailed out of the truck.

Trixie did what she always did in a time of crisis. She bellowed at the top of her lungs for Fred. She closed her eyes to avoid looking at Marcus's flapping arms and feet as the wheelbarrow careened down the bumpy road,

Flash trying to stop it. *God, what if Marcus falls out and dies?*

Trixie turned on the ignition, cursing under her breath as she backed up again and again, then managed to move the old truck forward. She gunned the engine and roared down the road in time to see Flash finally catching up with the wheelbarrow. She watched in amazement as the big dog tried to slap at the ON/OFF switch. Trixie wanted to cry when the wheelbarrow came to a stop about a hundred feet from where Fred was standing. He looked like his eyes were about to pop out of his head.

Trixie stopped the truck. She ran to Flash to praise him. Marcus was shaking. With laughter. "What'd he say? How are you, dear?" she said to Fred as though this was an everyday occurrence.

"I think he wants to know what you do for an encore. What the hell happened, Sweet Cheeks?"

"We need to fix that damn road, Fred. I hit a big hole, the tailgate came down, and out he went. That contraption is battery-operated. I want one. Marcus is all right, isn't he?" She hated how anxious her voice sounded.

Fred McGuire looked like a modern version of Santa Claus, with his snow-white hair, white beard, wire-rimmed glasses, and round belly. He leaned over. "You okay, Marcus? Welcome to McGuire Farm. Good to see you again. You wanna get out of that contraption?"

"I want a drink," Marcus mumbled, as Fred helped him out of the wheelbarrow. Fred looked at Trixie to see if a drink was in order. She nodded. "Make me one, too, sweetie. A stiff one. I want a cigarette, also. Never mind, I'll get it. Just help me get him into the house. You need to get started for Baton Rouge. Ah, Fred, I don't think there's any need to . . . ah, tell anyone about our little mishap. All's well that ends well."

Fred grinned. "I hear you, Sweet Cheeks. Are you sure that jalopy is going to make it all the way to Baton Rouge?"

"It got me here. You better buy some gas. I gotta tell you, the springs are shot. It's a real kidney crusher. Did you call the doctor?"

"I did. He'll be here in about fifteen minutes. I guess I'll see you when I see you. Nice to see you again, Marcus."

When the door closed behind her husband, Trixie settled her guest in the kitchen rocking chair. She knew she was twitching all over the place. If anyone needed a drink, it was her. She slopped Kentucky bourbon into two glasses and handed one to Marcus. Flash licked up the excess. Trixie finished her drink with one gulp and poured a second. "Bottoms up, Marcus!"

Using both hands, Marcus was able to bring the glass to his lips. He imitated Trixie, then held out his glass for a refill. Trixie obliged. "Now if I can just find a cigarette, we're in business. I quit. Fred quit. Then Fred started up when we retired, so I did, too. Then we started to train the dogs, and we quit again. Technically, we are off cigarettes," Trixie said, rummaging frantically in the

kitchen drawers. She finally found a crumpled package
of cigarettes and lit one up. Marcus held up his hand,
indicating he wanted one.

"I don't think that's a good idea, Marcus." When he
said "please," Trixie capitulated. "Okay, but no more.
Just one. Fred will kill us both if he finds out. So will the
doctor who's coming to check you over. Hurry up and
puff," she said in a jittery voice. She puffed furiously,
not even enjoying the cigarette. She watched Marcus,
who blew a perfect smoke ring, then gave her a lopsided
smile.

"Safe here?"

"Absolutely. Flash will guard you with his life. Seriously, we have it under control, Marcus. I don't want
you to worry. Just cooperate with the doctor, and we'll
take it from there."

Another perfect smoke ring sailed upward.

Trixie turned away so that she was facing the door,
Flash at her side. He pawed her leg. It was time to take
off his working gear. Trixie bent over to undo the straps
of his bulletproof vest. The huge dog licked her hand
before he trotted back to the man in the rocking chair.
He whined in pleasure when the man's hand dropped
down to stroke his big head.

"I forgot to put the wheelbarrow back in the truck,"
she muttered. "How could I have forgotten to do that? I
hear a car. It must be Elmo." She turned around. "Elmo
is retired now, but he stays up on what's going on. In the
world of medicine," she clarified. "He's bringing his

wife, who's also his assistant. He has a little clinic in his old offices, so they'll run some blood tests. That means they have to draw blood from you. Are you okay with all this, Marcus?" Marcus's head bobbed up and down. He looked tired.

"You aren't getting out of here until you answer a lot of questions, Marcus. Just so you know. I wonder if that dear, sweet, charming wife of yours reported you missing yet. I guess we should turn on the TV to check that out. I gotta tell you, Marcus, this was one of the most exciting snatches I've ever participated in. Fred and I really have to do one more book." She was dithering with apprehension as she stared at the small television on the counter. She jerked upright when she saw a banner running across the screen. A young woman who looked like she was sculpted from glass said, "This just in to our newsroom. Mrs. Bella Gunn, wife of Marcus Gunn of Baton Rouge, reported her invalid husband missing at one-thirty this afternoon. Mr. Gunn, in the company of his nurse, was having lunch outdoors in the garden, when he disappeared. At this time, we don't know if the nurse is missing or not. Our details are sketchy. It seems that Mr. Gunn either walked away or was taken away, because his wheelchair was left behind."

The lacquered, sculpted newswoman then proceeded to talk about Marcus and the good deeds he'd done during his lifetime. An old picture of Marcus in a three-piece suit shaking hands with the then-governor of Louisiana flashed on the screen. She finished up her segment by asking anyone with information as to Marcus Gunn's whereabouts to call the number listed on the screen. It was at that precise moment that Elmo Odam creaked into the room, followed by his wife, Tildy.

Trixie drew a deep breath as the retired doctor homed in on the picture of Marcus flashing on the screen. He looked over at Marcus, who held up his thumb, a sign that he was amused by what he was seeing.

"I assume you and Fred are coming out of retirement and are contemplating a new novel and what I'm seeing here is hands-on research. I'm honored, Trixie, to be part of that effort. Now, if you'll take Flash and disappear for a while, I'll do what I do best. Nifty-looking wheelbarrow you got out there. I've been thinking about getting one. I could wheel Tildy around the backyard." Trixie made her way to the door, Flash leaving his post the second she held up her hand. She turned back and reached for the last cigarette lying on the counter.

"I'm going to pretend I didn't see that," Elmo said.

"I'm going to *pretend* to smoke it, Elmo." Trixie turned back a second time. "I'd be happy to lend you the wheelbarrow to try out. If you don't like it, you don't have to waste the money buying one."

"Take the offer. Fingerprints. DNA," Marcus said smartly.

Trixie was stunned at Marcus's willingness to help his kidnappers.

Elmo walked over to the door. "I'd be happy to take it off your hands for a trial run, Trixie. Fred and I can load it up when we're finished here."

"Fred isn't here, Elmo. He had . . . uh . . . business in Rayne."

"Not a problem. Give us thirty minutes, Trixie."

Trixie walked away from the house. As soon as she was out of sight, she whipped her cell phone out of her pocket. Dodo picked up on the first ring. Trixie's words all ran together in one long rush. "We got here, Fred's on his way, the doctor is here. Marcus is okay. He had a drink and a cigarette. I forgot to send the wheelbarrow back, so Elmo is going to take it to his house. I saw Marcus on the news." She wound down like a balloon with a slow leak.

Trixie fired up the cigarette with shaky hands. She almost choked to death. Now she remembered why she gave up cigarettes in the first place.

Dodo's voice was just as fast and furious as Trixie's voice. "Lunch was fine. Ducky said Bella played it real cool. No unwanted visitors yet. We have an alibi for two o'clock, with those goons working on Bella's houses in the shoe. It's on the news here, but they're not playing it up. Yet. We haven't seen Darby or Ben yet either. We're just sitting here on the porch. Call me after the doctor leaves."

"Okay." Trixie snapped off the phone. She puffed

and coughed, coughed and puffed, as she walked around the yard, Flash at her side. She smoked the cigarette until it was down to the filter. She felt relieved when she was finished. She looked back at the house, wondering what the future held in store for her friends. She shivered in the humid summer air. She would be glad when autumn arrived. The new dogs would arrive for training in a few days. Or was that tomorrow. Damn, she couldn't remember anything anymore.

Trixie sat down on a small round bench that circled a monstrous oak tree that dripped Spanish moss. Over the years, she'd eaten lunch with Fred in this very spot more times than she could remember. The good old days. She sighed. These were good days, too. Fred and I have wonderful friends, friends that don't ask questions and help even if it means bending the law. Then there was her niece and godchild, Jane, and her husband, Mike, with the two little ones to round out her life. Yes, life was good. Flash was the dearest animal on earth, as were all the *newbies* who arrived four times a year for intensive police training. She crossed her fingers that the good life would continue.

Flash leaped to his feet, his head swiveling to stare at his mistress. They were being called. He pawed her skinny leg. Trixie took a long moment to observe her beloved companion. His last checkup revealed the beginning of arthritis in his hindquarters. Flash was aging just the way she was. A wave of sadness engulfed her. A shrill whistle from the back porch shook her from her reverie. She got up and followed the German shepherd to the house.

Elmo was beaming from ear to ear. "This young fella," he said, jerking his head in Marcus's direction, "is in surprisingly good condition. I'd like to see him get a little exercise. Start out slow. Let him walk with the dog but be close by or give him a cane to begin with. He's a tad wobbly. I'll get back to you with the blood results by late tomorrow. No reason at all I can see that he can't be on the same diet as Fred. I'm leaving samples of the meds he's on as well as a dozen insulin packs that I put in the refrigerator. Fred can give him his shots." He shook his head to show what he thought about what was going on. "Well, Trixie, my good and old friend, I'd say God is going to smile on you for what you've done." He leaned over, and whispered, "Your secret is safe with me. Obviously you knew that, or you wouldn't have called me. I'll give you a call later this evening. I just gave him his shot, so he's good till morning. Now, if you and my wonderful wife are of a mind, let's get that wheelbarrow into my trunk."

"Flash, keep your eye on our guest. I'll be right back."

Outside, the three oldsters huffed and puffed until they got the wheelbarrow into the trunk of the ancient Buick. Elmo tied it down with a ratty-looking piece of rope.

"Thanks for all your help, Elmo. Tell me something, why is Marcus's speech so slow?"

"Yours would be, too, if you had as much Valium in you as he does. He's going to be fine once it wears off. Trust me, Trixie. Say hello to Fred for me."

Still dressed in her cop uniform, Trixie walked back into the house. She smiled when she saw the shepherd on Marcus's lap. That alone was a feat that verged on awe. Both man and dog were sound asleep. Trixie dusted her hands dramatically as she left the room to go upstairs to change her clothes.

Yep, this was too good a plot to let fall by the wayside. When she returned downstairs, she put on a pot of coffee. While it dripped, she went into her office for a yellow legal pad. She carried it out to the kitchen and started to write.

And thus the sixty-seventh T. F. Dingle masterpiece was born. She knew as she made her notes that she had an instant best seller on her hands.

Oh, yeah.

13

The Lane sisters were sitting in Dodo's kitchen drinking strong black coffee, their eyes on the clock and Dodo's cell phone, sitting smack in the middle of the table. They were *not* so patiently waiting for the phone to ring. Diddy was pouring herself a third cup when she heard the sound of a car's engine. She craned her neck to look past the trailing green fern hanging over the kitchen window. "It's Ben." Her voice was flat yet jittery-sounding.

Dodo toyed with her coffee cup before she held it up for Diddy to refill. "I wonder where he's been all day. Do you know that for every cup of coffee you drink you have to pee three times. I read that in *Health Watch* when I was waiting in the dentist's office."

Ducky grimaced. "Thanks for sharing that little gem, Dodo. God, you don't think that old clunker broke down, do you? No, no, Fred would have called if that happened. Where the hell is he?"

"Unlike his wife, Fred does not have a heavy foot. He's probably going the speed limit. He'll be here soon. What is Ben doing?"

Diddy craned her neck, the fronds of the fern tickling her neck. "He's walking across the yard. I assume he's going to see Darby. Yep, that's where he's going. Willie just barreled out of the house. I think you're going to get your wish, Dodo. Something's going on between those two."

Ducky bounced across the kitchen. She turned on the television for the six o'clock local news. She looked over at the clock. "Two minutes till the news comes on," she said. "I'm really surprised that Bella hasn't called. She was too damn cool at lunch. I think she knew something was going on. She just couldn't figure out what it was."

Dodo scoffed as she gulped at her coffee. "You only feel that way because you feel guilty. Get over it. All you did was eat. Diddy, Trixie, and I are the ones who did all the dirty work. It's our rear ends that will go in a sling if Bella can nail us." She gulped at her coffee.

The phone in the center of the table rang just as the local newscaster appeared on the small TV screen. The Lane sisters looked at the phone. It rang four times before Ducky shoved Dodo's hand toward it. "Answer the damn phone already, Dodo. I'll watch the news."

Dodo's voice was a bare squeak when she said, "Hello. Yes. Ten minutes." Her sigh was so loud in the kitchen it literally drowned out the voice of the newscaster. "Go! Go! I'll fill you in when you get back," Ducky said, making shooing motions with her hands. The screen door slammed with such force, Ducky shuddered. She turned up the volume on the TV the moment Bella Gunn appeared on the screen, wringing her hands and sobbing.

Ducky pressed her face to within inches of the screen to better tell if Bella was acting or not. She decided she was acting when she didn't see any tears rolling down Bella's gaunt cheeks. One thing was being made clear between Bella's sobs. The nurse had had some kind of blackout and was currently being examined at Baton Rouge General Hospital. The cameraman moved his camera back to the newscaster, who said, "As we all know, the first twenty-four hours are crucial in a disappearance or a kidnapping. The police, at last report, are saying they have no clues as to Mr. Gunn's disappearance. We don't know yet if the FBI will be called in."

"Oh, God, oh, God!" Ducky said, running to the kitchen cabinet. With shaking hands she reached for a bottle of apricot brandy and guzzled till her eyes started to water.

Her back to the kitchen door, she turned when she heard the screen door creak. She whirled around, the brandy bottle in her hand. "Ben!"

"What's wrong?" Ducky pointed to the television screen. Ben's jaw dropped. "What the hell . . ."

"Bella . . . Bella . . . was just on, sobbing and wringing her hands. Your father either wandered off or he was kidnapped. They said . . . they said the nurse . . . they implied she had some sort of . . . of blackout or maybe a seizure of some sort. She's in the hospital. The nurse, not Bella," Ducky babbled.

Ben stood rooted to the floor. "Are you telling me my father's missing?"

"Well . . . I suppose that's a . . . the police don't have a clue. I'm going to have another drink. Do you want a drink, Ben? Maybe you should go over to Bella's. You are Marcus's son. Yes, yes, you should go over there."

"Why, Ducky? What can I possibly do?"

"I don't know why. Marcus is your father. You're his son. It's going to look strange if you don't . . . show some kind of reaction. What other reason do you need? The man is your father."

"He probably went for a walk and got lost. By the way, I thought you went to Rayne." The question that wasn't exactly a question hung in the air.

"I did . . . we did . . . but we came back. This morning. I had lunch with Bella today. The Garden Club is going to nominate Bella and Marcus's house for the Christmas Candlelight Tour. I had to interview her . . . but none of that is important." Ducky tried for a compassionate smile, but it wobbled on her face.

Ben narrowed his eyes; he wasn't buying her story. "Where are Dodo and Diddy?"

Ducky sucked in air. Brandy always made her belligerent. "Why do you want to know? I'm not their keeper just like they aren't my keeper."

Ben backed up a step, his hands in the air, palms outward. "Whoa. Look, obviously, I came over here at a bad time. Darby and I are going to order Chinese. She wanted to know if you three wanted any."

"No, thank you. MSG doesn't agree with me. I haven't had Chinese in *years*. No, thank you," she added again as an afterthought. Then she took another belt from the brandy bottle. "I really think you should go over to your father's house to . . . to . . ."

"To what, Ducky?"

"To help find him. He's your father. You are his son. That's why." She gulped again. She was getting lightheaded. She looked down at the bottle in her hand. She'd seriously depleted its contents.

"So, where are Dodo and Diddy?" Ben asked a second time.

"I told you, I don't know. I don't much care for your attitude, young man."

The screen door opened to admit Dodo and Diddy. They took one look at Ducky's red face and knew they were looking at trouble.

"Ben came over because he and Darby want to know if we want Chinese tonight. I told him no," Ducky said, slurring her words. "I told him his father disappeared, and he should go over there to see what's happening. He won't go." Ducky sat down with a thump on the kitchen chair, her hold on the brandy bottle tight and secure.

Ben frowned, certain now that Darby was right and the three of them were up to something. "Listen, I just got back from Metairie. I went to talk to the people at LOPA. Do you want to know what I found out?"

"Not right now. Tomorrow will be soon enough," Diddy said, taking charge and ushering their guest to the back door. "Right now we have some work to do for the Garden Club. I'm sorry about your father's disappearance. I'm sure . . . he'll . . . he'll turn up eventually." She gave Ben a final push, and he was out the door. She slammed the door, then locked it.

"What happened, Ducky?" Diddy and Dodo asked in unison. Then Diddy continued. "You look guilty, like you did something wrong. All you did was have lunch with Bella. We did the dirty deed. Now, what did they say on the news? Don't leave anything out either."

Ducky fondled the brandy bottle, her new best friend. "They said the nurse had some kind of blackout, and she's in the hospital. They still aren't saying if Marcus was snatched or if he wandered off. Bella was wringing her hands and sobbing, but there weren't any tears. Then Ben came in and saw the news report. Ben was shocked at the news. That young man really does care about his father. Right now he doesn't quite know what to do or how to act. He's been bitter for so long, these new feelings are alien to him. He has to work this out himself. All we can do is be here for him if he needs us," Ducky concluded, but then she saw that her sisters were rolling their eyes. "Don't look at me like that. I can read that young man like a book. I saw the concern in his eyes. And, his hands were shaking. What that means to us is when he next sees his father, Ben will convince him to turn on Bella."

"Ducky, are you sure that isn't all wishful thinking on your part? Did this brandy have anything to do with what you thought you saw in Ben?" Diddy said as she snatched the brandy bottle from her sister's hands and placed it on the counter.

"Not a thing. I heard his voice crack. The boy cares, no matter how he denies it."

"All right," Dodo said soothingly. "What exactly did Bella do or say that upset you?"

"She didn't have to *say* anything. You didn't see that woman's face. I did. She's going to come after us. Just wait, they'll be showing her interview all night long. Did Fred say anything?"

"No. We just switched vehicles, and off he went. Diddy, make Ducky some coffee. I'm going to cook dinner."

A statement like that was usually a cause for alarm between the sisters, but today they rolled with it and watched as Dodo got out bread, peanut butter, and jelly.

Darby sat back on her workbench to stare at the frame she'd constructed for the Scottish castle. She nodded to herself. The frame was always the hardest, the trickiest part of constructing a dollhouse or, in this case, a castle. She sensed a flurry of movement behind her. Willie. She turned to see Ben and Willie standing in the doorway. She didn't like the expression she saw on Ben's face. "What? What's wrong? What did they tell you in Metairie?"

"Have you had the radio or television on this afternoon?" Ben asked hoarsely.

"No. Why? What happened? You're scaring me. The aunts . . ." she said, her own face draining of all color. Willie woofed to be heard.

"The aunts are fine. Well, Ducky looks schnockered but . . . my father has disappeared. Either he wandered off or he was kidnapped. It was on the news," Ben said in a choked voice.

"Oh, God, I'm sorry, Ben. Is that why Ducky's tipsy? No, that can't be right. It would be Diddy who would have been drinking. I thought they went to Rayne. Obviously, they're back. Wait just a minute . . . you don't think . . . you can't believe . . . oh, God, yes, it does make sense. Did . . . did they . . . did they look . . . *guilty?*"

"Hell, yes, they looked guilty. And belligerent. They kicked me out of Dodo's kitchen. They didn't even want to know what I found out in Metairie. Which, by the way, was nothing. I was stonewalled every step of the way. Incidentally, your aunts don't want to share our Chinese."

Darby dropped to the floor and sat Indian fashion, Willie half-on and half-off her lap. "What should we do? Are you going to Bella's house? Should we confront the aunts? What? Talk to me, Ben."

Ben sat down next to her and reached for her hand. She leaned toward him just as flashing red-and-blue lights appeared beyond the workroom windows. Willie was on his feet, growling and snarling as he pawed at the door. The wailing siren died abruptly. Darby and Ben jumped to their feet. Holding hands, they walked through the house to the back porch, where they could see two police officers walking up the center of the shoe. Darby took a deep breath as she started down the steps.

"Let me handle this. I think I'm the one they want. Go over to your aunts," Ben said.

Darby sprinted across the lawn and around to the front porch where the aunts were sitting. They did *not* look like the three wise monkeys. They looked like three nervous old ladies, possibly capable of bluffing their way through anything. Sort of. Kind of.

"I heard you were back," Darby said breathlessly. "The cops are here! Ben's talking to them out back. He told me about his father. He's really upset."

"It's going to rain," Ducky said, raising her beer bottle to the sky.

"The truck broke down," Dodo said, upending her beer.

"Dodo cooked dinner. They were the best peanut

butter and jelly sandwiches I ever ate. That's why we don't want Chinese. Is that more than you wanted to know, dear?" Diddy asked.

Darby leaned over so that she was almost eyeball-to-eyeball with her aunts. "You snatched him, didn't you?" she hissed just as the two police officers, escorted by Ben, approached the front steps. Darby backed up, her eyes on the aunts, who suddenly looked like they were stone-cold sober.

Ducky took the initiative. Hands on her hips, she blasted the two police officers, her angry voice carrying in the humid air. "It's about time you showed up! We have a noise ordinance here in Baton Rouge and as officers of the law, you should be enforcing it. That's what I pay my taxes for, isn't it? That ridiculous rap music is still ringing in my ears. Now go up there and put a stop to it!"

"Ma'am, we're not here about the rap music. You have to file a complaint, then we'll come back out. We're here about the disappearance of Marcus Gunn."

Dodo stepped up to the plate. "We heard about it on the news. I don't blame him for running off. The man can't handle all the bad press. He knows he isn't going to get away with demolishing those houses."

"So what is it you want?" Diddy asked coldly.

The second officer stepped forward. "Mrs. Gunn said she had lunch with a Harriet Lane. Which one of you is Harriet?"

"I'm Harriet," Ducky said. "Yes, we did have lunch. I

can't believe she would tell the police *we had lunch*.
Did she call the newspapers to tell them, too? We had
salmon and a sweet-potato soufflé. Oh, and a glass of
wine. So what?"

"We have to check everything, ma'am. It seems Mr.
Gunn disappeared sometime between one-thirty and
two o'clock."

Dodo crunched up her face as she shrilled, "Are you
here to check to see if we have *alibis?* I haven't seen that
rascal Marcus Gunn in . . . Lord, I don't remember
when. We were up front going toe-to-toe with those people playing that rap music during that time period.
Those men can confirm it. We asked them nicely to
stop, and they refused. Go talk to them if you're serious
about us needing an alibi. And that, in itself, is probably
the most ridiculous thing I've ever heard of. Ask yourself, do we look capable of what you're suggesting?"

"I resent this inquisition," Diddy said, getting into
the act. "We have not associated with Mr. and Mrs.
Gunn in over twenty-five years. I expect we will not be
associating with them for the next twenty-five years either. You can just put that in your pipe and smoke it,
Mr. Police Officer."

The two police officers stepped backward at the hard
glint in Diddy's eyes.

The older of the two officers homed in on Darby.
"What about you, miss? Where were you between one-
thirty and two o'clock?"

"I was working in my workshop. No, no one but the

dog was with me. I guess I have no alibi. Oh, oh, wait. Actually, I was on a long-distance call to my client in Scotland. We talked for over thirty minutes. I think the call came in around 1:20 or so. You can verify that with the phone company. Now, if you'll excuse me, Ben and I were going to go out for Chinese. Please wait up for us," she said, addressing the aunts. "We'll bring you some fortune cookies."

The police officers shuffled backward. They were dismissed, and they knew it. It wasn't supposed to be like this. *They* were in charge. But, the commissioner himself had sent down word that they were to tread lightly when speaking with the Lane sisters.

When everyone was gone from the front porch, Diddy spoke anxiously. "Did we pull it off? Should we call Trixie?"

"No, we should not call Trixie, at least not from our phones. Wait a minute. I have a phone card because of all the traveling I do. If we use it, there's no way to trace the call. But wait until Darby and Ben are gone. It's next to the phone in the kitchen," Ducky said.

Ducky moved to the swing and started to pump her legs. Dodo moved out of range. "Do you think Bella is going to call us tonight?"

"No, she isn't, Ducky. Right now, she's trying to piece it all together. Not that she can do much about it. We pulled off a *clean* job. Listen! They finally stopped playing that awful music." Dodo almost swooned.

"I'm surprised I haven't heard from the private detective in N'awlins," Ducky said, swinging almost to the ceiling. "He said he would call late today." She slowed and hopped off to sit on the rocker. "This is so depressing, Dodo. Rocking on a rocking chair on the front porch is for *old* people."

Dodo snapped her fingers under her sister's nose. "Hello, there, Ducky! This may come as a surprise to you, but we are old. Rocking is a comfort to me. You, too, but you just won't admit it. I'm sure Marcus is going to be just fine. I hope Diddy can handle whatever it is he finally tells her. The good news is that Marcus is recovering and appears to be grateful that we snatched him. You know, we were so rude to Ben. He wanted to tell us about his trip to talk to the LOPA people, and we didn't even give him a chance to tell us. How could we have done that? We got into this mess because of dear Russell in the first place."

"That's all well and good but we still don't know if Marcus will turn on Bella and stop the demolition of the Gunn houses."

"We didn't let him talk because we were too damn busy trying to cover our collective asses, that's why. I'm worried about the FBI," Ducky whined.

"I'm not," Dodo said confidently. "The minute we hear they're involved, we call Trixie, tell her to buy a phone card, and then Marcus can call the FBI and tell them he's fine and he left under his own power. You're working yourself up over nothing."

"I'll remind you of that when they're carting you off

in handcuffs. I'll be left behind because I was having lunch with Bella." Ducky sniffed to show what she thought of her sister's plan.

"And how long do you think Honoria will keep quiet. She'll sing like a canary, and we both know it. You're as involved in this whole mess as Diddy and I are."

"I wish you'd shut up, Dodo. You're giving me a headache. Fred forgot to bring back the wheelbarrow. Ben and Darby are going to notice that."

"You're a sadist, Dodo. You didn't have to tell me that, now did you? You just want me to worry even more. So what if they notice it, so what?"

Dodo dropped her head until her chin was resting on her skinny chest. "I don't think we were meant for a life of crime. It's entirely too stressful."

"This was all your idea, you . . . you . . . ninja."

"I'm going to take that as a compliment," Dodo growled.

Diddy appeared at the bottom of the steps. She looked up at her sisters, giving them a thumbs-up. "Marcus is fine. Flash is with him, and he's sleeping for the night. The doctor called a half hour ago to check on him. Trixie said he's A-1. Said she gave him a drink and a cigarette. The doctor is going to check again in the morning. Fred got home okay, and the wheelbarrow is with the good doctor. She said we should go to bed and let the professionals take over. I think she means her and Fred. Being the professionals, that is."

"Go to bed! I can't sleep," Dodo said.

"Who can sleep with the thought the FBI is going to come into this at the end of twenty-four hours. Not me, that's for sure," Ducky said with a quiver in her voice.

"What do you suggest we do to wile away the night?" Diddy asked as she lowered her ample frame onto a rocking chair.

"What we do best, drink," Dodo and Ducky said in unison.

The hour was late, a few minutes past eleven, when Bella Gunn's doorbell rang. With the servants retired for the evening, it was up to Bella to open the door herself. She looked at the two police officers and motioned for them to enter the house. She prepared herself to play the part of the worried wife. She dabbed at her eyes with a lace-edged hankie.

"I hope . . . please tell me you aren't here to give me bad news." She sniffled into the hankie.

"No, ma'am. We said we would report any new developments. We spoke with the three Lane sisters. Miss Harriet Lane confirmed that she had lunch with you. The Misses Lydia and Vivian were up at the Horseshoe arguing with the foreman you hired at the time your husband disappeared. We weren't able to reach the foreman until a little after ten. He said they gave him a lot of grief about his men playing rap music. Miss Darby Lane said she was working in her workshop and was on an international call with a client from Scotland at the time. She said the client called her. We checked with the international operator and what she said is true. Your stepson Benjamin Gunn was in Metairie. He was there during the entire time in question. He has a complete record of every single person he talked with. The offices are closed now, but Mr. Gunn had enough material and notes to prove he was there. We will of course verify all that in the morning when the offices open."

"What offices are you talking about, Officer?"

"The Louisiana Organ Procurement Agency."

How interesting, Bella mused to herself. Ben could dig all he wanted but she'd still get her way—acceptance, finally, by the *Rougies,* inclusion in the Christmas tour, and a conditional license to refurbish the houses on the shoe. *Dig, Ben, dig all you want. You can't stop me now and neither can your father because he knows that I'll reveal his deep, dark secret. He'll be ruined. You'll be tainted, too, dear Ben. Even those snippy Lane sisters will be tainted by association.*

Now she was going to take a nice long bubble bath and dream about tomorrow and all the tomorrows yet to come. Life was certainly looking sweet at the moment. She didn't give another thought to her missing husband as she started to run the water into her Jacuzzi.

14

Ben Gunn slid into the booth across from Darby. He reached to take both her hands in his. He smiled, and Darby's heart rate quickened. She smiled in return. Ben was forced to release her hands when a waitress appeared with menus along with a bowl of hard noodles, duck sauce, and hot mustard.

"I missed you today, Ben. I thought about you all afternoon while I was working. I'm sorry I didn't go with you to Metairie. It was my place to go since I'm the executrix of Russell's will, but my little client won out. I have to finish her dollhouse-slash-castle on time. Should we talk about your trip first or should we talk about your father's disappearance and the aunts' possible involvement?" She felt breathless just sitting across from Ben.

Ben reached for her hands again. "I know how this

must sound, but I'm not worried about my father's disappearance. Wherever he is, I feel he's safe, and, yes, I think those three ladies took care of things. They're never going to make it in the criminal world. Their eyes give them away even though they bluster and posture. So, let's talk about my trip.

"I came up blank, Darby. I lost count of the people I talked to. I was shuffled from one department to another to another. I played that tape over and over. I hope I didn't wear it out. At one point I even threatened legal action. I made one lady cry, and I'm sure not proud of that. She was a volunteer worker, and her daughter was a kidney recipient a few years ago. Working for the organization was the mother's way of paying back for her daughter's life."

"Oh, Ben, I appreciate your staying in town to do all that to help me," Darby said. "I can only imagine how difficult it was for you. I know you . . . What I mean is, I know you didn't do it for yourself, you did it for me. I just want you to know I appreciate all your efforts."

Ben nodded. "Right now I feel like I'm some kind of authority on the donor program. Just here in our state of Louisiana there are 952 people waiting for a kidney transplant and 47,622 in the United States. We have 162 people waiting for a liver transplant, 244 waiting for a heart. The list is virtually endless. I read case histories of some of the recipients. They're just heartbreaking, especially the children. Damn, they haven't even had a chance to live yet, and here they are dying for lack of a

donor. I saw videos by the dozen of some recipients—
digitally altered, you know, with that blue dot thing over
their faces so no one will know who they are. I can't
fault the program for protecting both the donors and the
recipients' families. It's beyond sad."

Darby dipped a noodle into the hot mustard and
popped it into her mouth. Her eyes started to water. She
gulped at the small cup of tea, downing it all.

"I still want to know who has . . . I want to know the
recipients of Russ's organs."

"They will not divulge names, Darby. I talked to the
Match Maker himself. He's the doctor that matches up
the donors with the recipients. It's somewhat like the
lawyer-client privilege. We're *never* going to know. Like
you, that's the part I can't handle."

"There has to be a way. I just want to know something about them. I want to see them. I want to say hello
and good-bye even if it's silently. I don't want to invade
their lives or even let them know I know who they are. I
owe that to Russ. I do, Ben. I'm not going to be able to
live with myself if I don't know."

"I said almost those same words to the Match Maker,
and while he listened to me, viewed the tape, knew the
setback it would cause to the program if we went public,
he was adamant. He wouldn't give me a clue. Like I
said, I can't fault him or the program."

Darby squared her shoulders. "Then we're going to
have to go another route. I'll call Claire when we get
outside. She can get in touch with Russ's computer

hacker friends. Maybe they can hack into the donor record. If I go to jail, then I go to jail."

"Then I'll be there with you. Oh, here comes our dinner. Believe it or not, I haven't eaten all day," Ben said, and Darby watched as he ate with gusto. He cleaned his plate, then picked from hers.

Darby stared across the table at her dinner companion. She wondered what her future held in regard to Ben. She almost asked him but changed her mind. Time would tell. Suddenly, she felt like crying and wasn't sure why.

"What's wrong?" Ben asked, concern ringing in his voice.

Darby shook her head. "I cry when I'm happy. I cry when I'm sad. I'm both right now. Sad about Russ, happy that you came into my life, bewildered at the aunts' behavior, sorry about your father, sick over the little girl in Scotland who isn't going to live to see her tenth birthday. Emotionally, I have a very full plate."

"Then we need to start clearing it off. Trust me when I tell you my father is all right. The aunts are in the mix, and they're wise old ladies. They're going to be fine, too. I can help you with your castle for the sick little girl in Scotland so that you get it done on time. I'm thinking her days will be happier with her dollhouse. Just show me what you want me to do. I was always fairly good at building and repairing things. That brings us front and center to Russell. You're going to call Claire so those wheels will be put into motion. Everything's going to work out, Darby. Between us, we can make it happen."

Darby smiled, tears glistening in her eyes. "I knew I liked you for a reason."

Ben's chest puffed out. He felt like leaning across the table to kiss her. Instead, he said the words out loud. Darby laughed. He loved the sound. His thoughts traveled to the future and how the house they would live in someday would be full of laughter. He said that, too.

"Don't we have to get married first for that to happen?" Darby teased.

"Yeah. Absolutely we have to get married. Four children, two girls, two boys. Is that okay with you? A dog, a cat, some goldfish, and maybe a bird. I'll build the kids a tree house with electricity. Maybe running water from a hose. I can get a job here at one of the state parks. The big question is, where are we going to live?"

Darby was breathless when she said, "Where would you like to live, Ben?"

"In the house where my memories were the happiest. The first house on the shoe. If I could get my father to deed it to me, I'd use all my trust fund to restore it. Those houses came to my father from my mother's side of the family. I was to get one, Russ was to get the other, and Mary . . . well, they never said what Mary was to get. That could certainly explain Mary's attitude in regard to a lot of things. I'm not sure about this, but I think she was to get the house in

Crowley that belonged to my great-grandparents. I'm resigned to the fact that it isn't going to happen now because Bella is going to demolish it."

"What about Russ's house, the other one on the shoe?"

"She's out for blood. She'll take the wrecking ball to it, too. Can you see yourself living at the top of the shoe as opposed to having a room in Ducky's house?"

"Oh, yes. Yes, Ben, I can. Do you remember as kids how we used to run from house to house begging for sweets, never telling what we got in the one before. I think we were constantly on sugar highs until the aunts got wise to us. It all sounds wonderful but like you said, it isn't going to happen now."

"We can still get married in the middle of the shoe. That's where my mother and father got married. That's always been a dream of mine. Russ said the same thing to me last year," Ben added.

Darby's eyes twinkled. "First you have to ask me to marry you!"

"I know that, but I'm not going to ask you in a Chinese restaurant, that's for sure."

"We just met again after so many years apart, Ben. How can you be so sure . . ."

"That I love you? I've always loved you. Seeing you here was the most natural thing in the world. It was like those years we were apart never happened. I know you felt what I felt. Admit it," Ben teased lightly. He tossed her a fortune cookie, then opened his and laughed.

Darby started to giggle when she read hers. "Mine says 'You will find true happiness with a tall dark-haired man.' What does yours say?"

Ben was still laughing when he read his own. "Mine says 'a dark-haired woman is your soul mate.'"

"You made that up! Let me see!"

"Nope. You have to trust me."

"Okay," Darby said agreeably. She waited until Ben reached up to take the check from the waitress. She snatched the small slip of paper. She read the fortune: "A dark-haired woman will be your soul mate." She laughed as she scrambled out of the booth. Ben wrapped his arms around her. Nothing in the world had ever felt this good, Darby decided.

Twenty-three hours after Marcus Gunn disappeared, Trixie McGuire used her new phone card to call Dodo's cell phone. "What are you hearing on your news stations, Dodo?" she asked.

"They're just rehashing everything. No clues, no ransom demand. Mrs. Gunn is *demanding*, that's the word they're using, demanding they widen the search, call in the FBI. The twenty-four-hour waiting period will be up in exactly fifty-eight minutes. That's when they step in and take over. Ducky and Diddy think you should have Marcus call somebody to say he's all right. I agree. He is all right, isn't he, Trixie?"

"He's just fine. He ate a nice breakfast, and I'm preparing lunch as we speak. Fred is showing Marcus all the dog kennels and telling him what we do. I can see a change hour by hour. He slept through the night. Flash stood guard. To tell you the truth, Dodo, he's better than any of us have a right to expect. I'll run the phone call by him and see what he says. I'll call you back after lunch."

Dodo clicked off the cell phone and repeated what Trixie had told her.

The three sisters were eyeballing one another when Willie appeared, a piece of paper between his teeth. He dropped it at Ducky's feet. "Admit it, this is clever," Ducky cackled. "Oh, the private detective called on the house line and wants me to call him back. Things might be looking up, ladies. I wonder if he found out anything."

Diddy stared off into space, completely oblivious to the two squirrels Dodo had tamed and named Oliver and Olivia. They had come up on the porch for their afternoon treat of shelled pecans. They sat on the railing, the nuts clasped between their paws as they nibbled daintily. Dodo didn't notice either, her thoughts someplace else. Ducky shrugged as she reached for Dodo's cell phone and pressed in the numbers on the slip of paper that Willie had fetched.

Ducky identified herself to the private detective, then leaned back in the wicker chair to listen. She ended up agreeing to meet him at a seafood restaurant down by the river in an hour.

"Hey, wake up, you two. That was the private detective I hired in N'awlins. He's here in town. He said he has some good news. I'm going to meet him in an hour. We can all go if you want. Actually, that might be a good idea. I would have invited him here, but there's no need to raise red flags where Ben and Darby are concerned. Shake your booties, ladies, and let's see what a *real* private dick can do."

Seeing that the bowl was empty of the pecan delights, Oliver and Olivia waddled across the porch, tapped Dodo's shoes, their version of thanks for the nuts, then scampered off. Any other time, their antics would have brought a smile to Dodo's face. Not that day, though.

"We missed the noonday news," Diddy grumbled as she got out of the wicker rocker.

"There's nothing new, Diddy. Marcus hasn't been found. Finding him would be the only new news."

"Ben seems to be taking this all very well. He's spending all his time with Darby. I don't think he has any plans to go out to the house to talk to Bella."

"Well, that's where you're wrong, Ducky. We have other things to worry about. The twenty-four hours are up, and the FBI is going to be taking over. Now, *that's* something to worry about. You can't lie to those guys. We need to take a trip," Diddy sniffed. Neither Ducky nor Dodo responded to her ominous words.

"What do you think the detective found out?" Diddy asked.

"He didn't say, just that it was good news. He said it

was interesting. I suppose that could mean any number of things. Like maybe he found out where Bella came from. Or, maybe he found some relatives or friends that have loose lips. It could be anything. Whatever it is, it's something he seems to think is important," Ducky said.

Thirty-five minutes later the three women walked into a restaurant called the Barge in the old section of Baton Rouge. It was a seafood restaurant whose nautical decor was not unpleasing. Plus, the Barge had the best fried catfish in all of Louisiana. Ducky looked around for the private detective. When she didn't see him, she motioned to a hard wooden bench near the entrance. "I guess we're early," Ducky said.

Brandon Lautril appeared ten minutes later. He carried a brown folder that he slapped against his long leg as he strode up the walkway leading to the entrance. Ducky's eyes got big and round. He looked every bit as good as he did when she'd met him in New Orleans. She made the introductions. Lautril held the door while they walked inside single file.

Ducky's heart soared when the detective smiled.

The detective got right to the point.

"Mrs. Gunn did work as a nurse's aide at the Ochsner Medical Center for a year. Her background information was bogus. I guess the hospital didn't check up on their employees back then. I went there to see if by chance there were any old employees still working there.

"I hit a streak of good luck when I went to the coffee shop manned by volunteers. One of them remembered

Bella quite clearly. Thirty years ago this volunteer was a candy striper who continued with her volunteer work all these years. She said Bella always used to buy chewing gum and give the girls, meaning the candy stripers, a stick. For some reason she thought that was funny. She said Bella had a friend, a woman named Alice Avery, who was a nurse who is since retired. She said they would have lunch together in the coffee shop almost every day. She said she would do her best to find out the nurse's address or phone number and call me.

"I had the feeling as I was asking around that people knew or knew of Bella but for some reason didn't want to discuss her. It's just a feeling I have, but I always pay attention to feelings like that. While it isn't much, I would like to stay on the case to see what else I can dig up."

The three women nodded in agreement.

"We'd like you to continue, Mr. Lautril."

"Please, call me Brandon, Harriet."

"Mr. . . . Brandon, something's happened. Marcus disappeared yesterday. The news said he was having lunch outdoors. No one is sure if the nurse with him had a spell of some sort or if she just went to sleep. There is speculation that he was kidnapped. It's also possible that he just up and walked away. Mrs. Gunn made an appeal on television for her husband's safe return."

Brandon looked from one to the other of the sisters, his eyes speculative. They returned his gaze without blinking. "Now, I find that very interesting. What do you think happened?"

The three women shrugged in unison. Ducky chose to speak. "Marcus's son Ben came to Baton Rouge for his brother's funeral. He's staying with us."

The detective looked at the three women, a speculative glint in his eye. "Mr. Gunn's disappearance seems . . . rather convenient, given all the confusion that's going on. Do you ladies see it that way?"

Ducky could feel her face growing warm. A sound that could have been a giggle escaped her lips. Dodo kicked her under the table. She sobered instantly. "I suppose you could look at it that way," she said coolly just as she saw the waiter approaching with their food.

The crispy fried catfish platters arrived along with a huge salad bowl, another bowl of okra and corn, and a huge basket of golden corn bread, all served family-style.

"I hear my arteries snapping shut," Brandon quipped.

"This *is* the *light* version," Diddy said as she slid a catfish filet onto her plate. She went light on the okra and corn and heavy on the corn bread. She bypassed the salad altogether.

The foursome ate while making small talk about the weather, the horrendous humidity, and life in Baton Rouge compared to life in New Orleans.

It was three o'clock when Brandon Lautril paid the check, promising to stay in touch.

The Lane sisters settled themselves on the veranda. They sat silently, their respective gazes going to the top of the shoe, where the whine of the machinery could be heard. Ducky proceeded to fan herself with an ornamental fan dangling from the swing. "We need to keep our eyes on those . . . hoodlums up there on that machinery. If they even go near the houses, we call the police and everyone in authority. I don't object to them leveling the outbuildings because the next good wind that comes along will blow them down anyway. But Bella can't be stupid enough to go ahead with demolishing the houses without a permit, can she?"

"*She* might be that stupid, but that man Tigger knows he can lose his contractor's license if he removes even one board from either one of those houses. A provisional license is just that. That's not to say he won't try to pull a fast one. That's why we're sitting out here watching. He can see us watching him, so for now, I think everything is okay," Diddy said.

"I hope Brandon can find out something crucial that will get that woman out of our lives once and for all. He struck me as being extremely competent, Ducky said with a sly smile. If there's anything to find, he'll find it. Our little window of time is dwindling at an alarming rate. I don't like being the voice of doom and gloom, but this whole mess is not looking good for us. I had such high hopes when Darby took Russell's seat on the Preservation Board, but the other members have been brainwashed by Bella."

"Stop it, Ducky! It's not over till it's over. Things can still turn around. My, God, they *have* to turn around. I cannot believe *that woman* got the best of us. If Brandon and Marcus don't come through for us, we're dead in the water," Dodo said.

"You forgot about the FBI. The twenty-four hours are up. Bella will insist they look into her husband's disappearance. Even if she didn't insist, the police will have called them in," Ducky said as she fanned herself furiously.

The sisters sat silently, each busy with her own thoughts. The clatter from the top of the shoe mixed with the loud rap music irritated them, but there was nothing they could do about it.

Dodo finally broke the long silence.

"Now that the kids are gone, why don't you call Trixie using the phone card. Ask if you can talk to Marcus yourself just to make sure he really is okay. You know you've been dying to speak with him," Dodo teased. Diddy obediently trotted off.

On the front porch, Ducky looked at her sister. "We're no match for the FBI, Dodo, I guess you know that. We must have been crazy to do what we did. We didn't think it through. That's what happens when you get old. You lose your edge," Ducky said pitifully, wringing her hands in agitation.

"Speak for yourself, I haven't lost my edge. We might be able to *fool* them, though. I never thought I'd live to see the day when I'd say our old age might serve us in good stead. We'll need to mention our age from time to time. All we need to do is act vague, hard of hearing, and maybe drool a little. Severe memory loss should work well. I wonder if the *fibbies*, that's what they call FBI agents, call to make an appointment before they show up. Maybe they'll get frustrated and leave us alone. If not, we suck it up, then split for parts unknown. I have no intention of going to jail for Marcus Gunn after what he did to our sister. Why don't you bring out some snacks. I'm starving. We need some more beer, too. It's your turn, Ducky. Bring the tub and fill it with ice from the ice maker."

Diddy returned with Ducky, each holding a bowl of snack chips. "Trixie and Fred don't think Marcus's speech is clear enough to make the call yet. I talked to him myself, and I agree. By tomorrow most of the sedatives should be out of his system. He . . . he thanked us for . . . for *snatching* him. He was laughing. Do you believe that?"

"That's mighty good of him," Dodo snapped.

"Yeah, mighty good," Ducky agreed.

"Now what?" Diddy asked as she flopped down on one of the wicker rockers.

"Now we sit here and wait for something to happen," Dodo replied.

The time was four-thirty in the afternoon, twenty-eight and a half hours since the sisters snatched Marcus Gunn.

15

Russell Gunn's girlfriend Claire opened the door of the town house to Darby and Ben. She offered up a wan smile. "Before you ask, I'm okay. I'm going to the YWCA to take a quilting class. It's something to do. Jason and Mickey are in the study waiting for you. If you leave before I get back, lock the door, okay? I might go with some of the girls to get a drink or maybe coffee. It's just more hours to kill, so I don't have to think. By the way, how's Willie?"

"Willie's fine. Do what you have to do, Claire. I'll call you in the morning, and we'll talk. If you're up for breakfast, let me know."

Jason and Mickey looked like the computer nerds they were. Tall, lanky, sloppy dressers, eyeglasses, and long, skinny fingers. They were playing a computer game when Darby and Ben walked into the office. They clicked off the game and nodded at the introductions. Then they listened attentively to Ben's instructions. "Can you do it?"

Both young men, nineteen if they were a day, shrugged. Both flexed their fingers as they sat down at Russell's computer. The one named Mickey hooked up his laptop, then fanned out the papers Ben had provided.

"Sorry about Russ, man. He was a good friend." Ben nodded. "Some popcorn and a couple of beers would taste real good right now," the one named Jason said. "Not to be rude or anything, but we work best with no distractions."

"I guess that means you want us to disappear after we fetch the popcorn and beer, is that it?" Ben asked. There was no response, the two young men were locked in another world, one that didn't include Ben or Darby.

In the kitchen, Darby went to the small pantry for the popcorn. Sensing Ben's eyes on her as she moved easily around the kitchen, she said, "I was always the one who made the popcorn. Claire made the egg rolls, the kind you buy frozen and heat in the oven, and Russ opened the beer. Then we'd watch videos. It seems like so long ago."

Ben opened the refrigerator expecting to see empty shelves, forgetting that Claire had already moved in. Instead he saw a roasted chicken, a ham, all kinds of vegetables and fruit, milk, and juice. The shelves on the door were full of wine and Lane beer. He uncapped two bottles and set them on a tray. "Do you think those two guys are going to have any luck?" he asked.

Darby slit the popcorn bag with a knife, waiting for the steam to escape before she poured it into a bowl that was shaped like a watermelon. "I bought this bowl for Russ so he'd have some color in the kitchen." Her voice was so sad, Ben blinked. "But to answer your question, I don't know. The one named Mickey hacked into the Pentagon's mainframe somehow one time. According to Russ, he didn't look at a thing, he got out as quick as he got in, but he did manage to breach their security. I guess it will depend on what kind of firewalls are in place to prevent hacking. I'm sure their safety programs are good but not on the caliber of the Pentagon. Like Russ always said, there's always a back door to those programs, you just have to know how to open it. If there is a way for them to access the donor list of the recipients who received Russ's organs, these guys will find it. It's personal for them because they adored Russ."

Ben took the tray and carried it into Russell's study. Neither young man looked up, keeping their eyes glued to the huge flatscreens in front of them, their fingers tapping ninety words per minute. He closed the door when he left.

Back in the kitchen he found Darby wiping at her eyes with a kitchen towel. Ben didn't know what to do, so he sat down and stared at Darby across the table. He, too, felt like crying. He bit down on his lip.

"Want to go for a walk, Ben?"

Ben sighed in relief. He couldn't bear to see Darby cry and welcomed anything that might cheer her up. "Sure. I saw a running trail when we were here the other day; let's check it out."

"Ben, I want to thank you again for helping me in this . . . this endeavor. I know initially you didn't want to find the recipients. I'm so grateful that you were able to come around to my way of thinking. We both need the closure, so let's hope and pray the boys are successful. If they aren't . . . well, I guess we'll just have to live with not knowing."

Ben nodded, not trusting himself to speak.

Hand in hand, they started out. They walked until they were tired, then started back to the recreational area, where they sat down on a wrought-iron bench. Darby laid her head on Ben's shoulder. "I don't want to come back here. It's too painful."

Ben squeezed her hand in sympathy. He felt a lump form in his throat. He tried to clear it, but it seemed lodged for good. Finally, he was able to mumble, "Darby, just so you know, we're really flirting with trouble here, hiring these guys to hack into the donor database. The feds always come into play when someone hacks into something they aren't supposed to. They're right there when one of those hackers spreads a virus. On top of that, the Bureau is going to be looking into my father's disappearance. This little nucleus we're in is going to raise all kinds of flags. I'm all for pouncing on the aunts to get things cleared up. I also had another thought, which was to call Trixie McGuire and ask to speak to my father. Just to see if that will shake some apples from the tree. What do you think, Darby? I know in my gut, and you know, too, that the aunts snatched Dad and stashed him with Trixie and Fred."

A vision of the five old people being led off in handcuffs caused Darby to bolt upright. "I want to say yes, do it, but something tells me we should wait. Call it gut instinct, but I think the aunts can handle it. Stop and think about it, Ben. Even if they did snatch him, and we aren't a hundred percent sure about that, all it will take is your father saying he walked off on his own. The FBI won't be happy with the wasted man-hours, but the aunts will be home free. What you and I and those two guys in the house are doing scares me more."

Darby gasped. "I hadn't once thought about getting caught, Ben. Do you think there's any other way we can find out who got Russ's organs?"

Ben shook his head. "This is the only way, Darby; we've tried finding out the legal way. I can call them off. And then you have to let it go. Really let it go. If Jason and Mickey get caught, we go to jail, that's a given. Our family names won't help us one bit. What do you want to do?"

Darby looked up at the star-filled night, felt the warm summer air on her bare shoulders. Overhead the trees rustled with the faint breeze. If she went to jail it would be a long time before she saw another night like this. She wouldn't be able to lay her head on Ben's shoulder or squeeze his hand. It would be years before she'd be able to walk in a warm spring rain. Her custom-built-dollhouse business would go down the tubes. No one would want to hire a jailbird.

Darby looked up at Ben. "I want to continue. I have to do everything I can to honor Russ's wishes. Well, not wishes exactly. Russ didn't want to be an organ donor. He made a will to the effect and he trusted me to carry out his wishes so that would never happen. Thanks to Bella, that didn't happen. So in that sense, I failed my dearest friend in the whole world. All I know, Ben, is this, I need to know who received his organs so I won't feel like I failed Russ. I don't know if you'll understand this, but when someone trusts you with . . . with their life, you have to take that trust seriously. What kind of person would I be if I just shrugged it off and went about my business? I don't want to spend the rest of my life regretting that I didn't do anything. If we get caught, I'll take all the blame. I won't involve you or the guys."

"Like hell. Those two guys know what they're getting themselves into; they're willing to take the risk for Russ. We're all in this together. Don't get your hopes up, though. Let's go back to the house to see what's going on."

Bella Gunn looked at herself in the vanity mirror. She mentally ticked off the things that were a nightly ritual. Flossing. Night cream. Hair wrap and hairnet to protect her *poufy* hairdo. A spritz of cologne to her nightgown. Another spritz to her pillow, and she was ready for sleep.

Within minutes she was ready to slip between the satin sheets she loved so much. She hoped she would have a dreamless sleep. She hadn't had a good night's sleep in weeks because of all the stress in her life. She sighed wearily as her gaze went to the little white desk in the corner of her room where the forms for the Garden Club rested. How she'd anguished over those forms, Harriet Lane's words echoing in her ears that each and every fact would be checked and double-checked. Just about everything on the form was a lie. Would she be tripped up or not? And, why hadn't Harriet Lane stopped by to pick up the forms like she said she was going to do? Probably because of Marcus's disappearance. Everyone in this damn place was so polite it was sickening.

Bella almost jumped out of her skin when the phone on her night table chimed softly. Harriet Lane calling to apologize about not picking up the forms? Who else could it be? No one ever called her this late in the evening. Finally, on the fifth ring, she reached out to pick up the receiver. "Hello," she said coolly.

"Bella?"

Bella's jaw dropped. She would have recognized her husband's gravelly-sounding voice anywhere. "Marcus!" Her mind raced. What if her line was tapped. Such a ridiculous thought. Why would anyone tap her phone. Still, it paid to be cautious. "Darling, Marcus, where are you? What happened? Did you wander off? The police and the FBI are looking for you. Good Lord, Marcus, you gave us all the fright of our lives."

"Cut the crap, Bella, I don't want to hear it. I'm just calling you to tell you to call off the police. I'm going to call them myself in the morning, so I'll know if you called them or not. What I'm really calling to tell you is this. I finally came to my senses and your threats to expose me no longer scare me. A private detective I hired," he lied, "has told me he located your old nurse friend, and she is prepared to recant what you've been holding over my head for years. It's all over, Bella. I can hear all those dreams of yours gurgling down the drain. Sleep well, Bella."

Bella stared at the phone in her hand. Did she just hear what she thought she heard? Of course she did. Marcus was alive and well and threatening to expose her. She'd be the laughingstock of Baton Rouge. She started to cry. All her dreams were within her grasp. So close. And now with one phone call, those dreams were dashed.

Bella allowed herself five full minutes of panic before she straightened her shoulders. Maybe not. She raced over to the little white desk where she fumbled for her address book. She flipped through the pages until she found the name Alice Avery.

Even though it was close to midnight, Bella

punched out the numbers with a long, painted nail and waited as the phone rang on the other end of the line.

In Rayne, the K-9 was on his feet the minute Marcus Gunn swung his legs over the side of the bed and picked up the phone. He trotted down the hall to Trixie's room, jumped on the bed, and nudged her till she woke up. "What's wrong? Something's wrong, Fred, wake up. What is it, baby? Come on, show me." Flash leaped off the bed and raced down the hall to Marcus's room, Trixie and Fred trailing behind.

"Oh, God, Fred, you don't think . . ."

"Shhh, Trixie, don't even think about it."

Husband and wife stood in the open doorway just as Marcus slammed down the phone. Trixie and Fred both heaved a huge sigh of relief. Marcus turned to look at them, a grim smile on his face. "We need to talk. Let's go down to the kitchen and have some coffee."

"Marcus, it's after midnight. Are you sure you're up to this? Can't it wait till morning?" Fred asked.

"No, it can't wait. I need to clear my conscience, and I damn well need to do it now. I can handle the stairs as long as I take them one at a time. I'm not an invalid. What I am is a damn sorry, poor excuse for a human being."

Trixie shivered in the cool air-conditioning. She stopped in her room for her old flannel robe and slippers while Fred helped Marcus down the long staircase. Flash nuzzled up against her, waiting for Trixie's praise. Trixie didn't disappoint him. She stopped at the top of the stairs and sat down on the first step. Flash sat next to her, his huge head in her lap. "You did real good, big guy. The best thing I ever did in my whole life, aside from marrying Fred, was to buy you from the police department. The day you came into our lives was a special day, so special that Fred and I don't know what we'd do without you." Flash tried to crawl into her lap. He loved it when Trixie's voice dropped to a whisper as though she were telling him a secret. He lifted his head so Trixie could hug him. He whined softly, knowing instinctively that the tears rolling down her cheeks were happy tears. He licked them away and waited for his second hug. After the second hug they always got down to business. This time was no different.

Fred already had the coffee on when Trixie and Flash appeared in the kitchen. Marcus was chomping on a piece of toast as Trixie walked over to the kitchen table and sat down. Flash walked around the kitchen until he was satisfied nothing out of the ordinary was going to happen. Trixie reached across to the shelf and got a dog chew, a greenie, and handed it to the big shepherd. He woofed softly as he carried it over to the door and lay down. He woofed again in thanks.

"Talk, Marcus. This is almost thirty years overdue, so make it good," Trixie said coolly.

"I just called Bella and scared the hell out of her. It

was all a bluff, but I think she fell for it. Now, down to
the nitty-gritty. Bella has been blackmailing me . . ."

Darby's sweet dream of walking through a green
meadow filled with daisies was shattered by Willie's
shrill bark. She bounded out of bed, her eyes open
wide. She listened to see what it was that set Willie off.
Ben reared up, his legs swinging over the side of the
bed. "What? Is the house on fire?"

"I think someone is ringing the doorbell. Who could
be stopping by at eight o'clock in the morning? Even
the aunts know better."

Willie growled when he reached the kitchen door
and let out a bark as Darby pulled back the curtain to reveal Jason and Mickey. They looked tired and bleary-
eyed. Darby welcomed them in and Willie sniffed their
shoes, their pant legs, undoubtedly picking up the scent
from Russell's house. He whined, then growled when
they entered the house. The retriever, the hair on his
back on end, his tail between his legs, stalked both
young men until Darby ordered him to sit.

Ben entered the kitchen, his hair on end just like
Willie's. He looked questioningly at both Mickey and
Jason. Darby busied herself by cleaning the coffeepot
and adding fresh grounds.

"We did it, Mr. Gunn. We broke through around five
this morning. We would have been here sooner, but it
took us three hours to repair the firewall and cover our
tracks so the webmaster doesn't get wise to the breach.

We took a thirty-minute catnap and here we are. Is there anything else you want us to do?"

Darby whirled around. "Are you saying you know . . . that you know who . . . who got Russ's organs?" She started to cry, her shoulders shaking uncontrollably.

"Yeah. Yeah, we got it all."

Ben turned and ran upstairs for his wallet. He grabbed all the cash he had, a couple of hundred dollars, and thundered back down the steps. Mickey saw the money, held up his hands, palms outward. "No way, Mr. Gunn. We didn't do it for the money. Please don't insult us."

Ben stuffed the bills into the pocket of the tee shirt he'd pulled on before coming downstairs. "Thanks." He pumped their hands.

Darby hugged them, and whispered, "Thanks, guys."

"Anytime," Jason whispered in return.

"See you around," they said. A moment later they were gone. Willie barked until Darby got some sliced roast beef out of the refrigerator and gave it to him.

"Should we have our coffee first? Should I make breakfast? Or, should we sit here and read these papers. Oh, God, I never thought they would be able to get this information." Darby started crying again.

Ben took her into his arms. "I have an idea. Let's take a shower and go out to breakfast. We can talk about it, and you can make your decision. Whatever you decide will be all right with me. I don't think we should tell anybody about this. That means the aunts, Trixie and Fred, or Claire. We need to agree on that, okay?"

Darby nodded. "You're right. Okay, you shower first. I'll shower down here. Oh, look, the aunts have company. They don't usually get company this early in the morning. Wonder who it is?"

"Who cares? Shake it, Darby, I'm starved."

Darby decided to shake it since she really wasn't that interested in who was visiting the aunts at eight o'clock in the morning. She had other things to think and worry about.

Diddy woke first, startled that she was still on the front porch. She looked over at her two sisters, who, like her, had slept in their chairs. She looked down at her watch and groaned. Eight o'clock. If she looked half as messy as her sisters, she was in bad shape. "Wake up!" she shrilled.

Dodo jumped to her feet, startled and a bit disoriented. Ducky half rolled off her chair before she managed to slide backward.

"I should kill you for screeching like that," Dodo said.

"Yeah, she should kill you. What the hell is wrong with you, Diddy? I can't believe we slept out here all night." Ducky groaned as she rubbed her lower back.

"We have company," Diddy hissed. "No one in Baton Rouge wears that kind of suit at this time of year.

And they don't wear sunglasses at eight o'clock in the morning either. I think this might be serious."

"It's the feds. They're cloned to look alike. Let me do the talking, and for God's sake remember what I told you," Dodo snarled as she struggled to wake up fully.

"What? What did you tell us?" Diddy wailed.

"Act stupid," Dodo hissed in return. "That shouldn't be too hard."

The two men looked alike, meaning they were tall, slim, and dressed in suits with white shirts and striped ties. "FBI. I'm Special Agent Drew Warner, and this is Special Agent John Stephens."

"Yeah, right, and I'm Madonna. This," Dodo said, pointing to Diddy, "is Cher, and this," she continued, pointing to Ducky, "is Barbara Walters. Do you think we're stupid? FBI my foot. You're from our competitor, Fine Beer, Inc. FBI, get it? Don't even bother trying to deny it. I have to admit, you guys have some nerve to come here. Everyone knows you're floundering. No one wants beer that's made in one central location. Your operation is nothing more than a fad. Our beer is our beer, and the family plans on keeping it that way. That's another way of saying we don't want to buy your rinky-dink operation on Canal Street, so stop asking and buzz off. Now, get off our property before I call the cops."

Diddy, remembering her instructions, let her head roll to the side, her right arm dangling in the tub of melted ice. She picked up one of the empty beer bottles and blew into it for no good reason. Then she closed one eye and squinted into the empty bottle before she dropped it back in the tub. She wiped her nose on her sleeve. She wanted to scream her head off, but Ducky took that moment to slide off the chair onto the floor. She started to laugh.

Dodo turned around to stare at her sisters. It was hard not to laugh, too. She turned back to the agents. "It's early. We don't usually get up till noon. Please leave."

"We are not from . . . Fine Beer, Inc. We're from the FBI. Federal Bureau of Investigation." One of the "twins" flashed a badge for Dodo's benefit.

"I'm still Madonna. I still don't believe you. But just in case you are who you say you are, you should go after those imbeciles who thought they were going to put Lane Beer out of business by brewing beer on a storefront. Ha! Now they want us to buy them out. Ha!"

The second agent whipped out a small notebook. He shook his head as though to clear away a bad image. "Which one of you ladies is Harriet Lane?"

"Me! I am Harriet Lane. I was Harriet Lane when you woke me up," Ducky trilled as she rolled over on her stomach and proceeded to kick her legs up and down. "My friends call me Ducky, but you can call me Harriet," Ducky trilled again.

The agent winced as he scribbled in his notebook. "Which one of you is Vivian Lane?"

"Why do you want to know?" Diddy said as she up-ended another empty beer bottle. Instead of putting it back into the tub she said, "Why don't we all play spin the bottle? We haven't played that since . . . since last night. Actually, I'm Barbara Walters, but you can call me Diddy. No, no, just call me BaBa."

"I guess that must mean you're Lydia Lane," the agent with the notebook said, pointing his pen at Dodo.

"Aka Madonna. You aren't fooling us one little bit. Now, if you don't get off this porch, I'm going to have to *take you out* myself."

The jaws of both agents dropped as Dodo did a high pirouette and let loose with a wild, wicked, "Yeow!" Her arms and feet went in different directions as she socked one-two punches in all directions. When the agents' jaws dropped even farther, Dodo said, "I could kill you both in thirty seconds. What's it gonna be? You can be arrested for impersonating officers of the law."

The agents looked at each other. "Just out of curiosity, ma'am, what do you think we'll be doing while you're *trying* to kill us?" He sounded like he really wanted to know, infuriating Dodo. Sometimes people didn't take her seriously.

"Dying," Dodo said dryly. "There won't be a mark on you either. Are you going to leave, or should I bring it to a test?"

"A test, a test!" Diddy and Ducky squealed in unison. "We haven't had a test in a long time. Can you do it in twenty-five seconds? I'll give you a hundred bucks if you can do it in twenty-five seconds," Ducky said, gazing at the bloodred polish on her toenails.

"Two hundred if you can do it in twenty seconds," Diddy chirped.

"How about fifteen?" Dodo shouted.

Both agents scampered down the steps and ran to the top of the Horseshoe. The sisters ran into the house and collapsed on the floor.

"They're just going to come back," Ducky gurgled.

"We're crazy," Diddy cried.

"No, we're not crazy. We *fooled* the FBI. We really did!"

16

❧

Brandon Lautril rarely if ever made a mistake but he was thinking he'd just made the Queen Mother of all mistakes where this case was concerned. He should have left his position in the oleander bushes where he'd been hiding all night long before it got light out. Now there was no way to sneak away without being seen. If the gardener showed up, the police would be called, at which point he would have to explain why he was dressed all in black, complete with a black watch cap to cover his silvery hair, and hiding in Mrs. Gunn's bushes. He chastised himself for being so sloppy.

He looked down at his watch: six-fifty. Any minute now, the day workers who saw to Bella Gunn's wants and desires would be arriving.

He watched then as four different cars chugged up the hill and drove around to the back of the house. He waited five more minutes to see if there were any stragglers. Time to make his move and slither his way down the hill, hoping against hope that he wasn't spotted. Just as he made his decision he saw a gaggle of women walking up the driveway, when the front door opened to reveal Bella Gunn carrying a bright red satchel. In her haste to get down the steps carrying the heavy bag, she missed a step and landed on her tush, her long skinny legs shooting out in front of her. He heard her let loose a string of obscenities as she tried to right herself. That's when she noticed the gaggle of women staring at her.

Brandon continued to watch, mesmerized from his position in the oleanders.

For one second, Bella Gunn thought she'd died and went to hell as the women approached her. She could tell they'd seen her fall, heard the rough language that spewed from her mouth. How to make this right? "It's a little early to be visiting, isn't it, Honoria?"

"Ah . . . well, yes, it is, but I like to get an early start on the day. We thought we would pick up the forms since Harriet wasn't able to stop by yesterday."

"Forms? Is that what you said? My husband . . . and you want . . . I can't . . ."

Marcus Gunn's pride and joy—his Bentley—suddenly appeared, driven by the gardener. He got out and held the door open for Bella, who just looked at him. "Where's the chauffeur?" she screeched.

The gardener shrugged. "He isn't here."

Bella's cheeks flamed. She didn't have a clue how to drive the Bentley. She was already embarrassed beyond tears. She would be humiliated beyond belief if she climbed into the backseat and . . . and sat there waiting for a chauffeur who might or might not show up. She steeled herself to stare at the women, who were looking at her like she had sprouted a second head. Was there a way to make this right? Could she still salvage . . . ?

"Obviously, we've come at a bad time, Mrs. Gunn. We . . . we'll be in touch," Honoria said coolly.

"What about the forms?" Bella said just as coolly.

"Like I said, we'll be in touch. You understand, the forms are just for nomination."

"Oh, I see. Suddenly you're changing your mind. My husband . . . you know what, Honoria, screw your forms, screw you, and screw this town," she shouted to the women's retreating backs. The women ignored her as they trooped down the hill.

"Take this stupid car back to the garage and fetch my Cadillac," Bella shouted to the frightened gardener.

Angry tears streamed down Bella's cheeks as she kicked out at the red satchel. The minute the Cadillac came to a stop, she slung the red case into the backseat and climbed behind the wheel. She sped off, gravel spurting in all directions.

Brandon waited for a good ten minutes before he

stepped out to the driveway and sauntered down the hill to where his car waited.

Darby stood by the kitchen window, her eyes going to the gazebo where, as a child, she had played with Russ from sunup to sundown. Russ always looked out for her, protected her. She closed her eyes and saw a ten-year-old Russ with a butterfly on his index finger. His face was full of awe at the delicate yellow butterfly. "Look," he whispered, "it trusts me. It knows I won't hurt it. Miss McInerny said it's important to trust people. Do you trust me, Darby?" She remembered how her head bobbed up and down. "That's good because I trust you more than any person in the whole world." A second later, Russ had walked over to one of the camellia bushes to transfer the butterfly to one of the shiny, waxy leaves.

Darby blinked and walked back to the table. She squared her shoulders, wiped at her eyes again, sniffed, and reached for the stack of printouts. "I promised never to betray your trust but through no fault of my own, that's exactly what I did. I don't know if reading these papers can make things right or not. I have to go with my heart here."

She read slowly and carefully, absorbing everything she read. When she was finished, she had the names of the recipients, the names of the hospitals where the transplants were performed, and the names of the surgeons who performed the operations. What she didn't have was the family members' names or the home addresses. Maybe Mickey and Jason could get that information for her.

Darby reached behind her for the phone. She dialed Russ's old number from memory. She knew Claire would be up, and she was. She explained what she needed. It was her way of keeping Claire in the loop. Claire said she would take care of it. They made small talk for a few minutes, then Darby hung up the phone.

Darby's mind wandered to the day at hand. A smile tugged at the corners of her mouth when she thought about Ben. She was in love. Big surprise. She'd always been in love with Ben Gunn. Russ had known it, too. Once he'd said that Ben was her destiny but she was too dumb to know it. *Well, I know it now, and you were right, Russ,* she thought. Would Ben have come back into her life if Russ hadn't died? Probably not. Then again, maybe when she was too old to care anymore, he might appear.

She thought about the aunts then. How lonely they were with no men in their lives. Not that a man made a woman's life complete. They seemed content, yet she knew something was missing. Ducky was searching for companionship and her youth. Diddy still loved Marcus Gunn and would probably go to her grave never having loved another man. Then there was Dodo and the mystery of her life. There was more to Dodo's life than any of them knew. She felt it in her heart.

What would marriage to Ben be like? Wonderful,

she decided. He wanted what she wanted: a large family, pets, friends, a job to love. Just last night he'd said he couldn't wait to have a family Christmas. A real family Christmas, where a dog knocked down the Christmas tree, peed on the carpet, and bounded up and down the steps following the kids everywhere they went. He wanted the smells of a home, things baking in the oven, hampers full of clothes waiting to be washed. What he wanted, he said, was disarray. He didn't want anything perfect. He wanted the screen door to squeak, wanted the windows to stick, the lights to burn out, and the toilets to stop up. He wanted to be with her when she picked out just the right couch that would comfortably fit the two of them and the dogs—until the kids came along. Maybe even a leaky roof. He'd laughed. She'd agreed with him, and he'd hugged her so tight she had to squeal to be set free. Then they'd made love that was so sweet, so gentle, she never wanted it to stop.

Yessirree, she loved Ben Gunn. With all her heart. Tears rolled down her cheeks. And all this happiness and wonderment was happening because her best friend had died. All because Russ was no longer with them. There were no other options. She had to do what she had to do.

Darby turned around. Standing in the kitchen doorway, his hair tousled, his eyes full of love, Ben beckoned her to him. She stepped into his arms. "I settled it with myself and with Russell. I know what I have to do.

When it's my turn to go *up there,* I don't want to have to make explanations to Russ. I want him to know he didn't make a mistake in trusting me."

Ben kissed her lightly on the cheek. "Wise choice," was all he said.

Clean, dressed, and coiffed, the three sisters met up in Diddy's kitchen. It was a place of comfort for the three of them, filled with treasures from their youth and their lives in general. Diddy was the sentimental one of the three, the nester, the one they came to when they needed hot tea and comfort. Diddy was also the most motherly of the trio.

When Ducky and Dodo walked into the kitchen it was like they were walking back into their past. The scarred oak table with the colorful place mats was welcoming. Diddy had never made any effort to sand out the gouges or the scars, saying if she did that the table and chairs would have no character, and, besides, their mother and father shared their first married meal at this very table. The centerpiece was a huge ceramic milk jug full of brilliant purple crepe myrtles. Diddy was also the gardener of the three, which made Ducky and Dodo wonder from time to time what exactly they were good at.

Dodo flopped down. "I'm tired. We need to get our lives squared away so we can get back to normal. I might just be able to make Japan by the skin of my teeth."

Ducky's eyebrows shot upward. Today she had taken

the time to put on makeup, and she was dressed in a simple, sleeveless, persimmon-colored dress. Her curly hair was piled high on her head. She looked good, she thought as she stared at her reflection in the glass on the microwave oven door.

Diddy was wearing a pristine white apron over a simple shirtwaist dress as she bustled about the kitchen. "We're having eggs Benedict and ham. I have some cinnamon rolls baking in the oven. I know how you like cinnamon rolls, Dodo."

"By the way, I cleaned up the front porch, thank you very much."

"It's your porch, you clean it," Diddy snapped. "Just like this kitchen is mine, and I will clean it when I'm done cooking. Stop whining, Dodo."

The sisters glared at one another and were still glaring when the doorbell rang.

Diddy whirled around. "Oh, God, the FBI can't be back that quick!"

"Right," Dodo said, marching to the front door. A scowl on her face, she opened the door with a flourish. She took a step backward when she saw Brandon Lautril standing on the other side of the screen door. "Please, come in. We were just getting ready to have breakfast. My sister is making eggs Benedict."

The detective smiled. "My favorite breakfast in the whole world. I hope you're inviting me. I also have some excellent breakfast conversation I can share."

"By all means," Dodo said, opening the door for the

detective and calling out that they had a guest for breakfast. She noticed Ducky's face turn pink as she led the detective into the kitchen.

Diddy quickly set another place at the table.

"Good morning, ladies. Appreciate the offer of breakfast. Please excuse my appearance," he said, motioning to his wrinkled clothing and the stubble on his face. "I spent the night in the bushes at the Gunn's house. I was about to leave this morning when a group of ladies arrived just as Bella was coming out the door carrying a red satchel. It looked rather heavy. She took a misstep and landed on her derriere. She let loose with some very choice words that the other ladies heard. It went from bad to worse. To say Mrs. Gunn was embarrassed and humiliated would be putting it mildly. The ladies said they came for the forms Harriet didn't pick up. When they left they said they would be in touch. Mrs. Gunn streaked off in a Cadillac. I waited a few minutes and then I left. By the way, last night Alice Avery, the hospital volunteer I told you about, called me. This is just gut instinct, but I think that's where Bella Gunn went this morning."

Diddy served them one by one, then sat down with her own plate.

"Well, she's planning on going somewhere if she packed a bag. Maybe she sees things closing in on her and went to this Alice Avery person to warn her to keep whatever secrets she knows to herself. Or . . . maybe to make those secrets known. This is just my opinion, but I think she's coming back. I think you should stake out her house to see what her next move is," Dodo said.

Ducky and Diddy agreed.

"Then that's what I'll do.

Dodo suddenly jumped up and clapped her hands. "Did you hear what this man just said? He said Bella is . . . Bella is leaving. That means all that nastiness up at the shoe will stop. That's what it means, isn't it?"

Brandon stood up. "I think you might be right, Miss Lane. I'm going to go back to the inn to shower and change. I'll go back to Mrs. Gunn's house and stake it out. I'll call Miss Avery on my cell while I'm at the inn. How long do you want me to stake out the Gunn house?"

Dodo looked over at her sister. "As long as it takes. Ducky, why don't you keep Brandon company. It must be terribly boring to be on a stakeout. You might have some insight to contribute if things get . . . you know, hairy, if Bella returns. You might have to follow Bella if she decides to light out for good. Ducky is good company, Brandon. Don't you agree, Diddy?"

"Oh, by all means," Diddy said.

Ducky flushed again. What she really wanted to do was get up and hug her sisters for their suggestion. "Well, if you're sure you don't need me here, I'll be glad to go if you don't mind, Brandon."

It was Lautril's turn to flush. "I'll be glad of the company. I'll swing by and pick you up after I get cleaned up. It was a wonderful breakfast, Miss Diddy. Thank you."

"Put some perfume on," Diddy said to her sister.

"Get rid of those Birkenstocks and put on those slutty shoes you always wear. Play it cool, and you might be able to snag that guy," Dodo said.

Ducky huffed and puffed. "What makes you think . . ."

"Oh, get off it, Ducky. You're as transparent as cellophane. I think he has the hots for you. Don't you think so, Diddy?"

"I do, I do," Diddy said.

Ducky felt pleased with her sisters' assessment of the private detective's feelings. "What are you two going to do? This might take all day. You aren't up to anything, are you?" she asked suspiciously.

Dodo threw her hands up in the air. "We're going to sit here and wait for the FBI to show up. Then we'll decide if we should take a trip to Rayne or not. That's it. We have your cell phone number. If things change, we'll call you."

"The kids . . ."

"In case you haven't noticed, Ducky, they are busy with each other. Go! Put on your perfume and don't forget the shoes. I think that private dick is a leg man for some reason. Do you agree, Diddy?"

"Absolutely. A leg man. Definitely." She wondered what being a leg man meant. She promised herself to get out more.

Ducky grimaced. "There are days when I love you two, and days when I hate the both of you. Today I love you."

Diddy and Dodo shrugged before they separated to start their day.

Five days later, Bella Gunn walked into the Natchez Savings and Loan, a thick, heavy accordion-pleated folder under her arm. Years ago, eighteen years to be exact, she'd made a trip here to open several accounts in person. She'd fed those accounts regularly but had never been back. Eighteen years ago she'd also purchased a house, paying cash. It was a steal, actually, the owner dying suddenly, the heirs wanting to settle the estate immediately. Cash had been king that day. If she'd been religious, she would have crossed herself, but since she wasn't, she merely congratulated herself for thinking ahead to a time when she might need to retreat to a safe haven. That time had arrived.

She was now Margaret Puckett, but even that wasn't her birth name. There were days when she couldn't remember what her real name was. She'd learned a thing or two by reading T. F. Dingle books, Marcus's favorite author. Crime in all forms, according to T. F. Dingle, worked. Until you got caught. Only the murderers got caught in Dingle's books, never the clever, wily con artists. However, she considered herself more of an entrepreneur than a wily con artist.

Bella made her way over to one of the small glass-fronted rooms where a bank officer sat. He looked bored as he stared at the computer terminal in front of him. Well, she would liven up his day in a few minutes.

Bella looked around, surprised that nothing had changed in the bank in eighteen years. The furniture looked the same, even the rubber plants spaced throughout the lobby looked the same. While the bank officer looked the same, just older, she knew he wouldn't remember her. Today, she looked totally different from the way she'd looked eighteen years ago. She wore a brown wig and wire-rimmed glasses that were nothing more than window glass. She'd bought them at Iverson's Drugstore the day she'd arrived in Natchez. The wig was from a catalog and bought years ago. She'd masked her thinness by layering her clothes. The sensible inch-high shoes gave her a slightly frumpy look. No sense in advertising her arrival on the off chance the bank officer or someone else in the bank had seen the news, assuming people in Natchez were interested enough in what went on in Baton Rouge, Louisiana.

Bella seated herself demurely, crossing her ankles and looking straight at the bank officer. "I need to avail myself of your help this morning, sir."

"That's what I'm here for, ma'am."

Bella hated to be called ma'am. Really hated it. She smiled, her large teeth gleaming like polished pearls.

The meeting lasted exactly fifty-five minutes. Print-outs of her holdings were now safe and secure inside the folder.

The bank officer escorted Bella across the lobby and held the door for her. He beamed with pleasure.

A very wealthy, satisfied Bella Gunn smiled again, thanked the bank officer, and made her way to her new car, a Mercedes-Benz.

Humming under her breath, Bella thought about all the really big numbers in her accounts. Years ago the bank didn't have an investment division, now they did. All her eggs were now in one basket, all fourteen million of them. Invested wisely, the bank officer had told her she could expect a return of close to a million dollars a year and never have to touch her principal. Then there were the jewels that were worth another couple of million.

"Eat your heart out, Marcus," she murmured as she sailed down the road in the brand-new Mercedes that got eleven miles to the gallon.

Margaret Puckett allowed herself a few minutes to grieve for Bella Gunn and all she had endured. She wondered if she would ever be able to forget the humiliating experience in her driveway. To be so close to all her dreams and desires and to suddenly have them ripped away from her at the eleventh hour was almost incomprehensible. The haughty disdainful looks on the members' faces when she'd cursed aloud were seared into her brain. Even now, she cringed when she thought about it. But it had happened, and she had to live with it.

What bothered her more than anything was knowing she would be fodder for town discussions forever and ever. Well, she had to live with that, too.

Taking up residence here in Natchez would allow her to start over and not make the same mistakes she'd made in Baton Rouge.

Anything and everything was possible if you put your mind to the task.

17

The trio in the kitchen watched the weatherman drone on about the possibility of inclement weather throughout the day with flash flooding expected in certain areas. Trixie turned off the TV and looked across the room at her husband and Marcus Gunn. "Now, I want you to drive carefully. There's no hurry to get Marcus back to Baton Rouge. If the weather turns bad, Fred, I want you to spend the night and come back tomorrow. I can handle the new dogs when they get here this afternoon. Jane promised to be here in a few hours, so I don't want you worrying about things here at the farm."

Fred hitched his suspenders up over his ample stomach. He grinned, looking more like Santa Claus than he did Fred McGuire. "I know the drill, Trixie. Don't go over the speed limit. Stop for gas. Go to the bathroom. Don't miss the turnoff because I'm too busy blabbing to Marcus. Go straight to Diddy's house and park in the alley. I will remember to tell Diddy that you ordered her a new battery-operated wheelbarrow from the Frontgate catalog, and it should arrive in a few days because you are keeping the one you brought here along with Marcus. Did I get it all?" he asked with a twinkle in his eye.

Trixie pretended to grumble. "I guess so. Marcus . . . I don't know what to say to you. You have a rough road ahead, and I wish you the best. Be sure to call me when you arrive."

Marcus held out his arms to Trixie. One look at his miserable face allowed her to step forward. He hugged her. "I don't know how to thank you. Somehow, I'll find a way."

"It's not me you need to thank, Marcus. It was Dodo, Diddy, and Ducky who made it all happen. Good luck."

Marcus stooped over, wiped at his eyes as he stroked Flash's big head. "You know what, big guy, you were the frosting on this cake." He held out his hand, and Flash offered up his paw. The K-9 offered up a shrill bark as the two men walked out the door. He danced around, pawed at Trixie's leg, and barked again.

"He doesn't need us anymore, Flash. He's going home." Flash continued to bark and prance.

Trixie sighed, knowing there was only one way to divert Flash. "Okay, time to go to work! Get your gear while I change into my uniform." This time Flash's bark was joyful as he raced across the kitchen to the chest under the big window. His bulletproof vest was inside. He used his snout to open the lid, pawed it backward, and dragged out the vest. He trembled with excitement, Marcus Gunn a memory.

Dodo looked up from the computer she was using when her sister Diddy appeared in the doorway. Dodo didn't know if she should laugh or cry.

"Go on, say it! Go on, Dodo. Feel free to tell me I look like a clown. I know I do. Nothing fits. I look like a stuffed sausage. It's been years since I used this much makeup. Face it, at seventy, makeup doesn't do much. If anything, it just accentuates the problems. I cut my hair myself," she volunteered.

"Why, Diddy? Why are you doing this? Do you seriously believe Marcus expects you to look like you did when you two were in love a hundred years ago? Did you by any chance notice how much *he* has changed? The way he looked didn't bother you, so why do you think the way you look will bother him? He saw you, remember. Go back to your house, and when you come back here you better look like my sister Diddy, not some floozie."

"Are you sure, Dodo?"

"Diddy, you look silly. I know what you're trying to do. You can't fight the clock and the calendar. You are what you are. Don't try to pretend to be something you're not. A lot of years have gone by," Dodo said gently. "Don't cry, Diddy. Things are what they are and can't be changed. All we can do is accept it and hope for the best."

Dodo swiveled around in her ergonomic chair and put her feet up on the desk. She was looking straight at the photographs on the wall above the computer. Her eyes were sad. So many years ago. Suddenly the letter she had been typing didn't seem like such a good idea. There was never a response to the letters, so why bother. She didn't bother to consider the fact that she never put a return address on any of them. She hit the DEL key and turned off the computer.

Dodo sat perfectly still, her breathing slow and steady as she let her mind go back in time to the day she'd given birth to the boy in the pictures. How happy she'd been. All she wanted to do was shout the news to the heavens, but the Japanese didn't do things like that. And her family back in the States would never accept a child that was half-Japanese. It was a different time back then. Secretly, she thought Ducky and Diddy might have suspected something wasn't quite right in her life. They'd grilled her, quizzed her, argued with her, then fought with her about how much time she spent in Japan. But that was then, and this was now. The little boy in the pictures was now thirty-five years old, and he still didn't know she was his mother. And that was by her choice. She didn't want him tainted as he grew up. A white mother of a half-Japanese boy simply wasn't acceptable back then. In later years, when society changed a little, she saw no reason to upset her son's life. Fortunately for her, she had the wherewithal to pay someone to take care of her son and raise him the way all Japanese parents raised their children.

Over the years she wrote letters, sent money and gifts, and visited when she could. The boy, a young man now, thought of her as a family friend of the aunts who raised him. Many times she'd suspected that he knew she was more than a friend, but he never acted anything but respectful of the American lady who cared about him. The questions she saw in his eyes remained but were never voiced.

There were times when she thought she'd done the right thing and other times when she knew she'd made the biggest mistake of her life for denying her son a mother's love.

Dodo was jarred from her reverie when Diddy appeared in the doorway. She looked like Diddy, dressed in a sky-blue shirtwaist dress. She wore pearls, and her snow-white hair was pulled back into a prim bun, but her new cut allowed stray tendrils to frame and soften her round face. Her blue eyes twinkled behind the wire-rimmed glasses. "Let's just say I had a minor senior moment. Thanks for talking some sense into me." A sound escaped her lips. It sounded suspiciously like a childish giggle.

Dodo smiled. "That's more like it. How are dinner preparations going?"

Diddy sat down on a webbed red plastic chair across from her sister. "Everything is under control. The turkey's roasting. It will all be ready for dinner at seven. We're having Thanksgiving a little early this year. That means we're having all the trimmings." She looked down at her hands, glad she'd gotten rid of the bloodred nail polish. "Dodo, I'd like to return the favor. If you hadn't told me how silly I looked, I would have made a fool of myself." She deliberately raised her eyes to stare at the photographs on the wall above the computer. Then she looked pointedly at her sister. "I think I speak for Ducky as well as myself when I say it's about time for us to meet our nephew. No, no, don't say anything, Dodo. We just want you to think about it. We'd both be willing to go to Japan if that's what it takes. Oh, Dodo, we've known . . . *forever*. When and if you're ready, Ducky and I are here for you."

Dodo's eyes grew misty. "How did . . ."

"I have my ways. Your mistake was thinking I just sat in my house making quilts to sell on eBay, and eating red-velvet cake and fried chicken. I also know your attic is full of the quilts because you bought them all. I'm every bit as good on the computer as you are."

Dodo's eyes were wild as she looked around her small office, then at her sister. Her voice was fierce when she said, "I'm not admitting to anything, but I will think about what you said. Furthermore, Diddy, my attic is not full of your quilts, which, by the way are beautiful. I donate them every year to the Christmas Bazaar. One of them fetched over two thousand dollars."

"I know." Diddy laughed. "Let's see what Ducky and that private detective are doing."

"Oh, no, I'm not sticking my nose into *that* business," Dodo responded with a laugh.

Dodo and Diddy turned toward the door when they heard their names called. "It's Ducky! Oh, dear, something must have happened."

Ducky pushed open the screen door and took her seat on one of the rockers. Her sisters looked at her expectantly.

Ducky flushed. "My place is here with you two. I felt . . . well, it didn't feel right being with Brandon under the circumstances. I did invite him for a late dinner. I said seven o'clock. Of course, if he's still on his stakeout, he won't be joining us."

"Did you have sex with him, Ducky? Is that why he's not giving up, why he's coming to dinner?" Dodo blurted.

Startled, Ducky looked at her sister, flushing a bright pink. "None of your damn business, Dodo. Like I really had time!" she quipped.

"Will you two stop it. I can't stand all these squabbles, and nothing is ever solved." Ever the peacemaker, Diddy got up and started to pace the wide veranda. Since all the verandas on the shoe were the same, she felt like she was on her own veranda. She felt happy, sad, and anxious all at the same time. She wished she knew what the future held for all of them. She was sick and tired of going through life living off her memories. With whatever time she had left in her life she wanted to *live*. She sat down on the top step and hugged her knees, the wide overhang protecting her from the rain. Dodo looked over at Ducky. "You're right, your life is none of my business. I'm sorry. I really am sorry, Ducky. These last two weeks have turned me into someone I don't even like anymore. Do you . . . care about Brandon?"

"Yes."

"Does he care about you?" Dodo asked carefully.

"He said he does. I don't have a real good track record when it comes to men, Dodo."

Dodo smiled. "This time might be the charm. If it's what you want, I hope it comes to pass. I hear a car. Diddy, can you see if someone turned into the alley?"

"Yes, it's Fred. He tooted the horn. Should we go to the alley with an umbrella?"

"No," Ducky and Diddy said in unison.

"I'm not extending myself for Marcus one whit more until we hear his story. He has a lot of explaining to do before I can be civil to him. I don't care if you still have feelings for him or not, Diddy. Just keep thinking about those three kids we raised, who were his responsibility," Ducky said heatedly. Dodo's head bobbed up and down in agreement.

"Here they come, and Fred has an umbrella," Diddy said, getting up from the steps. "And here come Ben and Darby. They don't have an umbrella," Diddy said, her voice full of awe.

"When you're young and in love you don't need an umbrella. You don't need anything but each other," Ducky said softly.

"We're here!" Fred said from the bottom of the steps. A moment later both he and Marcus were on the veranda, hugging and shaking hands. "I have to call Trixie, if you don't mind. Looks like I'll be spending the night, if it's okay." He didn't bother to wait for a response but let himself into the house.

The sisters looked at Marcus and motioned to one of the wicker rockers. He sank down gratefully. He leaned his head back and sighed. "Do you have any idea of how often I've thought of one of these porches? In my mind's eye, I could see the plants, the flowers, the paddle fans. I could actually *feel* the rockers. But it's the scent that I remembered the most. I can smell the river, the marsh, the grass, the jasmine. A person can get drunk just on the scent alone.

"The trees are amazing," he said, opening his eyes. "I always loved the moss dripping down the branches." He stopped talking when he saw his son and Darby running up the steps, drenched to the skin.

Time stood still as Ben looked at his father but made no effort to go to him. His eyes were cold and dark. "*Sir*," he said by way of greeting.

"It's good to see you . . . *son*."

For a moment it looked like Ben was going to argue over the word *son*, but with a nudge from Darby, he simply walked over to a wicker bench and sat down.

Darby shook the old man's hand and went to sit by Ben.

"We were right all along about the aunts' involvement. He looks great. I'm glad he's okay," Ben whispered.

The silence was awkward and uncomfortable. The sisters glared at their guest, even Diddy. Marcus stared off into the distance, his thoughts in the past.

The awkward silence continued until Fred banged the screen door, a bottle of beer in his hand. "Trixie said hello."

Diddy looked at the watch on her wrist. "It's six-thirty. Dinner is at my house this evening. I suggest we all walk over now. Ben, you and Darby put on some dry clothes and bring some for your father. Dodo, get the umbrellas," Diddy said in a take-charge voice. Everyone gaped at her but hastened to do her bidding. Without a second look at Marcus, she snapped her umbrella open and walked down the steps and across the yard to her own house.

Marcus looked perplexed.

Ducky and Dodo looked bewildered but immediately started a search for umbrellas.

Darby and Ben flew down the steps and raced across the yard.

"If you were expecting an open-arms welcome, Marcus, it ain't gonna happen," Fred said as he handed Marcus an umbrella.

Marcus looked up at Fred, who was towering over

him. "Actually, Fred, I wasn't expecting anything. I am hoping they'll allow me to stay on for a few days until I can make other arrangements. Do you think it will happen?"

"For your sake, I hope so. If it doesn't happen, you can go back to Rayne with me in the morning. Ben turned into a mighty fine young man. I wish Trixie and I had a son like him. I'm not sure you deserve a son like him."

Marcus got wearily to his feet. "I'm sure you're right, Fred. Don't worry, I won't force anything. I'm ready if you are."

"Are you feeling all right, Marcus?"

"I'm fine, Fred. Thank you for asking. I'm just overwhelmed at the moment."

A smile worked its way across Marcus's lips as he and Fred let themselves in a side door. Diddy's house rocked with sound; the sisters arguing. *Some things never change,* he thought. Then there was Darby's laughter and his son's rich baritone. He thought about Russell at that moment. *I wonder where Mary is. Someplace in New York, Bella told me not too long ago. I suppose Ben knows.*

The sound emanating from the kitchen came to a sudden halt when Fred and Marcus entered through the swinging door. Fred sniffed appreciatively. He did love a turkey dinner with all the trimmings. He reached out to accept a pile of clothing from Ben, then handed it to Marcus. He pointed to the bathroom off the laundry room. All eyes followed Marcus's slow walk down the narrow hall.

"Everything's ready," Diddy said. "You've been elected to carve, Fred. Ben, you carry the turkey to the table. Darby, you're in charge of the wine. Ducky, I don't want any lumps in those mashed potatoes. Dodo, go easy on the marshmallow in the yams. Dis-perse!"

"Where is Brandon?" Dodo asked as she craned her neck to see if the detective had arrived in the alley.

Ducky shrugged. "He said he'd be here by seven. He said he has great news."

"He's here. He just pulled into the alley. He's looking pretty good from where I'm standing." Dodo grinned.

"You should see him without his clothes on!" For the first time in her life Ducky heard Dodo giggle. "What would you think of me living in N'awlins six months and here six months?"

"If it works for you, it works for me. What do you suppose Diddy meant by too much marshmallow? Guess you found time after all."

"Half a jar, not a whole jar." Ducky smiled from ear to ear when Brandon Lautril walked into the kitchen.

"I hope I'm not too late."

"Right on time." Ducky smiled as she scooped the mashed potatoes into a fine china bowl that had been her grandmother's.

Dodo took a moment to study her sister. She couldn't remember when she had looked so alive, so happy. Her shoulders sagged as she wondered if she'd ever be as happy. Ducky handed the potato bowl to Brandon and pointed to the dining room.

"Dodo, I'd love to go to Japan with you if you'll have me. I always wanted a nephew. Truly, Dodo. Let's not waste any more years, okay? Let's bring him and his family back here," Ducky said.

Dodo's heart swelled. "What about . . . ? "

"Screw them!" Ducky laughed. "We'll make him president of Lane Beer! Chairman of the board, the whole ball of wax! In this town it doesn't get any better than that."

In spite of herself, Dodo laughed. "Okay," she said softly. "Okay."

18

The three Lane sisters were in the kitchen, loading the dishwasher and tidying up. The others remained in the dining room, with their coffee and brandy. Ducky hung up her dish towel as Dodo added the detergent and closed the dishwasher.

"We want to give you a little . . . pep talk," Ducky said. "I saw the way Marcus has been looking at you, Diddy. I don't have a clue as to what he's going to offer up as an explanation for all those lost years. First chance I get I'm going to strangle Trixie and Fred for not telling us. They *said* it was Marcus's place to tell us. Don't let me forget to do that. What I'm trying to say here is, don't be easy, Diddy. He alone screwed up his life and the lives of his children. The three of us picked up the pieces. Just you remember that if he tries to sweet-talk you."

Dodo cleared her throat. It seemed to her all she'd been doing of late was clearing her throat. "Memories, Diddy, are just that, memories. You and I have been living with them way too long. We can't go back to that time in our lives. All we can do is go forward and hope we make the right decisions. Marcus is an old man now, just like we're old women. We're all looking at our mortality, and there's nothing wrong with that even though it's on the scary side. It's the order of things. If you want to forgive Marcus after he tells us whatever it is he's going to tell us, fine. It's Ben and Mary who really count. And don't forget for one minute that he has to answer for Russell. I don't want to see you get schnockered again, Diddy. We have things to do and places to go. Are you getting any of this?"

Diddy squared her plump shoulders, her eyes shooting sparks. "I'm getting *all* of it, Dodo. You two think Marcus wants my seventy-year-old body, wrinkles, warts, and all. You think I'm going to be sappy and fall for whatever he tells us and drop right into his arms. You don't have to worry about me, it's not going to happen. Now, let's go see what the old geezer has to say."

The sisters took their places in the old-fashioned dining room, with its pictures of relatives that dated back years and years. The huge dining-room table sat twelve comfortably, with six extra chairs for special occasions. The china closet and buffet held priceless crystal, exquisite china, and fine linens. Even though it was old-fashioned, the plantation shutters, the green plants, and the ankle-deep carpet made it a pleasant room to break bread with friends and family.

The coffee cups and brandy snifters were empty, the napkins wadded into balls. All eyes turned to Marcus Gunn. If one were into body language, it was clear his audience did not have open minds, especially Ben Gunn. He stared at the portraits of the Lane ancestors. All the men had high pompadours, their faces grim above their stiff-looking suits and starched shirts. The women wore simpering smiles and high-necked dresses. There wasn't one thing warm and fuzzy about any of them. It was a mystery as to how Diddy, Dodo, and even Ducky managed to be so different—warm, caring, and loving. He made a note to talk to Darby about having the aunts' pictures taken so they could hang them in their new house. For when they got married. His heart skipped a beat at the thought of marrying Darby. He swallowed hard and looked across the table at the man who was his father. Such a warm wonderful title. His heart skipped a beat.

Marcus looked around the table, his gaze stopping on Diddy. She eyeballed him, her eyes cold and hard, colder and harder than Ben's, if that was possible.

Marcus took a deep breath and launched into *his* story.

"I think you all know my wife Myrna was my whole life. She gave me three wonderful children. Life here on the shoe couldn't have been more idyllic. Gunn Industries was performing beyond expectations. I was proud of that because I knew in time it would go to my three children. Then Myrna got sick. You, Ducky, Dodo, and Diddy were Myrna's best friends. You know how our world was rocked at the doctor's final diagnosis. We all did everything we could to make her as comfortable as possible. If you remember, toward the end, we had round-the-clock nurses because Myrna said she wanted to die at . . . at home. She begged me on an hourly basis to . . . disconnect her life support. The day came when I couldn't take it anymore. I couldn't stand to see her suffer the way she was suffering. I waited until the nurse went downstairs for her dinner. I was going to do it. Myrna was watching me, begging me to . . . *do it*. I was just about to do what she wanted, but I just couldn't. I turned around to tell Myrna I couldn't end her life like that when the nurse, her name was Alice Avery, walked into the room and demanded to know what I was doing. I think I said something incredibly stupid, like I was just checking to make sure things were all right. I'm sure I looked guilty as hell because I *was* going to do it. I could see she didn't believe me. Myrna backed me up, but she was full of drugs. The next day, Myrna died."

"Dad, Brandon Lautril, the PI the Lane sisters hired, knows where Alice Avery lives. He might be able to convince her to recant her story. She'll clear you," Ben interjected.

Marcus Gunn straightened his shoulders. "No need for that, young man. I'm not afraid of Bella any longer.

It's time, way past the time where I step up to the plate and make things right for my family and friends." He looked over at his son and tried to smile.

All eyes turned to Ben, who let a wide grin rip across his face. "Good going, Pop," he said, using the name he'd called his father as a young child. "We're with you all the way." He reached down and felt Darby's reassuring clasp on his hand.

Marcus cleared his throat and began his story again.

"My world ended when Myrna died. When the nurse packed up her things she drew me aside and said I killed Myrna. She said I disconnected the life support, then when I saw her standing in the doorway, reconnected it. She said she was going to tell the doctor. At that point I didn't even care because I knew I hadn't done anything. For some reason, Alice never did tell the doctor, but she told someone else—Bella—but not until later. It seems Alice went back to work at the hospital where Bella was working as a nurse's aide. They struck up a friendship of sorts, I suppose. Eighteen months to the day of Myrna's death, Bella came to Gunn Industries and asked to speak to me. She told my secretary she wanted to see me about Myrna, so of course I agreed to see her even though I didn't know who she was. I assumed she was a friend of Myrna's."

"Myrna would never have been friends with a snake like Bella," Dodo snapped.

Marcus agreed. "But I still wasn't thinking straight. We were going global, and things were starting to make sense again. The children were being well taken care of by all of you, I was working eighteen hours a day, and my grief was lessening a little, thanks to Diddy, with whom I was slowly falling in love.

"Anyway, Bella came into the office and got right to the point. She said she had an affidavit from Alice Avery that said I had murdered my wife. She didn't ask for money. She said she wanted me to marry her, and she'd keep quiet about Myrna's death. I went crazy. I didn't want my children to think I was a murderer, but I couldn't prove I didn't do it. I saw Gunn Industries, which I wanted to bequeath to my children, going down the drain. I thought about Diddy and the life we'd planned to have together." He looked at Diddy then, and she turned away so he wouldn't see the tears in her eyes. "I didn't see that I had any choice but to agree to marry the witch. It was a marriage only on paper. I hated her, hated myself. I started staying at the office or taking a room at the inn just so I wouldn't have to see her."

"Pop, you don't have to go on," Ben said.

"No, no I have to tell it all," Marcus explained. "Things went from bad to worse when the good ladies of the town refused to accept Bella. She ranted and raved, threatened me every day, demanding I turn over this and that to her so she could try to buy her way into society. I did whatever she wanted, but nothing worked for her. She was a pariah, and she knew it.

"This doesn't say much for me, but I thought Bella was seeing to the children's care until Russell told me the way it really was. He came to the office one day and told me what he thought of me. It wasn't good. I wasn't nice to him, that much I do remember. That was about the same time attorney Bodene got me to go on the wagon. From then on, I took it one day at a time. Gunn Industries remained in top form. I worked round the clock. Bella got more and more demanding. She wanted the houses on the shoe. I refused because they were in Russell's and Ben's name. The house in Crowley was in Mary's name. I did stick to my guns on that because it was what Myrna wanted. Bella thought if she had those two houses, she would automatically become a *Rougie*. That was her goal in life. That and taking over the Gunn Foundation."

Ben stared at his father with compassion.

"That was my life. Then I had the stroke, and Bella stepped in and took over my care. I recovered, but suddenly I had a new doctor, new nurses, new everything. Then I had a mild heart attack. I know it was mild because I heard the doctor say so. All they did was pump me full of drugs. I was in a daze most of the time. Suddenly I had round-the-clock nurses, no access to a phone."

"Oh you poor thing," Diddy began, but Dodo silenced her with a look.

"I didn't know about Russell's death until it was too late," Marcus continued. "When Bella told me she'd donated his organs I had a ministroke. Then they doped me up even more. I had seen Russell's living will the day he dropped it off at the Foundation, knew how he felt about donor programs. I told Bella. I honestly don't think she knew even though she was heading up the Foundation. I can't be sure, but I don't think she ever looked at Russell's will. She thought that if she was this great humanitarian—the town would have to take her to its bosom. Every day she'd regale me with the news coverage, but she was afraid. I could see it in her eyes, but like everything else, she bluffed her way through."

Marcus looked at his son, seeing forgiveness there. He turned to Diddy, who stared at him with moist eyes.

Marcus turned to Fred. "Do you think you could take me to the inn? I'm rather tired."

"That's not necessary, Marcus. You can stay here a few days until you're really on your feet. Take the room at the end of the hall. *It's Russell's old room*," Diddy said. She told herself Marcus deserved to have to spend the night in his son's room.

Ben disappeared into the kitchen after his father left the room. He got a tray, filled it with beer, and carried it into the room.

Outside, the rain slashed against the windows. Thunder rolled across the sky. From time to time lightning could be seen through the plantation shutters. Ben felt sick at heart, sick to his stomach. Just plain old sick. Darby reached out to take his hand in hers. It didn't help.

Fred stood up, gave his bright red plaid suspenders a hitch, and announced that he, too, was going to bed because he wanted to get an early start home in the morning. "I want to call Trixie to say good night," he said.

Then it was just the three sisters, Darby, and Ben.

The sisters looked at Ben, waiting for him to say something. What he finally said surprised everyone in the room.

"Now that I know my mother wanted me to have the front house, I'm going to start using my trust fund tomorrow, find a historical contractor, and give the order to restore it. Russell's house across from mine belongs to Darby since Russell left it to her along with all his assets. She told me what she wants to do with it after talking to Ducky and Diddy this afternoon." He looked over at Darby, who squirmed in her chair.

Darby spoke softly and gently. "I'm going to hire the same contractor and it is my hope and Ben's that a new family might be interested in moving to the shoe." She looked pointedly at Dodo, who had tears streaming down her cheeks. "It was Ben's idea, really. He's the one who asked me about the pictures on your wall, Dodo. Then I asked Ducky and Diddy, and they told us your secret. We're family, Dodo," Darby said, getting up and walking over to her tiny aunt. She dropped to her knees to hug the little woman. "Family, Dodo."

Dodo struggled free of her niece's embrace and ran from the room. Ducky held up her hand to stop the others from following. "She's okay, trust me. She never thought we'd be so accepting. Why she thought that, I have no idea. Keeping that secret all these years must have been terrible for her. Now that the secret is out and the load is off her shoulders, we're going to see a much happier Dodo. I think it's time for all of us to turn in." There was no apology or shyness in her voice when Ducky said she was returning to the inn with Brandon. There was, however, a decided gleam in her eye that matched the one in Brandon Lautril's.

Darby and Ben helped Diddy clear the dining-room table, then they, too, left, leaving Diddy alone. She took off her apron, hung it up on the pantry door, checked to be sure she was leaving her kitchen clean and tidy for the morning. She walked through the house, sadder than she'd ever been in her life.

Fifteen minutes later, Diddy was in bed staring at the ceiling. At three o'clock in the morning she was still staring at the ceiling, the bedcovers in wild disarray. She finally got up, slipped on her robe and slippers, and went downstairs by way of the kitchen staircase, where she made herself a cup of tea. While the tea was brewing she opened the kitchen door. She liked hearing the sound of rain. Somehow it soothed her.

Outside, the rain dripped steadily from the drain spout at the side of the back porch. Crickets chirped, another soothing summer sound. Amazing that just by rubbing their legs together could create such a pleasing sound. The children used to capture the crickets along with the fireflies in the summer. She could see some of them now on the back porch, little pinpoints of light flitting about. The crazy urge to capture one of them was so real she gripped her teacup to stop herself from going outside. The tree frogs and the crickets, along with the fireflies, calmed her.

The scent of her gardenias was so strong it wafted through the screen door, enveloping her in the heady scent. The gardenias had bloomed twice this year. She always picked some and floated them in little bowls. She hadn't done that with the second blooming. She wondered why. Now with all this rain, by morning the small white petals would be bruised and turn brown. She sniffed again, savoring the rich smell. She did love gardenias.

Tears burned her eyes when she thought about all the years she'd hoped and waited for Marcus Gunn to come to her. Wasted. What a fool she'd been. She was still a fool because her heart beat just the way it had years and years ago when she was in his presence. Tonight had been sheer torture. She fought the urge to cry. Finally, a lone tear escaped her eye and rolled down her cheek. She swiped at it angrily.

She was so wide-awake it was scary. At any given moment she could go back upstairs and walk down the hall to Marcus's room and vent her anger at the man who had made her so miserable for what seemed all her life. The *best* years of her life. Yes, she could do that. But, she wouldn't. Because . . . because she still loved the man.

Maybe she should do a crossword puzzle or, worse yet, make a red-velvet cake. Or she could go out to the front veranda and sit there while she imagined the restoration that would soon begin at the Gunn houses. All of the above meant she would have to get up and move.

When Diddy looked at the clock on the stove again it was four-thirty. In another half hour she could get up and make some fresh cinnamon rolls. Fred loved her cinnamon rolls. She'd make an extra batch, so he could take them home to Trixie. All she had to do was get through the next hour and a half.

She heard a tree frog then. It sounded like it was right outside the screen door. Sometimes they got into the house. She didn't mind since they always found their way back out, and, if they didn't, she helped them.

Diddy sensed his presence before she actually turned to see him standing in the doorway. Her old heart kicked up a beat. It just wasn't in her to be inhospitable. She motioned to a chair at the table. She looked at the ratty robe he was wearing and wondered where he'd gotten it. Maybe it was one Russell had left behind. Yes, it was probably Russell's. It seemed to fit. "Do you want a cup of tea, Marcus?"

"Tea would be nice. Thank you. I couldn't sleep."

Diddy busied herself at the stove with the teakettle and pouring tea leaves into the little tea strainer. "Why?" she asked. "Because I put you in Russell's room?"

"I suppose," Marcus said wearily. "He seemed to be everywhere."

Diddy whirled around. "I loved that boy as though he were my own son. I don't have one iota of sympathy for you. Not one. Maybe in time . . ."

Marcus Gunn's shoulders slumped. He started to wring his hands, his lips trembling. "I know," he murmured. "What's going to happen to me, Diddy? I don't know what to do. Help me here."

Diddy plopped the teacup in front of her guest. "You're talking to the wrong person. If you're looking for absolution, you came to the wrong place. I'm fresh out of it." While the words were harsh, her tone was gentle.

Marcus raised his eyes to meet hers. "When did you get so hard and bitter, Diddy?" He sounded like he was going to cry any minute.

"The day you broke my heart, that's when. For years I dreamed about you. I prayed that you'd come to your senses. I lied and lied, we all did, to your children. You didn't come to your senses. I was such a fool," she cried, her voice breaking.

Marcus voice was gentle when he said, "You were never a fool, Diddy. You were the woman I loved. You were kind, caring, gentle, and you made my heart sing. I was the fool. When I saw you at the house the day you and your sisters rescued me, all the years came rushing back. I mistakenly thought you were coming for me because you wanted me. How trite that sounds now."

"In a way I *was* coming for you. I had such high expectations for all of ten minutes. We snatched you because of Mary, Russell, and Ben. Not for me. I finally locked all that baggage away." Diddy's voice was so cold it could have chilled milk. Her eyes were misty with tears. She turned away so Marcus couldn't see them.

"What should I do, Diddy?"

He looked so pathetic, Diddy took pity on him. "There's nothing in this world you can do to make Ben love you. Although I sensed forgiveness in him this evening. You have to realize that. Then there's Mary. Mary will never come to you. It will be up to you to get yourself well enough so you can go to New York to try to make amends with your daughter. This is just my opinion, but I think Mary needs you. Ben doesn't need you. Russell didn't need you either. Both of your sons figured that out a long time ago. You have to live with that. You have to tell Ben that half of the money to start up Gunn Industries came from Myrna, and it was always her wish that Ben and Russell take over the business when you retired. Ask him to take over. I don't know if he'll agree, but I tend to think now that he's going to marry Darby and restore the house he might be in the market for a job."

"I am so sorry, Diddy."

Diddy smiled, a wonderful, warm smile. "I'm sorry, too. Maybe when the shoe rings with laughter and small children things will be different. We'll be having birthday parties, pony rides, and picnics. I'll always make sure to invite you."

"And I'll accept," Marcus said smartly.

Hot tears again pricked at Diddy's eyelids. She

sniffed. "Then we both have something to look forward to." She looked at the clock on the stove. Time to start making the cinnamon rolls. Then she remembered that Fred and Marcus were diabetic. She wouldn't be making cinnamon rolls. Perhaps a fruit cup with yogurt. An egg-white omelet with green peppers, tomatoes, and onions. The possibilities were endless.

"It's five o'clock, time to start a new day, Marcus. Would you like some more tea?"

"What are you going to be doing, Diddy?"

"Ducky and I are going to Japan with Dodo to see if we can bring her son and his family here. It's our hope that they can move into Russell's house. Then the shoe will be complete again."

Marcus sipped at his tea. He looked confused. "I didn't know Dodo had a son. What's he doing in Japan?"

"He lives in Japan with friends of Dodo. He's half-Japanese, Marcus. He has two little boys, a girl, and a new baby on the way," Diddy informed Marcus. And, not knowing what Dodo and Ducky had decided, Diddy went on, "I just bet there's a job at Gunn Industries waiting for him. A high-paying job. I don't know how all that immigration stuff works. If he needs a sponsor aside from Dodo and us, I would expect Gunn Industries to step up to the plate. Are you getting my drift here?"

Marcus's eyes twinkled. "I can personally guarantee it. I guess I should be thinking about taking a shower and getting ready for the new day. I wonder what it holds for all of us."

"Hopefully, only good things, Marcus. Only good things. It's been a long, hard road, but I think we're at the end of it now. When you go upstairs, wake up Fred. He said he wanted to get an early start. I'll have breakfast ready when you come back down."

"I enjoyed our little talk, Diddy. Thank you."

Diddy nodded, not trusting herself to speak. She reached for a melon and started to peel it, her tears dropping onto the rind. This time she didn't try to stop them.

19

Darby stared at the castle in front of her. She'd made excellent progress during the past month. With all the family turmoil going on she'd had her doubts about finishing the dollhouse on deadline. But with the aunts in Japan and Ben spending his days at Gunn Industries, she had been able to devote all her time to the castle. All she had to do now was install the windows, put in the door for the drawbridge, then paint it.

Willie barked as he nudged her leg. Time to go out. Darby looked at her watch. Where had the time gone? The last time she'd looked at her watch it was one o'clock, and it was already six-thirty. She had to feed Willie, clean up, and meet Ben at the Shogun restaurant for dinner. If she put some grease on her shoes, she just might make it. She took one last look at the creation on her worktable, knowing that the little girl in Scotland was going to love it.

Darby tidied up and turned off the light. She opened the door for Willie to bound out when the phone rang. She debated answering it, but, thinking it might be Ben, she turned the light back on and picked up the phone. Her greeting was cheerful. "Jason!"

"I finally got it all, Darby. Do you want me to drop it off or wait till tomorrow? I can be there in ten minutes."

"Every single one?" Darby asked in awe.

"Every single one. They're all in Louisiana. Seems Mrs. Gunn did make that stipulation. Your call, Darby."

Darby's heart was beating so fast she had to take a deep breath before her breathing returned to normal. "Drop them off now, Jason. Come around the back through the kitchen door."

"Will do."

Darby hung up the phone, turned off the light, and left the workroom. By the time she made her way to the kitchen, Willie was at the screen door waiting to be let in. He raced to his empty food bowl and looked at it, then at Darby with reproach. She hastily opened the refrigerator and took out a deli chicken she'd picked up the day before. She picked off the white meat and mixed it with some wet dog food. She knew Willie would pick out the chicken and leave the dog food. Because she knew what the retriever would do, she picked more chicken until his bowl was full. Willie scarfed it down, nosing the dog food out of the way. When he was done he sat up on his rump and barked again. Time for dessert. Darby laughed the way she always did. Russell had always given Willie a strawberry Pop-Tart, the kind with frosting on the top. This treat Willie took his time eating, the tart between his front paws as he nibbled.

Darby washed her hands, ran upstairs, washed her face, brushed her teeth and her hair. She slipped out of her work clothes into a cranberry pantsuit. She was halfway down the steps when she realized she'd forgotten her shoes. She was back on the stairs when she heard Willie bark. It was the bark that meant company. Jason must be at the kitchen door. She flew down the rest of the steps, through the house, and out to the kitchen. She was so breathless, she had to lean against the door to open it.

"Jeez, Darby, where's the fire? I would have waited."

Darby eyed the bright red folder in the computer hacker's hand. Russell's *whereabouts* in a red folder. The thought was so crazy, she grew light-headed. Her hand was shaking so badly when she reached for the folder that she dropped it. Jason picked it up and laid it on the kitchen table.

"Everything you asked for is in that folder, Darby. You need anything else, call, okay?"

"I will, Jason. Thanks. Listen, you didn't . . . what I mean is, they . . .

"Nah. I know what I'm doing. You and I are the only ones who know. I didn't even read it, just printed it all out for you. Do us both a favor, though. When you're done with it, burn it."

"I will, Jason, and thanks again. I owe you."

"No, you don't. I did it for Russell. See ya."

Darby looked down at her watch, then at the red folder. She had twenty minutes till she had to meet Ben. Time to peruse the contents. She probably had time actually to read the contents. No. She wanted time to sit down someplace quiet to do that. In the end she carried it with her to show Ben.

Ten minutes later Darby parked her car and walked into the restaurant. She loved the ambience of this particular restaurant, even more so now that a new family from Japan would probably be coming to live in the shoe. She looked around to see if Ben was there. He wasn't. She sat down on a slatted bench next to a trickling fountain surrounded by miniature bonsai trees. A broadleaf tree behind the fountain held chimes that tinkled softly from the air gushing through the air vents in the ceiling. Darby closed her eyes, her thoughts on the red folder in her handbag.

Sensing a presence, Darby opened her eyes. "Ben!"

"President Gunn to you, ma'am." Ben laughed as he hugged her. Darby melted into his arms. "I missed you."

"Not half as much as I missed you. Are we going to have an argument over this?"

"Nope."

The hostess, dressed in a long scarlet dress with a mandarin collar, motioned for them to follow her to a long table where four other people were sitting. They settled themselves, smiled at the strangers across the table, ordered drinks, then sat back to talk to one another while the chef with a tall red hat and a set of wicked-looking knives took up his position behind the grill.

"Ben, Jason came by the house just as I was getting ready to leave. He . . . he brought me the profiles of the recipients along with their family members. I have phone numbers and addresses. At least I think I have them. I didn't actually look. Jason said he got everything I asked for. I don't know what to do, Ben," she whispered. "We talked about this a hundred times, and I'm no clearer in my mind now than I was when we first discussed it. I had a long talk with the aunts before they left for Japan, and they feel I should go ahead and search out the recipients and the families but not do anything about it. Sort of satisfying myself. This isn't about me, though. Do you see it any differently?"

Ben chose his words carefully. "I see it as a matter of a promise made to Russ. I thought about this a lot, Darby. Every person's last wishes should be honored. A terrible mistake was made, and nothing you or I or anyone else can do is going to change what's been done. If it takes you checking it out, seeing the recipient, then you need to do it for your own peace of mind. It's that simple. Which way can you live with it, Darby, checking out the recipients and their families or not checking them out and simply walking away? I can't do it, Darby, but I support you one hundred percent."

"I'm going to make my decision this evening after I read everything. Jason told me all the recipients live in Louisiana, that it was one of Bella's stipulations, and the donor program here in the state obviously agreed. I didn't know you could do something like that. Bella was literally holding the donor program hostage if you stop and think about it, since time was of the essence. Someone, say in West Virginia, might have been at the top of the list waiting for a kidney, but Bella said no, the person at the top of the Louisiana list gets it. I want to cry every time I think of it. Let's talk about something else. Ah, here's our Sapporo beer. I still say Lane Beer is better even though I like Japanese and Chinese beer."

"Do you have any idea how much Lane Beer Gunn Industries ships overseas?"

"Nope, no clue. How's it going at Gunn Industries? Do you feel like a president?"

"It's a hell of a lot different than being a ranger on Mustang Island. I have free rein, and I have plenty of ideas. Right now I'm just getting my feet wet."

"Have you heard from your father?"

Ben grinned. "Yes, I have. The last time we spoke he said he was going to New York to see Mary, and that was three weeks ago. I think he's still there. We just might become father and son again, but it's going to take time."

"I'm okay with that, Ben."

"Then we're both okay with it. Have you heard from the aunts?"

"Not since that initial call I had transferred to you. Were you able to help Dodo with immigration and all that stuff?"

"We did what we could from our end. If things move forward, Dodo's family should be here by Christmas. By the way, I've never heard her so happy. She said Ducky and Diddy are having the time of their lives."

"What's the news on the rebuilding? I get home so late I can't see anything, and I leave in the morning while it's still dark. How's it going?"

The chef took that moment to start banging his salt and pepper shakers and throwing them in the air. He swiveled and caught them behind his back. Everyone clapped in approval.

"I walked over this morning. All the wood rot has been replaced. The new roof is on, and the first floor is being Sheetrocked tomorrow. Believe it or not, the pine floors are intact and just need to be sanded and refinished. It's being rewired this afternoon. Then it's the plumber's turn. Most of the work has passed inspection. The new windows arrived yesterday. The double front doors are being repaired and will be beautiful when they're finished. Even the hardware is still good, believe it or not. The front veranda and the back porch are what's taking so much time. Most of the wood is rotted. Finding cypress wood isn't all that easy. Three more weeks and the house should be ready to be painted.

Then if they start right away on the other house, it is possible it could be ready by Christmas. The aunts are going to be *soooo* happy. Weather is going to play a big part in everything from here on in."

The chef waved his knife for attention to ask who wanted sesame seeds and who didn't. Six hands shot in the air. The chef stirred and swirled, then scooped the crunchy fried vegetables onto the plates. He started on the rice, adding eggs and finely minced carrots and scallions. Someone across the table asked for extra ginger sauce.

The next hour was spent eating and making small talk with the four strangers at their table.

Outside the restaurant, Ben kissed Darby soundly. "Are you sure you don't mind that I'm going back to the office?"

"Of course I don't mind. I'll wait up for you. Willie really misses you. Oh, I made such headway on the castle today. A few more days, and I'll have it finished. Then it just has to sit and dry. I made my own hinges for the drawbridge. And, I even made the pulleys that will allow the windows to be opened and closed. I'm thinking maybe I should patent that little device. What do you think of that?"

"What I think, Miss Lane, is that you are the marvel in marvelous." He pretended to groan at the thought of going back to the office. Darby gave him a shove toward his car. She waved and blew him a kiss.

It was a warm night, and Darby drove home with the

car windows open. The radio played softly, allowing her to think as she drove up one street and down the other until she came to the alley leading into the shoe. Even from this distance she could hear Willie's welcoming bark. She knew he was on the sofa under the front window watching to see which door she would enter through. Seconds later she saw him on one of the kitchen chairs that allowed him a clear view through the top half of the kitchen door.

A four-legged welcoming committee of one.

It was midmorning the following day before Darby took the red folder out of her purse. She wanted to be totally alone with no distractions when she read its contents. She hoped that someday Ben would want to meet the people listed in the red folder. Loving him as she did, she understood now just wasn't the right time for him.

She was at her worktable, the red folder in her hands. Strangely enough, her hands were steady, her breathing normal. Willie was being cooperative, lying at her feet, his golden head between his paws. He wasn't even panting. She thought it strange. For some reason or other, she thought the dog would somehow know what she was holding. She took a moment to wonder if she was teetering on the edge of a nervous breakdown. She discarded the idea almost immediately. Thousands of people every day were faced with moral or ethical decisions. Why shouldn't she have anxiety over what she was about to do.

What was bothering her most at the moment was how she would react and feel after she checked out the contents. Would she *really* be able to put it behind her? She would never know if she stopped now.

Darby took a deep breath and yanked at the papers. There were only four sheets of paper, but those four sheets were full of words from top to bottom. Russell's life reduced to four pages of copy paper.

Darby settled down to read the papers in front of her. She ran her fingers under the words to make sure she didn't miss a word or a meaning. When she finished all four pages, she looked around. Nothing had changed in her workroom. Willie was still lying at her feet. The sun had come out. That was the only difference. She shivered.

Darby bit down on her bottom lip. Time to move on this. If she left the house now, she could visit a family in Baton Rouge, a family in Lafayette, and a family in Slidell. Tomorrow she could drive to New Orleans and the other places on the list. She needed street maps so she wouldn't waste time. She called Willie and went into the small room off the library that held her computer. She sat down, typed in MAPQUEST. Fifteen minutes later she had a printout and precise door-to-door instructions on how to get to each of the first three houses on her list. She printed out the instructions and stuck them into her pocket.

These last weeks she'd mentally turned over several different game plans. At last she had to make up her mind which to use. The plan she liked best was the one where she stopped at a florist for a basket of flowers and some brightly colored balloons. She would deliver them personally to the recipient with a card inside that simply said *Have a good life*. Of course, there would be no signature or anything else that would lead the recipient and the family to think the flowers and the balloons came from the donor's family.

Enough time had gone by since the different operations so that most of the recipients should be home or back to work or, at the very least, recovering in the hospital. According to Jason's report, all the recipients except the liver and heart transplants were at home recovering.

Darby then made two phone calls, the first to a local florist to order the balloons and flowers, saying she would pick them up in an hour. The second call was to Ben, asking if she could trade cars with him. She would need Russ's Range Rover for the flowers and balloons, and she wanted to take Willie with her. Willie would . . . she wasn't sure what Willie would be able to do, but she was taking him with her anyway.

"C'mon boy, time to go out one last time. Then we're going for a ride." The golden dog stopped in his tracks, turned to look at her, not quite understanding the catch in her voice. Darby shooed him out the door. He was back inside in five minutes.

Darby stood still, contemplating what she was about to do. From outside the sounds of the heavy equipment assailed her ears. The hammering was almost as loud as the pounding in her head. She popped four aspirin, gathered up her purse and car keys. She checked her wallet to make sure she had enough cash for the flowers and balloons. She decided she didn't have enough and would have to stop at an ATM machine after she switched cars with Ben.

It was ten forty-five when Darby pulled into the driveway at 2246 Vandemeer Avenue. It was a tidy, sprawling ranch. Two cars sat in the driveway, a dark green Mustang and a white Honda Civic. There was no front porch, but there was a small stoop at the end of the walkway. Beautiful lemon-colored marigolds lined the walkway. In the center of the yard was a huge oak tree, whose lower limbs were lying on braces anchored into the ground. Two wooden chairs and a small table were underneath. Arthur Quinn was the recipient of one of Russ's kidneys. He was twenty-eight, married, and the father of two little boys. Darby was halfway up the walkway, the balloons in one hand, the flower basket in the other, Willie at her side, when the front door opened. A young woman in jeans and a sleeveless tee shirt smiled a greeting. "Oh, my gosh!" she said. "Those flowers are beautiful!"

Darby took a deep breath. "My delivery is for Arthur Quinn. Is he here?"

"Yes. Yes, he's out back on the patio. Come in, please. You can bring the dog. My husband loves dogs."

The house inside was just as neat and tidy as it was outside. Darby followed the young Mrs. Quinn through the living room, whose walls were covered with pictures of two laughing little boys. A fat, gray cat hissed at Willie from his perch on the back of a yellow sofa. Willie ignored him.

They walked into a family room that was littered with bright-colored toys and Tonka trucks. Mrs. Quinn opened the sliding door. "Honey, look," she said, pointing to the flowers and balloons. The young man named Arthur looked up and smiled. "Somebody sent me flowers and balloons! Who are they from, Tricia?"

Tricia plucked the card from the nest of ferns inside the flower basket. She read it and smiled again. She handed the card to her husband. He read it, his eyes filling.

"My goodness, where are my manners?" Tricia asked. "Would you like a glass of ice tea. I just made it."

"Tea would be nice," Darby said, and smiled nervously. "It really is still hot out here, isn't it?"

"I love it," Arthur said, when his wife went back into the house with the balloons and the flowers. "For a long time I couldn't get warm. This is like heaven to me."

Willie started to whine and Darby watched as the man stroked Willie's head. "Doesn't he like strangers?" Arthur asked, as Willie tried to nuzzle his side.

"Actually, he does. He's a very gentle dog. You said you love the heat—why is that, if you don't mind my asking?"

"I was on kidney dialysis for three years and on a donor list. I only had one kidney, and my days were numbered. Then an organ became available. I'm feeling really good now and in a few more weeks I can return to work. Because some kind person donated his kidney, I'm going to get a chance to see my kids grow up."

"That's . . . that's wonderful, Mr. Quinn."

"I'm not sure about this, but I want to believe those flowers and the balloons . . . I think they were sent from the donor's family. I'm going to do just what the card said, 'have a good life.' "

Darby smiled. "That sounds like a great idea."

"Yes. I really like this dog. As soon as my boys get a little older, we're going to get a dog. Oh, I hear them now!"

The sliding door slid open and two whooping five-year-olds burst onto the patio. "Hi, Dad!" they said boisterously. Then they whipped out pictures they'd made that morning in kindergarten. They suddenly noticed Willie and the stranger sitting across from their dad. They turned shy and grew quiet.

Darby noticed that they were miniature Arthurs. One of the twins looked at Darby strangely. "Are you going to do *that stuff* to my dad again?"

"No, no, Michael. This lady isn't a nurse. She brought me some flowers and balloons." He looked at Darby, and said, "This is Michael and Richard. They had a bad time when I was so sick. I'm trying to convince them that the day will come when we can play ball and take hikes again."

Tricia arrived with the ice tea. Darby took a few sips and stood up. Willie was still whining at Arthur's side. *Is it possible . . . ?*

Darby held out her hand. Arthur shook it. "Like the card said, Mr. Quinn, have a good life. Come on, Willie, we have some more deliveries to make. It was nice meeting you both."

"Look, Dad, he doesn't want to go with the lady. He likes you. Can we get a dog, huh?"

"Soon," Arthur said cheerfully.

This time Darby's command was sharp when she ordered Willie to follow her. He did so, but reluctantly.

"I'm not going to think about that visit until I get home. I know, I know, Willie. I'm going to think about you later, too. Now we're going to see a Mr. Prentice Carpenter."

It was two-thirty when Darby parked the Rover in front of Prentice Carpenter's duplex. Carpenter had been the recipient of a cornea transplant. He was a forty-two-year-old widower with a son in college and a daughter who was a senior in high school. Mr. Carpenter had been unemployed for several years. The family was living on public assistance. Mr. Carpenter opened the door and looked down at Willie through his dark glasses, and smiled. "Don't blame you for bringing a dog with you, Miss. You can't be too careful these days when making home deliveries," he said with a smile. "What have we here?"

"A delivery for Mr. Prentice Carpenter. Are you Mr. Carpenter?"

"I was when I woke up this morning. Come in, please. Are you sure these are for me and not my daughter?"

Look at me, Mr. Carpenter. Really look at me. Russ, do you see me? Darby asked silently.

"No, they're for you. Where would you like me to put them?"

"Right there on the coffee table," he directed.

Darby did as he asked and took a minute to look around. Everything was neat and clean but shabby and worn. "I wasn't sure if you would be home at this time of day. I was worried I would have to leave them with a neighbor."

Prentice Carpenter plucked the card from the flowers. He held it away from him and laughed, a sound of pure joy. Willie barked at the sound. Darby fidgeted, standing on one foot and then the other. *Look at me. Tell me you recognize me. Tell me something. Please.*

"There's no name on the card. Do you know who sent them?" he asked, and Darby held her breath when he stared at her long and hard. "Do I know you?"

Oh, God, oh, God. "I don't think so." She wanted to scream, yes, yes, you do know me. *Oh, God, Russ, it's me, Darby. Are you really seeing me?*

Carpenter turned the small florist card over and over

in his hand. Darby waited to see if he would tell her what it said. He didn't. "I needed these today," he said, indicating the flowers and the balloons. "A pick-me-up, if you know what I mean. There's no way you could know this, but I've been blind for some time. On Monday I'm going to be able to go back to work for the first time in years. I'll be able to drive again and see my children. I've never seen such beautiful flowers."

"I guess you must have had a successful eye operation," Darby said, moving toward the door, Willie at her side.

"Yes, you could say that. I never thought it would happen. I was reconciled to a life of darkness. I have to wear these sunglasses for a while, but I'm only too happy to wear them."

Carpenter held the door for her. "Thank you for making my day, miss."

Darby wanted to cry. She nodded as she made her way to the Rover. Willie hopped in and barked shrilly when the door closed behind Prentice Carpenter.

Darby slipped the Rover into gear and drove off. She turned up the radio as she talked to Willie. *One more, today. We'll talk about this later. Then again, maybe we'll never talk about it*, she thought.

It was after five o'clock when Darby walked into the Ochsner Medical Center. Much to his displeasure, she'd left Willie in the truck. This was going to be the trickiest visit of all. Lionel Williams was still in the intensive care unit, so that meant she wouldn't be able to see him. Mr. Williams was to be her final test. With Russ's heart, surely she would sense or feel something. She knew that wasn't going to happen since Lionel Williams, according to Jason, had suffered a setback because of an infection but was holding his own, with the doctors convinced it was just a temporary setback.

Darby walked over to the volunteer who sat behind the front desk. She smiled. "Can you tell me where I can find the Williams family? These aren't for the patient but for Mrs. Williams and her children. I'd like to hand them over in person, if that's possible."

The volunteer typed into her computer, then frowned. "For the family, not for the patient. Is that what you said?"

"Yes, ma'am."

"I don't see why not. Mr. Williams is in intensive care. The family sees him for a few minutes on the hour. Fourth-floor waiting room, follow the yellow arrows. The children just went up about a half hour ago."

Darby thanked her and hastened away before she could change her mind. She took the elevator and followed the volunteer's instructions. She recognized the family because of the three children who sat quietly, their schoolbooks open in their laps. Mrs. Williams was saying a rosary, her eyes glistening with tears. A pile of knitting in a bright-colored bag sat at her feet.

"Mrs. Williams?" Darby asked.

"Yes," she said dully.

"I have a delivery for you. Actually, it's for your husband, but I realize they don't allow flowers or balloons in intensive care. Can I leave them with you?" Darby asked gently.

"Of course. Now who would be sending Lionel flowers and balloons?"

Darby tried to smile and found it hard. "Someone who cares about your husband, would be my guess. There's a card in the flowers."

Mrs. Williams wrapped her rosary around her hand as she plucked the card from the flowers. She read it and tried not to cry. Darby fished in her pocket for a tissue and handed it to the little lady with the shining black hair. "Is there anything I can do for you, Mrs. Williams. A cup of coffee, a soft drink?"

The three kids were suddenly surrounding their mother. "Who are they from, Mum?" one asked.

"They're pretty. Maybe the nurse will let us hold them up to the window," another one said.

The youngest child, a dark-eyed pretty little girl with cornrows in her hair, started to cry. Her mother handed her the balloons and told her to go back to her homework.

"I have some extra time, Mrs. Williams. Would you like to go with me to the coffee shop for some coffee. I could certainly use some."

Mrs. Williams looked at her watch. "Yes, I would like some coffee. It's very nice of you to invite me." She leaned over her children, and Darby heard her say, "If there's any change, come and get me right away."

In the coffee shop Darby held a chair for Mrs. Williams before she walked up to the counter to order two coffees and some brownies. She carried the tray back to the table.

"Thank you. I don't even know your name."

For some reason Darby couldn't lie to this tired, sad woman. "It's Darby."

"That's a pretty name. My name is Lila. I hate this place. Lionel was doing so well, and they were talking about him going home. Then he got an infection. The doctors say he should be okay, but . . . I try to be positive, and I pray."

"How . . . how long has your husband been here, Mrs. Williams?"

"I've lost track of time. It's so hard. I don't know why the Lord lets these things happen. I try not to question Him. My husband is such a good man. He was good to his parents and my parents, too. All the man ever did was work and work. It's not easy for a black family here in Baton Rouge. He's the best husband and the best father. We couldn't believe it when we found out there was a heart for him. I think we had both given up. We were just plain worn-out. Lionel worked two jobs, and so do I. We want our children to go to college. Lionel didn't want no handouts. He said if we couldn't pay for our kids, then they weren't going. We had a nice little bank account, then his heart gave out. All our money's gone and . . . and . . . now why am I telling you all this? All you did was a nice thing, bringing those flowers and balloons to brighten our day. I'm sorry if I didn't seem appreciative. I just have so much on my mind. I don't know what I'll do if anything happens to my Lionel."

Darby's mind raced. There was no way she could go through with her charade where this woman was concerned. No way.

"Mrs. Williams, I want to tell you something." She told her about her friendship with Russell, about her life, and what had happened. The truth was cathartic. "I believe, and I want you to believe that your husband will be all right."

"You poor thing. How hard this must be for you. Thank you for telling me. I feel better already."

"Mrs. Williams, can I just see your husband through the glass? I don't want to take your turn or anything like that. I want to be able to tell Russ . . . I know how asinine that sounds but . . . I . . ."

"Nothing sounds strange to me anymore, and of course you can see my husband. He's hooked up to a lot of machines, so be prepared. I'll tell him everything you told me when he's well enough. That was a very good brownie, for a hospital coffee shop. My own are better, though." Mrs. Williams sniffed. "Come along now so you can see my Lionel."

Darby trotted behind the brisk little woman who suddenly looked more energetic, more alert, more hopeful.

"Two more minutes and we can go down the hall. You just follow me like you belong to my family, but I don't know how that's going to look since you're white and I'm black." Lila Williams chuckled richly to show what she thought of that. In spite of herself, Darby laughed.

Mrs. Williams donned a hospital gown, a cap, a mask, and gloves. She let herself into her husband's room. She motioned Darby to stand by the window.

Tears streamed down Darby's cheeks. *C'mon, Russ, kick up that heartbeat. Don't let this man down. C'mon, c'mon, give me a sign here. I need something, Russ. They're going to toss me out of here soon, so let's see what you can do. C'mon, Russ. You told me on your last physical the doctor said you had the heart of an athlete. Prove it!*

Through her tears she could see Mrs. Williams stroking her husband's cheek. Then she saw Lionel open his eyes and smile at his wife. It was the most beautiful sight Darby had ever seen. Lila Williams said something to her husband, and he looked at the window. An even bigger smile raced across his face. Darby wiggled her fingers in a wave. *Thanks, Russ.*

Darby turned and walked away. Out in the parking lot she sat in the Rover for a long time, Jason's papers in her lap. From time to time a tear rolled down her cheek. It was over. There was no need now for her to visit or check on the other recipients. She could live and walk away with what she'd seen. She thought about Lionel Williams's smile. Was it a sign from Russ? She didn't know. Better to believe it was than not to believe. The dark clouds hovering over her were gone. Tomorrow the sun would be a little brighter.

Deliberately or not, Bella Gunn had done a wonderful thing. *I'm going to go on with my life, Russ, believing she didn't know about your will. Wherever you are, I want you to rest easy. By the way, old buddy, no one is ever going to know about this, but me and you, and Mrs. Williams. Well, Ben, Jason, and Mickey, too, but not about this particular visit.*

Darby drove home, her shoulders straighter, her heart lighter. Willie hopped into the front seat and pawed her shoulder. Did he understand? Did he sense something? She would never know. That was all right, too.

When Darby pulled the Rover into the alley, Ben ran from the house to greet her. Willie woofed happily as he leaped from the car and raced around the shoe. She stepped into Ben's arms, a wide smile on her face. "It's okay," she whispered. "It's really okay now."

Ben didn't ask for explanations, there was no need. He kissed her, then picked her up and carried her over the threshold. A practice run for when they would truly be husband and wife.

20

The Baton Rouge Airport was teeming with the post-Thanksgiving crowds returning home. Ben, Darby, and Brandon Lautril stood at the security checkpoint waiting for the aunts and Dodo's son and his family. Darby was so excited she thought she was going to explode. Ben was no better, constantly looking at his watch and asking what was taking so long. Brandon just looked like he was in a daze.

Darby turned to Ben. "It just dawned on me, Ben, we're waiting in the wrong place. They have to go through Customs. C'mon. They're probably waiting for us." She sprinted off, the two men following.

Diddy came through first, then Ducky. Brandon moved fast and had Ducky in a bear hug in the blink of an eye. Then there was tiny Dodo, shepherding her son and his family toward them. She looked anxious and even frightened, but no more so than the cluster of people with her. "Dodo, over here," Darby squealed as she ran to her aunt. Ben was right behind her.

The kisses and the hugs were exuberant. Then it was time to meet the Japanese family. Her heart and her love were in Dodo's eyes when she made the introductions. "This is my daughter-in-law, Hisa, and this is *my son, Kiyo.*" Her voice was full of pride. "My grandsons, Koko, Kobe, and this little flower is named Gyn." Dodo stood back while everyone bowed and smiled. Darby was having none of that. She threw out her arms, startling everyone by hugging and kissing them. "This is how we greet family in America," she said, laughing, much to the startled family's delight. Ben picked up Gyn and put her on his shoulders. She squealed with pleasure as the two small boys giggled behind their hands.

They all spoke English but not fluently. Hisa, the mother, seemed exceptionally shy as she clung to her handsome husband.

"This is all so wonderful, so very wonderful," Darby babbled as she followed everyone to the exit, the baggage carts in the hands of a porter. "We brought three cars," she said.

"The house isn't ready, is it?" Dodo asked hopefully.

"Two more weeks," Ben said. "Wait till you see it. It looks just like it did when we were growing up." Gyn still on his shoulders, he looked over at Kiyo. A twinkle in his eyes, he said, "When will you be ready to go to work?"

His own eyes twinkling, Kiyo responded smartly, "Tomorrow."

Ben smacked his hands together. "Sounds like a plan to me." He looked around at the little group. "Darby and I thought you might all like to go to a Japanese restaurant for dinner." He looked down at the two little boys. "Would you like that?"

"Do they have hot dogs?" the older of the two asked shyly.

"Spaghetti," the younger boy said.

"Ice cream!" Gyn squealed.

"My family is more American than I realized," Dodo said softly.

"That means takeout. You all head home, and Darby and I will pick up everything."

Darby walked over to her aunt Diddy. She put her arms around her. "I missed you. Really missed you."

Diddy smiled. "You're worried about me, aren't you? Ducky has Brandon, Dodo has her family, you have Ben. I have three children, soon to be four, to raise now and fuss over. I couldn't be happier." The sadness in her eyes belied the statement.

"I don't know if you're interested or not, but Marcus is back. He bought a condo in Willow Springs. He came by the house last week. He and Mary are friends. In fact, Mary is coming for Christmas. I invited them both. Marcus said she's a different person these days, and that's a wonderful thing. He and Ben were affectionate to one another. It's a start, Diddy. Remember, Rome wasn't built in a day. He asked about you, Diddy. I told him a sumo wrestler had the hots for you, and you were thinking about sponsoring him. He laughed and laughed. He still has feelings for you, Diddy. Make your peace. Life is just too short. Look at all the years Dodo wasted because she was afraid to let us know about her family. Life is for the living. Russ always said that."

Diddy wiped at the tears gathering in the corners of her eyes. "Did you . . ."

"Yes, I contacted three of the recipients. I was satisfied and didn't feel the need to see the others. It's over now. The new year is coming up. We're all going to start fresh. Our lives are just beginning again. It's going to be so wonderful to have the kids in the shoe. I've been a decorating fool these past weeks, fixing up the bedrooms we used to sleep in at Dodo's house. It's time for a new generation to take over. Ben said we should all dedicate rooms to Dodo's grandkids. You know, a room in every house like we had. Even Mary agreed, if you can believe that. It's almost like a miracle, isn't it, Diddy?"

"Yes, child, it is. None of us would be here right now if it wasn't for Russell's passing. Russell is what brought us all together. All I've been doing is thinking about that for weeks and weeks."

"I know, boy, do I know. It's time for you to go home now, Diddy, back to the shoe." She linked arms with her aunt's and led her out to the parking lot of the airport.

Home.

The most wonderful place on earth.

Epilogue

Darby woke with a start to find Willie sitting on the bed staring at her. She knew instantly what day it was and what lay ahead of her. Christmas Eve. She bounded out of bed, raced downstairs to let Willie out. She took a minute to stare at the huge Christmas tree Miguel and two of his nephews had set up a week ago in the middle of the shoe. To her mind it was almost as big as the tree in Rockefeller Center. It was even decorated. At night it was one of the most glorious sights she'd ever seen.

The shoe was quiet, everyone still asleep. Ben was living in the Gunn house, which would become their house on New Year's Day, when they got married. Until then, they waved to one another from their respective porches. She went into a fit of laughter each time they did it. She looked forward to giving Ducky back her

house so that she and Brandon could spend their six
months here and the other six in New Orleans. They'd
eloped to Las Vegas on the fifth of December. To avoid
fanfare, Ducky had added.

Their new Japanese family was now settled in across
the way, and loving everything American. Grandma
Dodo, happier than Darby'd ever seen her, hustled and
bustled, driving the children to school, taking her new
daughter-in-law for driving lessons and to the doctor
and to the supermarket.

She knew if she ran across the yard to Diddy's
house, she would find her aunt wearing her white
apron cooking up a storm for tonight's festive dinner.
Darby also knew there would be a bounce in her
aunt's step because Marcus and Mary would be attending dinner.

Willie ran into the house and followed Darby upstairs, where she showered, dressed, and was back
downstairs in less than twenty minutes. She had something important to do that day. Something she'd been
wanting to do for a very long time but just wasn't
ready. Today, she was ready. But before she took care
of that little matter, she had something else to do.
Something very important. She just hoped she could
get out of the house and on the road before the others
woke up.

Darby made coffee, fed Willie. She looked at the
clock. It was still early to make a house call, but she
didn't have any intention of actually visiting. Last night,

actually in the middle of the night, she'd loaded up her car so no one would know what she was doing. This was a private matter, not to be shared.

Little did she know every eye in the shoe was on her as she carried her basket and a tote bag out to the car. Willie hopped in, and they were off.

It was ten minutes past nine in the morning when she made her last trip up to the Williamses' front door. She tried to be quiet as she did her best to position the last of the gaily wrapped presents. She was huffing and puffing from the exertion and the weight of some of the boxes. She almost fainted when the door opened and Mrs. Williams, clad in her robe, greeted her as she bent down to pick up the morning paper. Willie inched forward to be petted.

"I . . . I thought you might still be sleeping. I didn't mean to wake you, Mrs. Williams."

"You didn't. What is all this?" she asked, looking down at the gift-wrapped boxes at her feet. "Now, there was no call for you to do this," she said, pointing to the pile of presents. "It's pretty chilly out here. I just put some coffee on. Would you like a cup?"

"I . . . I have to go . . . thank you but no. How is your husband?"

"If you come in, you can see for yourself. He's been fretting and stewing ever since he got home, wanting me to call you. I told him I couldn't do that. Now that you're here, it might make his Christmas all the more memorable if you speak with him. We weren't sure we'd have a

Christmas this year. You can bring the dog. Lionel loves animals."

Darby, her heart thundering in her chest, walked into the small living room, where Lionel Williams was sitting in what looked like a comfortable chair. It was probably his favorite chair, the chair he'd always sat in when he got home from work. Darby smiled, Lionel smiled, and Willie whined.

"Merry Christmas, Mr. Williams," was all Darby could think of to say.

Lionel Williams's voice was husky and low when he said, "Thank you." He patted Willie, who was practically salivating at the attention he was getting from this stranger. Then he threw back his head and let loose with the most unholy sound Darby had ever heard in her life. She ran to him and swore later that the golden dog was crying, and she was babbling that Willie had been Russell's dog. Her own eyes burned unbearably. *He knows. Willie knows.* She had to get out of there. The lump in her throat felt so big she thought she was going to choke to death.

"Come, Willie. Time to go." She managed to utter one more "Merry Christmas" as she bolted for the door. She turned back and thrust the tote bag into Mrs. Williams's hands.

"What's this?" Mrs. Williams asked.

Darby managed to smile. "Just a little something to help you have a good life. From Russ."

The little something turned out to be a check to tide

the Williams family over for a few years and three full scholarships for the Williams children when it was time for them to go to college. The boxes to go under the tree were computers, Palm Pilots, prepaid cell phones, VCRs, and bicycles that only needed assembly. This, after all, was the electronic age. For Lionel, there was a sixty-inch plasma TV that would be delivered at noon. And for Mrs. Williams one of Diddy's beautiful quilts, along with a monster gift certificate to Foley's Department Store.

"You did good, Russ," Darby whispered to herself as she drove away.

Ninety minutes later she was at the cemetery. She opened the door for Willie, who didn't know what to make of these strange goings-on. He circled Darby and watched as she tugged the big basket of flowers from the backseat. It wasn't a flower arrangement, though; it was a basket of freshly cut daisies.

If she hadn't been so intent on what she was about to do, she might have noticed the group of people standing off to the side of the gates. Even Willie didn't seem to be aware of them.

The ground was wet and cold, but Darby didn't mind as she sat down and gathered the daisies to make her daisy chain. When it was finished, she started to cry. Hating herself for blubbering, she fished for a tissue in her pocket and blew lustily. She was on her knees by then, trying to loop the daisy chain over the wing of one of the angels on Russ's headstone.

It fell off.

She replaced it with shaking fingers.

It fell off again.

Frowning, Darby worked her fingers around the sculpted wing. She wedged the delicate daisy chain tightly.

It fell off again.

Willie threw back his head and howled. Darby shivered when she picked up the daisy chain. For some reason it felt like it was glued to her fingers. She looked around, sniffing the air like Willie did. No breeze. Maybe she should just lay the daisy chain at the foot of the stone.

In the blink of an eye, Willie had the chain in his teeth and was walking toward the little group who had gathered by the gate. Darby smiled as Ben led her family toward her. Willie stopped in front of Ben and dropped the daisy chain. Ben picked it up and put it around his neck.

Darby ran to him. Ben reached for her, and whispered, "We are *never, ever,* going to talk about this. Never, ever. Do you understand me, Darby?"

"Willie knew. He knew all along. Every place we went, he knew. Damn it, Ben, *he knew.*"

"It's incredible, Darby, but somehow it still makes sense."

Darby looked around. They were all there, even Marcus and Mary. Dodo's son and his family were smiling shyly. She was sure Dodo had explained what they were all doing there. The American way of saying say-onara.

Everyone stood back to allow Marcus, Mary, and Ben their moment. At the last second, Marcus reached for Diddy's hand to draw her alongside.

"It's as right as it's ever going to be, family," Darby said, walking away.

An hour later the long caravan of cars reached the top of the Horseshoe. Everyone piled out to stare at the magnificent sight in front of them. The tree was so fragrant it was heady. The five pristine white houses gleamed with the miles of garland covering the banisters and columns on the verandas. Monster evergreen wreaths with huge, red-satin bows graced all the doors. Scarlet poinsettias lined the porches and steps. The gazebo sported more evergreens and satin bows. Even from where they were standing, Diddy's Christmas Eve dinner permeated the air. And inside, under all the five Christmas trees were bicycles, wagons, doll carriages, and baby dolls. There were games and puzzles and books, along with the requisite boxes of necessary but unwanted clothes. For Gyn, a special present. Darby's old dollhouse, with a new coat of paint and a little remodeling, now looked like a Japanese dollhouse complete with black-lacquer furniture and a miniature pagoda serving as a front gate.

Darby nudged Ben. Then she nudged him again.

Wearing the daisy chain he swore he'd never take off,

Ben approached his father and sister. "Merry Christmas, Dad. Merry Christmas, Mary."

Everyone beamed with pleasure, their smiles as bright and shiny as the star on top of the Christmas tree in the middle of the shoe.

"Merry Christmas, everyone!" Darby shouted at the top of her lungs. *And to you, Russ, wherever you are, for making this all possible.*

Pocket Books proudly presents

THE MARRIAGE GAME

Fern Michaels

Available now
from Pocket Books

Turn the page for a preview
of *THE MARRIAGE GAME*....

Samantha Rainford, just hours away from her thirtieth birthday and forty-eight hours away from being served with divorce papers, looked around the tiny apartment she'd lived in for the last five years. It was tiny but cozy and comfortable. For the most part, all she did was sleep here. Every piece of furniture had been chosen with care. Every knickknack meaningful. Even the plants had been chosen with regard to light and temperature. Translated it meant she was a home-and-hearth kind of gal. So much so that her husband of three weeks had just served divorce papers on her.

Sometimes life was a bitch.

Sam took another look around the tiny apartment. She'd sold off the furniture, the knickknacks, and even her luscious plants to the new tenant who was moving in tomorrow, at which point she would move into the condo she'd been in the process of buying when she'd been caught up in a whirlwind romance with Douglas Cosmo Rainford, III.

Samantha gathered up her coat, her purse, and the carry-on that contained what she referred to as her "life," and made her way through the living room to the front door, where her bags waited for her. She shoved them one by one out into the hallway. The manager would have them in the garage waiting to be loaded into her BMW by the time she took the elevator to the garage. Then she would take them to her new condo a mile away in Alexandria, Virginia. The condo was a spacious, two-bedroom, two-bath, up-and-down condo that she'd furnished in two days' time. It even had a fireplace, the main reason she'd bought the condo in the first place. The fireplace was part of her nesting home-and-hearth personality. The kitchen had new appliances and ample counter space. She could hardly wait to cook her first dinner and mess up the place. Best of all, she had an unlisted telephone number that she'd given out to only a select few, including her closest friend Sara, otherwise known as Slick, who was a super, glossy, high-fashion model, her employer, and, of course, the bank where she had her checking and savings accounts. In addition to those accounts, she had several CDs that she'd taken out with her modest inheritance from her grandmother years before and all the savings bonds she'd gotten as gifts during her lifetime. She was definitely solvent.

An hour later Sam was lugging her bags into her new

home. The minute the bags were in her spacious living room, she locked the door and danced around the room, clapping her hands in glee. It was all hers. No one could cross the threshold unless she invited them in. All hers. She started to cry then because it wasn't supposed to happen like this. She was supposed to start her new life with her new husband, not alone in a condo just three weeks after her honeymoon.

She swiped at her eyes with the sleeve of her shirt as she looked at her watch through tear-filled eyes. She had one hour till her appointment with Douglas's attorney. What *that* was all about, she had no clue. The call had come in yesterday, just an hour after she'd been served with divorce papers, *inviting* her to the offices of Prizzi, Prizzi, Prizzi and Prizzi.

She thought about blowing off the Prizzi law firm but decided to keep the appointment so that when she returned to her new nest, her past would be just that, her past. Her lawyer could handle the divorce, and she would simply move on. She needed time to grieve, to cry and sob, to stomp her feet and get down and ugly. The honeymoon must have been some kind of test that she failed. How crazy was *that?*

The honeymoon was everything a honeymoon was supposed to be. She'd loved every minute on the exotic island. Loved the togetherness, loved making love on the beach under the stars. Loved hearing her new husband whisper sweet words of undying love in her ears. She had every right to expect that she would return home and have a normal marriage. Instead, she'd returned home to be served with divorce papers. Even a stupid person could figure out the divorce papers had to have been drawn up and filed while they were still on their honeymoon.

Sam looked around for her purse and car keys. The little mirror by the front door showed her that her eyes were red and puffy. As if she cared. Minutes later she was on her way.

As she maneuvered the BMW up and down the streets, she wondered what this particular summons was all about. Something to sign, undoubtedly. She'd called an attorney who was a client of the accounting firm where she worked to represent her, but he'd been out of the office taking a deposition. His secretary said she would have him return her call later in the day.

She was on K Street with two blocks to go. She found a vacant spot, parked, buttoned her coat against the cold wind, and moved toward the entrance to the building that housed the Prizzi law firm. She signed in, showed her ID, and headed for the elevator that would take her to the eighteenth floor.

The law firm was one of the most prestigious firms in the DC area, befitting Douglas Rainford, III, who liked to say he measured everything in life by dollar signs and beauty. "I have an appointment with Mr. Prizzi. Is it one, two, three, or four? Prizzi I mean," Sam asked.

The receptionist looked up at Sam with a blank expression before she looked down at her appointment book. "Which one?" Sam prompted as she looked around the shiny, marble lobby with the expensive furniture and luscious green plants. She looked down at her watch. "I'm in a hurry," she said coolly.

"Isn't everyone?" the receptionist responded just as coolly.

"Yes, but I'll leave if Mr. Prizzi doesn't see me in the next . . . three minutes," Sam said, her eyes glued to her watch. *What am I doing here? I never should have come. My lawyer can handle things.*

The phone console buzzed. The receptionist listened attentively. She hung up the phone, and said, "Mr. Prizzi will see you now. Go through the door on the right. Mr. Prizzi's office is the third door on the right."

Sam unbuttoned her coat as she walked through the open door and down the hall. She took a second to look at the nameplate on the door. Emmett Prizzi. The worm. Number Four in the pecking order of Prizzi brothers. Smallest office off the long hallway, one tiny window, no secretary. It could only mean one thing, Emmett Prizzi was the runt of the litter. She felt insulted.

Emmett Prizzi was a smallish man, thin and wiry. He wore large, thick glasses that magnified his eyes and seemed to engulf his thin face. He didn't bother putting his jacket on, nor did he bother to stand up to greet her. A worm. She felt more insulted. Without waiting to be asked, she sat down across from his desk. She felt bold and aggressive. She also felt wounded and sad, but this worm didn't need to know that. She wished she'd put on some makeup. "I don't have much time, Mr. Prizzi, so let's get right to the point." That's when she saw the folder on his desk. Even though it was upside down, she knew it was the prenuptial agreement she'd signed before she married Douglas. She waited.

The attorney was just about to speak when a knock sounded on the door and it opened almost immediately. A secretary handed over a sheaf of papers, which the attorney ignored.

Emmett Prizzi shuffled the papers in a folder that had her name on the flap. Sam saw a blue check work its way out of the folder. The lawyer picked it up and waved it around, then wet his lips as he tried to decide what he was going to say. Sam lost her patience. "Yes?"

The lawyer took a deep breath. "Your husband said I was to give you this check and to tell you he's sorry things didn't work out. The check is for five thousand dollars as per the prenuptial agreement. As you know, if you and Douglas had remained married after the five years stipulated, you were to get ten million dollars. Since that isn't going to happen, this is your payoff." He slid the check across the desk. Sam looked down at the blue check and wanted to cry. Five thousand dollars for a three-week honeymoon. The man she'd married, the man she'd thought she loved, certainly moved at the speed of light. She made no move to pick it up because she was too busy fighting the tears that threatened to roll down her cheeks. She leaned back in the leather chair and forced a laugh that sounded hysterical to her own ears.

"I don't find this a laughing matter, Mrs. Rainford," the worm squeaked. Another paper slid across the desk. "All you have to do is sign the release, and the check is yours."

Sam laughed again as she stood up. She started to fasten her coat. All she could think about was the new cozy condo she was going to return to. She was going to cook a wonderful dinner, build a fire, and settle in with a good book. She didn't know if that would be before or after she cried her eyes out.

"I don't want it. I don't need it. Is there anything else, Mr. Prizzi?"

"You have to take it," the lawyer sputtered.

"No. No, I don't have to take it. I'm not signing anything either. From here on in, you can talk to my attorney.

The lawyer snorted. "That's what the second Mrs. Rainford said. It didn't get her very far."

The second Mrs. Rainford. Surely she'd heard wrong. She shrugged. "Ask me if I care."

"That's exactly what the third Mrs. Rainford said. In the end she *did* care."

The third Mrs. Rainford. That had to mean she was the *fourth* Mrs. Rainford. She had to get out of here *immediately* so she could think about what she'd just heard. She was almost to the door, the lawyer following her, when she turned, and said, "What did the *first* Mrs. Rainford say?"

Prizzi started to sputter again. "She said she didn't give a good rat's ass what her husband wanted, and she would take him to the cleaners. Of course, that didn't happen."

Sam opened the door and sailed through. Douglas had had three other wives he hadn't seen fit to tell her about. Prizzi caught up with her at the elevator. Up close and personal, he still looked like a skinny worm. He reached out to touch her arm. Sam jerked away. "You have to sign the paper or you don't get the check, Mrs. Rainford. The bank in the lobby is giving a free blender if you open a new account," he said.

Sam pierced him with one scathing look before she stepped into the elevator. "I have a blender, Mr. Prizzi. Tell Mr. Rainford he can just kiss my ass."

Hysterical laughter bubbled out of Sam's mouth as she rode the elevator to the first floor of the office building. She dabbed at her eyes, not caring if anyone saw her or not.

Three ex-wives. Three!

Forty-five minutes later, just as Sam was fitting her key into the lock of her new home, her cell phone rang. She clicked it on, jiggling her shoulder bag and the key. "Slick! Wait, wait, I can barely hear you. Let me get inside. What's wrong, you sound terrible. Then again you're half a world away. You're not half a world away? You're at Reagan National? Of course you can come here. Wait, I'm not in the old apartment. I moved into my new condo today. You have the address. You're crying, Slick. Get a cab, and I'll have the coffee on."

Sam shrugged out of her coat and hung it in the closet. Her best friend in the whole world was coming to visit, and she was crying. Slick never cried. Never. Ever. Crying made the eyes puff, something no model could allow to happen. Something must have happened in her love life, and she was coming home to lick her wounds. They'd curl up by the fire and cry together, then talk it to death. At least with Slick here, she wouldn't have to think about Douglas and his three ex-wives and getting dumped the day after her honeymoon.

In her bedroom, which was painted a delicate peach color, Sam shed her business suit and pulled on a navy sweat suit and heavy wool socks. She turned up the heat as she made her way to the kitchen to prepare her first dinner in her new abode. Stew and homemade bread. Perfect for a cold, blustery November day.

Don't think, don't think, she cautioned herself as she dredged the meat in flour, then browned it. In minutes she had the vegetables chopped and the stew set to simmer. The bread machine took an additional few minutes. She was proud of her pantry and stocked refrigerator and freezer. *Don't think about Douglas and the three wives that came before you. Don't think, period.*

All the dinner preparations had been taken care of with an economy of motion, the way Sam did everything. The oven was on, but it hadn't yet reached the temperature required to bake the frozen blueberry pie compliments of Mrs. Smith. While she waited, she made her first pot of coffee in her new coffeepot. It was a bright cherry red machine.

Done. Sam smacked her hands together. *Three wives, and I never had a clue. Don't think about it. It's over and done with. Think about Slick and whatever her problem is.*

This was the perfect, warm, cozy place for Slick and herself to lick their wounds. Sam looked around the kitchen. She'd taken pains with it, hanging ferns and settling potted plants in colorful clay pots in the corners of the counters. The maple table and chairs by the bow window were inviting, allowing for a full view of the garden outside. It looked barren now, but in the spring and summer it would be beautiful. She did love the color red, and all the accent pieces in the cozy kitchen reflected that love. She couldn't wait to have her morning coffee and frozen bagel right here in the morning.

Sam slid the blueberry pie into the oven, set the timer, and moved on to the living room, where she built a fire. Douglas was divorcing her after a three-week whirlwind courtship, a justice-of-the-peace wedding, and a three-week honeymoon. What did that say about her? What were the three Rainford wives that came before her like? *Why did Douglas divorce them? More to the point, why did he marry me?* she wondered.

Sam stared into the fire, looking for the answers to her questions, finding nothing that would satisfy her. She turned around, savoring the tantalizing smells wafting in from the kitchen. There was nothing like the smell of baking bread to remind her of the times she spent at her grandmother's when she was a little girl. Thursday was always bread-baking day. Of course her grandmother hadn't had a bread machine. She did it the old-fashioned way. Everything Grandma had done, she'd done the old-fashioned way. She'd hung clothes on the line outdoors, ironed her sheets and pillowcases. She'd stretched her curtains on a contraption that was a killer on the fingers. She'd canned vegetables, made her own root beer, and kept a fully stocked root cellar. She was gone now, having died, Sam thought, of a broken heart soon after Grandpa had died after a long illness.

One of these days she was going to return to Pennsylvania, and the old house with the big front porch that her grandmother had left to her. But not yet. She simply wasn't ready to beard those old ghosts. She paid the nominal taxes every year, paid the neighbors to mow the lawn in the summer and shovel the snow in the winter.

Sam almost jumped out of her skin when the doorbell rang. It was a five-note chime. She ran to the door and threw it open. "Slick!"

"Oh, Sam! Thanks for letting me come here. God, it's cold out here!" Sam stepped aside for the taxi driver to carry in Slick's bags.

"Oh, it smells *sooooo* good. And that fire is great. Can I sleep in front of it? Let's have a sleepover the way we used to do in college." Slick gave Sam a quick hug, then wiped the tears from her eyes. "They fired me,

Sam. Sheer Delight fired me! They replaced me with a nineteen-year-old girl whose legs go all the way up to her neck. She's Scandinavian and weighs ninety-three pounds. Just like that, they fired me! Do you believe that? I was so upset I packed up when the shoot was over and for two months I ate my way across Europe. I put on eighteen pounds. What do you think of *that!*" She burst into tears, not caring if her eyes got puffy or red. "My whole life is over!"

Sam waited until Slick paid the driver, then led her over to the deep comfortable sofa in front of the fire. "What I think is you look wonderful! You don't look like a plank of wood. Your bones aren't showing. You look *healthy*, Slick. Your life is not over, it's just beginning. I'll get us some coffee. Then we'll talk."

"Four sugars and cream," Slick said.

"What happened to black coffee?"

"I left black coffee with the Scandinavian. By the way, her name is Grette." Slick started to cry again.

It was midnight when Slick finally asked the question Sam dreaded. "What are you going to do now, Sam?"

"I'm going to work for the FBI after all. I was going to sign on, but then I met Douglas, and everything changed. They gave me ninety days to make up my mind. They've been actively recruiting for the past few months. Want to join up?"

"Hell, yes. It's got to be better than strutting down a runway throwing my hips and pelvis out of joint."

"Then we'll sign you up tomorrow," Sam said.

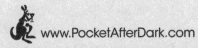